Witch of the Winter Moon

Stuart Mascair

To the 588th "Night Witches" Women's Bomber company
who flew on wings of canvas without parachutes.
Also to my mother, who was my first fan.

Witch of the Winter Moon

Part 1

1
Flight

Nadia had spent four months working on this broom. She gathered the materials and bound them together when the moon was at its fullest. She made the bristles with strands of wheat, with a shaft of hemlock. The sacred oils that covered the broom's surface gave it a lacquered shine and made it smooth to the touch. She spent many days in the forest to get the plants and herbs needed to extract the oils. She made sure not to draw too much attention, as the government saw spies everywhere, and in a time of war, that meant the clutches of the secret police.

Her earlier attempts at constructing a broom had failed, and she had to start over from scratch. It took her three months to prepare her current broom. With the war on, she didn't know when she would have another chance to attempt a flight. She had to fly this time.

Nadia took a deep breath as she gripped the neck of the broom. Her hands had been caressing it on her walk over to her mentor's home in the forest. The witch Olivia had known Nadia her entire life and even acted as a midwife during her birth. Within a few short years, Nadia was practicing with her. It took Nadia eight years to get to this point. Her graduation ceremony. When she had finally constructed her broom, she could call herself a full-fledged witch. Olivia had said the ceremony was a necessary formality. It stressed the symbolism of leaving the nest and becoming independent.

Olivia sat in her rocking chair, chain-smoking factory-made cigarettes while petting her ancient cat, Petrenko. Nadia took several breaths as she stood in the garden of her mentor's cottage.

She mounted the broom, eschewing her usual skirt for trousers. When Nadia first showed up wearing the state-made unisex work pants, Olivia laughed at her, saying she didn't teach boys witchcraft.

Nadia said the first thing she would do was show the people in town what she had done. She wanted to awe them, not have them laugh as they looked under her skirt. Olivia shook her head. That was four attempts ago. Now Nadia knew she would finally fly. She would leave this tiny village with its disapproving peasants, away from the advancing fascists, and finally be free from the life that had trapped her. Nadia took a deep breath and called the magic that weaved into the broom. She didn't grip the neck too tightly. She used her breath to awaken the magic in her broom. She began to rise, slowly lifting off the ground. She was excited, and in control. Wind emanated from below her, sending waves of ripples that buffeted Olivia's garden. She hovered off the ground. Nadia couldn't help but laugh.

A loud crack erupted through the garden, and Nadia realized that she had failed again. The broom had split apart, and Nadia began to shake as it attempted to throw her off. The broom bucked and soared above the tree line. Nadia held tight as it thrashed like an angry bull. The broom tore apart, and flowers and vines grew from the handle. The bristles thrashed. Nadia was squealing as she saw the broom split in two, each pulling her in different directions. She tried to think of a spell to get the two pieces to meld or stay under control. She was flailing about, her legs kicking the air. Something sharp dug into her palms as the broom's pieces began to grow spiny thorns. The stinging pain was too much for her, and she let go.

She had fallen before, on her third attempt, but no higher than Olivia's house. Now Nadia would surely die. She made her peace with the sun and moon and closed her eyes. With a sudden jerk in her body, she was caught on what she thought was a tree branch. She opened her eyes to see the ground, just a cat's tail away from her. She was floating in the air, with Olivia watching her from her porch, scratching the head of the old cat Petrenko, and smoking.

"You should really just enchant a factory broom," said Olivia, exhaling a cloud of smoke. Nadia floated back to the ground. The pieces of the broom had dug into the earth, planting themselves. Any hint of Nadia's design was gone as the broom was now a pair of miniature trees. Nadia stood, brushing herself off, feeling very foolish and very frustrated.

"It wouldn't be the same. I want to make my own broom. It doesn't matter; I don't know when I will have another chance to get more herbs from the forest, even if I were to use a premade broom. This curfew is suffocating me."

"Such a stupid thing like a curfew shouldn't stop a young witch," said Olivia. "Now come inside, I made dumplings, and I don't intend to eat them all myself." Nadia followed her mentor, pulling the stinging nettles from her palms. Olivia's cottage was in the old style. Many of the modern amenities didn't extend to her part of the forests. There was no electricity to light the home, no plumbing to wash the dishes or flush a proper toilet. But the cottage remained warm and cozy and smelled strongly of spices and herbs.

Olivia placed the old cat Petrenko on the table, where he immediately curled up, resting his head on his paws. Nadia had known that cat for years, and he always looked old and tired. Olivia placed a bowl of dumplings in front of Nadia. Sprinkled paprika popped out against the yellow broth.

"I want you to eat all of that, the famine is done, no need to hide it away," said Olivia, sitting back down. The ashtray that sat on the table was filled with burned tobacco, mixing with the smell of garlic and pepper. Nadia ate as she was instructed. She was starving, having skipped breakfast. She had been sucking on a button to reduce her appetite, but that only worked for so long.

"Do you know what went wrong?" Nadia asked. Olivia took a deep breath of acidic smoke, brushing her grey hair aside. Her limbs were thick, heavy, and strong enough to pick up a starving girl from the woods.

"I do, but I want to know why you think you failed," said Olivia, playing with the old cat's tail.

"I think I didn't pick the right branch for the broom. I better go with spruce next time or maybe just find a thicker branch," sighed Nadia, resting her chin on her hands. "I really thought I got it right this time. I was so sure I was going to fly."

"Your failure had nothing to do with the broom's construction. It was quite well made. A lot of time and effort was put into this one."

"Not for lack of choice. Ever since the war started, I can only spend a few hours each day hunting for herbs."

"Is there another war? Is it a civil war or an invasion?" asked Olivia.

"Invasion. The German fascists invaded mouths ago, the whole Soviet Union is making a valiant defense. Don't you read a newspaper?"

2
The Examination

Nadia clutched the small vial of oxen bane to her chest. Olivia had added lavender and wildflowers to the elixir to help the taste, but Nadia dreaded taking the potion. The concoction would have terrible effects on her body.

She walked out of the forest on a dirt trail. The sights and sounds of nature vanished as she made it to the main road. Nadia was taken aback by the number of soldiers marching in shambled columns. Soon she was forced to leave the road as a tank covered in sleepy, brown-clad soldiers rolled by.

All were headed to the train station in the village. Their brown uniforms looked drab and utilitarian. To some girls, these uniformed men looked gallant and brave. All Nadia could think of were those soldiers coming into her home, taking the family's livestock and grain, and raiding the larder, leaving her family without so much as a morsel. When Nadia's father fought back using an old pistol, he was beaten mercilessly before being dragged away. To Nadia, those men meant collectivization, kidnapping, and hunger.

"Hey, pretty girl," shouted one of the soldiers. Nadia was shaken out of her contemplation by a soldier riding on top of a tank. His military cap rested on cropped hair. The red star of the Soviet Union was the most striking thing on his person. "Give me a kiss on the cheek. I'm going to kill the fascists and I need something to keep me warm at night." Nadia looked back at the road and tried to ignore him. "Don't ignore me, pretty girl, I just want to protect you from those dogs."

"Ignore them, sister." Nadia turned to see a blond-haired woman exit from the line. Her oversized pants were stuffed in her boots. Her belt was on as tight as it could be, and her rifle had a scope. "They are farm boys with none of the culture of the city; they are harmless," said the woman soldier whose hair was cropped like the rest of the men.

"Aren't you worried about the other soldiers? I can't imagine being around so many rowdy men."

"Ha! They're not so bad, and between us girls, it helps that I'm one of the untouchable sharpshooters," she said, grinning and holding up her rifle. She sighted down the gun as if she were posing for a photograph. She smiled like one of the happy farmers in one of the ubiquitous propaganda posters.

"I thought you might be. My father was a sharpshooter in the last war," said Nadia. "What makes you untouchable?"

"Well, I'm a better shot then any of my comrade brothers. When we sniper girls went to join up with the regiment, the officer made a big show in front of the entire company." The sniper dropped her voice, imitating the officer. "'These girls are the untouchables. If any one of you bastards lay so much as a finger on them, then I will have every tenth man in front of a firing squad.'" She laughed. "After that none of the men even looked at me, let alone tried anything stupid. But between you and me, if they did try anything, surprised her when the commissar trotted up in his signature round hat and brown uniform. His buttons were gold, and he had a disapproving sneer that he wore so well that it gave the impression that he could make no other facial gesture. Beside him stood a woman soldier in a brown uniform with cropped red hair and an army cap. She had a pistol on her hip and a broom in her hand. Nadia could tell she was a sister of the craft, but it felt wrong seeing her wearing a Soviet uniform.

"Is this the applicant?" asked the commissar. His stare was disapproving. The witch remained silent.

"Yes, comrade commissar," said the sergeant.

"What is wrong with her, she appears as weak and sickly as a spring lamb."

"I don't know, comrade commissar, but I think she is lying to get medical attention. But following mandate eighty-seven, all persons claiming magical aptitude are to be reviewed even if their condition is suspect."

"Don't recite regulations, comrade, it makes you sound like a bureaucrat, not a soldier of the Revolution." The commissar walked around Nadia, sizing her up. "Tell me, girl, did your family come from bourgeois stock before the Revolution?" he asked.

"No, comrade commissar," said Nadia as she looked at the uniformed witch. Her grey eyes reminded Nadia of the moon.

"I ask this because only bourgeois brats of the upper class would have the audacity to use such a sneaky and underhanded method as claiming to be a magician to try to steal medicine from the army. Are you trying to con valuable medicine from the war effort? Is your local state doctor, not suitable to your needs?" he asked, leaning right into Nadia's face. "Don't look at her, applicant! Look at me! I'm the one who has the power to accept you in the army or send you to a firing squad for your malicious lies." Nadia looked away from the other witch, whom she assumed to be Anna. "Good, now follow me, and we will put you under review."

Nadia followed the commissar away from the hustle of the train station and the ant-like activity of the soldiers. The three went to a field behind the station where a goat chewed on a bale of hay. The other witch sat on a bale and watched as the commissar checked his watch. "Now is the time to admit any malfeasance you may have."

"I don't understand, commissar?" said Nadia. Her body ached all over. The commissar stood in front of her, careful not to step in any goat droppings.

"To admit the truth, of course!" he said. "Lying to an official of the state is not only illegal, but it is also high treason in a time of war. If your so-called magical talents are false, then I will have you shot by the end of the day. But if you were to admit to any perjury now, then I can reduce your sentence to work in a state camp out east." Nadia looked at the ground. Denying being a witch would make her worse off than before.

"I'm a witch, comrade commissar. I have reported to the army, as ordered by the colonel," Nadia said, having rehearsed the lines.

"Then let the review begin," he said, checking his watch. "Let the record show it is 1227 hours. I, Commissar Vladimir, and first-class magician Anna have begun our review of the applicant. What institution did you graduate from?" he said, pacing back and forth.

"Institution?"

"Yes, did you graduate from the universities of Moscow or Kiev, or perhaps the illustrious college of Leningrad?" he said in a mocking tone.

"None of those universities, comrade. Do we have to do this questioning in a field?" asked Nadia.

"Yes, we do. After an incident a few months ago with a fire slinger, all applicants are to be reviewed in a suitably open location. No exceptions." He then turned to Anna. "Make a note the applicant has had no education in a magical institution." Nadia looked at Anna, who was more interested in the goat than the examination.

"Now what, would you classify as your area of magical expertise?"

"I know how to brew potions, and I can speak with beasts," said Nadia.

"Is that all?" he asked. "You claim to be a witch and I get a hackneyed response. We don't have time for you to make a witch's brew with cauldrons and herbs, and what good is an animal in combat? Will speaking to birds help blind the Germans? Can you convince a German attack dog from tearing your throat out?"

"No, comrade commissar."

"The validity of these claims is also questionable. How would we know you are actually speaking to an animal? As for potions, mixing herbs and roots would hold no scientific and combative value."

"Not true, commissar. A well brewed potion can give a man or woman extraordinary abilities," said Nadia.

"Oh really, and what, pray tell, can these potions do? Will you make a brew to put the fascist armies to flight? Could you make a potion to knock German planes out of the sky or halt an advancing column of tanks? Maybe a vile poison to put Hitler to sleep until Prince Charming gives him a kiss?"

"No, comrade, but I can brew a potion that will keep a man awake for days, or keep a man fed for a week, as well as many different healing salves."

"Could you make those enough to supply a battalion?" he asked, suddenly very curious.

"No, comrade."

"What about a company?"

"No, comrade."

"A platoon? What about a squad?" he barked.

"No, comrade."

"Then you are next to useless. Amphetamines can keep a soldier fighting without sleep. The state's farms can feed the men. What good are these potions and brews if they can't be disseminated to a large group of soldiers. How long would these potions even take to brew?" he shouted at her.

"Some an hour, others at least a week."

"At least a week! Are you mad? Right now, the Nazi hoard is taking hundreds of kilometers a day. Assuming you are not a fraud, what good are you? Have you no hexes, have you any incantations, anything to keep a man from killing you?" The commissar then drew his pistol and pointed it at her head. "What if I was a German soldier? If I don't shoot you on sight, what are you going to do to stop me? Have you any idea what they do to female soldiers? What will you do to stop me from shooting you?"

"Comrade, please don't!" Nadia said, panic in her voice. She looked at Anna for support. The other witch just stared at her. Her grey eyes flashed like the glow of the moon. For a moment, she forgot about the man with the gun, forgot about the war and her small village life. She knew only the moonlight and the strength within. Time slowed, her eyes darting back to the man with the gun. His face was red and belligerent. On his cap was the red star of the Soviet Union, a symbol of power emulated by a tribe of the Kievan Rus.

She saw past the static metal symbolism of the pendant. She looked up a moment and saw the shining sun above. The bright light overhead, a blazing nourishing beacon, while the Soviet star that sought to emulate its power was a smoldering, dark red star. An arrogant symbol, a symbol of power without life. This man drew strength from the symbol he wore and the gun in his hand. He cocked the pistol and placed it between her eyes. Nadia's world became crystal clear, the oxen bane a dull roar in her body. She drew the moon out from Anna's eyes and placed it within herself. It had mysteries and secrets. The moon was willing to tell her if she listened.

Comrade Commissar Vladimir counted down from three. She could barely hear him as the world went quiet. A sudden pure epiphany flashed in her mind like lightning in the dead of night. The simple mechanism of the pistol followed a set of rules. Whenever those rules were broken the machine would fail. All she had to do was tap it with a little magic.

"Break." The spell was half made in her mind and focused on her word. The gun in the commissar's hand clicked without firing. The commissar, still all fury, pulled the trigger again to no effect.

"What the devil?" He took the gun from her head, pointing it skyward. He checked the chamber, and then the pistol exploded in the commissar's hands. The pair both recoiled as the powder from the cartridge sprayed them both. The commissar got the worst of it. His hands were twisted and blackened, his fingers hanging on by strips of skin. Exposed bones jumped out of pulped red meat; all the while, the commissar screamed and cursed. Then the oxen bane reminded Nadia that it was still in her system. It was this gentle reminder that caused her to vomit. The dumplings and oxen bane were expelled from her body with the acidic spit dripping from her mouth. She looked up to see Anna with her grey eyes staring right at her.

"Wretched pistol," grunted the commissar as he held his fingers. He began to wrap them up with a white handkerchief that quickly turned red.

"I can confirm the validity of the applicant, comrade commissar," said Anna, speaking for the first time.

"Are you saying that she was the one who did this?" he said, holding up his hand. "Looks like I will get my firing squad after all. Assaulting a political officer is a capital offense, witch."

"The girl had nothing to do with the explosion. I saw the spell she used. It was a simple jinx. It was your fiddling that caused your sidearm to explode, comrade." Nadia knew the spell she used was to destroy it. Not to simply jam it.

"Are you trying to protect her?"

"My duty is to the people. Anything else would be negligent of my duties."

"What does that mean?"

"It means that while the applicant holds magical aptitude, I do not think she has the skills to properly deploy them in combat. A proper jinx would have kept that weapon from any sort of harm. This is amateur hour."

"Could she be trained up, possibly use that jinx on a tank or a battalion of Germans?" asked the commissar, forgetting all about his injury.

"Given a couple years maybe, but as you said, the Germans are taking kilometers. I doubt we have time to train her to be effective. And this one looks to be a delicate sort. She won't be able to deal with the rigors of combat," said Anna, looking down at Nadia.

"Then I hereby declare this examination over with the rejection of the applicant," said the commissar.

3
The Story of Tanya

Nadia's skull pounded as she drank a glass of water. Her empty stomach tightened and contracted as the liquid-filled it. She felt wretched. The oxen bane had worked through her body, leaving her an exhausted mess. All she could do was sit on the stoop of her home, holding the cold glass to her head.

The water tasted of earthy minerals, having been drawn from the well underneath the town. The sickness of the oxen bane faded slowly as Nadia watched the sunset. There were sporadic cracks of rifle fire in the distance as soldiers did their target practice. Nadia hoped they weren't firing squads.

Nadia finished her glass of water and stepped inside. Many of the village structures were very drab. Official buildings were brutal concrete boxes, and most of the village homes were from the last century, with only the main street showing any hint of modernity. However, Nadia's home was blooming with color. Blankets threaded with reds and yellows covered hard furniture. While the kitchen had all manner of herbs and plants, wildflowers and roots rested next to bowls of berries and mushrooms.

Her mother, Katarina, was lying on the couch, a bottle of vodka on her lap. Nadia sighed; she had obviously been there all day, and it looked like Nadia would be handling tonight's meal.

"Mama, wake up," said Nadia, gently stroking her mother's head.

"Alexander, is that you?" her mother asked, speaking her father's name.

"No, Mama, it's just me, Father has not yet come home." After nine years, Nadia's mother still dreamed of a returning husband. Many people were taken away by the state, few had ever returned. "Mama, have you been drinking all day?" Nadia asked, reaching for the bottle. Her mother recoiled, her grip tight and desperate.

"Yes, my darling, the state forced me to dismantle the town's factory with the other women. Now there is no work for anyone. Mark my words, this is just the start of the bad times."

"Yes, Mama," Nadia said, bringing her mother to a sitting position.

"It starts off by closing the factories, then the food vanishes, and then boyars, or the reds, or the capitalists come riding in on horses, cutting down the small folk. Our lot in life is to suffer, my darling."

"Don't say such things, Mama."

"I see they haven't trussed you up in a uniform like a boy. To think they are asking for girls to serve in the fighting. The world has gone mad. We had our troubled times with the tsar, but he would have never asked my Nadia to fight in a war."

"I met one of those woman soldiers today; she was a sniper," said Nadia.

"No doubt she is being constantly harassed by the other soldiers, poor thing. Women were never meant to be near such men for a long time, at least groups of them. That's how I met Alexander. You know your father was an oafish animal when he was with his comrades during the Great War.

I told him off more than once. Yet when he left the company of soldiers, he became very sweet. A completely different man. He became civilized again. A soldier by himself is a noble dignified figure. But in a pack, they are like wild animals, no better than mad dogs."

She took a drink, wincing as she exhaled the potent liquor. Nadia had heard this story uncounted times. As well as her mother's opinion of soldiers. But this talk made her nervous.

"Mama, we are at war. You can't be talking like that," said Nadia.

"You worry too much about the secret police. They have better things to do then harassing one tragic woman." She waved dismissively. "Where is Peter?"

"He is playing with friends; he should be back soon. I told him to be back before curfew."

"That's good. Children should be children, they should play. I couldn't as a girl. I had to work and pull cold turnips out of the ground. That was when we still had a tsar."

"I know, Mama." Nadia had put on an apron and was getting the oven going. She filled the stove full of propaganda pamphlets and newspapers, exhorting the people to smash the fascist invaders.

"Were you able to fly today?"

"For a moment," Nadia said, preparing turnips and beets. "Olivia said that I didn't really want to fly and that's why I couldn't. That I really want to stay here and that is what is keeping me from flying."

"I like that. You should stay here with your brother and me, find a nice young man. Motherhood has been the most fulfilling thing in my life." Katarina stood up from the couch and crossed the room with careful steps. She made sure she was planted before taking another step, eventually sitting down at the kitchen table. "Like that Mykola. He is rather handsome; he reminds me of Alexander."

Nadia was thankful for the knock at the entrance. Upon answering the door, she found a pair of soldiers holding Peter between them.

"Are you this boy's family?" barked the short one.

"I'm his sister. Is something wrong?"

"This boy was out past curfew. Don't you know that there is a war going on, sister?" said the tall one.

"What's going on, my darling? Is that Peter?"

"Yes, Mama! I thought curfew started in an hour."

"That was yesterday, today is now. If this boy were any older, he would have been shot on sight for being a fascist spy." Peter was crying, his eyes red and blotchy.

"Don't let it happen again; others might not hold as much restraint as we have," said the short one.

"Thank you, comrade, we will be mindful of the curfew from now on," she said as the soldiers let go of the boy, who grabbed ahold of Nadia's leg.

"See that you do." The pair then spun on their heels and began patrolling again. *At least they didn't take our food,* Nadia thought as she breathed a heavy sigh. She hadn't realized she was shaking. "Go sit with Mama; dinner will be ready soon."

"I'm sorry, Nadia, I didn't mean to get in trouble. I was just playing. I didn't do anything wrong," Peter said, squeezing her leg.

"I know you didn't," said Nadia, leading him to the kitchen table next to their mother. Katarina hugged her son. She was too drunk to say any words of comfort, so she just held Peter. Nadia's mother looked at her. There was pleading in those eyes. Her brown eyes begged Nadia to say the words she could not communicate. The words that would give her young son courage. So that he may stop his weeping. Eyes that asked for Nadia to speak about anything but the war and the turmoil. All the while, Peter wept into his mother's arms.

"Peter, have I told you how the witches of the steppe first learned of magic?" Nadia said, cutting vegetables. Nadia looked over her shoulder and saw Peter, teary-eyed, peeking out from Katarina's arm. He shook his head while sniffling. His weeping was momentarily halted.

"No, I don't think so."

"Well, once upon a time, long after the first people were birthed from mud, and only a short time after the sparrow stole one of the sun's golden hairs to make fire for man, a great migration of people from the steppe rode through the land. At first, they rode to find better hunting grounds, but as they moved over the vast grasslands, they lost sight of what could and could not be hunted. Soon they began raiding the peaceful herders and farmers."

"Like the Nazis?" Peter asked, grimacing. Katarina's eyebrows furrowed at the story's subject. Nadia's mother was a devout Christian after all, and the story of war didn't help the mood.

"Not quite. The steppe peoples of that time were very different than how armies and people interact now. They were more concerned with stealing food and gods."

"Who were these people then, the people that raided?" asked Peter.

"Their name is long forgotten, so we shall call them the Horse Lords of the Sun. For they grew their own strands of the sun's hair to make arrows of fire. But one day the Horse Lords raided a village of the small folk. Their lives were dominated by the tilling of the land and the worship of their local god. The Horse Lords attacked the small folk and stole all their grain, and of

31

course, their god," she said.

The vegetables were done, and a soup was boiling; the smells of savory vegetables combined with the smoky tinge of burned propaganda pamphlets.

"How can you steal a god?" Peter said, perplexed. His eyes were still red and blotchy, but his crying had ceased. He still held on to Katarina's arm.

"The gods were also very different back then. They had not grown large and powerful and tended to be much smaller like a sculpture or tree, or a special amulet."

"That's silly," he said. Their mother nodded in agreement.

"I'm sure our customs may seem rather silly in a thousand years. What was I saying? Oh yes, so the Horse Lords had stolen the god of the small folk, and they threatened to destroy their god if they didn't offer a tribute. The small folk offered their tribute but had very little food for themselves. It came to the point that all the food of the small folk went to the Horse Lords. This way of living was at odds with their way of life and the harmony they once had. So, they elected a member of the village to leave and fend for themselves out in the steppe. They all cast their vote with a lock of hair. Each was thrown into a fire and the first locks to burn blue were to be sent away."

"Hair does not burn like that."

"Well, maybe not your hair, but hair was much different back then." Nadia had sat down at the table by now, her head resting on the bridge of her hands. "You see, Mama, I told you he learns new things. The chosen person was named Baba Tanya, a young woman who had lost three children and four husbands. How they were lost is another story involving an Ogre, but that is a story for another time. Tanya was given a leather satchel and a bird's feather and was sent away. Tanya traveled for three days and three nights, and on the third night, she collapsed in hunger and fatigue. She pulled at grass and dirt and ate them as if they were succulent morsels of grain. That is when the Moon sat down next to her. The Moon was full and pregnant, ready to give birth to another darkness.

"'Little one, why are you so far from home?' asked the Moon.

"'The Horse Lords have stolen our god and have demanded tribute. Our village can no longer feed everyone, so they have done away with me, for the good of the village.'

"'Well, little one, you can't eat earth anymore. You gave up that gift for the power of words,' said the Moon feeling the kick of her child."

Katarina had fallen asleep, her head drooping as Peter sat in her lap. The boy was enraptured with the story, his head resting on his arms on the table.

"'But how will I eat? I have no time to grow any grain, and the steppe has naught but nettles and grass, and I know not how to hunt like one of the men.' The Moon rose slowly as she does when she is in the sky.

"'You are a cup that has been emptied of purpose,' said the Moon. 'Your old knowledge is useless out here. Do not lament your expulsion from the village, for you have the chance of becoming something new.'

"'How can I become something new if I'm to die out on the steppe?'

"'Because, my little one, you have forgotten how to speak with beasts and plants, you have forgotten the real names of things, I will teach them to you again because I love you, as I love all things in their way. Listen to my words every night. My first gift is to show you how to hear the names of plants.'

"The Moon then showed Tanya how to listen to the names of plants, and soon Tanya was able to find a fat turnip below the grass of the steppe. Tanya learned much from the Moon. She could only speak with her when the Moon was bright and full in the sky. For when the Moon gave birth to her dark children, she had to recover from the endeavor. Most nights, the Moon could only spare a word or two. After many years of speaking with the Moon, Tanya had learned much, but she missed her village terribly.

"'Mother Moon, who gives birth to the eternal dark, I miss my home I miss my loved ones.'

"'Then return to them,' said the Moon.

"'It is not so simple, for without our god, the village will spurn me. As long as the Horse Lords extort tribute from the small folk, then there will be little food for the rest of us.'

"'Then you must rescue your pudgy god. Speak to the Horse Lords in a language they do not know, with the words I taught you.' Tanya kissed the hands of the Moon before crafting a clay pot. She spoke the secret word of birds and gave the pot flight. Tanya traveled many leagues as quickly as hopping over a puddle of mud. She found the Horse Lord's camp. She approached their Chief, a large, arrogant man who wore the strands of the sun's hair in his own burly mane so that he looked like a lion given the shape of a man.

"'Please, oh lord of the open steppe who uses fire like a spear, I ask that you return the god of the small folk.'

"'Which one? I have many idols. I have the idols of those who live in the trees like the birds. I have the icons of those who can float on water and drink the bounty of the sea. No, you look like one of the small folks who pull the fruits of grain from the earth. Well, you shall not have it. While your food is not fit for a warrior, it can be turned into a potent alcohol that we use in our celebrations.'

"'That is not a wise decision, oh Horse Lord. Know this: until you return our idol, I will speak the words of truth until my god is returned.'

"'What good is speaking? I have uncounted warriors at my beck and call, and more horses than all the peoples of the world. I hold more arrows than there are blades of grass. What good are your words in the face of such might?'

"'I speak the words of the Moon, she who gives birth to the dark. A force even the sun fears. So, I shall speak my first word to you.' Tanya then beckoned the children of the Moon, the ever-present darkness to cover the Horse Lords in perpetual night. Before the Horse Lords could slay Tanya, she had already stepped into her pot and flew into the sky.

"The Horse Lords all mounted their many steeds and began to give chase across the darkened steppe. The Horse Lords made great bonfires to find their way in the dark. Tanya, in turn, whispered the word of the storm that brought rain. So, they could not travel so quickly, as the mud would suck their horses into the muck. The Horse Lord laughed. His men ran to all the villages of the small folk and forced them to make a road of stone, so that his army could ride without trouble.

"Meanwhile, Tanya was teaching the words to other small-folk women who were marked by the Moon. The Horse Lords soon found it more challenging to extract tribute as the small folk began to use those words to keep the army at bay. The Chief of the Horse Lords was furious, for he had felled many tribes and made vassalage of many more. Yet, a single woman was destroying his violent reign.

"So, the Horse Lord sought out fell creatures in the ever-present dark. He traded flesh for his own words. For every soul he offered those foul creatures, he learned a word, and after a month, he had learned a whole language. Soon Tanya's language of the Moon had no effect on the Chief and his Horse Lords. With his new words, the Chief made villages of the smallfolk into his subjects by naming them slaves. He controlled the seasons by naming them. For all those bearing words of the Moon, he named concubine.

"The winds sent to batter the Horse Lords and their animals had no effect. When Tanya convinced the horses to flee, the Chief had them captured and bridled. Soon the steppe was conquered by the Chief with the strand of the sun in his hair, yet the dark things he had made deals with were always hungry and always willing to teach crueler words.

"Tanya knew several ways to deal with unruly spirits, so she sought out all those cruel creatures who traded foul words for flesh. One by one, she bound them with the words of the Moon. She tied one to iron. The spirit hated water, which is why iron rusts the way it does, and why iron always seems to make fine weapons. She bound another in the earth, and that is why the ground has earthquakes. She secured a third to the water; where once we could breathe it freely, we would now drown. Tanya knew she was changing the world by binding these spirits to various elements. It was a necessary act, as the Horse Lords could no longer commune with the elements of nature. The wicked spirits raged, sowing havoc in the world, but Tanya made deals with them. If they taught her some of their words, she would lessen the time in their prison. Soon, Tanya added many of the spirits' dark words to her own language of the Moon. This new language had subtle nuance as well as vulgar curses and foul quips. When she felt that she was fluent in this new language of the Moon, she hopped in her flying pot and sought out the Horse Lords. The Chief had lost all his spirit tutors, and he used his cruel words to exact a crushing tribute on his steppe empire. Tanya landed in front of the Chief during a celebration of a recent conquest.

"'I have sealed away your spirit allies; you will learn no more dark words from them. I demand that you release my god as well as all those you have subjugated with your profane speech.'

"'I will not,' said the Chief. 'Your ugly language has convinced me naught. You drown me in dark, I brighten it with fire. You put fear in our horses, then we bind them with bits and bridals. I have named many slaves and they are at my beck and call. Through their labor and suffering, I prosper. So, I name them in turn, I name you enemy. I name you witch.'

"'A suitable name and I will wear it well for it makes me the master of my destiny, a foe of all the profane. In kind I will name you as well. I name you wretch.'

"The Chief with the fire in his hair was made deaf, blind, and mute. His limbs lost strength and withered, and the food in his mouth turned to ash. The Horse Lords abandoned their leader, each taking a portion of the vocabulary he knew. Each of his captains took to one of the four directions, spreading those foul words wherever they went. Tanya took up her god and reflected that he was rather pudgy. She returned to her village of small folk.

"'It is I, Tanya the witch. I return with our stolen god and have vanquished the Chief of the Horse Lords.' The village elder took the god in his hands and smashed it on a rock.

"'We have no need for such a pitiful god anymore, for we have the language of the Horse Lords to make our own gods. Soon we will be the ones with slaves and vassals. Soon we will be the conquers of the world.' Tanya now understood the curse of her name, for she realized that now anyone could become a tyrant with the right words. She realized that she would oppose tyrants for the rest of her days, for she was named witch. For she was named enemy. So, Tanya devised a poem that would shatter the understanding of the steppe.

"People across the steppe soon found that they could no longer speak to one another, their language made obscure and unintelligible. Soon none knew the words of power from any of the strange noises they made. That is why there are so many languages, so the dark terms of power are no longer tied to potent words but to many lesser words.

"Tanya's own language of the Moon and dark spirits remained pure. That is why witches can speak to animals, and the elements, that is why we can use magic."

"Did that really happen?" asked Peter, yawning, his eyes still puffy from his tears.

"It might have," said Nadia, getting the stew ready. She set the table and then gently shook her mother awake.

"It's time to eat, Mama."

"I must have dozed off," Katarina said, adjusting Peter on her lap.

"Nadia told me how magic was made."

"Then we shall read the Bible tonight as well. Maybe the tale of how Jesus made all the bread and fish."

"Yes, Mama," said Peter.

"Where is your meal, Nadia?"

"I ate earlier, so I'm not that hungry," she lied.

"You must eat if you are to survive winter. Having a little extra fat is the best thing for a girl, and it drives the boys wild."

"Mama, I'm fine, I'm just not hungry," Nadia said with a slight blush. "All the boys think I'm too strange anyway."

"Nonsense. A young pretty witch like you? They must be frightened of your dread powers," said Katarina. Nadia was thankful the subject had changed, even if the new topic made her feel inadequate. What kind of dreadful witch can't even fly?

"Give it a year of good eating, and you will have all the boys wrapped around your finger. You will have your pick of any of them."

"Yes, Mama." Nadia nodded, not believing any of it.

"That is only if you eat; you're too scrawny," said Katarina, placing Peter in his own seat before getting another bowl of vegetable soup. Katarina then put a large dollop of sour cream in it before placing it in front of Nadia.

"Now I'm going to read a story from the Bible to Peter, and I want you to have finished that bowl when I'm done."

4

Anna the Red

The harvest was the most fruitful in years. The wheat and rye had grown tall, with immense yields of potatoes, beets, onions, and apples. Soviet farming was a strict and ordered affair, with a specific plot of land devoted to one crop. However, the cold was setting in, making the ground hard and implacable.

Nadia broke the earth with a pick to loosen the dirt. In a single column behind her, dozens of her classmates, laid-off factory workers, and all her former teachers dug a long trench that was to become a tank trap. A commissar watched the gangs of workers, reciting platitudes on how the war was to be won with the working arm of the people and the striking arm of the army. Nadia had done state work before. It was both expected and mandated that young people would "volunteer" to help dig irrigation for farming, dig a well, or flatten a stretch of land for a road. She knew several spells that would make the work easier. But she remembered what Olivia said about flaunting magic in front of the uninitiated peasants or state officers, as it made them nervous and therefore dangerous. So, she struck the earth with a mundane pick. Her limbs ached, and her back screamed. She could already feel blisters growing on her palms.

Around her were her former classmates, peers she had known for many years, all working side by side. The state reduced them all to cogs in the machine. However, those cogs were alive, and unlike a machine, could act unpredictably.

"Hey, witch." Nadia turned to see Ivanka resting on a shovel, glaring at her. Ivanka loved dresses and candy. Once upon a time, she and Nadia were friends. However, a mixture of time, the famine, and the village's prejudice slowly put pressure on the two. Now Ivanka looked at her with contempt and scorn.

"Why don't you use one of your spells to dig this ditch for us? So we can all go home."

"I can't do that," Nadia lied.

"Can't or won't? It doesn't matter, I bet you find some sick joy in coming into the dirt and working with the rest of us like some bourgeois tourist."

Nadia said nothing and returned to digging. She just wanted to get the work done and not draw any more attention to herself. Attention only brought trouble for a witch.

"Don't ignore me, you arrogant sow!"

"Let it go," piped in another from the line, a quiet girl named Sofia. Nadia and she were never close, but the two were of a similar temperament. Sofia lost everyone during the famine: her mother, father, and all her brothers and sisters. She lived with her aunt now. It was said that the two were the most voracious eaters in town. That might have been the reason why they were never close. So much food made Nadia uneasy.

"No. Sofia, right now my father and three brothers are off at the front giving up everything to protect our people while this witch, toils in the ground like the rest of us. She should be at the front as well. I read the paper; all wizards, witches, and occultists have been called upon by Premier Stalin to fight the Nazis. So why isn't she fighting?"

"Lay off, Ivanka," said David, a young man who was tall and strong, the first in the village to try to enlist in the army when war broke out. He was turned away for not meeting the necessary requirements, meaning he was Jewish.

Witches were not the only persecuted minority in the Soviet Union. Jewish pogroms were still within the living memory of every Jewish family. Nadia had a crush on David. Once upon a time at least. He rejected her. After all, Jews don't marry witches. Regardless, it made her feel good that someone was standing up for her.

"I saw her at the recruitment office yesterday," he said.

"Then why isn't she at the front right now?" asked Ivanka. "What was it that put you here instead of helping on the front? All the men in my family are off risking everything, while yours do nothing. So why didn't the army accept you?" Nadia hated this. She looked past Ivanka, her eyes pleading to be rescued by Sofia and David. "Don't look at them. Tell me right now, why you are still here?"

"I was sick," she said, not meeting Ivanka's eyes.

"Sick! You're a witch! Who ever heard of a witch getting sick?"

"She used one of her potions." Everyone looked up to see Mykola standing above them, looking down on the three in the trench. "You drank one of your strange concoctions, to get out of conscription. We should have thrown her out into the woods with that old hag long ago. After all, lies come as easily to a witch as snow comes to winter."

There wasn't a youth in town who hadn't been on the receiving end of one of Mykola's torments. It was public knowledge that once Mykola stabbed his sister's favorite goat in the neck. It was rumored that he did it because it bleated in front of his window in the morning. He claimed it was sick, and he had to put it down.

He was attractive in the way a sharp dagger was attractive. Even so, the village elders doted on him, and all the teachers loved him. This kind of respect from the older members of the community allowed Mykola to torment his peers and juniors.

"So, what was it? Some herb you brewed with that hag in the woods to make you look more pitiful then usual? Some forest mushroom that turned you into an utter wretch?"

"Mykola, this is unnecessary. We should get back to work," said David, stepping beside Nadia.

"Shut up, Jew, I bet she consulted your family for the right poison to use. I can only imagine the dreadful concoctions you people have thought up over the years," said Mykola, his attention turning to David. Nadia quickly backed up into the trench wall.

"You take that back Mykola," said David. His cheeks and neck muscles were tense. Mykola, by contrast, was loose and calm. The whitening of David's knuckles told Nadia he was ready to use that shovel to smash the back of Mykola's head.

"Forget the Jew, Mykola. If the witch did weasel her way out of fighting, I think we should teach her a lesson," said Ivanka, eager to switch Mykola's target. Mykola turned, his head twisting like a snake.

"You're right, Ivanka," said Mykola, stepping back into Nadia's face.

Nadia was pressed up against the dirt wall of the trench. "What should we do with the little witch?"

"We should cut off her hair," whispered Ivanka, while Sofia stood back, nervously chewing her lip. David looked like he was going to attack Mykola. Nadia grabbed a fistful of dirt and began to form a spell in her mind. She was improvising, but she had a feeling it would work. After all, if David attacked Mykola, his life would be over. If Mykola didn't kill him, the commissar certainly would. Any sort of fighting in volunteer work was punished harshly. While some offenders were shot, most were consigned to a penal corps, and others simply vanished.

"I have a better idea. Why don't we break her hands? I heard some soldiers say that if civilian women can't work with their hands or on the line, then they would work on their backs. Apparently, there are mobile brothels. Some women service fifty men a night."

Sofia gasped, and even Ivanka took a step back, shocked by the cruelty proposed. The moon was once again fixed in Nadia's mind. Things became clear for Nadia. The sweat from her palms mixed with the dirt.

"Mud," whispered Nadia, and the dirt in her hands turned to thick brown mud.

"What was that?" said Mykola.

"Silence," shouted Nadia and slapped Mykola in the mouth with her hand full of mud. The mud on his face crawled over his mouth before hardening to the strength of steel, sealing his mouth shut. Mykola recoiled, falling to the ground. Sofia gasped. David's anger turned to fear, and Ivanka dropped her shovel, stepping slowly back as if she was the next target. Everyone was looking at her like sheep do when they realize a wolf is amongst them. Olivia always said it's best to say something witchy when in a pinch.

"Next time you try to bully me or anyone else, I will make it so every word you say swells your tongue up, I will summon venomous insects to sting and bite you, and I will get a flock of ravens to peck out all your hair. Do you understand me, Mykola?" He nodded his head.

"What the hell are you yokels doing? Get back to work!" shouted a soldier, advancing on the small, frightened group. He looked down and saw Mykola with his mouth sealed shut and a young woman standing over him.

"What happened to him?" he said, pulling his pistol out and pointing it at them. Sofia was now crying.

"It was the witch." Ivanka pointed. "She cursed Mykola because he said she faked her illness to get out of conscription. Everyone saw it." She turned to Sofia and Mykola, who nodded in assent. "Right, David?" For his part, David looked like he wanted to tell the truth, that Ivanka had pestered Nadia, drawing the attention of the cruel Mykola. However, he didn't want to draw any attention from the soldiers, either. He looked at Nadia, and they both knew what he was going to say.

"Yes, she used her witch magic on Mykola," said David.

"Get your hands up," said the soldier. "Get your hands up, or I will shoot you where you stand!"

Nadia complied as the others recoiled. They moved away from her as if Stalin's own giant boot would come down and crush her and anyone else nearby. However, the red-haired witch who was at her examination yesterday was floating on her broom above everyone.

"Stand down, soldier. All magical infractions are to be analyzed and judged by the committee of the occult." The soldier turned around, saw Anna, and saluted. The Red Army witch floated down. "You! Get out of that hole. We need to talk."

"What about the boy who was cursed?" asked the soldier as Nadia climbed out of the hole.

"It will evaporate at midnight. Regardless, they should get back to work. The Nazis aren't exactly taking their time."

"You heard her, get back to work. The Germans move like lightning, so we, in turn, must work like thunder." He then turned to the pair of witches. "What is to be done with this one?"

"I will handle it, for now she is exempt from work," said Anna, sitting on her floating broom.

"The colonel will have to be informed," he said.

"If you think distracting the colonel while he is forming his defense to tell him about one girl who's not working, then by all means do so."

"I see your point, comrade sister." He saluted and went back to patrolling the trench.

"Come, there is a cafe in this village that I hear has the most delightful tea," said Anna.

The pair walked through the town as the Soviet troops bustled about. Every tenth man didn't have a rifle and just held tight to a clip of ammunition. The sharp crack of a firing line could be heard every so often as some poor unfortunate soldier met their end. They passed laundry women, who washed with their hands, and cooks, who had set up seven large ovens in the town square and carried heavy flour bags with their strong arms.

Every time Nadia tried to explain herself or speak, Anna would hold a finger and bid her wait. When they crossed the street, people veered out of their path. Most wanted nothing to do with the pair of witches. When they reached the cafe, Nadia saw it was Trotsky's Cafe.

"Sister, this place doesn't serve witches," Nadia said. Anna waved her hand as if batting away a bug.

"They will serve us, sister." The confidence was reassuring. A few soldiers were sitting at tables outside the cafe. As soon as the pair sat down, several people threw money on the table and left. The few soldiers that stayed either smoked or drank tea but ignored the two witches.

"One advantage of being a known witch is that I'm never crowded." Anna smiled. Nadia tried to return it, but she felt more ostracized than comfortable. Trotsky's wife, Vera, stepped out of the cafe and saw Nadia and Anna sitting at her table. Visible outrage reddened her face, and Vera marched over to the pair of women.

"Get out of here. We don't serve witches or any other sort of conjurors of Satan," said Vera, crossing her arms. "I told you that ages ago," she said, glaring at Nadia.

"Sister, our Soviet Union is an egalitarian state, that does away with such simple superstitions, and discrimination. Now you will serve us two cups of your house tea," said Anna.

"No. I'm willing to serve the soldiers, but I have limits. No black magic harlots, I must draw the line somewhere. Now get out or I shall have the police throw you out," said Vera.

"Sister, you may do so, but I must tell you your establishment is a luxury in a time of war. In fact, it reeks of bourgeois living. If I'm thrown out, then I might have to have a word with local party headquarters. Have them reevaluate the establishment. Maybe it needs to be closed and everyone who works here moved to more necessary fields of work. Like mining. The war needs steel after all. I don't think it needs tea."

Vera's nose went up, her face became bright red, and her powerful arms flexed.

"What can I get for my sisters today? You said you wanted the house blend?"

"Yes, sister, that would be lovely," said Anna, all sweetness and smiles now. Vera returned to the kitchen, and the soldiers around them breathed a sigh of relief that the local cafe was not to be closed.

"Was that really necessary, sister?" asked Nadia, leaning in.

"Yes, she made it necessary. I most certainly would have preferred to have drunk our tea in peace, yet as you know old grudges are hard to shake. A witch must employ many tools to navigate the world. The Red Army, for instance, has given me a powerful belligerent bureaucracy. My position gives me some leeway on how to deal with spiteful peasants. It is known they fear the state more than they fear a witch. Now, I'm a part of the state." Anna then shrugged. "Strange times we live in."

"Indeed, sister." A quiet fell over the pair. Nadia didn't know why she was here. She suspected she was in trouble for flaunting her magic or faking her sickness. After all, she was not sick anymore.

"You're not going to report me to the commissar, are you? For what I did to Mykola?" Nadia blurted out. Anna examined Nadia with those grey eyes. The younger witch felt uneasy with this scrutiny. Anna was much too lovely—a bright and beautiful flower scrutinizing a weed.

"No, sister. I may have joined the Red Army with all its chauvinism and thuggish buffoonery, but my bonds with our sisterhood is far greater," said Anna. Nadia looked away from Anna and her intense gaze and saw her broom. Its shaft was oak, and its bristles were beautiful straw. It was the kind of broom any babushka would have, yet Anna was no older than herself. Vera returned and placed the two cups in front of the pair of witches. Despite her fury, she was still delicate with the cups. She then backed away like a chained wolf.

"So why are we having tea?" asked Nadia, taking hers and smelling the aroma. There was a note of sourness to it.

"If you can call this tea," said Anna after taking a sip. "She must have added spoilt milk to it."

"The locals do this to me all the time. Here, let me freshen up for you." Nadia took her spoon and tapped Anna's cup. "Purify." She repeated the small spell on her own cup. Once again, she smelled the lavender within, and any hint of spoilt milk was gone.

"Lovely." Anna smiled. "For such a miserable owner, this cafe has wonderful tea."

"Between you and I, mine is better," said Nadia.

"Of course. That is the reason we are here," said Anna.

"What reason is that?"

"A conversation with a fellow witch, interaction between peers talking of trials and tribulations, as well as learning a new spell or two. Yes, I could have told the commissar that you were fit for duty and ready to learn how to fight, but you obviously went to some effort to stay out of the army. So, I will take a pleasant conversation and a cup of tea with a sister of the moon."

"Oh, I can't be much of a peer, I haven't even been able to construct a decent broom."

"Really? I'm surprised to hear that; you are obviously an accomplished spell crafter and herbalist. What was in that concoction that made you so sick but allowed you to bounce back so quickly?"

"It was oxen bane," said Nadia.

"Oxen bane? Of course. You are a clever witch, aren't you?"

"I'm afraid I can't take credit for the potion, it was my mentor's doing," said Nadia, feeling embarrassed. She was so very out of her depth.

"So, who is your mentor, little sister? A quite clever witch, if she brewed such a potion out of oxen bane," said Anna, taking a deep sip of her tea.

"She is Baba Olivia," said Nadia. Anna almost choked on the tea, placing it gingerly back on the saucer. She took a napkin and wiped her mouth.

"Baba Olivia? As in Olivia Yosonivitch? The Mockingbird is your mentor?" Anna said, leaning forward.

"I've never heard her called the Mockingbird, but yes. Baba Olivia taught me the craft of the moon," said Nadia. Anna stood up, moved her chair around the table, and sat down next to Nadia before taking her hand.

"You are apparently the witch to know. I didn't even think there was another witch in town, let alone one of the greatest witches of our age and her lovely apprentice."

"I don't know about that last part or even that first part. She is just Baba Olivia to me."

"So humble. Has she told you anything about her exploits?"

"She once told me how she saved her cat from a pack of wolves," said Nadia.

"Your mentor was a fighter back in the day. She fought the tsarists, the reds, the whites, the Germans, practically everyone in the first great war. It is because of her that Russian witches are renowned the world over. She is the reason that American girls dress up as witches for their harvest festival."

"I find that hard to believe," said Nadia, imagining the old woman who chain-smoked being an unholy terror.

"It's true. It is a little odd that she hasn't taught you how to make a flying broom."

"She has, but I'm terrible at making them. Just two days ago my broom split apart when I tried to fly it," said Nadia.

"Cheer up; you must be a late bloomer is all. Some flowers only bloom at midnight after all," said Anna, squeezing Nadia's hand in reassurance. "I imagine it can't be easy to get ahold of the proper ingredients and oils to enchant a broom with the war going on."

"It took many months to get a chance at flight. Now with the war, and the fascists getting so close, there is no telling when I will get to make another attempt."

"Well, since you have shown me that delightful purification spell, and have revealed an effective use for oxen bane, as well as demonstrating that machine hex. I will give you a few things as well," said Anna. She then pulled out a small vial of amber liquid and placed it into Nadia's hand.

"Is this flight oil?" asked Nadia.

"Yes, it is."

"Thank you, sister, I had not expected such kindness," said Nadia, embracing Anna in a hug.

"You are my sister; there is nothing I would not do for you. Now I have another gift to give you," said Anna, taking Nadia's palm. "Before I was with the Red Army, I was part of a traveling circus. I had a fortune teller's booth. I designed my craft with kitsch and theatrics. I made a living telling peasants and factory workers and bureaucrats their future. Mostly happy futures, as they rarely want to hear that misery is coming. It's amazing; everyone wants to know they are something special, destined for great things. If a fortune teller says so, then it confirms their happy future. I will read your palm and tell you what is in store for you, unvarnished. I will tell you exactly what I see in your palm."

Anna examined the lines on Nadia's hand, using her finger to trace curves and splitting paths into the lines of her hand. Her fingers brushing the callouses on her palm.

"You have very delicate fingers," said Nadia. "Mine are so boney."

"They're fine, sister," replied Anna. She then sighed, putting her hand over the lines in Nadia's future. She closed her eyes. "I'm so sorry, Nadia."

"Why, what did you see?"

"Most people have branching paths on their palm. You have those branches as well but in very short twigs. You are burdened with great purpose. Any deviation from that purpose will be the end of your life. At some point, the person you are will die."

"I have no illusions about my own mortality."

"That's not what I mean, sister," said Anna. "Everyone changes into different people throughout their lives. You are not who you were when you were a child, that is not you now. You will experience something akin to death. The complete erasure of who you once were. Your life may or may not continue afterward, but it will be a new you. The witch that sits before me will be no more, and I'm afraid that moment is coming soon." Anna then embraced Nadia.

"I leave for a more active part of the front soon, most likely tomorrow. I now know I made the right call keeping you out of the army. I wish I could stay in this village a little longer so I could learn more about you and maybe even meet your mentor. However, the army demands much of my attention. I have very little room in my world besides fighting and identifying magicians for the war. Our craft does not grow in such a fetid pool. You must learn all you can, on your own terms."

"Sister, you speak as if we won't see each other again," Nadia said. A small tear formed in Anna's eye before she rubbed it away.

"The men hate it when we cry; it doesn't matter if you're a hated witch. Sometimes, I feel as if that's all I can do; it is the only thing I have left that the army can't take from me. The storm is coming, and I want you to know that whatever you do, just know, you can follow the moonlight that shines eternal in Grandmother's Forest."

"I don't understand what that means," said Nadia.

"You will, provided you asked the right animals, or witches," said Anna, then wiped the tears out of Nadia's eyes.

"First-class magician Anna, what are you doing weeping with this yokel?" The pair of women turned to see a stern-faced colonel. It was as if the man had shown up with a hammer and crushed that moment of tenderness. Anna stood up and saluted, along with every other soldier in the cafe.

"This magician was enjoying a moment of rest and respite before she was to be shipped out, sir," said Anna with a practiced response.

"Well, that's over, the Germans are not going to wait while you lollygag with one of your girlfriends. Now you are to report to central headquarters in Kiev immediately. I know you have other means of travel beside the rail yard, so grab your things and get going."

"Yes sir." She saluted her superior officer before mounting her broom. She gave a smile to Nadia before taking to the air like a leaf blown on the wind. The colonel looked over Nadia and gave a sneer.

"You! Don't fraternize with my soldiers any longer, I need them fighting fit and I can't have their heads muddied with thoughts of yokels." He puffed out his chest for emphasis. "And shouldn't you be working on digging trenches? I made a specific order that all students of appropriate age were to report for work assignment."

"My apologies, comrade," said Nadia. "But my sister Anna needed to have a few words with me; I was only following the direction of a member of the military."

"An order that came from a lower stratum of the military. The order of a state magician does not supersede a colonel of the people's Red Army. Now return to your dig site."

"Yes, colonel."

After the colonel had departed, Vera grabbed Nadia by the arm.

"You may have the slight protection of the state, but when the Nazis come to liberate us from the yolk of Communist tyranny, I will be sure to let them know who you are. I will tell the Germans that you are a bride of Satan," she whispered.

"Get your hands off me, Vera, or I will turn your womb into a wasteland and leave you vomiting blood for the rest of your days." Vera recoiled in a moment of panic before rage set in once again.

"A reckoning will happen for your insults today, witch. Be afraid, harlot of Satan, good Christians are coming to fix this land. Be afraid."

Nadia threw some money on the table for the tea and left without saying a word.

5

A Cat in the Night

The rest of the day was filled with hard work, digging at the ground. The rest of the workers gave Nadia a wide berth. She hacked at the earth alone. She rolled Anna's words in her mind. *How am I going to transform? What did she mean by the moon shining on Grandmother's Forest?* There was something ominous about how she was going to experience a death or an experience something like death.

She had never heard anything like this before. Now it stuck in her mind like a beam of light through a cloudy horizon. She needed to talk to Olivia, but she could only see her during curfew. It would be impossible to see her tomorrow as she would be working the trenches once again. It had to be tonight, but how to get there unseen? If she had her broom, it would be simple enough to fly over the patrolling soldiers. As it was, she had to find a way to hide in plain sight. She crafted a spell in her mind. Piece by piece, she remembered the words of darkness and avoidance. The terms of mice and rats, as well as swooping owls. By the time everyone was sent home, she had a spell in her mind. She had only a cup of tea today and water that was over purified and tasted like minerals and iodine. When she made it home, she found her mother and brother had fallen asleep at the table.

"Peter, Mama, it is time to go to bed," said Nadia, gently shaking the pair. An empty bottle of vodka was on the counter. She expected that it was a new bottle. Katarina usually had a glass of vodka at night and drank heavily when she was not working at the factory. However, she never drank this much. Nadia expected this was a way of dealing with frayed nerves. She didn't begrudge her mother that, but she hated how much of the domestic work fell to her.

"Nadia, why did it take so long for you to come home?" Peter said, rubbing his eyes.

"The army is keeping us busy, that's why. Now, come on, you have obviously been up for too long." She then picked Peter up and carried him to his bed. Her arms and back roared in pain while moving the boy, but Nadia gritted her teeth and placed her brother in the small bed that she once slept in.

"Nadia, please tell me a story," asked Peter.

"I thought you were a man now. I heard men don't get bedtime stories."

"Even men still like to hear a good story," he said, peeking out from under the covers.

"Please, Nadia, then I'll go right to bed."

"Alright, my little knight, what would you like to hear?"

"A witch's story," he said, his eyes droopy. *It better be a short one*, she thought. *He is not going to be awake for much longer.* Nadia wanted nothing more than to curl up with him in the small bed and sleep away the uncertainty and fatigue of the day.

"Well, once there was a girl named Misha, a fat and happy girl who lived on a sunny farm that grew apples. She spent many days and nights running through the apple orchards, chasing away the village boys and girls from eating all the fruit. One day Misha found one of her family's trees was barren of apples. In their place were left dozens of nesting dolls, and inside each was an apple core. The next day another apple tree was picked clean, and once again, a dozen nesting dolls were placed around their base.

"Misha decided to stay up all night and find out who exactly was stealing her apples. So, she took one of her mother's black veils and placed it over herself and laid flat on the dirt. When night came, Misha was practically invisible." Nadia smiled. She could tell Peter was already falling asleep. His eyes were fluttering to stay open.

"When she heard the chomping of apples, she crept along the orchard floor. She saw no one, but she followed the sound of chewing. When she looked around, she saw an old woman in a flying mortar and pestle. She took huge bites out of the apples, devouring each in three bites. She threw the cores into a large sack. Little Misha then jumped from her veil and shouted at the strange old woman. 'Stop eating my family's apples,' she cried, 'or I will have the troll that lives atop of the Ural Mountain to come down and eat you.' The old woman laughed as she took another bite.

"'Silly girl, I'm Baba Yaga. I do as I please. You didn't plant these apple trees, for that was me. Your miserable family threw a fence around it and called it theirs.'"

"Chicken house," Peter muttered, eyes now completely closed.

"Yes, Baba Yaga has a house that travels on chicken legs. However, this night her home was far away, and nursing its leg after a bear mistook it for a tree to scratch on. Now where was I? Oh yes.

"'Well, you better stop, or I will call the troll, for he is always hungry,' said Misha.

"'I know this troll you speak of, and he is a cranky and lazy sort. He won't be able to help you,' laughed Baba Yaga, eating another apple.

"'Why does a witch even eat apples? I thought witches only ate children,' asked Misha.

"'You got it all wrong. I don't eat children. I eat *for* children. Each of these nesting dolls was once a child, but they have grown up to be terrible men and women. Their childhood is no more, so I eat apples so they might remember the taste of their childhood and become better people.'

"'Well, if that's the truth, then I suppose a few apples is worth it to make the adults think of childhood again,' said Misha. 'But what do you need the apple cores for?'

"'Simple, my little piglet. I'm going to take the seeds and make arsenic from them. Then I'm going to poison those terrible men and women.' Baba Yaga then flew off into the night."

Nadia saw that Peter was asleep. The end of the story would have to wait for another night. She adjusted his blanket and kissed his forehead.

Nadia returned to the kitchen, to where her mother still sat. She nudged her shoulder to awaken her.

"Mama, it's time to go to bed," said Nadia.

"Alexander is that you?" asked Katarina, hope in her eyes before recognizing her daughter. The hope shattered against the rock of reality.

"No, Mama, it's just me." She helped pull her mother to her feet and took her toward their room. Nadia and Katarina shared a room and a bed. The house was too small for Nadia to have her own room, so when Peter became old enough, he took up Nadia's old room and she moved in with her mother. Nadia had put her mother to bed many times.

"You know, with this war as bad as it is, they are going to need sharpshooters like your father. Maybe they will free him so he can fight in the war. They gave him a medal for his skill. Once he is done, he could come home. Who ever heard of imprisoning a war hero?"

"No one, Mama."

By the time she had gotten her mother into bed, she wanted to crawl in herself. But she had things to do tonight, dangerous things. She looked out the window into the dark. The few streetlamps in town had already been put out. Only the odd flashlights from the odd soldier could be seen in the night. The glow of the moon gave everything a slight iridescent aura, like an afterimage of the world when you close your eyes and your mind tries to fill in the gaps with imagined colors and shapes.

"Mama, do you still have that black veil you wore when Father disappeared?" Nadia asked, turning to her mother, who had already turned on her side.

"It's in the top drawer of my dresser, my darling. Please don't start mourning, someone has to take care of this family," said Katarina.

Nadia opened the dresser and found the black veil, but something else had caught her eye. It was hidden underneath the clothes. Adjusting her mother's dresses and veils, she followed the object's contours to discover a trigger. It was a rifle, with several war medals next to it. Nadia closed the drawer in case a spy was at the window, ready to report the illegal weapon.

"Mother, why do you have a rifle in your dresser?" Nadia asked, sitting on the bed, the black veil clutched in her hand.

"It's your father's from the Great War. When the Revolution was happening, he simply kept the weapon. Now leave me be, my darling, I need to sleep."

"Mother, if the army knew that we had such a thing in the house, we could get in big trouble. We could get sent to prison or worse, and Peter would have to be raised by the state," whispered Nadia.

"I know that, my darling," Katarina said, turning on her back before propping herself up on her elbow. "But it was the last thing of your father's I had left. I just couldn't get rid of it; there were many opportunities. During the famine it would have fetched a good price to buy a month's worth of food."

"You let us starve so you could keep a memento!" Nadia wanted to shout and scream.

"Don't get angry with me. I sold my jewelry, I sold the fillings in my teeth, I even allowed soldiers into my bed so they would skip our house when they came to take food." Katarina grabbed her daughter's shoulders. "When your father was taken, I had to do things to keep this family alive. When everyone was dropping dead in the streets from hunger, and while I grieved for your missing father, I did what I could to keep this family living. I couldn't get rid of that rifle; I still can't. If I do, that will mean he really is gone. He always said, in a world like this you can burn down your house, let the water go foul, and have the crops turn to thorns, but if you have a rifle, you have opportunity. You have your destiny, so my dear, I can't get rid of it."

"I think I understand, Mother," said Nadia. "If no one has found it by now, no one will."

"That's right, my dear, now give me a hug." Nadia felt the bulk of her mother's arms around her. They were reassuring, yet her mother seemed like such a small and frail woman. She was twice Nadia's age, but at times she looked like an old grandmother.

"Now I must sleep. The drink has gotten to me."

"Alright, Mama, get your rest, I will see you in the morning."

"What did you need my veil for, and why aren't you dressed for bed?"

"Don't worry, Mother, I just have to settle a few things before I come to bed."

Nadia stepped out of the bedroom and went to the door of the house. She took the veil and began to whisper the spell she had been working on all afternoon. The black cloth began to shimmer, the fabric melted away, and what remained was the darkness of night in her hands. The veil would look like pure darkness, with a hint of moonlight for good measure.

In the forest, she would be invisible. In the city, however, that was different. It would help hide, but if anyone touched Nadia, she would be discovered and most likely shot for espionage. A voice in the back of her mind told her to just go to bed, don't risk it. But Olivia had answers to her questions. She wrapped the veil around herself and found that her body looked like it was covered in darkness. After taking a deep breath, Nadia put out the candles and stepped outside into the dark.

She had to cross through town to get to the road that led to Olivia. So, Nadia kept to the back roads and alleyways. She moved slowly, looking down each street to make sure no soldiers were crossing. Whenever she did spot a soldier, she pressed herself against the wall, the veil hiding her in night's shadow. The darkness, however, worked both ways.

Nadia didn't see the cat. In an instant, Nadia tripped over the yowling feline and knocked over a trashcan. The veil was pulled off of her, exposing Nadia to the world. The cat hissed and cursed.

"Curse you and your giant feet," the cat muttered. The cat she had run into was the tomcat Dasha, a Russian grey that fought with everyone, even the dogs.

"I'm sorry, Dasha," whispered Nadia.

"Nadia! You trundle foot, why did you step on me?" the cat hissed.

"I'm sorry, I didn't see you," Nadia said, rubbing a nasty scrape on her arm while her hand throbbed with pain, having hit the hard earth.

"Not good enough. Nighttime belongs to cats; you should be asleep. A witch should know that. Now I demand reparations," said Dasha, hopping into her lap and pushing his nose right into her face.

"Reparations? I don't have time for this," said Nadia, standing up and looking down the alleyway. She could hear a high-pitched whistle and soldiers shouting.

"Fish is the customary payment for insulting a noble breed such as myself, but any meat will do."

"Quiet, Dasha, soldiers are coming." Nadia could see the light of the soldiers coming down the street.

"Oh, I'm sorry, am I being an inconvenience to you? I was on my way to make kittens with the young and feisty Polina when you ruined my coat with your magic. I stink of it now. That means no kitten making! It will take all night to get it off."

"I'm sorry, but if you don't be quiet, the soldiers or the secret police will have me shot and you will get nothing at all," she said in an angry whisper. Three soldiers were at the mouth of the alley. On the other side, two more sealed her in.

"Reparations!" yowled Dasha.

"Fine, but I need to hide," said Nadia, squeezing into a spot by the trashcans as the soldiers moved in. They only heard the yowling of cats. Nadia had just enough time to throw the veil over herself as she pressed against the wall.

"I expect a big fish," said Dasha, wagging his tail before hopping up on another trashcan.

"It's just a cat," said one of the soldiers. "We got all worked up for nothing."

"Let's double check to be sure; something knocked over this trashcan."

Nadia huddled against the wall, tightening the veil around her body. She held her breath. The light passed over her as a trio of soldiers walked over to her.

"I found blood," said one of the soldiers.

"What do you think? Local or saboteur?" asked a man. He was right in front of her. She put her hand over her mouth to keep herself from breathing too loudly.

"Does it matter which?"

"Yes, it does. If it's a local, we shoot them; if it's a saboteur, we beat them until they are pissing blood. Then we give them to the secret police, where they will know true suffering."

"I have a blow torch that begs to differ."

"Well, check the other back alleys; maybe they are hiding somewhere else."

"It might have been just the cat."

"No, there is definitely someone else out here, and if we don't find them the commissar might have us lined up against a wall and shot." The soldiers left the alley, the lights shining on every corner looking for someone, anyone, to do violence to.

"Lucky witch," chirped Dasha. "Now let's get my reparations. Sardines are quite tasty, but so is pig. I'm also partial to mutton."

"That will have to come later," said Nadia. She cast a spell to remove the blood from the ground. The blood on the pavement sizzled and evaporated like water on a hot pan.

"Nadia, if you renege on our contract, then I will tell all the animals in the town and forest that you are an oath breaker," said Dasha, his tail puffed out and his back arched.

"I'm not breaking our agreement. An agreement made under duress, I might add. You will get something nice to eat, just not now. I need to first speak with my mentor, Olivia."

"Fine," said Dasha, his tail returning to its usual sleek look. He gave a small chirp, indicating he expected food. "But I insist I follow you around so you may pay your reparations at the earliest possible opportunity."

"Do whatever you like, but if I get captured by the soldiers, you get nothing from me," said Nadia. Dasha gave a chirp of acknowledgment.

The cat and the witch crept through the village, with Dasha occasionally advising which alley to take. In the distance, Nadia could hear the faint sound of artillery bursts. The sounds carried over the horizon. There was something else on the wind: the smell of magic, a mixture of fresh rain and burned autumn leaves. Little known to most, but magic burned like fire and flowed like water. It clung to an individual like mud and was light enough to be carried on the wind. Someone nearby was doing magic, and it got more intense the closer she came to Olivia's home. It didn't take long for Nadia to get to her mentor's home once she found the main road. Even in the dark of night, she could see it. She found Olivia's hut and felt like the area was drowning in magic. It was everywhere. It was pungent like wet cheese with the acidic tang of viper venom.

The smoke of burning wood billowed from Olivia's chimney, and the glass from her windows was fogged over. September was almost freezing at night, so cold that steam puffed out of Nadia's mouth. Yet Olivia's magic made the air around her house quite warm like a summer's day. Olivia had once said her door was never closed to Nadia. But if she ever came when Olivia was practicing a ritual, certain precautions had to be taken. Before touching the handle to Olivia's door, Nadia placed a finger on her forehead and pictured the moon. She brought down the moon in her mind and neutralized the magic that clung to her. The veil shimmered back to its original color and hue. The cloth would have residual magic, but nothing that would interfere with a spell. When she felt she was clean of any errant magic, she stepped into Olivia's hut.

Her mentor knelt in the center of a circle marked with runes and astrological signs. Sage and lavender burned from an orthodox censer that Olivia held in her left hand. In her right, she held a knife skyward.

"That better not be Dasha in my house," said Olivia, turning and looking back. A red rune was written on her forehead, painted with mulched herbs.

"Apologies, Baba, he insisted on following me so that he can get reparations," said Nadia.

"Well, if I catch him trying to fight Petrenko, I will feed him to the wolves," said Olivia. Nadia looked over at the grey tomcat, who looked bored. He simply went about cleaning his fur. "So, what brings my pupil to my home past curfew?"

"I have questions, Baba, but that can wait if you are in the middle of your incantations," said Nadia, sitting down at the table.

"My spells are proving fruitless," said Olivia, hanging the burning censer on a hook by the fireplace that bellowed a wave of heat. Olivia sat across from her pupil.

"What is making them so fruitless? Are you working on a new spell?"

asked Nadia, petting the elderly Petrenko.

"There is no fault in my spell work. More to the point, someone has concocted a clever way of hiding from me."

"Are you looking for something specific? Maybe I can help," said Nadia.

"I fear that the problem is that we don't know what we are looking for. If we had a third witch like the one that left town today, we might be able to pinpoint the disturbance."

"You know of Anna? I met her today."

"I thought it was her. Anna the Red, once known for her brilliant hair, now known for helping the regime hunt our sisters. She placed her sigil in the aether as a courtesy when she came to our town. I saw no reason to do the same."

"I have never seen a more lovely and independent witch in my life, Baba."

"It was bought at a price, my dear," replied Olivia. "Zaida of the Coiling Marsh, Tatianna the Swarm Weaver, and Nikita of the Wondering Wood. All witches apprehended by Anna the Red and turned over to the state."

"But all of those witches were dangerous members of our craft; I have heard you say that both Tatianna and Nikita practiced infanticide in their magic, and Zaida bargained souls for more power,"

"True, they are dangerous and formidable witches, all of them. The world is better off knowing that they are locked up, but it is not our place to interfere with another sister's craft. Our way is one of intuition, not orthodoxy. Without a certain degree of freedom, a witch is practically blind. I know Anna may see what she's doing is morally right, but we cannot police our own. If we do, we are no better than the practitioners of the vulgar craft of the academic schools, an institution that makes machines of war and limits the exploration of magic."

Nadia was quiet as she digested her mentor's words and evident mistrust. Olivia seemed to sense this and took her pupil's hand.

"My apologies. This scent on the wind has me on edge."

"What has you so upset?" said Nadia.

"Scratch my head," meowed Petrenko, and Olivia scratched her cat's head.

"When you said there was a war on the other day, I did some spell work. It was routine things, checking the ley lines, some scrying of old friends out west, and to get the lay of the land. As well as projecting into the spirit realm. What I found disturbed me, my child. For one, our western sisters have gone silent, those of Poland, Germany, Czechoslovakia, Romania, the Balkans. Our Norse sisters and all the western witches, even as far away as France, have also gone silent. This could mean they have gone into hiding and don't want to be found. But I have heard tales of such things happening before, in places like Spain, the Americas, the Holy Roman Empire, and Old England. Witches were rounded up and killed.

"When I checked the ley lines, I found them choked with foul and harmful magic. As if there is something feeding on pain and suffering and spitting it directly into the magic of the world. Finally, I went into the spirit realm. In that mental landscape of the world, I saw a colossal eagle gripping a black sun in its talons. In the sun's heart was a bleeding swastika. I once spoke with a witch from the Far East. I learned how that was once a symbol of peace. Now it has been tortured, corrupted, and perverted into a new shape of arrogance, hate, and violence.

"These Nazis and their polluted ideology have sunk their teeth into

Germany and seek to foul all magic. They aim to twist everything into their own evil form. This is a regime that is using black magic and corrupted symbols to reinforce its grip on the mind, while using violence and persecution to reshape the world."

"The papers have said that that Nazis have been proclaiming themselves the ideological enemy of the Soviet Union. That the Slavic people are sub-human, and that Jews are pulling the strings. Utter nonsense, of course," said Nadia.

"Of course it is, but it still has power," said Olivia, who looked prominent in the flickering shadows. Someone primal and dangerous, yet loving and powerful. "Regardless, if an idea is ludicrous or insane, for some it can hold great comfort, and link by link, with each bias, people become a slave to the idea. If someone were to pull those chains, they could control these enslaved minds to a terrible purpose.

"But, my dear, there is something else. As I searched, I caught the whiff of something. It was magic, but not any magic I had ever seen. It was metallic and oily. It tasted of blood and rust. I caught just a whiff of it, for but a moment, then it vanished. My dear, have you ever been walking through the forest and run into a single strain of spider's web? The thin gossamer the clings and tickles your face before its snaps and vanishes."

"Yes, Baba."

"Well, it was like that. Someone had set a single thread, and I felt it cling to me. This magic is not easily shaken, either. I have been trying to track it all evening, yet it eludes me. If only I knew who laid the line, I could find out more. However, with recent developments I fear that whoever that magician is, they are definitely working with the Nazis and whatever has been polluting the ley lines."

"So, what do we do, Baba?" asked Nadia.

"I don't know, my child. I fear doing what we have always done might not work this time. Gone are the days of hiding and fighting only when necessary. This new foe is not something I fully understand. In the same turn, I understand it all too well. For now, we wait, and you must gather herbs to make a new broom. The sooner you get your broom flying, the sooner we can flee if needed."

"Baba." Nadia reached into her pocket and pulled out the vial of flight oil. The amber liquid trapped the fire's light and flickered.

"My dear, where did you get this? Did you perhaps store some from a previous batch?"

"No, Baba. Anna the Red gave it to me when we spoke earlier today; she said it was in exchange for learning of the oxen bane."

"At least Anna remembers some of the old ways. You must make your broom before the waning moon. When the sky is dark, we are at our weakest."

"I understand, Baba."

"Now, if I remember, you had some questions for me. Here I'm filling you with dread and my own worries, and I have not been a good teacher and answered your questions."

"Well," started Nadia, tucking the oil back in her pocket. "Anna told me some things. She said you fought in the Great War. Why have you never told me this?"

"That was a long time ago," she replied. Olivia seemed to have wilted. "I was following my own teacher, who thought that this was the moment. A moment to strike at the old systems of oppression. In many ways it was in line with the Communist Party of Marx, not this deranged thing Stalin and Lenin had made. We thought if we could overthrow the kings of this age, a more egalitarian world would emerge. However, greedy men wanted power for themselves, and we couldn't join them. The Bolsheviks killed my mentor. In my anger I struck out at everyone. I tried to tear down the world with my own two hands. I suppose that Serbian boy from the Black Hand did a better job of tearing down the old world then I ever could. Ancient history of a naive girl who has become disillusioned. I will speak no more of this. It hurts me to this day."

"I understand, Baba," said Nadia.

"No, you don't, my dear, but that's alright. The longer you remain ignorant of such things the better for your soul. What is your next question?"

"Anna said something peculiar to me. Where does the moon always shine on Grandmother's Forest? She said I should follow the light to it."

At Nadia's words, Olivia became silent. She sighed and stood; she looked down on the magical circle in the center of her floor. The chalk outlines, with its strange symbols and geometric lines, interlocked the whole.

"I have nothing more to teach you," said Olivia. "You are no longer my student."

"Baba, what do you mean, have I done something wrong?" Nadia stepped over to her mentor.

"No, my dear, but you have been recognized by an established witch. More importantly, you have been invited to a coven."

"A coven? I think I would have remembered something like that, Baba," said Nadia.

"I'm no longer your Baba. I'm your sister. You were invited into a coven. The Coven of the Ever-Shining Moon. One of the most revered and oldest covens of the East. Some covens like the Star's Thorns and the Owl Talons are well known amongst the uninitiated, but the Ever-Shining Moon has been around before there was a written word. Now you are a member of that coven."

"Baba."

"Olivia, my dear sister. I have no more use for that title."

"Fine, Olivia, my sister, I can't go off and join some coven! I barely know anything about the greater witch community, I don't know the etiquette, or anyone in this coven. I didn't even know I was invited to one until you told me."

"It sounds like you're throwing this kitten out into the woods alone," said Dasha, his ears twitching. Upon hearing this, the elderly Petrenko stood up and hobbled to the edge of the table.

"Quiet, you rogue, I have known Nadia all her life. If my Olivia says it's time to push her into the woods, then it's time."

"Not from where I sit," said Dasha.

"Dasha, be quiet," Olivia hissed. Dasha went back to licking himself.

"He is right, sister. I'm not ready to join a sisterhood of such an illustrious coven."

"Bah." Olivia grabbed the black veil that Nadia held in her hand. "This veil is covered in applied magic. I presume you used a spell of concealment of some sort so that you could get out here tonight. I have never taught you such a spell, and yet you made it. Improvisation, imagination, and execution are a sign of an accomplished witch."

"Baba, I'm not ready!" said Nadia. "I still need you. I can't even fly on my own broom without it ripping apart or throwing myself into the garden."

"A broom does not make the witch, my dear," Olivia said, grabbing Nadia's shoulders. She then pulled Nadia in for a hug. Olivia squeezed Nadia's thin frame. Nadia embraced her former mentor after a moment. "A witch makes herself. She lets no one else define that for her."

"Baba, you just said I was recognized by a coven, and now you're saying I must define myself as a witch. You're speaking in contradictions."

"Is there anything more witchlike? You are ready to become a full-fledged witch. When Anna the Red, a member of the Ever-Shining Moon invited you, it was a clear sign to me that my task was done. Yes, you could stay a couple more years, learn some spells here and there, but I fear it will keep you from growing into your own. I can no longer keep you in the tiny garden of my tutelage. I must insist you grow."

"Baba, I don't even know where Grandmother's Forest is. Could you tell me that, at the very least?"

"I'm afraid I can't, my dear. There are a great many forests, most ordinary, others sacred. The Ever-Shining Moon has never been open about such information." Nadia parted from Olivia's arms and held her hands. She felt abandoned. She knew from Olivia's words that she meant well, but Dasha was right. It was like she was being thrown into the woods. Even worse at a time when mad dogs approached her home. "Now, Nadia, my sister. I must insist you stop calling me Baba. It is making me feel old."

"Alright, Olivia, so what coven are you a part of?" asked Nadia, feeling overwhelmed about her new expanding horizon.

"A witch never reveals her allegiances. Not openly, at least."

"I guess there is nothing more for me here," said Nadia, taking back her mother's black veil.

"There is, but not for long. I will always be your sister, and friend. I will be preparing to leave. Whatever forces or things the Nazis are planning, I want nothing to do with. You will be wise to make your own preparations for leaving as well."

"I don't know if I can. My mother and brother are here, and the government is refusing to let anyone flee, so as not to cause a panic."

"Then you must help them flee. War is harsh on all of us, especially witches and their families."

"You ask so much from a newly ordained witch."

"Are you two done?" Dasha yawned. "My night has already been ruined and I would like to get my reparations paid as soon as possible."

"Stuff your reparations, Dasha," hissed Petrenko.

"You take it back, old man, or I will scratch you from tail to tongue."

"Dasha, get out of my home this instant," shouted Olivia. The grey cat's tail puffed out and his back arched, and he began to hiss and yowl. He then ran out the front door as he smelled the magic being summoned. "One more piece of advice, my dear. Learn to keep better company then Dasha."

"Yes, sister," said Nadia.

"Now go home. It would do us no good if you were arrested by the military for espionage."

"Goodnight, sister."

"Goodnight, Nadia."

"Well, that was a waste of time," said Dasha, licking his paw as Nadia stepped out of Olivia's home.

"Come on, Dasha," Nadia sighed. "Let's go see what I have in the pantry."

The return to town was uneventful. With Dasha's help, the pair made it back home with none the wiser. It was late when Nadia came in and collapsed on the puffy chair by the dying fire. The long workday and two conversations with witches had drained Nadia of all her energy. Fatigued boiled in her brain, and all she wanted to do was sleep before another long day of mandatory work tomorrow. *Should a witch even bother with state labor?* she thought.

"Hey, it's time for repayment," yowled Dasha in her face.

"Let me rest my eyes for but a moment, Dasha. You will get your reparations."

"No, Nadia. I have been as patient as I can be with you. Now it is time to fulfill your end of the bargain."

"A bargain made under duress," said Nadia. She felt Dasha on her chest.

"A bargain is a bargain, especially with a cat," said Dasha. "You do remember that, right, or am I going to have to tell all the animals in town that Nadia the newly minted witch breaks her promises?"

"Fine." Nadia stood up and went to the pantry. Since the war started months ago, meat was hard to come by, with most of it directed to the war effort. There were a few cans of sardines and canned beef leftover. She took the sardines, as that was what was traditional. She opened the can, and the salty oil smell of fish hit her nose. She took a fish and ate it. Her stomach still growled in hunger, but she found it was best not to overeat. She then placed the can in front of Dasha.

"What is this?"

"Sardines. It's traditional. You said so."

"I don't know what you think this is, but fish is alive and wriggling. While it smells good and I will eat it, it is not good enough reparations."

"Whatever, Dasha. For all I care, my end of the bargain is complete," said Nadia, sitting at the table.

"I want something fresh. Something decent. I can get canned food at any human house. I want something fresh!"

"Fine, Dasha, but you won't get it any time soon. The war has seen to that. I don't know when I will have a chance to pay you back."

"Then I have no choice but to escort you until I'm repaid."

"Fine, but right now I'm going to bed. The day has been too long," said Nadia, returning to her shared bedroom with her mother. Dasha ate the fish, licking his chops of all the oil and fish pieces before continuing to lick away all the magic that he had on his body.

"This girl is going to be trouble," he muttered to himself.

6
Little Soldiers on Parade

Nadia's night was short, for in the early morning, the sound of airplanes could be heard over the village. The planes sounded otherworldly and terrifying. The only thing worse was the concussive sound of explosions.

"My God, they're bombing us!" shouted Katarina, looking out the window. Nadia pulled herself from the bed.

"Mama! Didn't you read the pamphlets? Stay away from the windows," cried Nadia, pulling her mother away. Shrieks of terror could be heard from Peter's room over the chattering of machine guns from a passing plane. Nadia and her mother both ran to Peter's room to find him hiding under his bed.

"Peter, get out from under there. If a bomb hits the house, you will be buried!" shouted Nadia.

"If a bomb hits the house, there will be nothing!" shouted Katarina as another loud explosion went off. Peter crawled out from under the bed and hugged his mother and sister. The small family huddled close as everything turned into screams and explosions. Their world rocked with another explosion outside the house. The toys on Peter's dresser fell on the floor while the lamp by his bed fell and shattered. The crashing sound was devoured by the howling cacophony outside the house. Nadia only knew that she held the warm bodies of her family and prayed that one of those whistling bombs would not hit her home.

The roar outside was deafening as the planes soared overhead with their unearthly wail. Nadia's jaw hurt as she gritted her teeth; her eyes held tight as she hugged her family. Something in her chest was constricting. It became too much. That was when she realized she wasn't breathing. She inhaled and exhaled and counted the breaths as the world rumbled and shook. Then the bombing and shooting stopped, with the rumble of the planes fading as they left the village. The small family held each other tight. After a minute, the cries of the injured could be heard. Nadia let go of her brother and mother. She realized she was shaking. She tried to make a fist to cease the shivering, but her body wouldn't obey her. Peter was pale and had a faraway look in his eyes, an obvious sign of shock. Only her mother remained with any degree of levelheadedness.

"We need to make sure the house is alright," she said, standing up. "We need to get dressed and prepared for the day."

"What?" said Nadia, hearing her mother's words but not their meaning.

"We need to get dressed quickly. In case we need to run to an air raid shelter. Nadia, go check the trunk in the closet."

Nadia returned to their shared bedroom to find that half the room had collapsed. Singed and splintered wood covered the floor, and part of the roof had fallen on the bed, crushing it. *If we had stayed in here, we might have been killed,* thought Nadia. She checked the trunk that her mother mentioned.

It was leaking. When she opened the trunk, she saw five bottles of liquor rested on their winter blankets. The bottles were shattered, with alcohol and glass soaked into the fabric. She closed it and started getting dressed.

The action felt ordinary and unreal in the destroyed room.

"Nadia? Get out of there! The roof could collapse and crush you!" her mother shouted from the doorway. Nadia realized that she was staring at a crack in the mirror, her mother's voice snapping her out of her fugue.

"Did you check the trunk?"

"They are all broken, Mama," said Nadia. Her voice was hoarse. *When was I screaming?* she thought.

"Damn. Now sit with your brother. Hopefully I can get my clothes."

Nadia drifted into the main room of the house to find her brother sitting at the table. with Dasha on his lap.

"Nadia! The world has erupted, what's going on?" the cat yowled.

"I think we were attacked by airplanes," said Nadia.

"Airplanes! Those things? Why would they ever want to attack here? What did you humans do to anger them?" asked Dasha.

"We didn't do anything, Dasha, they are piloted by the Nazis, other humans," said Nadia.

"Humans can fly?" he yowled. "This is what you do with flight! Make explosions! Shooting at people on the ground! If I could fly, I would never do such a thing," he growled.

"It's okay, kitty, the planes are gone," Peter said, petting Dasha's back.

"Peter, why do you have your school bag? You can't go to school on a day like this."

"I don't know, Mama packed it," he replied.

"Nadia, we need to get out of here before those planes return," growled

Dasha.

"You can go anytime you wish, Dasha! No one is keeping you here!" snapped Nadia.

"You are keeping me here! I want what is owed."

"What is Dasha doing here?" Katarina said, trundling in with two more bags.

"He must have run in when the bombs came," said Peter, a bit of his color returning.

"It doesn't matter. We need to leave so we can get a seat on the train," said Katarina as she foisted a long object wrapped up in canvas into Nadia's hands. "Whatever you do, don't lose that rifle, my child."

"A train! We can't leave here. This is our home!" shouted Nadia, cradling the firearm. It was heavier than she expected.

"I have been listening to the radio for months, my child. If the fascists get into this town, they will do unspeakable things to us. I want to get us out of here. I wish the alcohol wasn't gone. I could use a drink to calm my nerves. It would have been handy to bargain our way onto the train. Now come on, grab as many of the canned goods as you can and throw them in your satchel."

Nadia followed her mother's instructions, the simple directions giving her purpose. Nadia filled her satchel with canned food, as well as several bundles of herbs and vials. With these things, she could make medicine if needed.

"Don't forget something for me," meowed Dasha.

"Can't you hunt for mice?" said Nadia.

"Not always!" replied Dasha.

"Nadia, focus. Stop it with the cat noises."

"I'm trying, Mother," snapped Nadia. "He is being very demanding."

"Well, let's get going. There is no telling how many people are at the train station now," said Katarina.

The family left the house and found a small, unexploded bomb in the middle of their garden. There were multiple fires across the town. People cried or moaned in pain from injuries. Someone in the distance was wailing. All the while the morning sun crept over the horizon. Katarina held Peter and Nadia by the hand. The family made their way to the train station, with Dasha following behind. The streets were pockmarked with bullet holes that led to the corpses of people Nadia knew all her life.

A commissar stalked the streets with his pistol drawn. His brown uniform and wide-brimmed hat looked spotless and pristine amid the destruction around them.

"Do not panic. We must show resolve in the face of the jack-booted fascist. Order will be maintained at all costs. Any looting will be met with summary execution, public drunkenness is to be met with summary execution, any talk of surrendering to the fascists will be met with summary execution!" shouted the commissar into a megaphone.

The family moved past him, and a minute later, they heard the double tap of a pistol going off, followed by the screams of some poor unfortunate who broke one of the new, deadly regulations.

The train station was a smoking mess. Soldier swarmed around train cars, with gangs of horses pulling destroyed cars off the tracks. Men heaved supplies off cars and threw them in the street to make room for escaping soldiers while a crowd of villagers steadily grew.

A line of soldiers separated the growing crowd from the train while a commissar paced back and forth with a megaphone to his lips.

"Evacuation is only permitted for military personal. We are not taking any civilians. You must brave the coming fascists, you must not show fear, you must not panic. We may be relocated temporarily but we will come and lift the siege of the village," the commissar shouted in his megaphone as he paced. He was young, only a little older than Nadia. Not like the grim-faced old man she usually saw. Katarina pushed her way to the front of the crowd of citizens. Nadia, for lack of purpose, followed her through the crowd. She was jostled as she squeezed through the warm mass of people.

"Please, you must at least take my son and daughter with you. They must escape!" Katarina pleaded to one of the uniformed soldiers. He looked oddly familiar. It was only when he spoke that Nadia realized it was David.

"David, what's going on? And why are you in a soldier's uniform?" asked Nadia, squeezing between burly villagers.

"Nadia, thank goodness you're alive. The army is relocating to Kiev. It is under siege. All across the front the fascists are everywhere. The battalion has been ordered to regroup with the rest of the army, I don't know where. But they're taking all the young men who volunteer with them. With the Nazis a day away, I'm getting out while I can. I heard they are hanging Jews when they come into a town. At least in the army I have a gun to shoot back," he said.

"What about your family?" asked Nadia. David looked pained when she asked him that.

"They went into the forest. Now please don't ask me anymore about them," he said.

"Nadia, we need to get you and Peter on that train," Katarina said, gripping her daughter's arm. Peter had tears running down his face, but he wasn't sobbing.

"Mama, I don't want to leave you alone," said Peter.

"Hush, my darling. Nadia, I have seen war, it is not a thing a young woman or small boy to see."

"Mama, I can't leave you behind, I'm not ready to leave here. Don't ask this of me," said Nadia.

"I'm sorry, but we can't take anyone, army only. We are going to be short on train cars with the Nazi air raids," said David.

"Nadia." Her mother squeezed Nadia's arm; anguish and near panic were on her mother's face. "I have been a poor mother, languishing for a man that may never come back, but I can't see my children chewed up by this war. I don't know how, but you must use your magic or something to get you and Peter on the train."

Nadia wanted to tell her mother that she couldn't, but she remembered what her mentor had told her. Olivia had said, "Never let anyone know you can't do something; as a witch you must find a way, and often times you will get unexpected solutions." Nadia looked at her mother's anguished face and drifted over to look at David and the young commissar. Everyone was so young, too young to be in uniform. She then looked down at Peter, also too young to be fleeing from home. Then it occurred to her.

"David, Peter forgot his uniform," said Nadia, taking her brother and pushing him in front of her former classmate.

"What? No, he is too young for the army," replied David.

"Nonsense," said Nadia. "No doubt his paperwork has all the right details, he just forgot his uniform. The army can't take children with them. But they can always take more soldiers."

David was perplexed for a moment, then he caught on.

"Commissar!" he shouted. The young political officer came over. "This soldier is not in his uniform, but the family assures me he is a member of the Red Army," said David.

"You block-head, this is a child. I said no civilians on the train."

"Yes, comrade commissar, I'm aware of the orders. Private..." David for a moment drew a blank before snapping at Nadia to get his answer.

"Oh, Peter. Peter Voloshyn."

"Yes, Private Voloshyn is not a civilian, and we can get him on the train, away from the marauding fascists."

"I think I understand what is going on," said the commissar, furrowing his brow. He turned to the family and put his hand on his hips. "Private Voloshyn, do you know what the punishment for desertion is?"

"No, sir," said Peter, looking at his shoes.

"It is execution by firing squad, so it's a good thing you reported to me before we left, otherwise you would have to be punished." Peter gasped. "Disobeying an order is an equally harsh sentence. If a civilian was discovered impersonating a soldier, then they would have to be sent out far, far, away from the front line. That way, they don't try to sneak into the army again. Some place with food, and warm beds, and a place to learn their letters," said the commissar. Despite his stern face, a bit of humanity crept past the uniform. Concern could be seen in the young man's eyes. He was not old enough to be thoroughly indoctrinated in the party ideology. Nadia could see that.

"Thank you, sir," Katarina said, throwing herself on the commissar and kissing his cheeks.

"Get off me, woman, this is indecent," he said, pushing Katarina off. "Alright soldier, say goodbye to your family and get on the train." Suddenly, all eyes were on Peter. On realizing the attention, and the fact he was about to leave his family into an unknown future, he began sobbing.

"I don't want to leave you alone. Why can't Mama or Nadia come?"

"Because, my darling," said Katarina, hugging her son. "This world is complicated, and sometimes we must face challenges alone. Where you go is a mystery, but God willing. He will keep you safe, my darling, but for now we must part. I'm happy that you are going someplace safe. Now give me a hug." The two embraced, Katarina squeezing her son as tight as she could as if letting go for a moment would cause him to disappear forever. Nadia then crouched down to her brother and hugged him as well.

"Peter, be brave, be my little knight you said you were. You may not face a dragon, but remember, I will find you. When Mama and I are safe, I will find you."

"Promise?"

"Promise." She then kissed his cheek before standing up again and guiding him to the commissar.

"Commissar!" shouted someone in the crowd. "My son is out of uniform as well. The villager then pushed the child forward.

"Mine as well," shouted another.

"My son will need one of the others to change their diapers."

"Does a little girl soldier count?" A torrent of parents, all clamoring to convince the commissar their children were soldiers, stepped forward.

"What have I gotten myself into?" the commissar said, rubbing his head. "Alright, all soldiers step forward. I'm going to get shot for this." One by one, children left the crowd and passed the line of soldiers. One little boy led his sister, who was still a toddler. An older boy held a baby. Like Peter, they all shuffled off to the train.

"Now, the rest of you disperse. If you don't have soldiers out of uniform, we don't want anything to do with you."

"What about me? I'm a soldier, let me on that train!" said someone in the crowd.

"I said disperse!" The commissar fired his gun in the air. "Men if this crowd doesn't disperse by the count of ten, you are to open fire on them. Is that understood?" he shouted. The soldiers remained silent, looking at each other. David was looking confused. Not too long ago, he was one of the villagers. "I said, is that understood, or do I have to shoot you all for insubordination?"

"Yes, commissar," shouted the soldiers. David then raised his rifle to point it at Nadia and Katarina. Nadia realized at that moment the horror of the party. It made accomplices of ordinary people with the threat of violence. That moment of humanity was just crushed by a steamroller of power.

"One, two, three," shouted the commissar as the people ran. Katarina and Nadia were pushed and jostled everywhere. It didn't matter where they went, as long as they were moving away from those guns.

7
Marauders

The pair found themselves in front of the town's school. All around them, the world they knew was both familiar and unrecognizable. The streets were pock marked with bullet holes. The government building was on fire, having been hit with several bombs. It smoked and burned while a few sparse walls still stood. The ringing of the fire brigade as it tried to battle the wave of destruction could be heard throughout the city. The school they leaned against was somehow untouched from the morning air raid. Stalin's image loomed over Nadia and her mother. They watched one of their neighbors, a kind, quiet woman named Ludmilla, trudge down the street holding her dead son in her arms, blood leaking on her face from a head wound, one of her eyes sealed closed from the swelling. The town's priest, Ivan Chernoff, was dead in the street, a trail of bullets leading right up to his corpse. Nadia and the priests had never gotten along, as Ivan thought Nadia's practice of witchcraft was the work of the devil. She remembered when Ivan found out she was getting tutelage from Olivia. He berated her in public until her mother was able to rescue her. She hated him for a long time because of that, but now he was dead.

Her stomach growled. She had eaten little the past two days, and amid the death and turmoil of the air raid, her stomach reminded her she was alive. Her hunger made her feel guilty; she felt guilty being alive when so many others perished, and now her brother was gone. Put on a train to who knows where. Nadia pulled her face into her knees and began to cry. A muffled sob released the tension that was in her arms and legs that sent her shivering. She was no different than any of the dozens of other people sobbing in the street. War had come to her home. A home that was ugly, mean, and intolerant, but it was safe. Now it wasn't even safe. She could hear the trains whistle from across town, most likely taking off east. Katarina grabbed her shoulder and held her tight.

"There, there, Peter is safe on the train now. We have done our part. Let it out, my darling. Don't think I don't hear that stomach of yours growling. We will eat here," Katarina said, opening her bag and pulling out a can of peaches. "Now eat the whole thing, my darling, we don't know when we will get a proper meal."

Nadia wiped her eyes and did as her mother said. She pulled the ring on the can, opening it up, and the sweet smell of peaches hit her nose. The fruit was sliced and swam in sticky juice.

"We should go home and make some proper food, Mama. At the very least get some proper utensils," said Nadia.

"We can't go home; there is a bomb in our garden. It could explode any time and kill us."

"So where are we supposed to sleep?" Nadia asked, looking at Katarina. It was all happening so fast. A brother sent away, a home abandoned, and not a single utensil in sight.

"What about Olivia? Would she take us in?" Katarina asked, opening her can. She grimaced when she realized it was mashed beets. "I really need a bottle soon. I'm going to get the shakes by midday."

"I don't know, Mama. Olivia recently said I was no longer her apprentice," said Nadia, eating the peaches. Her stomach twisted up when the sweet juice hit her gut. She felt queasy eating the fruit, but she continued, knowing that Katarina would scold her if she didn't eat enough.

"Why, what for? Was it because of the broom?" Katarina asked.

"Apparently, I graduated. I'm now a full witch, according to Baba...I guess it's just Olivia now. It feels as if the whole world is conspiring to take away everything I hold dear." Katarina then grabbed her daughter's ear and dug into the cartilage with her fingernail. The pain was sharp and stinging, and Nadia squealed as her mother pulled her close.

"Do you not see what has happen to our town? Do you not see the body of the priest, or the piles of rubble? You are not the only one who is suffering, Nadia. We must be grateful that we do not have it worse. We have our lives, and we know that Peter is headed somewhere safe. We have food for the moment; we are already much better off."

She let go of Nadia's ear, and the young witch winced and rubbed the sore spot. In the distance, she could hear rifle fire and the concussive sound of tank shells. A chattering of machine guns rose.

"I'm sorry, Mama."

"I'm sorry, too, my darling." Katarina hugged her daughter. "Hardships are coming. We may suffer, but suffering is universal. We must not forget that."

"Do I get anything from the bag of food?" asked Dasha, rubbing against

Nadia. Hearing the tomcat's meow, Katarina looked up at him.

"Dasha, shoo, we have nothing for you. Leave us alone, alley cat."

"I'm afraid he won't," said Nadia, rubbing her eyes. "I promised him reparations because I interrupted his date last night," Katarina looked at her daughter and shook her head.

"Foolish girl, never get indebted to a cat. They have long memories and never forgive a slight."

"I'm starting to realize that."

"Don't talk about me as if I can't hear you. Give me something to eat," he yowled. Ludmilla had collapsed on the sidewalk holding her dead son, weeping and rocking him as if he were still a baby.

"You can finish mine," said Nadia, watching the tragic episode in front of her. "I don't feel like eating anymore. It doesn't seem appropriate."

"Stop yowling like a cat," said her mother. "It's strange when you talk to animals like that. Now, will Olivia help us out?"

"There is only one way of finding out," said Nadia, standing up, taking her father's rifle in its canvas cover in her arms and her satchel of canned food.

"Fine, I'm going to find a mouse. I will find you later," said Dasha. "Nadia, if you try to skip town, I will find you. You won't get away from me that easily." Dasha ran down the street toward the secret place were cats go hunting.

"If only your father were here now," said Katarina, standing up.

The pair headed down the road that led out of town to the forest. When they heard the sound of airplanes, they hit the ground. The planes rumbled at low altitude, their propellers slicing the air as they flew overhead. No planes shot at them, for whatever reason. It became evident that the planes had no interest in a pair of women. It was no less nerve-wracking for the pair, having just been bombed that morning. The sun was much higher in the sky at almost midday, and they were getting closer to Olivia's cabin. Already Nadia could tell something was wrong as a column of smoke rose above the tree line.

"I have just realized I have never been to Olivia's home. I doubt she would have accepted me in, being a Christian woman. I hope for our sakes she will let me in now."

A rumble could be heard in the distance, like the sound of a great mass of people. Ahead of Nadia and Katarina was the forest edge, and a rolling rumble came from deep within.

"Hush, Mama, what is that sound?" asked Nadia, adjusting the bundled rifle in her arms. Katarina's eyes squinted, looking into the wood.

"Hide your father's rifle, my darling. I hear horses. Maybe they are mounted troops. I don't know if it's the Red Army or the Nazis. I doubt either will be pleased that we have a weapon." The two moved off the road and into the ditch, their feet sinking into the mud. Nadia quickly took a fistful of dirt and whispered into it.

"Mud of the earth, and water of the sky, hide this away from prying eyes." She then wiped the mud on the canvas cloth of the rifle and placed it on the ground. The weapon sank into the earth. There was no trace of the land being disturbed at all.

"Here they come. Lean against the ditch wall," said Katarina. The two women leaned flat against the ground as the rumble moved toward them. Out of the forest rode dozens of horses, and camouflaged riders. They galloped down the road, kicking up mud and dirt in their wake.

"Grass of the fields, grass of the muck, hide us in your sweet embrace," Nadia whispered, the spell leaving her tongue with the taste of wildflowers.

The grass wrapped over the pair as the horses drew closer. Katarina gasped as the grass wrapped her arms and legs, and she put her hand over her mouth so she couldn't be heard. In a short time, the grass had covered both women.

Nadia could still see the road and the passing riders. They carried rifles and machine guns; grenades and daggers hung on their belts. Menacing helmets with a twin lightning bolt emblems covered their heads. One of the riders stopped right in front of Nadia and her mother. He was tall and made taller by his fierce black horse that chomped and snarled when it stopped. The beast pawed at the ground, its hooves digging into the earth like a sharpened shovel. The man didn't have a helmet. He wore a cap and a black leather coat, with a wrought iron gauntlet more akin to knight armor than a soldier's glove. While the other soldiers had the hint of stubble from the campaign, this man was clean-shaven. His hair was grey, but he looked to be in his mid-thirties.

He smelled the air, breathing deep the fumes of the world. He unclipped the cover of his pistol before he reached into his pocket. The man took another deep breath, as if he was trying to locate something by scent. With his gauntlet-clad hand raised in the air, he dropped a small crystal on a silver chain. It fell like an executed victim with a sudden jerk. Nadia saw the insignia on his breast. A swastika within a circle. A member of the German Thule Society.

Adolph Hitler paraded his magicians about the Reichstag in 1934, after reestablishing the Germanic college of magic, and again in 1936, during the Olympic Games. Olivia had always said they were a strange and diabolical breed of magicians and best to be avoided. For their minds were polluted with offensive symbols and ideology. Now one was right in front of her with a blood-red crystal that made Nadia's blood run cold. The crystal began to rotate. When it gained enough momentum, it started to spin. She held her breath.

The crystal began to move more linearly, focusing on Nadia's position. *Is he looking for stray magic?* thought Nadia. One of the other riders rode up to the magician and said something in German. The magician responded. He was distracted for a moment, and Nadia prayed that they wouldn't be found.

The magician smiled, spoke some more German, and rode off with the mounted soldiers.

The tail end of the troop finally made itself visible. The riders rode at a slower pace. Behind them, tied with ropes, were a dozen people. They were half pulled, half dragged across the road.

To Nadia's horror, she recognized David's parents. Nadia then noticed that all the people the riders had tied up were David's Jewish relatives. One of the people pulled along was very old. Nadia thought it was David's grandfather. His rope was stiff as he struggled to keep up.

The old man made a misstep, and he fell. He yelled as he hit the ground and was dragged along the road for several meters before resting in front of the pair of women. One of the riders shouted, broke off from the others, and circled back, his horse shaking its head as he turned around. This man didn't have a captive; he shouted at the old man on the ground.

"Please, sir, my leg, it is twisted," said the old man. The rider got off his horse, his boots squishing into the mud. Nadia could see the silver spurs on his boots, a filigree designed with swastikas of gold.

"Please, he is an old man, he shouldn't be running," said David's mother. The rider shouted back in incomprehensible German. Nadia wished she had some babble root to chew, then she would be able to understand precisely what he was saying. Right now, she may not have known the words, but the intent was clear. He shouted again.

"Sir, my leg is twisted," said the old man, raising his hand while pleading. The rider sighed before pulling out his sidearm and shooting the man twice. David's mother started screaming when the rider pulled out his pistol. When she tried to go to the body, the others held her back. Nadia had seen people die slowly from malnutrition, but the sudden death almost made her gasp.

She held her voice in check, biting into her bottom lip to keep from shaking. She was horrified, yet she couldn't look away. The rider looked at the corpse for a moment before laughing. He spoke in German, then the other soldiers started laughing. All the while, the women wailed. The rider who shot the old man began to do a mock convulsion in imitation of the death spasm of the man on the ground. The riders began to applaud. The shooter then fired twice more into the old man's body. He holstered his pistol, pulled out the long knife at his belt, and cut the rope. The shooter then grabbed the old man's hands and started dragging him to the ditch. One of the other riders said something. The shooter shrugged, dropped the body at the edge of the ditch, and remounted his horse. Again, the troop and the prisoners were off. The wailing grew quieter in the distance. Nadia and Katarina were left staring at the twitching old man in silence.

After several minutes, the two stood up, shaking off the grass. Now that they were safe, their horror could find expression.

"Why did they kill him?" sobbed Katarina. "Why did they have to commit such casual cruelty? I have never seen such a thing. Even the brutes who took your father had a reason."

"It's too much," replied Nadia, her feet sinking into the mud. Such concerns were going unnoticed. After a minute, Nadia said, "What should we do with him?"

"It seems undignified to just leave him on the road," replied Katarina, wiping her eyes. "Could you bury him the same way you did with your father's rifle?"

"Yes, it would be the least we could do," said Nadia.

"Get your father's rifle first. It may seem insensitive, but I want to know it's safe," said Katarina.

"I understand," she said as she found the patch of mud that she hid the rifle in. "Mud of earth and water return that which belongs to me," Nadia whispered. The mud began to boil, and up from the ground the canvas-covered rifle emerged without a single splotch of mud, like it was pulled out of the dresser that morning.

When Nadia returned to the road, she found her mother already dragging the body off the road. Katarina had placed her headscarf on the man's face, hiding the grisly wounds underneath. It didn't hide the blood that oozed into the scarf and into the mud. Nadia grabbed the man's legs to help pull him. He was frail yet still heavy.

They fell several times from loose footing or moving too quickly and losing their grip. In one of these instances, the headscarf fell off, revealing the gunshot wounds in the man's face. She could see wet bone and pulpy red brain. His eyeball had ruptured. The ugly sight of death combined with her stomach cramping made Nadia turn and vomit in the ditch.

She stopped breathing as her stomach contracted and forced the sweet peaches from her mouth in an acidic spray. She was already tired of disgusting and horrific images. Nadia wanted nothing to do with them, but the grotesque and ugly were becoming increasingly standard sights.

"Nadia."

"One moment," she replied on her hands and knees. The acidic taste clinging to her tongue. Her dress was soaked, her shirt was muddy. She hated that she was in a ditch vomiting, that she had to bury a gentleman who never hurt anyone. She hated the riders who brought such discord into her life. She put her hate aside and returned to help her mother with the body. They found a flat stretch of grass to bury him. The sun was high in the sky, and a cold wind blew, making the two women shiver. Nadia crouched down by the dead man and whispered into his ear.

"I'm sorry this happened to you," she said before crossing his arms. She didn't know any of the Jewish funeral rights, or any witch funeral rights, for that matter. So, she improvised.

"Four winds watch over this man's soul so that he might find peace, earth reclaim that which has been borrowed and may his water nurture the life around him. Take this body in your humble embrace and let him find peace." She pulled a stalk of grass from the mud and placed it on his chest. "I lower this body into the earth but release his spirit to wherever it may go." She put both hands on his chest and pushed down on the body. The earth swallowed the dead man, sucking him into the mud.

"It's done," Nadia said, standing up. The two women returned to the road. They were shivering. The sun did little as autumn had come early, making everything colder. They trudged on the road over the hoofprints of the horses. Soon they were in the forest proper, taking the side path that led to Olivia's cottage. Nadia's heart clenched as she realized that the smoke column was coming from Olivia's direction. Other signs made her chest tighten up. Hoofprints in the mud, and broken branches and shell casings. The spider webs that signified magical wards had been torn up. Nadia had not realized she had started running, had not recognized her mother was calling her name to wait for her. She ran, knowing what she would find at Olivia's cottage while hoping that Olivia would be alright. That she would be safe.

It was not to be. Nadia discovered a scene of utter horror. Olivia's cabin had been burned down. It smoldered as the wood billowed white smoke into the air. Nadia, as if in a trance, walked into the garden of her mentor. She entertained thoughts that her mentor had gotten away. Escaped. These thoughts were helped by the strange wicker men that stood in the garden. They wore the same uniform as the camouflaged riders she saw earlier. They pointed rifles at the smoldering cabin.

Then Nadia found a sight she could not explain. It clashed with her worldview. What she saw made the young witch collapse into the damp earth.

"Oh Lord, Jesus Christ protect us," she heard Katarina whisper when she arrived. She placed a hand over Nadia's eyes. "Don't look anymore, Nadia." Nadia pushed her mother's hands away to stare at the corpse of her mentor.

Olivia was tied down to several pegs in the ground with a bloody butcher's apron thrown beside her. Her shirt was torn apart. Her stomach had been cut open, and someone had removed her organs and placed them next to her body. The red meat was arranged anatomically. Her insides had been completely removed. Blood was everywhere, and it pooled into sticky coagulated puddles. Nadia's eyes danced over the scene of butchery, not knowing where to let her eyes rest. Something Olivia couldn't do now, even if she was alive, as her eyes had been cut out of her head. The blood around her mentor's mouth made Nadia suspect her tongue had been cut out as well. Several organs were missing. The heart, and eyes, and tongue.

To see her mentor this way made Nadia shake. She wanted to weep and cry, but more than anything, she wanted to scream. She wanted to hurt those who had done this to her mentor.

"Look away my dear," Katarina said, turning Nadia away. Nadia caught sight of the cat Petrenko. He was hanging from a tree with a bootlace around his neck. For the second time that day, she burst into tears. The grief had been exhausting as she dealt with one emotional gut-punch after another. She collapsed in the dirt, clawing at the mud. Her anger, fear, and grief had nowhere to go.

She balled her hand into a fist and struck the ground repeatedly. It felt good to strike and hit something, even if it was ineffectual. She felt someone grab her armpits and pulled her to her feet.

"That's enough," Katarina said, hugging her daughter. "She is gone."

"I just spoke to her last night," replied Nadia. "I feel I'm in a terrible dream and I just want to wake up, and I know that won't happen."

"I know. Right now we have an obligation. An obligation to the dead. We must keep on living. It is our lot to suffer, but we must stay standing, we must persevere despite the cruelties of this world."

"Where are we to go now?" Nadia asked, holding on to her mother.

"I don't know, but we can't stay out here. We must go back to town for a short time. If the fascists catch us out in the open, I suspect they will do horrible things to us," said Katarina. Nadia looked at her mentor's body again.

"Things like that?" Nadia asked, jaw clenched and fists balled up.

"No, this looks like something else entirely, something I don't understand. But I do understand soldiers, and the other horrible things they can do to us. I dare not say them," said Katarina. Nadia saw that her mother was remembering something. Something from long ago.

"I need to do something first," said Nadia, letting her mother go.

"You plan to bury Olivia. Like the man from earlier?" asked her mother.

"Not entirely. Mama, I must do something. Something that might offend your Christian sensibilities," said Nadia.

"Witch things?" asked Katarina. Nadia nodded. "Alright, I will go count the cans of food we have." Katarina then walked toward the forest before turning back. "What kind of witch things?"

Nadia was looking at the body of her mutilated teacher, then looked over her shoulder at her own mother.

"Do you remember the story of Jesus Christ and Lazarus?" asked Nadia. Katarina went pale with disgust. She then returned to the woods.

Nadia took a deep breath and wiped the mud off her face. The wicker soldiers around her still had their armaments of grenades, and ammunition pouches hung at their hips. What Nadia wanted was one of those daggers. She unhooked the dagger from the wicker man's belt and went over to the tree that Petrenko hung from. Nadia cut the dead cat down and cradled him for a moment. She wanted to cry for the elderly cat, but no more tears would come. She then pulled a leaf from the tree branch.

She returned to Olivia and placed the body of Petrenko at Olivia's side. She then closed her mentor's shirt. The buttons were gone, the shirt having been violently pulled open. She cut the ropes that held her to the ground. The thin cords had cut into her flesh. Nadia threw them away before adjusting Olivia into a sitting position.

"What happened to her?" Dasha had arrived using the routes that only cats knew about.

"She was killed," replied Nadia, sticking the leaf in her mentor's mouth.

"That's a shame," meowed Dasha. "I take it Petrenko has met a similar end as well?"

"Yes.

"Poor old fool, I can smell the fear musk all over him. You have it, too, now that I think about it," said Dasha, sitting down next to Olivia.

"Be quiet," said Nadia. The tomcat yawned before lying down.

"Mama always said stay away from witches," murmured the cat. Nadia ignored him as she organized the spell in her mind. Nadia was about to practice magic she had only ever done under Olivia's supervision. A spell of darkness. Any spell of darkness was fraught with danger. The wrong pronunciation could end up jinxing the user or bringing something horrid to the physical world.

Spells of darkness were the domain of the dead, daemons, and other strange entities that were outside the realm of human imagination. Nadia saw now that the dagger had a letter written on the blade: "Meine Ehre Heibt Treue" in deep grey letters while the curved pommel almost wanted to bite into her palm. Nadia gently placed the dagger's point on her thumb, right over several other scars. She sliced her thumb open before placing a bloody thump print on Olivia's forehead. Nadia glanced at her mentor's empty sockets. She looked away, her eyes closed, trying to get the image out of her mind. The smell of burned wood and grass was everywhere in the darkness of her closed eyes. Nadia realized that the smell of feces and stomach contents were not present. A sign that whoever murdered Olivia and took her organs was better with a knife than even her local butcher. When Nadia opened her eyes again, she saw Olivia's organs had clean cuts. She was hesitant about doing what she was about to do, but she had to. She had to speak to Olivia one last time.

"I call upon the spirit that resided in this body. May no daemon, or malignant spirit of this world or the next inhabit this flesh. I call upon the witch Olivia Yosonivitch, also known as the Mockingbird. She who fought the tsarists, the reds, the whites, and the German empire. The woman who saved the cat Petrenko from a pack of wolves. Baba Olivia, return to your body for no longer than a conversation." She then leaned in and kissed her dead teacher on the lips. It was a way of reminding the dead about life.

Nadia then sat on her knees, readying a spell to burn the body of Olivia into cinders, should another entity possess her dead body. Olivia began to subtly undulate, as her soul returned to it corporeal form, like a hand adjusting itself inside a glove. Her head rolled forward. Her hands began to twitch and contort. Olivia then began to moan and drool. Nadia could tell she was trying to speak. But the lack of tongue made that impossible. Nadia then grabbed Olivia's face and whispered a spell into her mouth.

"May this leaf act as your tongue. May it give you voice and may it speak no lies."

"I can't see," said Olivia, her voice took on an echoing quality. Like the bouncing echoes in a cave.

"They have cut out your eyes, Baba," said Nadia.

"By the nine tailed god of cats," said Dasha, realizing a corpse was now speaking next to him. He got up and trotted away. He sat on the outside of the garden. "Let me know when you're done with your black magic," hissed Dasha. Nadia ignored him.

"I see a great flow of corruption erupting from the west. Like a fire giving off smoke. It is horrible, yet beautiful. I wish you could see this, my dear Nadia. My sweet little sparrow." The dead were easily distracted, except the vengeful dead who were singular in their thinking.

"Baba, I need you to focus. I have some questions for you, and I only have so long."

"My poor hungry little sparrow. Always with your questions. Have you eaten today? I hope you have."

"My appetite is not important right now. Olivia, I need to know who killed you, and why," said Nadia, grasping her mentor's cold hand.

"Oh, but it is important. Eating is an act of living. If you don't, then you're no better than a corpse." Olivia's head rolled and bobbed as she rocked about, her movements were stiff as the rigor took hold of her muscles.

"Olivia, who killed you, what was his name?" Nadia said, trying to help her remain focused. The lips of Olivia's mouth pull back, revealing teeth and gums.

"His name is Rudolph Becker, a Thule sorcerer attached to the Einsatzgruppen. A band of killers sent to murder all the undesirables of the Nazi Reich. I'm only one among thousands who have met their end from that unit." Olivia's hand shot out and slapped the side of Nadia's face. The young witch recoiled, but the hand still kept reaching out, trying to touch her face.

"Don't pull back, my sparrow, I just wanted to feel the life in your veins. I want to feel your warmth in my body." This was one of the problems of the dead. Left unchecked, they would do anything to feel even a little bit alive, and sometimes that meant getting close to another person. Other times it meant eating them.

"No, Olivia, behave yourself. Now, why did this Thule sorcerer kill you? I know that people have feared and persecuted witches, but your murder seems different. Why did he kill you?"

"Rudolph's mind is infected with the Nazi ideology. He spoke to me as he cut. He needs special organs so that he might craft another Philosopher's Stone. An item that can find magic. He believes that his people are the reclaimers of a lost legacy."

"I thought the Philosopher's Stone was just a myth. An impossible task meant to keep medieval alchemists busy."

"It was, my dear, but magic has a funny tendency to match the will of the user. If there is a will, there is a way," cackled Olivia. "Now, come closer, child, I want to feel the pulse in your neck, I want to hold you close and feel your warm, soft body."

Olivia lurched forward, her shirt spilling open, revealing the horrendous mutilations beneath. Nadia crawled backward.

"I'm so empty now, Rudolph took all of my organs. I need you to fill me up, my little sparrow. You hardly ever eat so you won't be needing that stomach of yours." Olivia was lasciviously licking her lips with the green leaf Nadia had placed in her mouth. Drool and blood leaked down her chin. Nadia struggled to her feet, backing away from the crawling ghoul.

Olivia's mind was degenerating faster than Nadia expected. The longer her spirit remained in her corpse, the more feral and bloodthirsty Olivia would become. Olivia's lower lip curled into her mouth. She bit the lip off, chewed, then swallowed before letting out an orgasmic moan. "Nadia, oh, Nadia, oh my dear sparrow."

There was nothing she could say to this thing anymore. She was no longer Olivia, just a hungry dead thing. Nadia stuck her thumb into her mouth and sucked hard onto her cut thumb. The metallic iron taste of blood filled her mouth; she watched as the ghoul sniffed the air, searching for her. A death rictus pulled Olivia's mouth wide, showing her bloody teeth and empty eyes searching for warm flesh. *She's going to attack soon,* thought Nadia. When her mouth was full of enough blood and saliva, she spat on the ghoul. The glob of red spit hit Olivia's hair.

"Our conversation is at an end. Return to the realm that you came from. I recite the three-part incantation of the restful dead. Banish, cleanse, burn." Nadia's throat dried up when these words left her mouth. It was only a lesser spell of shadows, but it took a toll on her physically, sapping her strength and energy, leaving her fatigued. Other spells of shadow had more dangerous costs. That is why most shadow spells have a victim that stands in for the caster.

Olivia went rigid as the glob of blood in her hair began to fizzle and boil. Olivia started to shriek. It was not a human voice but an otherworldly wail that hissed and yowled as the ghoul thrashed in the mud. Olivia hit the ground with her fists. She pulled at the long gash in her body. Olivia pulled and snapped the bones from her ribcage and clawed at the skin on her face. Before she could do any more self-mutilation, she stopped, convulsed, and became still. The banishment was complete.

Black smoke poured from the corpse's mouth, roiling around the body before shooting skyward. Then the body started smoking, igniting internally, and a jet of flame shot from Olivia's mouth. The fire spread across her flesh and clothes. The heat was so intense that Nadia had to retreat further back. So great was the flame that it turned flesh and bone into ash in a matter of moments.

"Well, that was dramatic. Was there any point to that?" Dasha asked, wagging his tail in a twisting swish.

"Olivia told me who I need to kill." Nadia looked over at the wicker troopers. She saw the grenades at their belts. She unhooked two and placed them in her bag.

"You aren't going to declare some magically enforced oath of vengeance, are you? Because that would really cut into time spent repaying your debt to me."

"Don't be foolish. Doing such thing is asking for trouble. I wouldn't want the string of fate to tie this Rudolph or his bloodline to me. But I will kill him. It may not bring Olivia back, but it will keep him from killing others."

"I think you should let this one go," said Dasha.

"What do you know? All you care about is your stupid fish," snapped Nadia.

"I know not to fight something bigger than me!" hissed Dasha. "You are like me. You are a cat who doesn't care what the rest of the town thinks of you. This Rudolph sounds like a wolf. Cats don't fight wolves, they get eaten. If you hadn't noticed, your Olivia was just eaten by a wolf. No matter how angry or sad or vengeful a cat may be, a cat cannot kill a wolf, especially not a wolf in the middle of its pack."

"I'm not a cat, I'm a witch. He has wronged my kin, his people brought violence and bloodshed to my home. If I do nothing he is just going to keep killing, until there is nothing left of us. I'm tired of letting bad things happen to me. I want to fight back."

"So, what are you going to do, hmmm? Are you going to fight all the human invaders by yourself?" asked Dasha, with a mocking chirp.

"No, but I will at least kill this man. I'm going to blow him up," she said, patting her bag. Dasha then walked forward, his tail aggressively swishing.

"Alright, but I want you to promise me something."

"Fine, what is it?" Nadia said, crouching down to be closer to the grey tomcat.

"If your plan doesn't work, then you run. You can't repay me if you are dead," meowed Dasha.

"This is a little bit more important than a fish dinner," Nadia said.

"Not to me. I want to see tomorrow. I want to see what strange and tasty fish a witch can conjure up." said Dasha. Nadia gave a small smile, a sad smile. This day had thrown her from one emotional extreme to the next. She had to say goodbye to two important people in her life. She couldn't foresee what the future held. Let alone the next day. But Dasha had his priorities all figured out.

Nadia felt cast adrift on the sea. With only violence ahead of her. *That's not true,* she thought. She remembered the Coven of the Ever-Shining Moon and the face of Anna the Red. Maybe all the coven witches were as bright and energetic as her. Perhaps she could find a future with them.

"Alright, Dasha. If I don't succeed, we will run." She sighed. "Come on, let's put these bad visions behind us," she said, walking away from Olivia's burned home. The flame crackled and sparked, a reminder of what she had to lose.

8
The Einsatzgruppen

Katarina said nothing as the two walked back to the village. The mud that stuck to their dresses and skin was hardening, yet their feet remained damp. The route felt longer as their feet squished in the soft ground. In parts of the country, the mud got so thick it could suck a truck up to its headlights. It was only the cities and highways, with their well-maintained, paved roads, that avoided this problem. For the rest of the Soviet Union, it was dirt roads that turned to liquid muck.

"You will want to hide that dagger and your father's rifle," said Katarina.

"What?" said Nadia, lost in thoughts of vengeance and remorse.

"Those weapons are bound to draw attention. Especially that dagger."

"I hadn't realized I still had it," she said, placing the dagger into her bag next to the grenades.

"What about your father's rifle? Do you have another means besides just hiding it in the mud? I don't want it to be lost." Nadia pulled the rifle off her back. Besides a bit of mud, the canvas remained clean.

"There is a way, but I need a lock of your hair," said Nadia.

"My hair? Why would you need that?" asked Katarina.

Nadia's mother had always been supportive and loving about her daughter practicing the craft. But she was still a Christian woman, and superstitious about any magic done around her. A few years prior, she had refused any potions that would have helped her with a cold, only accepting medicine from a mundane doctor.

"I just need something to hold the charm in place. I would use mine, but the spell prefers an older, more experienced person. A more seasoned pot, so to speak," said Nadia.

"I'm not that old, Nadia. Shame on you."

"No, Mama, the magic is flighty and lasts longer when it knows it is in experienced hands. If this spell sees my hair, it will unravel much faster. A lock of your hair, even a small one, will anchor the spell much more efficiently. It's silly and strange, I know, but I didn't make the spell, it's just how magic works."

"Alright Nadia, give me the dagger." Nadia did so, reaching in the bag, past the grenades, food, and to Nadia's surprise, the flight oil. She must have left it in her bag from the previous day. She handed the dagger to her mother, and in a quick motion, she cut a long strand of black-grey hair.

"Thank you, Mama," said Nadia, taking the dagger and the lock of hair. She focused the spell and thought of the woods and meadows and babbling streams, of moss, and the rising moon.

"Let this object crafted by the hand of man relinquish its image. May it take on the guise so it appears as it once was, so that all may remember what it is," The canvas-covered rifle shimmered and distorted like it was being submerged in a river. Nadia reinforced the magic and solidified it into a stick.

"What did you do to Alexander's rifle?" Katarina asked, gripping her daughter's arm.

"Nothing, Mother. It's still the same rifle, it just looks like a walking stick."

"As long as it remains intact, I will be happy," said Katarina. "I wish he were here now. I hoped so much that he was with that parade of uniformed soldiers, that he would find time to see us before he fought the Nazis. But…" Katarina turned and looked at the rolling fields of swaying grass and countryside. "I know he is never coming back. They either locked him away forever or dragged him out back behind a prison and shot him. He was a war hero after all. You don't see a lot of the old guard in the military."

"Mama."

"It's nothing," she said, advancing down the road. "Let's go. More soldiers could be coming."

The two picked up their pace as they made their way back to the village. Smoke and fire billowed up from the bombing, and there were several houses where nothing remained but chimneys and a pile of smoking wood. Aside from the bombing, there was minimal destruction. After seeing Olivia, Nadia expected rampant scenes of bloodshed and torture. There was none of that. Then the pair turned onto the main street and found where all the horrors were.

The Jews of the village hung from streetlamps, along with the Soviet officials. The bodies swayed with a slight breeze. The knot of people milled about, looking at the dead, while a much larger group surrounded the horsemen that Nadia and Katarina had seen earlier. They had assembled a wagon, with two camouflaged soldiers standing on top.

"This is horrible, ungodly, the work of daemons, not men," whispered

Katarina.

"Of one daemon in particular," said Nadia. She gripped the rifle in her hand. It was reassuring. The magic gave it the texture of wood. The only thing that could give it away was the lock of hair tied at the top. For the moment the rifle was useless, as she had no ammunition. She did have the grenades. When that monster showed himself, Nadia would blow him up.

"They look like they are going to say something. Let's get closer," said Nadia as the pair joined the crowd around the wagon.

Half of the town was jostling for a position in front of the cart. All collectively holding their breath as the tension mounted.

Someone climbed onto the wagon. It was the same man with the pendulum from the road. The silver-headed skull on his cap outshone all his other insignia except for the Thule medallion and the wrought iron gauntlet that had the look of tarnished silver. He spoke to the men on the wagon. Nadia couldn't hear him over the crowd and the occasional rapid cracks of gunfire in the distance.

The crowd was a mix of smiling jubilance and barely contained anger. Not everyone in Ukraine was pleased with being part of the Soviet Union. It was hated, feared, and loved in equal measure. Places like the Baltics had celebrated the overthrow of the Soviet regime in their country. But the state also bred die-hard loyalists who had fought the world in the chaotic times after the Revolution. Now those tensions were being played out in her village.

The man Nadia presumed to be Rudolph Becker stepped forward, clearing his throat. He placed his arms behind his back, the very picture of an autocratic Nazi.

"I once again thank you all and your humble community, for helping us root out the Jews and their Bolshevik puppets," he said, gesturing to the streetlamps. His pronunciation of Ukrainian was perfect but filtered through a thick German accent.

"I would also like to thank you all for the humble gift of bread and salt, symbols of peace I'm told commonly given to liberators. It pleases me greatly that so many of you are welcoming us with open arms. I regret that in my experience, there will be those among you who hate our presence. These are sick men. Their minds have been poisoned by the lies of the Jews and their Communist thugs."

Nadia had reached into her bag held the grenade tight. She knew there was a pin on the bottom and that once pulled, it would explode. Nadia didn't know if there would be a chance like this again. She pulled the grenade out of her bag, letting it fall to her side. The hefty wood handle made the whole explosive feel heavy. The crowd made it difficult to use it, however. She would have to put a spell on it only to affect one man or find some way to scare off the crowd.

"I'm afraid that there is no negotiating with these animals, for there is no negotiating with Communists. As a result, we Germans must assume the mantle of the stern father." Nadia mulled over a spell in her mind. While she fingered the pin of the grenade, she was nervous.

"The partisan must be dealt with harshly to discourage any future action against the German soldier and their allies. Any partisan discovered will be summerly executed. Anyone caught with a weapon will be executed. Anyone caught aiding these saboteurs, partisans, or their Jewish masters will be executed. Any family of the saboteurs will also be executed." People gasped on hearing this. Nadia looked at her mother, who was staring at the Nazi on the wagon. The grenade in her hand felt so heavy. If she threw that grenade, she might get away. Katarina most certainly wouldn't.

"These measures may seem harsh, but it is this type of stern hand that has turned the German people into what it is today. It has allowed us to be the masters of science, culture, and magic. It is this sternness that has allowed the German people to resist the taint of Communism, capitalistic decadence, and the effects of profane magic. Through the guidance of our Fuhrer, we will make a world Reich where all will be happy, healthy, and mighty. That is why I call upon all of you to do your part."

Nadia heard him. She realized she couldn't go through with it, not in so public a fashion.

"Do your part turning in any saboteurs, partisans, or practitioners of evil and profane magic! Heil Hitler," he shouted, and all the other soldiers shouted in unison while saluting the sky.

"Heil Hitler," they shouted, repeatedly. Nadia gripped the grenade and moved to place it into her bag. But someone grabbed her wrist and hoisted her arm skyward.

"Here is a witch, and she has a grenade!" said Mykola, waving Nadia's hand so all the soldiers could see. Nadia was shocked at how suddenly all the attention was on her. The crowd backed away from her and Mykola. Katarina on instinct pulled back as the group fled from Nadia like oil in water.

"This bride of Satan has poisoned our community for too long now," Mykola shouted.

Nadia tried to pull away, but the boy was too strong. Several soldiers moved in on her, pulling the glamoured rifle out of her hand and punching her in the gut. Nadia doubled over, her insides cramping up, forcing her to start dry heaving. The soldiers ripped the grenade out of her hand, and then Nadia felt a rain of punches and kicks hit her. She curled up on the ground, unable to think through the assault. She was hoisted up and repeatedly struck in the face. Someone grabbed her arms and held her up. Nadia felt her blood run down her nose and into her mouth. It took several moments to realize what was happening. Her eyes fell on her mother in the crowd, who had her hands over her mouth, and tears rolled down her face. An explosion of fear and grief had gripped Katarina. Nadia realized that her mother was about to see her daughter die. She was about to die. She struggled to get away from the man who held her, but she was struck again for her effort.

Every part of her hurt as they dragged her closer to the wagon.

"Grab everything that she dropped!" shouted Rudolph, pointing at the enchanted rifle. The soldiers ripped her bag from her shoulder. *I'm going to die,* she thought. Olivia's mutilated body came into her head. She screamed and redoubled her efforts to get away, but the men held her tight and hit her for her efforts.

"Thank you, young man. What is your name?" shouted Rudolph to Mykola.

"Mykola, sir."

"You have the features of an Aryan. Are any of your relatives Germans?" asked Rudolph, stepping down from the wagon.

"My parents were born here but my grandparents where from Switzerland," he said with pride.

"Wonderful. It shows that even a place as rough as this, greatness shines through. Now as for you," Rudolph said, turning to Nadia. "I thought there was another witch around here. The one in the woods was very insistent about being the only one here. I thought there maybe another when I caught the scent of magic on the road. I should trust my instincts more. I almost wrote it off as stray magic from the woods," Rudolph then grabbed her chin with his iron gauntlet, forcing her to look at him. Nadia could feel his firm grip digging into her face. He squeezed her battered cheeks.

"A young one too. Even beaten bloody you can see how pretty she is." he smiled. "Apologies. The academic in me is always willing to praise aesthetics." He patted her face twice like an affectionate father. From his pocket, he pulled out the crystal pendulum. She could see a red bead of blood inside a tiny cage of silver.

"Do you know what this is? It's a Philosopher's Stone, or at least a crude one. It looks for magic," he said, holding it up to her eyes. The red jewel seemed to pulse like a heart. The silver wire dug into the bead. "We made it by killing the enemies of the state. A tad crude but wonderfully potent."

"You used sacrificial blood magic?" said the horrified Nadia. Rudolph laughed at this before dropping the crystal. It immediately pulled on the chain and pointed at the enchanted rifle.

"Distasteful, I know, but a hog butcher's profession is rather gruesome don't you think? Someone must do the unpleasant things if a proper civilized society is to take shape. Now let's see what you have done to this stick. Could it be your staff? Like Merlin?"

The crowd watching her was staring intently. Some looked pleased, knowing the witch among them had found such a humiliating end. Other showed pity, if not outright sympathy, while others showed only a bored amusement. Rudolph looked the rifle over, only seeing the illusion. His gauntleted hand was running across the illusioned wood.

"Superb quality," Rudolph said. Nadia didn't want to look at him, but one of the soldiers grabbed her head and pulled it back to face the sorcerer. It hurt immensely and only added to her humiliation and pain.

"Did your crone make this? Hmm, perhaps not. Not her hair color. I remember these sorts of things you understand." He then pulled on the hair,

over his shoulder. Nadia licked the blood on her lip, a necessary part for her next spell. The submachine gun in the Nazi's hand exploded, killing the man when a shard a metal went through his neck.

"Kill her now!" shouted Rudolph, black lightning sparking off his gauntlet. A sudden impact threw Nadia to the ground. She was free of the soldier's grip, and she saw her mother tangled up with one of the guards.

"Run, my darling!" Katarina shouted. Nadia inhaled and blew out the air in her lungs as she transformed the blood in her mouth into a black cloud of smoke that covered the area.

The crowd began to panic at the open display of witchcraft. The smoke was harmless, but it was sticky and thick. It blinded everyone: the Nazi soldiers, the crowd, and herself. Nadia charged through the smoke at the place where she thought the soldier with her father's rifle was. She ran into the coughing man. He tumbled over, and the gun hit the paved street. All around was the sound of frantic coughing and panic. She dropped to the ground, blindly groping for her father's weapon. She found the metal barrel with its wood stock. She picked it up and crawled away from the coughing of the soldier.

"Nadia over here!" Dasha yowled. The cat had wisely hidden itself during the display of Nazi might.

In the blackness of the stinging smoke, Nadia's head was throbbing. She wasn't used to casting so many spells in one day. She had to endure. She crawled on the ground through the black smoke.

"Don't let her escape," Becker shouted. "The last thing we need is a magical partisan about." Nadia ran into one of the soldiers in the dark. He threw his total weight on top of her. The soldier was shouting in German, and Nadia was overwhelmed with his mass and body odor. His hand searched, grabbing at her arms and pawing at her torso trying to hold her down.

In the blackness, she couldn't see him, and the thick smoke made it impossible to breathe without coughing. She tried to think of a spell, but nothing came to mind. Nadia couldn't think straight. All she could do was struggle, her fists striking ineffectually at hard muscled flesh. She searched around, hand groping in the dark. She found his belt and a handle. *His dagger! All these riders had daggers!* she thought. She unsheathed the blade, and with all her remaining strength, stabbed into his gut. The assailant's grip faltered and loosened. The man sounded like he was punched in the stomach. She stabbed again, blood covering her hands.

He was still alive when she threw the man's bulk off her.

"The bag! He has your bag!" yowled Dasha as Nadia groped around. When she found it, she could see that the smoke had begun to clear. Nadia stumbled to her feet. Before she could pick up her father's rifle, someone grabbed her arm.

"I've got her," Mykola shouted. In blood-pumping desperation, she slashed at her onetime classmate and now Nazi collaborator. He recoiled and screamed as she drew more blood with the dagger. The smoke had cleared enough that she could now see Mykola's outline. He reached for her again, and Nadia slashed at him with fearful desperation. The blade hit only a tiny part of Mykola's neck, but it was the part that gushed blood. Mykola gripped his neck, collapsing to the ground. Nadia froze in horror as Mykola's body went limp.

"Run, my darling!" shouted Katarina. She could see how her mother was surrounded and being beaten by the Nazi soldiers. She was about to jump in and help when she felt the sledgehammer blow graze her arm and the resounding thunder of a gunshot. Enough to cut flesh, but not hit bone.

They might hit something more critical with the next shot. She grabbed the rifle from the street and escaped in the vanishing cloud of smoke. Another gunshot whizzed by her as she became exposed again. Dasha tensed up. His tail bristled out. She could see that the crowd had dispersed, running down the streets.

"Follow me," shouted Dasha. She followed the cat, which led her down a back alley, gunfire following in her wake.

"Get the horses!" she heard Becker shout. "She can't have gotten far! Run her down!"

"I can only get us so far!" shouted Dasha. "I know this town's every back alley but how are we going to escape? Those horses are far too fast."

"Get me back to the house," Nadia shouted. "I can enchant the broom in the kitchen, and we can fly out."

"I thought those things needed a ritual with the moon?" shouted Dasha.

"The moon is out now, it should be fine," she shouted.

"Should be? We need a way out!"

"This is the best plan I have, Dasha!"

"My mother warned me about witches. She said stay away from them or they will sweep you away with their nonsense!" yowled Dasha. Nadia could only think about her mother in the clutches of Rudolph. So much violence in such a short amount of time. Her face and arms hurt. She felt like she was on fire.

When Nadia's home came into view, her speed was faltering, but she ran as fast as she could. Dasha made it to the door before she did. The small bomb from the plane was still there in their garden. She ran past it, trying not to think too hard about the explosive. When she opened the door, she heard horse hooves coming down the street. Turning around, she saw that two riders were galloping at full speed to her house. She slammed the door and locked it, for what good it would do. Instead of coming into the house, the riders set up on the other side of the street. Nadia watched them as they dismounted their horses. They pulled a bundle off the horse. A tripod and a long gun were fitted together and with mechanical speed it was assembled and aimed at her home.

"Machine gun!" shouted Nadia. The house suddenly became a maelstrom of screaming bullets. The two soldiers poured hundreds of rounds into Nadia's home. The remaining windows shattered, and hundreds of holes appeared in the walls, sending dust and splinters everywhere. Nadia jumped to the ground, wincing in pain from her injured arm. She kept her head down as the cyclone of bullets tore everything apart. Shells destroyed all the dishes in the kitchen, shot up all the icons of Jesus and Mary; family pictures fell off the wall and crashed to the floor.

The guns paused for less than a minute to reload before firing an intermittent burst into the house. Nadia felt it was safe to crawl to the kitchen. She looked around for the broom she had planned to enchant. The young witch always wanted to use this broom. The bristles were perfect, and the shaft smooth. It was the ideal broom. Yet when Nadia found it, it had broken in half. A bullet caught the handle and tore it in two. It would be useless to use as an instrument of flight.

"Nadia!" shouted Rudolph from the street. *How did he know my name?* she thought as she crawled back into the living room. "Witch!" he called again. Nadia peeked up to look out on the street. Most of the riders were outside her house. Easily two dozen. All were holding their rifles in hand, with the machine gun still aimed at her home. Rudolph was gripping her mother by the hair. Katarina looked battered and bruised, blood leaked out of her nose, and both of her eyes looked like they were sealed shut.

The machine gun opened fire once again at the place where she peeked out from, and once again, she dove for cover. Her father's rifle was right in front of her; she grabbed it. To hold onto if nothing else.

"Hold your fire." The guns went silent. "Now, Nadia, I want to show you something." Slowly Nadia glanced out the window. She could see Rudolph holding a delicate-looking pistol. Without ceremony, he placed it against Katarina's head and fired.

Nadia wailed as if the bullet pierced her flesh. Katarina slumped on the ground like a sack of flour falling over.

"I said earlier that the families of partisans would be held accountable. However, you Slavs are a dimwitted people and even harsher measures are needed." Nadia was now shaking as she realized she was trapped.

"I hear them coming Nadia, three of them," whispered Dasha. Nadia peeked over the window. Sure enough three riders were crossing the street into the garden.

As they approached the bomb, Nadia crouched back down slowly, bringing her knees up, her skirt still covered in dry mud. She was dirty, scared, and hurt. She closed her eyes and thought of the bomb.

"Spark," she growled through bared teeth. A moment later, an explosion went off as the bomb detonated with Nadia's magical help. Her ears started ringing as she looked around. Part of the wall was gone, and so were the advancing troops. Large shards of wood were in her flesh, with a particularly stinging one through Nadia's cheek. But that was nothing compared to the mental backlash of the spell. It felt like her head was hit with ten years of migraines all at once.

"For every one of my men you injure, Nadia, I will have to kill fifty people in this village. If you're keeping tally, we are at over two hundred people. If I run out of people here, I will just have my men go to the next village. All because you keep using your foul magic."

She didn't want to answer him. She just clutched the rifle in her hands. She thought she couldn't cry anymore, but tears started flowing freely. These were tears of rage. She hated those men outside. It wasn't enough that they kill her, but they had to turn the knife every chance they could. She vowed to herself that she would take as many of those men with her. She would kill them in so many awful ways. She would make them regret ever coming to her village.

"Nadia, how are we going to fly out, we have no broom?" asked Dasha, his ears down and tail tucked underneath him.

"Olivia said we don't need a broom, that a stick would work." She didn't know why she was humoring Dasha. They were dead. Rudolph just needed to finish the job.

"Would that gun work?" he asked. Nadia looked at the rugged rifle, and her breath caught in her throat.

"Dasha, you are a genius!" she said as she fumbled around in her bag and pulled out the flight oil that Anna had given her. She then looked out the window. An enormous crater replaced her garden, and across the street, Nadia could see two soldiers putting large liquid tanks on their backs. Her mother's body still lay in the street. She couldn't look anymore.

"It's okay, Mama, I will get out of here." Nadia uncorked the vial of amber liquid and poured it into her hands. A hole in the roof revealed the moon above in its waning state. She rubbed the oil across the rifle barrel and wooden butt. She did this several times until all the oil was gone. Plenty to cast the ritual. Ritual magic tended to be less burdensome on the caster, unlike off-the-cuff spells. She may not be able to throw out anymore quick spells, but she was very good at flight enchantments.

"I smell burning fuel," said Dasha as he peeked outside. The doorway was blown off its hinge, giving him a clear view of the street. "Nadia what are those men doing?"

Nadia looked, and two men advanced on the house. Bulky tanks on their backs led to a hose with a grip on a nozzle. A flame protruded from the tip of the nozzle. One of the men pointed it skyward, and a giant whoosh of flame erupted like a volcano. The flame arced and landed on the house next to her own, setting it ablaze.

"Oh God, they are going to burn us alive," she said. "Quickly get to the bedroom away from the front of the house." She got up and ran, expecting to be gunned down by the machine gun or incinerated with the flamethrower.

"How long will it take to make the gun fly?" the cat asked.

"I just need to recite the incantation. Hopefully, it will work."

"Hopefully! Nadia, I don't want to be burned alive. I need more assurance that we can get out of here."

"I promise you right here, Dasha, as a witch, we will fly or die trying."

"That is not very reassuring!" he hissed. She sat down. The rifle was wet and oily. It smelled of the woods and moss and the earth after it rained.

"Rifle of wood and metal, you are of the earth. I must ask you to take on the aspect of air. Under the light of the sacred moon, I empower you, and I enchant you. I offer you this gift of flight."

A blast of flame engulfed the front of the house. The door to the bedroom smoked and hissed as any moisture trapped inside its wood evaporated. Smoke began to creep in from beneath the door.

"Spirits of the air, recognize this tool and let it fly as you do." She took a deep breath. She had taken all the necessary steps. She tried not to think of all the earlier brooms that threw her off before tearing themselves apart.

The flames began crawling across the roof of the house. Nadia crouched down, away from the harmful black smoke that stung her eyes and sent her coughing.

"Dasha, get over here." The cat obeyed, getting as close to her as he could. He yowled and hissed at the heat, and fire began to blacken the door to the bedroom and ceiling.

"Alright, we are going to fly out of that hole in the roof," she said, mounting the enchanted rifle.

"That one? The one with all the jagged splinters?" he yowled.

"The very same." She then picked up the cat and put him on her lap as she crouched down on the floor. She took a deep breath and closed her eyes.

She exhaled and used her will to push off the ground. A gust of wind began radiating outward, pushing the smoke away. Circular waves pulsed out from Nadia. An upward draft blew her hair up. The rifle started to lift the young witch and the tomcat off the floor.

They hovered, and Nadia blew out a nervous breath. She looked up and saw the sky above and the moon facing the arrogant sun.

She rose up slowly, being careful not to push things. The heat was becoming too much. She positioned the rifle's snout upward toward the hole in the ceiling and leaned forward over Dasha to make herself as narrow as possible.

"Fly," said Nadia, and the pair shot out of the hole like a bullet from a gun. They were above the tree line much faster than Nadia expected.

"I hate this," yowled Dasha, digging his claws into her legs as he squished himself into her stomach.

"You're right, this is too high," said Nadia, looking down at the village she had only ever known from the ground. She could see where all the bombs had dropped on the town. As well as her house as it burned up while Rudolph and his men scrambled to mount their horses. In the distance, she could see a flash of artillery lines erupting. All the horrors of the war around were made small at this height, almost made insignificant at this distance. That's when the sound of machine-gun fire brought her back to reality. The men from Rudolph's squad had taken aim at her as they rode. Bullets whizzed by in a hail of inaccurate fire. She realized how vulnerable she was. One sharpshooter could knock her out of the sky in no time.

"Hang on, Dasha, it's time to get out of here." Nadia was astonished at how easy it was handling the rifle as she flew. She dropped their altitude, falling downward much too fast for the tomcat's liking. He yowled as they slipped below the tree line, a meter off the road. The act sucked the air out of Nadia's chest.

"Wow, I can't believe we haven't crashed yet," she whispered.

"What was that? Did you say crash?" asked Dasha. "Please tell me you know how to fly this thing."

"I'm getting there. I'm feeling it out as we go. I always lost control of the broom before this," said Nadia. They were just outside of the village now. Turning around, she could see that the horsemen were turning up the road, galloping at full speed.

"Well, let's see if we can outrun a herd of horses," said Nadia, shooting off toward the forest. She veered off the road into a field. She could hear a hail of gunshots from behind. The riders took inaccurate shots at her, hoping to land a lucky hit. Some held back and stood up in their saddle to take standing shots.

tossing it aside. The illusion dripped off the rifle like melting snow splashing to the earth in droplets before vanishing. "Wonderful. I have never seen such a high-quality glamor; then again, I'm not a very good liar," he said, holding the canvas. "Now what do we have here." He opened the canvas.

"Don't!" Nadia shouted. He pulled the canvas off her father's rifle.

"Well, well, looks like she is a partisan as well. Quite clever this one." One of the guards said something in German and showed Rudolph the other grenade before placing it back in the bag. The flight oil remained in her satchel with the cans of food. He also had the dagger. "Our little witch is armed to the teeth. Do you think she planned to take on the whole German army?" The soldiers chuckled while Mykola stood behind the Germans. "In such a brief time you armed yourself and at once decided to kill me. At least, that's what I assume you were trying to do. Why else would you come here? While I wish I could use you for my research, you are obviously too dangerous to keep around." He handed the rifle to one of his troopers before turning around and marched back to the wagon. "Shoot her in the head, and string her up on a lamp post."

The world froze for Nadia as one of the Nazi troopers advanced on her. His machine gun adjusted in his grip. All she could hear was her breathing. The sun was high in the air its radiance shining on all. But she also saw the moon. *Was the moon supposed to be out in the daytime today?* she thought. An omen. An omen of defiance. The moon can be in the light of day, but the sun must hide during the night. The gun's muzzle pressed onto her head, and she could hear her mother screaming. She remembered the commissar days ago who had done the same thing.

"Break," she whispered, keeping the moon in her mind. The weapon clicked. The Nazi trooper examined his gun. Rudolph stopped and looked

"Hang on, Dasha, I'm going to try to shake their aim a bit." With one hand, she grabbed the scruff of Dasha's neck and held on to the rifle's barrel with the other. She turned sharply and dug her heels into the butt of the rifle. The weapon kicked into high-speed, shooting her across the field. She did another sharp turn and almost lost her balance as the weapon corkscrewed. She didn't have control over the flying weapon, but she was getting the hang of it with each maneuver.

"Now is not the time to be doing fancy flying! Just get us out of here," shouted Dasha. When she righted herself, she looked back to see that the horses and their riders had made it into the fields at full gallop. Nadia realized that they were gaining on her as well.

"You're right let's see how fast this rifle can go," she said, digging her heels into the rifle butt. Nadia almost lost her grip when the weapon picked up speed. Then the wind blew directly into her face, and all the tiny things that floated in the air hit her face and eyes, causing her to wince.

"Nadia, pull up, we're going to crash!" shouted Dasha. Nadia was still momentarily blinded, so she yanked up on the barrel, sending her skyward—at least, that's what she hoped. She rubbed her eyes, trying to get the grit out of them. It gradually began to get colder and colder. Dasha sank his claws into her leg.

"Too high! Too high!" he chirped. When Nadia finally opened her eyes, she saw the world just below the clouds. It was freezing, and she was shaking.

But it was quiet. The bright and fluffy clouds stood in stark contrast to the wide-open horizon of the earth below her. She could even see the earth's curve, and all the buildings and forests below were made almost unrecognizable. Her teeth chattered, her hands gripping white-knuckled on the rapidly cooling metal of the rifle's barrel. She felt exhausted and spent.

Yet this view of the world she had never seen brought her a sense of serenity. She wanted to tell Olivia and her mother. But they were no more, and Peter could be anywhere. Now she felt more alone than in her entire life. She didn't think what she was seeing was real. A bad dream, ending with a peaceful view above the clouds.

"Can we get down now?" said Dasha, breaking her out of her reverie. The blood in her nose had frozen hard. She couldn't stay up there. So, she picked a direction and flew slowly down to earth. The Nazi riders and their Thule sorcerer were nowhere to be seen.

9
Sanctuary

Nadia flew for the rest of the day. The gun was not a comfortable mount as the butt of the rifle dug into her leg, and the barrel grew very cold. Her feet kept getting tangled up in the strap that hung off the barrel of the gun. Dasha wriggled and adjusted himself, his claws occasionally digging into Nadia's leg or arm. It was a long and exhausting journey. Now she saw unfamiliar fields, roads that twisted in strange ways. As night approached, she picked a large forest to hide in. When Nadia finally landed, Dasha jumped from her lap and started rolling around on the earth.

"That was terrible, Nadia, just the worst," he said. Nadia's rump hurt from so much wiggling on a weapon never made for travel. She hoisted the rifle over her shoulder and saw a sturdy tree to lean against.

"So, what's the plan?" Dasha said, rubbing up on Nadia, shoving his head under her hand. She absentmindedly started petting him while closing her eyes to rest.

"There is no plan. Getting out alive was the plan," she said. "I just want to rest here and sleep."

"Well then, let's eat," he said, climbing into her lap. "I heard your stomach grumble practically the entire way here."

"Why don't you find a mouse or something? I just want to sit here for a bit."

"You're not going to eat?" he asked once again, nudging her hand.

"No. Not right now." On hearing this, Dasha thought for a moment and then bit Nadia's hand.

"Ow," shouted Nadia. "What is wrong with you."

"You're acting foolish, so I bit you," he said. "What have you actually eaten today? You've had a very turbulent day, so eat something."

"Turbulent?" said Nadia. "Turbulent! My life is gone! This has been the worst day of my life. Worse than seeing my aunt and uncle waste away. Worse than finding my cousin dead in his crib and having to tell his mother and father that their child was dead. It was worse than watching my father get beaten bloody by the state he idolized for years. Much worse than watching him get dragged away, never to be seen again. Worse than the daily humiliation by the village elders for being a witch! No, Dasha, today was not just turbulent. Everyone I have ever loved has been killed or sent away!" She stood up and was yelling down at the cat. "Now I'm kilometers away from my home, with bloodthirsty murderers at my heels! I'm hurt everywhere, I'm very cold, I'm covered in mud! I just don't…" She collapsed again and began wailing. There were no words, just a blubbering sob. An outpour of grief and frustration.

In her village, she couldn't show emotion about anyone who disappeared. Frustration with the state and life under it was always behind closed doors. But the woods were far from everyone. She was free to just be. Free to release all the pent-up emotion that had been pushed down so she could survive.

"I'm sorry, Nadia," said Dasha when her wails quieted down to a low sniffle. "You have gone through a lot. But I wanted to remind you that you are still alive. You need to do things to keep you going. There will be the snowy months soon. Where good things will be hard to find. You need your strength to deal with the challenges ahead. As the holder of your debt, I have vested interest in your wellbeing so that you may pay me back."

"It's just a stupid fish," she blubbered.

"A stupid fish you owe me. I aim to collect, and if I have to bite you so you will focus on your own health, then so be it."

"You are talking like a witch's familiar," she said, sitting up and wiping her eyes.

"What! Take it back! My litter would disown me if they found out. I'm in enough of a jam just having you in my debt," he yowled.

"You're a contradiction," said Nadia.

"That's a cat's business. Now, are you going to eat something, or do I have to bite you again?

"Alright, alright," Nadia said, feeling very tired. She pulled a can labeled beets out of her bag. This would do. She pulled the ring off to expose the dark red beets inside.

"I don't have any utensils."

"Well, make do," said Dasha, shaking his tail. "I'm going to find a bird or a mouse. When I get back, that can better be empty." Dasha ran off into the underbrush, leaving Nadia alone. She sighed, looking at the pickled beets. They were a dark burgundy color. She reached in and ate with her fingers. As soon as she started, she couldn't stop.

She finished off the meager meal by drinking the liquid at the bottom of the can before sending it back into the earth's depths. Sleep and fatigue clawed at her, forcing her eyes shut.

If it wasn't for the cold, she would have fallen asleep right there. Dasha returned, licking his chops.

"Did you catch your mouse?" she asked.

"I found a bird, much more filling. Alright, make a fire, it's cold," said Dasha.

"I'm afraid we can't. We don't know who are in these woods; there could be hungry refugees, Red Army soldiers, or Nazi spies. A fire might also draw the attention of an airplane," said Nadia.

"So, no fire?" said Dasha. Nadia shook her head, bringing her knees to her chest for warmth. "Hmm, we need to find some shelter for you. As a cat, I should be fine, but what about you?"

"Well, if we can find a large enough tree, I can request the sanctuary of wood," she said, standing up and shaking her dress of dried mud.

"What are you talking about?" asked Dasha, watching Nadia pick up a rock.

"It's a very old spell, one that every witch must learn quickly at the beginning of their training. It allows the caster to merge into the belly of a tree. In the old days, witches were often the targets of pogroms. If it wasn't a pogrom, it was bandits out in the forest where a witch might take up residence."

"Crafty, like a cat," Dasha chirped.

"Where do you think we learn these tricks from?" Nadia held the stone and rubbed in furiously. She kept rubbing until it was warm.

"What's with the rock?" asked Dasha. Nadia then cupped the sone and breathed into her hand.

"I don't know this forest; the rock will be our guide," she said, breathing on the rock again.

"This should be good. What would a rock possibly know?" Dasha asked dismissively.

"Some would say the same thing about a cat."

"I know what I need to."

"So do stones. They're kind of a pain to wake up." The surface of the stone was now warm. It would be sluggish, but it would do the job.

"Little drop of the earth, wake up, wake up, little drop, I need help. I wish to find a large tree. One that can fit a witch and her companion; in return I shall offer the moisture of a kiss. Will you help me?" The stone began to roll around in her hand. "The deal is struck." She then kissed the small stone and placed it on the ground. It began to slowly roll to the north.

"If I can barely see that stone, I don't know how you will. Especially with night coming." said Dasha, following the stone.

"Hmmm." Nadia looked up at the sky to see the first glimmer of stars overhead, as well as a few stray sunbeams coming from the west. She reached into a sunbeam and grasped a shard of light. Like the snapping of a branch, she pulled the sunbeam off and held it in her hand.

"Borrowed light is the best thing to get," said Nadia, then walked up to the rolling stone and placed the light on its surface. Now the stone could be seen clearly in the approaching dark.

"Show off," muttered Dasha.

"Why would you think that?" asked Nadia. She was too tired for any real conversation.

She also couldn't stop tonguing the cuts on her lips from the beating.

"From what I heard, most magicians spend a lot of time and effort to do the things that you do."

"If you say so," sighed Nadia.

The stone had picked up speed now and was rolling at a walking pace. Nadia adjusted the heavy rifle over her shoulder, thinking she would have to get a cloth to wrap around the uncomfortable weapon sights.

"I'm just saying, you grabbed a shard of light and threw it onto a rock that you had just brought to life. Most people walking around couldn't do that if they spent their entire lives trying."

"Says the cat who until recently stayed away from witches."

"I'm just saying no one likes a showoff," said Dasha.

"Who says I was trying to show off? You suggested, and I acted with the proper tools."

"I'm just saying, is all. Wait a second, we just passed a perfectly good tree. Why couldn't you have cast the sanctuary on that?"

"The stone must have a certain tree in mind," she replied. Dasha continued to grumble to himself as they walked. Nadia kept wincing with each splinter pulled from her skin. They walked until night had fallen and the air became freezing. Nadia kept rubbing her arms, careful not to touch the bullet graze. She wished she had grabbed a jacket as the long sleeve shirt could only do so much. Eventually, the stone stopped in front of a large tree that sat on a dirt overhang.

Its roots stuck out of the sides and bottom of the dirt bank with a small creek beside it. The rock stopped in front of the tree before jumping into the stream and laying still.

"I guess this is the one," said Dasha, looking unimpressed. "Will this thing fall over if we get inside?"

"No, it won't, it's wonderful. I wonder how long it's been here. It must be a hundred years old, maybe older," Nadia said, climbing the bank, using the roots to pull herself up.

Nadia ran her hands over the rough bark of the tree. Its twisted limbs and long branches overhead felt like protective arms, like a mother. *My mother is dead. My mentor is dead.* She pushed those thoughts away, taking a deep breath and placing both hands on the tree's surface. She took a moment to organize her thoughts, closing her eyes and doing her best to ignore the cold that sank into her bones and made her shiver.

"Well, go on, do it," meowed Dasha, his tail swishing with anticipation.

"Be patient, I'm choosing the right words."

"Right words? Just cast the spell so we can finally get warm."

"What if someone crawled in your guts without permission?" asked Nadia.

"They wouldn't dare. I would claw their eyes out," replied Dasha.

"Well, the same sentiment applies with a tree. I'm invoking an ancient pact with the trees of the forest. But any misgivings or impoliteness could ruin a future witch's chance to find sanctuary. Trees are terrible gossips and will tell everyone they know about a rude witch that climbed inside their trunk without asking."

"Wasn't this spell used to get away from people trying to kill witches?"

"Well, yes, but I'm being polite. If there were, say, fascists at our feet, we could hop into the tree and be forgiven for such a breach of etiquette. While the night is very cold and the forest very dangerous in a time of war, I'm still going to perform the proper courtesies."

"Well, do it quick. Riding that gun has been exhausting, and I don't look forward to riding it in the future," replied the tomcat. Nadia put Dasha out of her mind before clearing her throat.

"Tree of the forest, my companion and I seek sanctuary in your wooden trunk. Through ancient compact with the green man of the forest, I invoke asylum within, for I'm unequipped for the wilds of the forest. If you offer me this kindness, I will take your seeds and plant them wherever I may go. I will remember you always." The tree rumbled and creaked as the belly of the trunk split open. The gap widened as the internal wood bent and swelled, creating space for Nadia to climb into.

"Climb in, little flower," said the tree with a voice of snapping wood and rustling leaves. "The night is cold; within my trunk you will find safety and warmth. By ancient compact with the green man of the forest, I accept you."

"I'm having second thoughts about this; it seems unnatural," said Dasha with a nervous chirp.

"It's completely safe, and just because you have never seen it happen doesn't mean it's unnatural," said Nadia, climbing into the hollow of the tree.

"Says you," muttered Dasha. "Magic dabblers always make everything unnatural." Nadia let the quip slide as Dasha hopped inside the tree. With a slow cracking, the opening closed. There was enough room inside that Nadia didn't have to scrunch her legs up against her chest, but it was unfortunately not roomy enough to lie down. Darkness was absolute within the hollow of the tree. Now not even the thin crack of sunlight from dusk could light their way. For Nadia, it was perfect. She could finally find rest.

"You know, with that creek by the tree you might be able to get me a fish in the morning and repay your debt," said Dasha.

"I bet I could," muttered Nadia, her eyes already closed as she leaned against the wooden hollow.

"Maybe not a big one but a fish nonetheless," he said. "Or maybe I should hold out for later and get an even bigger fish. Oh, I can taste it now," he said.

"Hmmm," replied Nadia.

"I should definitely wait, but I would like a fish tomorrow. It won't cover the debt but will be sufficient to pay off the interest."

"Whatever you say, Dasha."

"We have a plan then. In the morning you get a small fish from that little creek, and then we go about our business, and we can plan to get a bigger fish and repay that debt you owe me. How does that sound, Nadia?" asked Dasha. He was met with quiet breathing. "Nadia?"

It was clear to the cat that the witch had fallen asleep. He twitched his tail, pondering on whether he should wake her up to continue his conversation. Instead, he placed his head down and fell asleep as well.

10
Kindersnatch

Nadia dreamed of flying. She was flying on a broom made of feathers and bone over a vast ocean. Nadia had never seen the ocean or a sea in her life. Every direction she looked was nothing but an ever-expanding horizon. If Nadia stopped flying, she would die. She looked down and saw bodies floating in the water. Thousands of the dead bobbed with the tides. A pair of suns, one black, the other red, rose from the waves. They rose in the sky as the sun's flares attacked and struck each other.

"Nadia, we have something to tell you," said a voice. She looked around to find Katarina and Olivia flying on the same broom.

"Mother, Olivia! I thought you died! I'm so glad you are both safe," she said to the two women.

"That's not important right now," they said in unison. The twin suns rose up behind them, turning the pair into shadows.

"We have something to tell you," they said.

"What is it?"

"Death comes for you."

Nadia felt a sharp pain in her hand that pulled her out of her dream. She awoke in the darkness of the tree, shocked and scared. She looked around for any source of light but was met with all-consuming dark.

"Where am I?" she asked.

"Inside the trunk of a tree in a haunted forest apparently!" yowled Dasha.

"What do you mean?" said Nadia, her sense of self and location catching up with her.

"Feel my fur! It only reacts like that when there are ghosts about! My teeth are on edge, this forest is haunted!" said Dasha. When Nadia ran her hand over the cat, she found that all his fur was puffed out. He was bristling with fear.

"Tree, can I get a view of outside your trunk?" she asked. The tree rumbled and rustled, and a small hole opened, letting in the night's freezing air. "I don't see anything," said Nadia. The cold seeped into the warm hollow, making her shiver.

"Trust me, there are ghosts about. Cats know when there is a ghost around, and there are a lot."

"Is this something unusual?" asked Nadia, pulling the dagger from her belt. She had a spell in mind. It would mean adding another injury to her battered body.

"Yes, it is unusual. Ghosts don't just hang out in large groups. Even on battlefields. Maybe in a building, but no more than a dozen at most. There are easily a hundred of those spooky things just floating about. So creepy! Why do humans do that? Tell me that, miss witch."

"Do what?" Nadia hissed as she dug the dagger's tip into her palm. The cut stung, and for a moment, Nadia thought she could see red.

"Become a ghost. You never see a ghost cat. Humans just don't seem to have enough sense to just move on when they die."

"I don't know," said Nadia, wanting to just get back to sleep. She also didn't want to get bitten again. So, it looked like she had to resolve whatever was going on. With a simple knock on the hollow of the tree expanded. With two fingers, she took the blood from her palms and dabbed her eyelids. A simple spell if a tad discomforting. "Specters, reveal yourselves to my eyes," she whispered.

When she opened her eyes again, the world became bright with glowing luminescent figures floating through the trees. Hundreds of ghosts floated along the ground or in the trees, glowing with a pale, sickly light as they moved at odd angles. They wailed in silence like figures in a silent film.

Nadia took two drops of blood and put them in the crevice of her ears.

"Words of the specters, let me hear you." A cacophony of wails erupted in the forest. What shocked Nadia most was that she recognized these people. She saw Vera from the tea shop, and Boris the baker, and Mark, who made candy. She saw the entire Volskya family burning with spectral fire as they wailed in pain.

"Let me out," whispered Nadia. The tree portal widened enough for Nadia to exit.

"Nadia, don't go out there!" yowled Dasha, but Nadia had already exited, taking her gun and bag of food. The light of the spirits lit up the forest with sickly incandescence. Nadia moved through the undergrowth, her dress sometimes catching onto stray sticks and leaves.

"Nadia, we should go back to the tree, just wait them out till morning. They won't last under daylight," said Dasha.

"It's Ivanka!" gasped Nadia. Her clothes were ripped and torn, revealing her breasts to the night sky. Several bullet holes snaked up from her belly to her chest. Her face had been severely beaten. "What happened?" said Nadia, following the ghost as she drifted through the underbrush. Ivanka floated into an upright position and looked at Nadia. All of Nadia's hair stood on end as the phantom advanced on her.

"They killed us, witch," said Ivanka, the air getting colder as she closed the distance with Nadia. "When you left, the Nazis rounded us all up and killed us. Because you had to raise your fist in defiance!" said the ghost, pointing at Nadia.

"That's not fair. They were going to kill me," shouted Nadia, recoiling from Ivanka. Frost was gathering wherever the spirit passed. She didn't realize that she had run into another ghost. It felt like being doused in ice water. The apparition passed through her and joined Ivanka in front of her. It was Sofia, the passive, plump spectator. Her clothes were also torn and shredded. Her wrists were bound with wire, and a large bruise formed around her neck.

"They killed us, Nadia. They killed the men out of hand," said Sofia.

"We were not so lucky," said Ivanka.

"That's terrible," replied Nadia. "I never wanted that to happen."

"But it did, Nadia," said Ivanka, floating in the air above the witch, pointing at her.

"Nadia, stop talking with the dead. It's bad luck," said Dasha, leaning against Nadia's leg.

"You're right," said Nadia, turning away from the ghosts. "I can't do anything for them now."

"Don't you look away from us!" Ivanka said, passing through Nadia to face her once again. Nadia hissed as the freezing cold covered her again, sending her teeth chattering. Other ghosts were now congregating around the living pair.

"Rudolph did this to us because you attacked his men. It was a lesson for the next village," said Sofia. "He said that this was your fault."

"Rudolph Becker ordered this?" said Nadia, her fists balling up. The recent cut she made on her hand screamed in pain.

"When we would not join the others in the square, they burned our house down with us in it," said a group of burning ghosts.

"They said I was too old and ugly, so they released the dogs on me," said Vera, her arms, legs, and neck mauled with savage bites.

As more and more ghosts arrived, they each spoke of how they died until they became a single roaring cacophony. The witch shrunk down as the whole town descended on her. It was too much.

"Silence!" shouted Nadia, enforcing her word with a spell. The ghosts were blown back several feet by the force of the magic. "I was not the one who did this to you. You think that Rudolph killed you because of me? No, they were looking for an excuse. You think I wanted this, that I was acting selfish? We were all fighting for our lives!" The ghosts remained silent. Nadia sighed. She grounded herself.

"Dasha, you said a gathering of ghosts is unusual, right?"

"Unheard of," replied the cat. He hissed at a passing ghost.

"Then we need to figure out why they are here," she said.

"Do we? I think we should leave well enough alone and just be on our way.

"These ghosts traveled many kilometers to accuse me of their death. I need to know why." She undid the spell of silence, and once again, the ghosts began to speak. "Be quiet, all of you. I need to know why you are here?"

"The commander, Rudolph, ordered us to follow you," said Ivanka.

"He tapped us with a dagger that had your blood on it; he bound our spirits and commanded us to find you," said Sofia.

"We followed your blood," said Vera.

Of course, the first dagger she used to awaken Olivia from her death. She should have cleaned it off. Now that monster had a bit of her blood, and he used it to direct the ghosts. How could she be so stupid as to leave a thing like that behind? Then she had to remind herself she was running for her life. Rudolph obviously wasn't willing to let her escape and was hunting her.

"I can't change what happened to you. While I feel guilty that I survived while you all perished, I can't change the fact that you were killed. All I can offer is release from your chains so you may find final rest."

The collective ghostly host sighed in relief. Nadia couldn't use the spell that sent Olivia to the other world. That one was made for the walking dead. What she was about to do needed a bit more elegance. With the butt of the rifle, she drew a circle around herself. She crouched and drew the four symbols of the cardinal directions. She put the Greek symbol of the sun in the east and the moon in the west.

"Dasha, do not leave this circle under any circumstance."

"There better be a good reason," he said, hissing at another ghost.

"Because you could get swept up in the vortex." In truth, the spell she was about to use would simply disperse the spirits like a strong wind on a gust of steam. It was one of the few ways she knew how to deal with rogue spirit entities that had become detached from their source. Dasha, fearing he would be consumed in the spell, squeezed up against Nadia's leg.

"Have you ever done this before?" Dasha asked, sounding very nervous.

"I cast a variation of it once to get rid of the spirits that were bringing dust into my room," she said. Nadia took the dagger from her belt and made sure to wipe the blood off this tip with her dress. Nadia centered herself, pushing out the cold that made her shiver. She ignored the hot breath that came out in small clouds of steam that shined with the ethereal light of the dead.

"Are we going to heaven?" asked the meek ghost of Sofia.

"I don't know if you will go to heaven. I don't know what happens to the dead when they disperse. It is mystery you must find out for yourself," said Nadia, grasping the dagger with both hands and pointing it skyward.

"I'm afraid," said Ivanka.

"Don't be," said Nadia. "For at the very least I know you all will find peace."

"So did the spell with the dust spirits work?" asked Dasha.

"Well, yes, but I still had dust," said Nadia. "Now be quiet, everyone, I need full concentration for this." Nadia turned to the north and pointed the knife eastward.

"From the east wind I invoke the warm winds to rise to my command." She then pointed the knife south.

"From the south I call upon the violent southern storm to my command."

As she spoke, the wind from those directions began to pick up. The cold night air began to move and blow against her skin, almost making Nadia lose her concentration. She pointed the knife to the west.

"From the west I invoke the dying hot wind that fades with the sun's descent."

A sudden warm wind blew on her and clashed with the frigid winds buffeting her. With both hands, she pointed the dagger north.

"From the north I invoke the powerful wind of winter to my command." She was met by the freezing bite of a gale. The forest was a mighty torrent of rushing air that pushed and blew on the ghosts. She felt magic move through her. It was warm and vibrant and coursed through her limbs, guiding her as water searches its way for the easiest path.

"With these four winds present, I beg your aid." She again pointed the dagger to the east. "Birth is like the rising of the sun." She began to raise the knife over her head following the sun's arch. "We live our lives like all living thing and then we die." The dagger faced the west. "Our end is like the setting of the sun. Here before me are those that linger in the twilight, seeking to walk in the daylight of life. I beseech the four winds to carry these lost souls to the land of the dead." The knife was now pointed at the earth. Nadia was no longer in control of the ritual. She was merely the vessel for the magic that flowed through her.

"Four winds of the cardinal direction take these souls with you on your journeys so that one day they may find themselves in a new dawn of life." The winds swirled around her. Now the ghosts would be swept up in a current of air and whisked away. Being laid to rest. Nadia collapsed as the magic left her. Dasha yowled as Nadia almost fell on him.

The spell was done, and Nadia was shivering and weak. Bringing down the four winds was a difficult task that required a tremendous amount of energy and focus. Weather magic was temperamental and needed a strong hand to keep it on course. She had her eyes closed.

"Ow, ow Nadia stop that," yowled Dasha. Nadia opened her eyes and realized something had gone wrong. Instead of being swept up in the wind, the ghosts were as still as a photograph.

"Nadia, stop your stupid magic, it's two loud!" he hissed. Nadia couldn't hear anything, but Dasha's paws were clutching his ears.

"I'm not doing any more magic. What do you hear?" said Nadia, feeling a great deal of unease. If the spell had gone wrong, she would have felt the mental backlash like sudden migraine or nosebleed. This was something different.

"Can't you hear the ringing? It's like glass shattering inside a ringing bell." Dasha's grey ears were flat, and his tail was tucked between his legs.

"I don't hear it. Are you sure it's shattering glass?" Nadia crouched down next to Dasha and put a hand on his back.

"Oh, of course, you can't hear, stupid human ears. Yes, it's like breaking glass or ice or splitting wood and ripping paper."

"Oh no," whispered Nadia, looking at the ghosts. She could see a red rune on their heads. A red light started to appear on all the heads of the spirits. A cross of bleeding light took shape before four lines sliced on their skin in the form of a bloody swastika.

"Oh no, he knows." She picked up Dasha in her arms, spinning around to see all the other ghosts with the burning swastika on their foreheads. She kicked the circle, breaking the lines, and the four winds died down at once. The forest was left silent. Now Nadia could hear the faint sound of a bell.

"Who knows?" whined Dasha.

"Rudolph! He knows I tried to lay the souls to rest. Now he is doing a counter spell. I'm so stupid. Rudolph was using the ghost to find me. Olivia said she sensed something in the aether. This must be one of the ways he finds witches. Now he is doing something to the ghosts."

The red light grew brighter, tearing apart the ghosts like it was peeling off an eggshell, leaving a bloody burning light in their place. The red spirits opened their mouths and screamed. The high-pitched scream forced Nadia to drop Dasha and grip her ears.

Hot air swelled across the forests. It was now as hot as high summer. Nadia looked up to see the red ghosts stretched like taffy and sucked to a point above her, forming a pulsing black sun. She grabbed Dasha and ran away from the black sun that boiled in the air above her ritual site. It grew more grotesque with each ghost sucked inside it. When all the spirits of the village were no more, there was the floating sun the color of smoldering coal.

The screams vanished, leaving an unbearable silence, with Nadia feeling like she was submerged underwater. Circular ripples appeared on the point of the sun like something was tapping the surface.

"We should be running, right?" said Dasha. The ripples stopped. "Nadia?" She was transfixed.

"I'm trying to see if there is a way of stopping whatever comes out of it."

"Is something going to come out of that? I don't want to see it! We should leave."

"No, whatever is going to come out has to be dealt with," said Nadia. The sun bulged, sending off spurts of solar flares. The sun distended, stretched as something tried to get out.

"Like hell it is! There is an adage among cats: take what you can, and don't fight anything bigger than you, especially if you don't know what it is."

"The problem is that I do know what it is. I was warned very early on never to bring one of these things in our world. Olivia said there are beings one must never consort with, must never make deals with, and must never make demands of. For it is our lot to shun the daemon."

"A daemon! Do you have some sort of death wish? Don't tell me you are planning on fighting that thing!" Another solar flare burst from the side of the sun with the smell of rotting flesh and rusted metal.

"Dasha!" she yelled at the cat. "I can't just run away! A daemon is being brought into this world to do great evil, most likely to me. It will not stop, and it will do terrible things as it pursues its task. Daemons are beings of pure evil that leave torment and suffering wherever they go. We have to banish this creature before it can do anything too terrible. Do you understand?"

"But it's not our responsibility," whimpered the cat, his ears folded back.

"Unfortunately, I think it is mine. The ghosts said their deaths were my fault. In a way I feel it is true. I survived because I fled, leaving them behind. I can't have others die at the hands of a daemon because I won't act. I must fight back so others won't have to."

The sound of ripping and tearing could be heard as a bulge in the sun swelled like a pimple.

"You can leave if you want to. I'm not asking you to stay here, not that you will do much to a daemon anyway. But I must stay, Dasha. I don't know if I will survive this, but what I can see from the size of the sun, that it's not a powerful daemon."

"Regardless of how powerful it is, I don't think you have any of the tools to fight a daemon. I don't think there is enough salt in that bag of yours and last time I checked that tiny dagger is made of steel, not cold iron," said Dasha.

"I have a spell that might work. I used it when I banished Olivia. At the very least it incinerated every remnant of her body. If the banishment itself does not work, then the fire should do the trick." A loud rip came from the sun; a deep tear formed on the pulsing bump.

"I'll be here when you decide to run. We can just fly away and never have to think of this creature again," said Dasha. "I don't want to die after all the trouble we had trying to escape the village."

"I suppose that is as close to 'good luck' as I'm going to get from a cat," sighed Nadia.

The tear in the sun expanded, and a hand ripped through the surface. A hand with too many fingers that were as thin and delicate as a stick. More like the legs of insects than actual fingers. It was followed by an arm covered in wiry hair and three elbows. A second hand appeared and gripped the side of the tear before both hands pulled it apart. The daemon fell out of the pulsing black sun, and the baleful orb started to fade. The creature began to right itself. It was covered in a gooey substance that had the sheen of blood and mucus on a freshly born goat. The light from the sun faded into a whisp of smoke that smelled of rotting meat. Nadia could see the daemon in full. It was a bulky creature covered in wiry hair. Its nose looked like it had been turned inside out. Its mouth had the shape of a boar with protruding tusks. The creature stood on two legs with feet facing backward. Nadia knew daemons lied every chance they could, especially about where they came from or where they were going.

This daemon was male, or at least manifested as one. Daemons had no need for sexual organs unless it was a way to torment or unsettle their victims. Over its shoulder, it carried a sack that dripped with red mucus. With the last of the dying light of the sun, the daemon inhaled through its strange nose. Then Nadia was plunged into darkness, unable to see the dangerous entity near her.

"Dasha, touch my hand, quickly," Nadia whispered. The daemon made several loud, grunting sniffs, like a pig searching for truffles. She touched her cat companion in the ink of the night, feeling his fur.

"Sorry about this," she whispered again. Nadia pinched a patch of hair and pulled hard, pulling the pinch of fur with it. Dasha yowled and winced in pain. The daemon's snuffling stopped.

The forest was quiet and dark. Nadia took the lock of Dasha's fur to deal with one of those elements. The creature began to sing. It sounded like the high-pitched melody of an opera singer and the cooing lullaby of a mother to her child. It was a decidedly feminine voice. It sounded so familiar and haunting. Then she realized that it was her mother's voice.

"Come little child, come play with me, come to my arms and you will see, I'll show you a place unknown. A place where the other children dream. For I'm the Kindersnatch, and I'm the best playmate you will ever meet," sang the beast. Nadia pushed herself up against a tree as the daemon continued to hum. Now at least it could not sneak up on her. She took the tuft of fur and swallowed it.

"Eyes of the night," she whispered, eating the hair, and cast the spell. Soon the darkness shifted to grey hues. Objects in the dark now had definition, and she could clearly see the daemon. It had gotten much closer now, its strange nose quivering in the night air as its long fingers tapped the ground while its male member dragged in the dirt. Now Nadia could see some of the details of the beast. She could see its wiry hair and strange warts and moles on its body. A swastika was tattooed in black ink on its chest. There was little doubt now that this was Rudolph's handy work. The fact he could summon a daemon from so many kilometers away was terrifying.

"My dear sweet girl, I can smell your fear. Don't you fret or shed tears. I have some candy. I have come with treats. Don't you want to be friends with me? Come to me and sit in my lap. We will have so much fun before I put you in my sack."

The daemon was much closer now, almost within grasping distance. Nadia tried to keep the tree between them. As quietly as she could, she sucked more blood from her palm. Her mouth was filled with the coppery taste of blood and saliva.

"Oh, there you are, sweet thing." The daemon jerked, looking right at Nadia. It had no eyes. The nose on its head seemed to quiver and point at her. "A little old for my liking, but we will have our fun, then that sorcerer can have the scraps."

Nadia spat on the daemon, a bloody glob of spit and blood landing right on the snout. The monster opened its mouth, and a long thin tongue snaked out, taking the magical blob, and rubbing it along its nose as it inhaled in euphoric ecstasy.

"Young enough," it whispered, gargling in beautiful melodic song.

"Daemon of the lower plains, I cast you out! Return to whatever world you came from. I recite the incantation of the cleansing of evil. Banish, cleanse, burn," she said. Her throat burned when she cast the spell. The blood on the daemon ignited, consuming the monster in a fiery conflagration. The creature began to scream, not in pain but in orgasmic ecstasy. The fire was doing nothing as it rolled across the daemon.

"That's not how it's done, my dear," laughed the daemon in her mother's voice. *That was my one shot,* she thought. She didn't know any spells that could vanquish it. She had hoped that changing the spell for banishing restless spirits would work; now she had nothing. She backed away from the creature as it laughed and screamed with joy as the fire slowly faded.

"Better start running, little girl. If I catch you, your soul will be mine for all time. You get to play with all the other children in my garden."

Nadia followed the creature's advice and ran.

Nadia ran back the way she came from, and she noticed that Dasha was running beside her in the undergrowth.

"So, are we leaving or not?" he shouted. "That thing is just playing with us, like I do with mice! I don't want to be a mouse, Nadia!"

Neither did she. While running, she pulled her rifle off her shoulder and quickly mounted it. She scooped Dasha in her arms, looking back for the daemon. Ice ran in Nadia's veins when she realized the nightmare was nowhere to be seen. *Now or never,* she thought as she kicked off the ground. The tangle of branches was no trouble to get through. As the pair went above the canopy, a wave of relief washed over Nadia, having escaped the jaws of a lion.

It was at that moment that the daemon attacked. Nadia felt a sudden jerk from the back of her dress and shirt.

She was pulled back with such force that she came off her enchanted weapon. She and Dasha were in free fall. The darkness overwhelmed her as she went tumbling down. Nadia fell through the branches and leaves that slapped and hit her end over end. It was in utter disorientation when she hit the ground. She landed wrong with one of her arms outstretched. A bone in her arm snapped, and several fingers were twisted. Nadia screamed and writhed on the ground. The pain in her body shrunk her world into those moments. Forgotten was the daemon trying to capture her. It was in this moment of agony that the monster began to sing again.

"Hush, my sweet darling. For you are my baby and you are all mine. I will not let you leave me. I will not let you flee. For you are my darling, you now belong to me."

Nadia fought through the pain and looked around for the daemon. Her arm was bent at a wrong angle, with several twisted fingers and pieces of bone sticking out through the skin. A part of her mind told her how to fix it, and what herbs and elixirs and incantations were needed to guide the misaligned piece back in place. The same part of her brain told her that she was still in mortal danger.

"Nadia! Run!" She heard from above her. Looking up, she saw the muted grey form of Dasha in the trees. Her vision was made blurry by the spell that gave her night vision. Dasha was struggling to get his feet on a branch. But to Nadia's horror, the daemon was above them in the canopy.

The Kindersnatch was climbing down the tree. One of its arms was held skyward as those long fingers had stretched out and made even longer. Now they retracted. She didn't know where her rifle was. Her only course was to follow Dasha's advice and run. For a moment, she didn't know where to run to. Panic began to set in as she looked around the dark of the forest. She pulled herself up, hissing and screaming as every tiny movement in her arm felt like glass was twisted up inside it. She held her arm close, desperately looking for any sign of refuge as panic began to take hold of her. It was above her. It was getting closer. Then she saw the tree on the collapsing bank above the stream. Hope, fear, and agony mixed as she saw the prospect of safety. She ran, this time with a limping gait. Her whole body suffered from the impact. Every step she took was a painful and challenging task, only made easier with the knowledge that sanctuary was just a little closer.

"Where are you going, little one? Is this a new game? How fun! Know that I always win these sorts of things. Hide under the bed, in the cupboard or attic, hide in a trunk, or in a barn. I always find my little darlings. After they have had their fun, I get to have mine. So have your fun, my sweetling, have fun. For soon I will have mine," laughed the daemon. It was the lovely, sweet laugh of her mother. As if Katarina were still alive. She hopped over the creek, the impact sending convulsions of pain in her arm.

Whenever Nadia made a noise of pain, the Kindersnatch giggled. She could hear it overhead as branches bent and snapped with the weight of the daemon. Nadia was frantic when she arrived at the steep dirt bank. She had little trouble climbing earlier when she had both hands. Now she didn't know how to get up with her brutalized arm. It was not something to think about, however. She grabbed a root and frantically pulled herself up. Her shoes dug into the cold, crumbling dirt that collapsed as she pushed down.

At the top of the embankment, she pulled herself up with one arm. Just before she was completely up, her foot stepped on her dress, causing her to slip. She fell hard on her injured arm. She screamed in the cold night air. The broken bone in her arm bit into torn flesh.

"I almost have you, my sweet!" sang the daemon. A loud thump could be heard as the monster fell from the tree. Nadia couldn't think as fear and pain drove her to desperately to throw herself over the edge of the embankment. The tree was only a few short steps in front of her. Looking back, she could see the daemon was a few quick steps away as well, as it crossed the embankment, its long, crooked fingers extended toward her. Its nose was fully flared out, giving it the appearance of large eyes. The little tendrils of the nose quivered as it inhaled her panicked scent. She pushed through the pain and ran for the tree that had stayed open and throwing herself inside the warm hollow of the tree.

"Close it! Close it!" she shouted, wiggling around to see the daemon effortlessly hopping to the top of the embankment. The opening of the tree quickly closed shut as the daemon's long bony fingers raced toward her, plunging Nadia once again into darkness. The spell she made with Dasha's fur gave her the vision of a cat, but not even cats could see in such complete darkness. It was only in the safety of this hollow that she found relief in screaming. The confined nature of the hollow made her howls of pain pierce her own ears, feeding the cycle of agony. All she could do was take quick sharp breaths while grinding her teeth. The pain faded slightly. Just enough for her to think. She leaned against the hollow of the tree, panting, as her hand gently explored her broken arm. It was in this gentle prodding that she remembered Dasha was still out there. While the creature certainly seemed more interested in her, every action was a calculated move to torment her, from using her mother's voice to just letting her almost escape before pulling her off the rifle. Even its strange song was meant to send her running in terror. *What if it let me get in the tree?* she thought.

Regardless of the motives of the infernal creature, she had abandoned Dasha in the darkness. Then again, he was a pretty resourceful tomcat and was probably much safer running about the woods than she was in the hollow of this tree.

A simple rhythmic tapping could be heard on the hollow of the tree, always an odd number of taps. In a sequence of seven, one, nine, a rapid tapping of eleven, then back to one. She could also hear the creature practicing its singing, as if it were doing vocal warmups. She ignored this the best she could, as her fingers soon found the bone jutting out of her arm. It felt like a painful shard of glass that wriggled and writhed with fresh waves of pain. She struggled to remember the spell she needed to fix her broken arm. It wasn't just the jutting bone but her twisted fingers as well. She did her best to concentrate, focusing on the magic in her mind.

"This tapestry is undone, make it whole, reknit," she said. The daemon's singing raised in pitch and oscillation. She felt the mental backlash of the magic as it rescinded. It was like a slap to the face and a punch in the gut. Her nose began to bleed. She heard that some creatures could turn spells back on the user. Creatures of magic and the other world often had specific knowledge of such things. She kicked the hollow of the tree in anger and frustration. She was so frightened. She felt as if she were at the bottom of a well filling up with water.

It was in the darkness that she heard a whisper. A whisper that carried on the wind of magic. Nadia could smell burning leaves and autumn grass. The taste of springtime honeysuckles as it pushed through the song, and the daemon fell silent. A dim light appeared above her, like the coiling spark on a burned log. It grew in brightness. Slowly a ring of cold fire blossomed above her head.

"Who are you?" It was a woman's voice. It sounded like Olivia's when she first found Nadia, mad with hunger in the woods.

"Why can I see you in my hearth?" It was so gentle, so calming. From outside the hollow, a gargling howl could be heard. The singing dropped to that of a squealing pig.

"You are in danger, what is your name? You can trust me," said the voice above her. Nadia saw that there was an image inside the halo of fire above her. It was the calm, serene face of an older woman with the whitest hair Nadia had ever seen.

"Nadia, Nadia Voloshyn," she said.

"Nadia, I should not be seeing you in my fire. But it appears that you are in grave danger. I can do little from where I am; it must be you who rescues yourself."

"But how? The Kindersnatch won't let me cast any spells," said Nadia, wincing. The taps were replaced with blows that echoed through the small hollow.

"A daemon! My child, how did you find such a thing? Never mind. The beast is adding impurities to your magic. It poisons the stream of magic fed to the spell, that is why your spells failed. If you can, use the moon's light to wash the impurities away."

With a high-pitched song note from the Kindersnatch, the ring of fire then collapsed, leaving Nadia in the dark. The impacts on the tree became heavier, and the tree began to rock and creak. It felt like the daemon was throwing itself against the tree repeatedly.

With each impact, Nadia was jostled, making her wince in pain. She was frustrated, thinking she might be losing her senses. There was no way the fiery apparition had actually appeared. How could she even seek the moon in this wooden coffin? She collected the magic in her mind, focusing everything on keeping it still. Her head throbbed, and she felt sick. *The woman told her to seek the moon*, thought Nadia. The thumping stopped. The daemon began its high-pitched singing. Now that she knew what was happening, she could see the magic being polluted as she tried to use it. She closed her eyes and thought of the moon, the bright, bountiful white-blue sphere, and the pain in her head rescinded. The singing from outside the tree halted, and a gargling growl replaced it.

"You horrible little slut," howled the Kindersnatch in her mother's voice. "You disgusting little viper, you are ruining my fun! You had to bring her into this! When I get my hands on you, I will have your rump scorched with burning hot coals, I will rip off those disgusting breasts of yours. That Thule sorcerer will be getting a book of your own skin that describes the horrible things I have done to you!" the creature screamed, but Nadia had tuned out its voice as the moon washed away the poison in her magic.

"This tapestry is undone, make it whole, reknit." This time, there was no backlash. Nadia's words carried the magic that found its way into her arm. She had not expected any pain from the mending. The magic had other thoughts on that matter. The spell forced the bones back into flesh. The spell rudely formed the bones and torn muscle back to its original place. Nadia could do nothing but grit her teeth and scream. Her broken fingers snapped back into the sockets, reknitting the fractures. It felt like many large rocks were repeatedly slamming together inside her arm and hands, leaving her limbs sore. The bullet graze burned like hot fire, as tissue melded together, while the cuts on her hands and face closed shut.

The daemon outside had continued hurling itself at the tree, making Nadia's tiny world disorientated. When the pounding and twisting pains in Nadia's arm vanished, they were replaced with searing, burning pain. Like someone had set her entire arm on fire. The breaks in her bones were being welded and knit back together. Nadia hit the hollow of the tree, while gritting her teeth. Anything to deal with the overwhelming pain in her arm. She felt like she was falling within herself, losing touch with the world around her. Then the pain vanished like a shadow under sunlight. The witch was left shaking and panting. Her body ached, and her arm was weak. She couldn't even make a fist with her formerly shattered hand, most likely a side effect of the spell.

She didn't have long to recover or plan her next move. The daemon's relentless assault was finally bearing fruit as the tree pushed from the embankment, its roots no longer able to hold it in place. The tree fell, with Nadia tumbling inside the protective cocoon. She was on her back now with one weak arm unable to support her. A sudden impact caused the tree to quiver. Something heavy had landed on top of it. The daemon had mounted the tree. The tapping resumed. The inner hollow echoing with repeated uneven taps.

"Ah ha, I found it!" the daemon shouted. Nadia could hear what sounded like tearing wood. She heard the tree scream. A low howl of pain resonated in the wooden sanctuary. The daemon was doing something that was causing great distress to the tree. That is when one of the daemon's long fingers poked its way through the tree, sending small splinters down on Nadia's face.

The creature was rapidly tearing open a larger hole into the hollow of the tree while the tree groaned all around her, sending chunks of wood falling on Nadia's face. Nadia gripped the knife, trying to think of any spell to use against the daemon. But infernal beings followed their own rules. Nadia could now see the Kindersnatch's face as it grinned and leered. Nadia gripped the dagger, ready to strike if it reached for her. The monster grabbed the rough openings of the tree and began pulling. The sound of splitting wood overwhelmed the small hollow as the daemon used all its strength to rip open the wooden sanctuary.

The Kindersnatch pushed its head in the opening, its tusked mouth drooling as it licked its lips. Nadia slammed the dagger into the daemon's pulsing nose, throwing all her weight behind the attack. The blade went right through the nostril of the creature. The beast looked perplexed. It snorted and sniffed in confusion by the sudden intrusion of a dagger in its skull. It seemed to not be in any pain. It jerked its head back, ripping the handle out of Nadia's hand.

"I suppose this is the end of our fun," said the daemon, as it licked the handle of the SS dagger. "I have you now like a pig troth full of honey and I will devour you at my leisure. Sting all you want. I have my reward for winning the game." Its tongue shot out and began licking Nadia's face, trailing fresh blood from its nose and smearing saliva across her face. The creature smelled of sweet candy, and its saliva was as sticky as molten sugar.

The feeling was nauseating.

"My poor broken friend," she said in the speech of wood. "Help me escape this beast." The tree groaned, and an opening appeared at Nadia's back, causing her to fall.

"No! My prize!" shouted the daemon, its greedy words still mimicking Katarina. It reached out with its long arms to grasp the falling witch. It only managed to grab Nadia's satchel.

The strap, unable to handle the jerk of Nadia's weight, snapped. She fell to earth once again, this time landing in the freezing creek. She had only a moment in the freezing water before cans of food began to rain down upon her, hitting her head and arms. One weighty object landed on her injured wrist as she tried to shield herself, sending a sharp pain across her brutalized arm.

"This is why I only deal with children," growled the daemon above her as it threw the bag aside. "So much easier to catch. There is great fun in the chase, but I want the fun of actually having you in my hands."

The object that had hurt Nadia's tender arm was now resting in her soaked lap. A long wood-handled grenade, seen in the dark muted grey of magical night vision. She grabbed the grenade and tried to push herself up with her weakened left arm, submerging her once again in the freezing creek.

Surfacing, she could see the daemon pulling itself off the hollow, readying itself to jump down. Nadia quickly rolled over and used her legs to push off the riverbed. She ran out of the stream. A heavy splash crashed behind her. She frantically tugged at the cord on the bottom of the grenade, but her weakened left hand couldn't grip the cord tight enough, let alone pull it.

"I'm right behind you little one!" the daemon shouted. The Kindersnatch's heavy feet splashed through the river. Nadia cursed. She was frustrated and scared. Gritting her teeth, she turned on her heel and threw the grenade at the daemon. The grenade crashed into the creature's chest before falling into the creek. The monster stopped, confused, noticing that Nadia was not running. It reached into the river and picked up the grenade.

"What is this curious bobble? I think I will stick it someplace rather uncomfortable." The daemon laughed with her mother's voice.

"Sparks," hissed Nadia, focusing on the grenade. The weapon exploded a moment later. The force threw Nadia back into the cold creek. She then pulled herself out of the icy water, and saw that the daemon was no more. Just a rapidly flowing water and several trees filled with entrails and viscera. The forest was once again silent, with only the ringing of the explosion in her ears. She shivered from the cold. The stillness of the forest felt very safe now.

She felt the tremors following the aftermath of terror. She was fatigued beyond measure. She also felt hate. A sort of hate that she was not familiar with. Hatred for the daemon who attacked her, hate for Rudolph, who summoned the monster. She hated the Reich for finding such men and putting them to horrible use. She hated the mothers of the men who had brought such terrible things to her life. She wanted to find those German mothers and berate them for making such evil men. She crouched down in the river and let out an agonized scream, just to get the hate out of her body.

"Is it dead?" meowed a scared Dasha. "There was a lot of noise coming from over here. Are you alive, Nadia?"

"Yes," she croaked. "Yes," she said, louder this time. A soft thump could be heard, and Nadia saw the grey Dasha sneak out to the edge of the river. His ears were folded back as he moved low.

"Are you alright?" he meowed. Nadia nodded as she shivered in the icy river. "Well, you won't be for long if you stay in there."

Nadia pulled herself out of the water. Her dress had a new layer of mud added to it. She was shivering, from both the adrenaline and the cold.

"You're going to freeze to death before dawn. We need to make a fire. I don't care if people spot it. You need to get warm this instant."

"No fires," she croaked. "This will take a moment." Nadia grabbed the top of her skirt and shook it. "Dry this garment," she said, pushing a spell into it. The cold water steamed off instantaneously, leaving her dress dry. She did the same for the rest of her clothes, leaving her socks and shoes for last.

"So, what do we do now?" asked the tomcat as they sat beside the creek in the cold night air. Nadia was still freezing, but at least she would not freeze from the river.

"I don't know. I guess we have to pick up the pieces the best we can," said Nadia, standing up. Her torn bag was easy to find. A simple mending spell was all that was needed to fix the strap. The food in the creek would have to wait till morning. It was not going anywhere. Nadia retraced her steps, following the Kindersnatch's big heavy footprints to the place where the daemon had pulled her out of the air. It was a short search before Dasha found the flying rifle.

"Let's go see if our tree friend is alright," said Nadia.

"We should just make a fire, since humans are so good at it," mumbled Dasha.

"No fires, Dasha. We don't know what's out here, and if the horde of ghosts from my dead village can find me, who knows what else might. No, we sleep in the tree after making sure it's okay."

"I don't know how okay it's going to be, having fallen over," said Dasha when they got back to the creek. The tree was at an angle, its base sticking out of the embankment, its broad trunk across the stream.

"It still lives," Nadia sighed. She went up to the fallen tree. "I'm sorry you had to be put in such a state on my account," said Nadia in the language of wood.

"I'm glad you live," groaned the tree. Nadia could tell it was in great pain. The savage wounds of the Kindersnatch were slashed across its trunk. "I could use spells and mend some of the damage, but I can't put you back on the embankment. I don't know how long you will live like this on your side. Your weight alone will have you split in the center and fall into the creek."

"It was going to happen sooner or later," replied to the tree. "For many seasons I watched this embankment crumble underneath me from rain and snow. I'm pleased that my end was at least in service of the ancient pact." Nadia embraced the tree. The hard bark could not protect it from the coming years as it sank into the creek.

"If it's any consolation, I could take some of your seeds so that I may plant them wherever I find my new home," said Nadia.

"The sentiment is appreciated, but I'm well past the season of growing seeds. No, the sentimentality of your kind is not prudent for us trees. We make our life in one place, and we die in one place. The only thing I ask of you is to climb in my hollow that you may continue to live."

"I understand," said Nadia, kissing the bark; her rough lips stung slightly with the contact.

"Did you just kiss that tree?" Dasha asked, looking perplexed.

"It has done us a great kindness that we cannot repay. It has given its life so we may continue," she said, climbing up the tree with Dasha following behind.

"This tapestry is become undone, reknit," she said, placing both hands on the ragged tear. The wood groaned and snapped back into place. The spell was much easier for wood than human injuries. The tree sighed with relief as its wood melted back into its shape.

They crawled once more in the hollow of the tree. Nadia wiped the night-vision spell from her eyes, putting her back into darkness. Her eyeballs throbbed from the spell. Her arms were tender and weak from her fight with the daemon. Her body ached with the fall and the beating from the Nazis. She was so cold that even just a little bit of heat from Dasha's fur was a godsend. It wasn't long before Nadia had once again fallen asleep. The protective tree closed shut, shielding the young witch and cat from the cold night.

11
Deserters

It was midday when Nadia finally awoke and stayed awake. The darkness of the hollow made her fall back asleep numerous times, and the frightful night had left her body and mind fatigue. When she finally awoke, she dropped into the creek and said farewell to the tree before taking flight. Dasha rode on top of the canned food in the bag so that he didn't have to constantly worry about falling to his death. Nadia thought it was an excellent idea. Her weakened arm could not be spared to hold him during their flight. She could make a fist now, but not for long, and it still hurt immensely when she did. Such quick healing had its own set of problems that didn't exist for those using slower magical remedies. The most obvious was the significant scar now on the spot where her bone had sliced through flesh. Such scars tended to disappear with slower healing magic. She also didn't have the luxury of the slower methods that would have made her arm stronger and more resilient after the injury. These were ancillary thoughts, concerns that needed only the briefest attention. She was like so many autumn leaves set adrift from their home tree. Her goal was to discover the location of the Coven of the Ever-Shining Moon. She didn't know where to start. The only member she knew was Anna the Red, and she could be anywhere.

There were other pressing questions as well. There was the woman who contacted Nadia last night in her confrontation with the Kindersnatch. The freezing autumn nights would be coming, and Nadia was still in her summer clothes. It was also becoming clear that it was dangerous to travel. All she had now was a rifle with no ammunition, an unsheathed dagger that was constantly cutting at her belt, and a head full of spells that couldn't hurt anyone. Not directly anyway; Olivia had never taught her any of the darker hexes.

She knew there were spells of blindness and deafness, spells that would cause their victims to wither in sickness. Some curses would make every animal enraged with the bearer of a cursed mark. There were even frightful killing spells that stopped the heart or caused convulsions. A dark spell that would make nests of poisonous insects in the bowels of the targets. Hexes to steal a voice. To age a person to infirmity. Spells that could steal a person's sanity. These hideous spells were rare things, confined to the blackest of magic. So cruel that they would leave a permanent mark on the user's soul, so that all would know of their misdeeds.

Nadia couldn't cast any of these spells. She had her wits and a Nazi knife, no more grenades, and an empty flying rifle. She thought of how proud Olivia might have been to see her now. Her thoughts then turned to lining up Nazis and shooting them one by one. Slowly pulling the bolt back so they could see that she was about to kill them. She had never had such thoughts before. Even on her worst day in the village, she had only ever wished for someone's hair to fall out. Maybe have their milk curdle so it would stink up the house. But now, after yesterday, her thoughts turned to brutal ways to hurt the Nazi invaders.

"Not that I don't love flying above everything at a height that would surely kill me if I fell, but where are we going?" Dasha asked, adjusting himself inside the bag.

"I don't know, I have never left the village before. Well, there was that time we went to Kiev, when Mother went to the central Komsomol to figure out where Father had been taken to, but we were only there for a day," said Nadia, her throat still hoarse from all the spells and cries of agony from the previous night.

"So, we are just aimlessly flying around?" asked Dasha, resting his head on the lip of the bag. His ears blew back as the wind hit his face. He did look quite content in the bag while Nadia was still freezing from the altitude and the cold September weather. She really wished she had a jacket.

"I guess I'm looking for the Coven of the Ever-Shining Moon. The problem is I don't know where they are. They live in Grandmother's Forest, only I don't know where Grandmother's Forest is. I doubt it is written on an official map," sighed Nadia.

In the distance, she could see several large airplanes flying high above her. With several small planes escorting them as they flew. If she had to guess, they were bombers. She remembered as a child watching propaganda films about the vaunted Red Air Force and its state-of-the-art bombers and dogfighting planes. Yet she hadn't seen any Soviet airplanes. Only the broad, round-edged German planes. Nadia descended a little lower so as not to draw their attention.

"Maybe you can ask for directions," said Dasha, yawning. "Maybe ask a rock or a tree. Maybe a squirrel would know."

"You wouldn't happen to know where Grandmother's Forest is, would you?" asked Nadia.

"A good cat shouldn't know such things or consort with witches. So, no, I do not know where your forest full of witches is."

"If that's true about good cats not consorting with witches, then there must be a lot of bad cats out there. Having a cat is almost synonymous with being a witch now."

"We cats are nothing if not contrarian," said Dasha.

"Well, stopping and asking for directions is not a bad idea. I remember Anna the Red had told me that the creatures of the woods could guide me to Grandmother's Forest," said Nadia.

"Who?"

"A witch I met the other day," sighed Nadia. There was no forest in sight, just vast farmland with sporadic fighting and vast columns of men and machines on the road.

"So, when you went to Kiev, did you find out where your father went?" asked Dasha.

"No. They had no records of them ever arresting him. They just made him disappear. Like he never existed. They didn't even have a birth certificate, a record of employment, or tax records. Have you ever heard of a government that erases its tax records?"

"I don't even understand what tax records are. It's all just a bunch of human nonsense to me," said Dasha. "Wake me up when we land. There is a can of sardines I want you to open up. If I'm not getting a big fish, I aim to get an occasional can of that salty goodness."

They flew till the midday before they could find a forest of any decent size. A long and winding forest that hugged a row of hills that went on for kilometers. She could see that lumber encampments had been slowly pushing the forest back bit by bit, chewing the ancient grove up in the unrelenting march of modernity. These lumber yards were empty of men, with droves of women taking their place hoisting giant logs on large circular saws that cut the lumber on site. Nadia wanted nothing to do with these people, and she doubted she would be greeted openly by the workers. Just because her own village tolerated a witch or two didn't mean the other Soviet towns and cities would.

Nadia landed in the most remote part of the forest she could, near the northern end, many kilometers away from any of the numerous lumber camps that belched hot steam in the air. Nadia took a minute as she stretched her legs and back. Dasha hopped out and began to lick his long legs.

"Time for a snack. I want you to eat all of it!" said Dasha as Nadia rummaged around in her sack.

"How about we just split the can of sardines? You get some fish, and we save on food. And you don't bite me like this morning," she said, pulling the can of fish from her bag.

"You thought you could just skip breakfast without me knowing. Well, I'm sharper eyed then that," said Dasha, hopping up on a nearby log. Nadia joined him as she turned the key that slowly peeled back the can's metal cover. The pungent smell of fish oil hit her nose and made her salivate. "Now gimme the fish," he meowed continuously.

"I'm a little worried about how much food we still have. What are we going to do when we run out?" said Nadia, placing several of the oily fish on the log in front of the grey cat. Dasha greedily began eating the fish, barely chewing before swallowing.

"It's alright, I can hunt for mice and birds. I do love eating birds," Dasha said, taking a moment to lick his chops.

"That's fine for you, but I have never hunted before, and I doubt I could convince game to give up their life for me."

"I don't see a lot of animals taking that offer. Don't you know some sort of spell that could help you with hunting?" asked Dasha.

"No, I don't. I should probably stick to herbs and mushrooms of the forest. I can find those with some time," said Nadia, sucking oil off her fingers.

"Can I lick the oil in the can?" Dasha asked.

"No, you will get the runs, and the last thing I need right now is a diarrhetic cat in my bag," she said, using a spell to sink the empty can back into the earth. "Come on, I want to keep moving."

"Who are you looking for anyway?" Dasha asked, trotting behind Nadia. His tail swooshed as he ducked beneath plants and fallen branches.

"We start with the trees, they always know someone who knows something, or one of the birds," said Nadia, spotting a woodpecker tapping away at the tree overhead. "Stay here, I don't want you to scare it." She mounted the rifle and flew up to the bird.

"Like I want to talk to a potential meal," muttered the cat as he returned to licking himself.

"Excuse me, woodpecker!" tweeted Nadia in the beast speech.

"Go away, witch, I'm busy," said the woodpecker before tapping the wood with its beak.

"I won't be long. I just need a minute of your time to ask a question."

"Ugh, what?" the woodpecker said, fluttering over to a nearby branch.

"I was wondering if you knew where Grandmother's Forest was. A sister of mine said that I should ask the animals of the woods. That is, if you're not too busy."

"Well, I am. Go ask Eldernaut, that old tree trunk would know," said the woodpecker sounding exasperated.

"Who is Eldernaut? I don't know this forest at all."

"Eldernaut, the oldest tree in these woods. If he doesn't know, he can direct you where you need to go. More importantly he has more patience for tourists and their stupid cats!" yelled the woodpecker.

"Well, I'm sorry for being such a bother, but could you tell me where Eldernaut is?" said Nadia.

"That way, down the hill, in the swamp. If you find the bear cave you have gone too far," sighed the woodpecker.

"Thank you, miss, is there anything I can do for you?" asked Nadia. The bird paused and thought for a moment.

"Well, there is one thing you can do," she said, tilting her head.

"Yes, what is it?" Nadia said, leaning in close to the bird.

"You can go away!" yelled the bird. The woodpecker flew back to the spot on the tree and continued pecking. Nadia followed the bird's wishes and returned to the ground.

"Rude bird. Want me to eat her?" asked Dasha, shaking his butt in the air.

"No, she directed me to someone to talk to. Eating someone after they have given their help is impolite," said Nadia.

"Says you," said Dasha, licking his chops.

The pair went their way through the forest, occasionally running into thick swamps, a terrain that would have slowed them down had it not been for the enchanted gun that allowed them to fly right over such obstacles. The journey down the hill was made on foot, much to the chagrin of Dasha, who hated moving through the occasional puddles of mud. The hill in question was not rugged compared to the others in the region. What it had were thick swamps and thick undergrowth, and some of the oldest trees Nadia had ever seen were growing out of the turgid black ponds. Eventually, it got to the point where they could no longer traverse on foot, opting instead to fly at canopy level, occasionally asking for directions from the nearby trees.

"Do you smell that?" asked Dasha in a hushed voice. Nadia took a deep breath, only smelling the moist, mossy air that had been giving her the chills.

"No, is it something good or bad?" asked Nadia.

"Don't know, smells like human food," he said, his nose wiggling as he sniffed the air. "We are almost at the bottom of the hill, so whomever it is, is close to that tree we're looking for."

"Well, we best move carefully then," said Nadia, then rose to just above the canopy. The rifle moved without a sound as it swayed between the reaching tree branches.

When they made it to the base of the hill, they found the source of the cooking. A Red Army soldier was stirring a pot over an open fire. Nadia landed on a neighboring tree branch, looking down on the lone man.

He worked in a clearing in front of a giant twisted tree that had been relentlessly pruned. Many of the larger branches were made into a small hut that one had to crouch to get into. Many more of the smaller branches had been chopped into kindling. The lone soldier was disheveled with a sprouting beard and his greatcoat covered in dried mud. There were several other packs beside the lone man's own. He seemed to be only armed with a pistol.

"Who's that?" whispered Dasha. Nadia had to steady herself with her good arm. If she fell, she would only have one arm that could help to grab on to anything. So, she kept a sure grip on the branch above her.

"It looks like a Red Army soldier, possibly a deserter. I count three other packs, but there is no way to tell if he just stole them or if he has comrades. What's worse is I think that the tree we need to speak is the one they have been using for kindling."

"Is it dead?"

"I don't think so," replied Nadia. Her arm was getting sore, and her legs were starting to cramp up. "But that tree is not doing so well, I don't know if it will survive to next year."

"Well, go talk to it. I hate this swamp. It's wet, and it is far too cold to be traipsing around in the mud."

"I don't think I can. I really don't want to have anything to do with that man down there. I don't know if he is friendly, but if he is a deserter, then I really don't want to have anything to do with him."

"Well can't you use some spell to talk to the tree from here?" asked the cat.

"No, not really. But I think I do have a way of dealing with the man."

"Some clever spell, I would imagine. Why don't you ever use some sort of death curse?" asked Dasha.

"I don't know any. I don't think I could kill anyway like that. That sort of magic comes at a high cost. I'm not a killer."

"Yes, you are, you killed those men in front of the house when we were escaping," said Dasha.

"That was different," she said.

"No, it wasn't. They were dangerous so you killed them; it's not that hard to understand."

"Let's not have this conversation now," said Nadia, looking over the tiny camp.

"Fine, just do your trick so we can get out of here. I just want to be dry `again."

"Alright," she said. "Get in the bag. I don't want to have scoop you up like last time if we get into trouble."

"Fine, but I'm expecting caviar when you finally get me fish," said Dasha. She closed her eyes and centered herself. The spell Nadia was thinking of was a strange one. It demanded that she become someone else for a time. She had to channel the aspect of the mother moon, the side that had to do with sleep and dreams. The aspect that rocked babies to sleep. It was something everyone knew in their hearts when they were born yet forgot when they grew up.

A sleeping lullaby that can put the unwary to sleep. A valuable spell to have when you have a little brother that has a nightmare. Nadia massaged her throat. She whispered the first syllables of the spell, a melody that didn't come from Nadia's own voice but a different, more primal one.

"Good night, my darling, sleep, sleep now, for I'm by your side, the sun has gone down to rest for the night, I'll be here to wake you. For now, sleep, forget this place, for you will be dreaming where you are free, and held in my arms tonight."

Nadia's voice carried through the woods, echoing, and reverberating through trees and puddles of water. She seemed to be singing from nowhere and everywhere. Her dark eyes had become silver as she channeled the aspect of the moon. The soldier continued stirring the pot, but slowly he began to nod off. His head drooped before bouncing back up. He carefully put down the metal spoon he was using to stir before propping his head on his chin. It wasn't long before he was sleeping. Nadia hopped on her gun and silently glided into the camp.

"Why didn't you use that on the men who destroyed the town?" asked

Dasha, sticking his head outside the flap of the bag. "Could have saved us a lot of trouble. Just put all the invading humans to sleep, then slice their throats."

"When you're trying to kill a mouse, do you feel like taking a nap?" whispered Nadia with a soft landing. Her shoes sank into the mud. "Spells are like tools. You wouldn't use a hammer to sew a thread, as you wouldn't use a needle to fix a post. Think of spells like various cups or glasses. The liquid you place in them can be any type of magic, but the cup reflects the power."

"I still don't understand," meowed Dasha.

"And probably don't even care," sighed Nadia, looking at the sleeping man. "This man was at rest, and I nudged him to sleep. I don't know how long he will stay like that, so don't wake him up."

"Like I would want to," meowed Dasha. "You should take some of their things."

"No!" admonished Nadia. "I just want to talk to the tree, so we can get going."

"Nadia, I see you shivering right now. They have a spare jacket right there, and a few extra bullets as well as a few spare cans of food. Maybe they have a sheath for that knife that has almost cut your belt off," said Dasha yawning, shaking off some of the effects of the spell.

Nadia looked at her belt, which was indeed slowly being cut by the unsheathed dagger. The naked Nazi blade had been a nuisance for a while. As for the jacket, she wanted it more than anything. The padded jacket with its fur collar would prove invaluable for the cold nights to come. However, she might be mistaken for a Red Army trooper. As for the bullets, she had no idea how to operate her father's rifle. She didn't know how the mechanism was cleaned or how to load it quickly. She could picture herself desperately fumbling with a clip of ammunition as a Nazi attacked her. Then she remembered the Kindersnatch and how helpless she felt as it befouled her magic. Other means of defense might be necessary for the coming months.

"You're a terrible influence, you know that?" she told Dasha, taking the heavy padded jacket and putting it on. The cold still stuck to her, but now she was bundled up. Even if it stank like a sweaty man, it was a satisfying moment. If she only had a cup of tea.

"I'm the best influence on you; you're like a weak kitten on shaky legs. It's good that you have an experienced tomcat like me to guide you."

"Why are men all the same, no matter the species? I'm older than you by at least twelve years."

"Details are for humans. Oh! If they have any sausages, I want them," he said, giving a slight chirp. Nadia picked a pack that was furthest away from the sleeping man. There was a bandolier of ammunition inside, as well as several cans of food. She only took one can; she didn't want to completely deprive these men. There was a bayonet sheath in the bag that wouldn't fit her own dagger. So instead, she wrapped the dagger in a pair of socks. That least would keep it from cutting her belt. Looking through the other bags, she found various things like canteens and letters to loved ones. She took spare things she could easily carry.

She took as many grenades as she could. The fist-sized grenades were more compact than the bulky German grenades she had, and after the Kindersnatch she wanted as many as she could carry. When she finished looting the soldier's supplies, she felt significantly heavier with the extra padding and weight. If she had to walk with even half of what these soldiers were carrying, Nadia wouldn't last long. Yet, the flying circumvented this disadvantage, and she doubted the gun would care about a few extra pounds.

"Alright, let's ask that tree where my new home is." Keeping an eye on the sleeping man, Nadia approached the tree with its shorn branches. She touched the bark and could feel the tree's pain.

"Excuse me, are you Eldernaut?" she said in the language of wood. She could hear the creaking of the wood inside as a face grew out of the tree.

"I am, young witch. Pardon my appearance, I have been shorn and the pain is great," said the tree in its slow, creaking language.

"I'm sorry that you had to bear such pain. We humans often forget that the trees are living beings as well, I hope you don't begrudge me or these men too much," said Nadia.

"I care not for the views of men. I have lived so long, that I now see that I'm but a small twig under a spinning sky. My life is one of constants; these pains are a teacher in a new way of being that I have not had in a long time. It will be hard adjusting to this new way of living. I will endure as long as I can before my frame goes still and once again collapses to dirt."

"You hold great wisdom within you; I'm sure the forest will grieve for your passing," said Nadia.

"Trees do not grieve. We do not think of things that were. We only care what is and would be. What was, is no more." The tree grimaced in pain, its eyebrows furrowing and mouth curling. "Now, what can this old oak do to help a young witch?"

"I'm lost and cast adrift. A seed with no patch of earth to put roots down. But I know of a place that can help. I'm looking for Grandmother's Forest where the moon shines eternal. A woodpecker said you would know where to find this place. I would be appreciative if you helped me."

"I know where this place is. It is good that woodpecker sent you my way." The tree gave a pained smile. "It is the oldest forest on this ever-expanding steppe."

"How do I find it?" Nadia placed her hand on the wooden cheek of the old tree.

"It rests on one of the nerve clusters of the world. Many ley lines of magic flow through there. It is a place where the magic of the moon is quite strong.

"Well, where is that?" asked Nadia. The tree furrowed its brow.

"You must follow the ley lines. Surely a witch knows how magic pulses through the world?" said Eldernaut.

"But I never learned that skill. How do I find what I cannot see?"

"I'm sorry, I cannot tell you. You must learn to open your eyes to the spirit realm. To open your inner eye. I cannot teach you how. But if you learn this, I'm sure you will find Grandmother's Forest."

"Hands up!" someone shouted behind her. *Had the soldier woken up?* Nadia looked behind her and saw two men emerging from the trees, their rifles pointing right at her. Nadia slowly raised her hands.

"Why didn't you warn me?" whispered Nadia to the tree and Dasha.

"I couldn't tell the difference. The coat you're wearing is overwhelming my nose," meowed Dasha. As for Eldernaut, his face melted back into the wood of the tree.

"Follow the ley lines," the tree groaned before falling dormant.

"Markov, wake up, you idiot," shouted the closest man. The sleeping man, Markov, jolted upright when he saw his comrades pointing guns.

"Goddamnit man, you had one job. Protect the camp while we forage. Now this thief is wearing half our supplies."

The man named Markov swore, pulling a pistol off his side and pointing it at Nadia with the other two soldiers.

"Apologies, Sergeant Kolkov; it's a good thing you stumbled in," muttered Markov.

"What do we do with the thief?" said the rifleman. He had a large bandage over his arm. It was dark brown with dried blood. The brown blood had darkened his padded jacket, and he was very pale.

"Turn around," barked Sergeant Kolkov. Nadia complied slowly, trying not to make any false moves.

"A woman!" said the injured man, who sounded too excited for Nadia's comfort.

"Now slowly take off all the things you have stolen from us," said the sergeant. Nadia slowly took off the bandoleer of ammunition and leaned her father's rifle against the tree. They only relaxed when she also put down her bag and jacket. That was when Dasha took a moment to run.

"What the hell was that?" shouted Markov, his pistol following the grey blur as Dasha fled into the woods.

"My cat," said Nadia. The injured man and the sergeant looked at each other before taking several tentative steps forward. The injured man took a rabbit that he had on his arm and placed it by the fire, the muzzle of his rifle pointing at Nadia.

"You're obviously not part of the army. No unit would carry a cat around," said the sergeant. "So that means you're also not a deserter. So, the question we should ask is where did she get that rifle?"

"It was my father's," said Nadia.

"She must have stolen it," said Markov.

"Are those my socks?" The man stepped up to her, keeping his pistol leveled at her chest. Markov pulled the dagger from her belt that was wrapped up in the man's socks. Nadia gritted her teeth, having been stripped of her last weapon.

"Holy hell," muttered Markov as he unwrapped the dagger. "The whore is a Nazi spy!" The next thing she knew, the man punched her hard in the belly. Nadia collapsed to the ground. The contents of her stomach threatened to emerge once again.

"Grab that rifle and bag; looks like you get a proper weapon after all, Markov," said the injured man.

"Cheap bastards give me a clip of ammunition. Send me into the fight with nothing but the hope that some poor bastard bites it," said Markov. Nadia saw the man pull a clip of ammo out of his breast pocket before pushing it into her father's rifle.

"So, what do we do with the spy, sergeant?" asked Markov, looking down the sights of her father's gun. This outraged her immensely, but she could do little as she was still sucking in air.

"We don't know that she is a spy," the sergeant said, walking up to Nadia. His boots squished into the mud with each step. They were almost soaked up to the leg. He crouched down and grabbed Nadia by the chin to look at her face.

"She could be any number of things; yes, she could be a German spy. But she could easily be a member of the partisan forces. Who's to say which one? Maybe a lying deserter throwing away her uniform, but then why steal another? Plus, her hair isn't shaven like the other cadets. She could also just be a scavenger, picking the battlefields clean of supplies in hopes of trading them for some food. So, what is it, girl?"

Olivia had once told her that a lie is always better than the truth. Even when they assume you are lying. Her identity as a witch was the most significant detriment when dealing with these men. It was a secret weapon. A head full of magic was often more important than a whole battery of artillery or a thousand men.

"I'm a spy, but I work for the Kremlin," said Nadia. Both the injured man and Markov backed away with almost panic on their faces. "My mission was to get behind the German lines and assassinate German officers."

"Oh shit, first desertion now attacking a state agent," said Markov as he paced back and forth. "Why does God hate me so?"

"He doesn't hate you," said the sergeant. "Spies don't bring cats with them on missions. This is a farm girl hiding in the woods."

"So, what do we do with her?" asked Markov.

"She could be our camp wife," said the injured man stepping forward. "She isn't a cow, and her cooking can't be worse than Markov's."

"Shut your mouth, Victor."

"I'm serious. How long has been since anyone of us have been with a woman?" Nadia grabbed a fistful of mud. She didn't like where this line of talk was headed.

"I will hear no more of such talk," said the sergeant turning to Victor. "We don't have any place for that pre-revolutionary behavior." He turned away from Nadia. For a moment, all eyes were off her. This would be the time to escape the clutches of these men.

But they had her father's rifle. They had her food. This Victor and Markov sounded like greedy men. But the sergeant had something cold about him.

"Last I checked we were all deserters. Just because you bossed us around in the army does not mean you can now," said the wounded Victor.

"Deserters by circumstance. If I had a choice, I would still be with the rest of the column taking the bayonet to the fascists," said the sergeant.

"And while we wear these uniforms, I'm still your leader. It is the only thing keeping us from being armed bandits." The mood in the camp was tense. The men had become more aggressive.

"Nadia," whispered Dasha. It seems he stealthily returned hiding behind the tree. "Let's make a break for it. While they are distracted."

"I can't, not without the rifle. They would catch me or just shoot me," whispered Nadia.

"Maybe there is nothing wrong with that," said Victor, his hand over the trigger. "We have guns, and grenades. We can find a farm and hold out till the Nazis win the war and start our lives over."

"That's not a bad idea," said Markov. "We can just put the uniforms aside and live fat and happy for a couple of months. When the war is over, we can just bury the weapons. No one would ever know."

"I will hear no more of this talk; the plan remains the same. We wait for an opportunity to rejoin with the army. Then we do our part in crushing the invaders," said the sergeant, adjusting himself so that the two men were not flanking him.

"That's the thing. Victor and I have been talking. You're the only one who believes in that party nonsense. Had we our druthers, we would be back home. If we wait long enough, the Communist Party will just be a bad dream. No more forced work, no more bad harvests, no more Joseph Stalin."

"This isn't mutiny anymore, this is treason," growled the sergeant.

"Things are about to get bad, Nadia. If things turn, I can escape but I don't know if you can," said Dasha.

"Well, then I'm going to need your help to get away," said Nadia.

"Seriously? What can I do to help? They aren't exactly mice."

"No, but you can help me cast a spell," said Nadia, slipping her hand toward Dasha around the tree. "Scratch my palm, enough to bleed."

"Alright but be careful. If you die, then I will be left out here all alone." She felt his paw resting on her palm, and before she knew it, claws dug four bloody furrows in her skin.

"We are not following your lead anymore. We are taking the girl with us. Even beaten to hell she's a looker. Right now, we are throwing you a lifeline. Don't make us cut the rope," said Victor. The officer's eyes had narrowed as he realized the situation he was in. Briefly, his eyes fell on Nadia. All the tension and immediately faded. All the anger he was carrying moments before fell away.

Nadia saw how old and tired he looked. She remembered that same look on her father's face before he attacked the soldiers stealing her family's food.

Then Kolkov punched Markov in the gut, sending the man falling to the ground. Victor tried to bring his own rifle up, but he was jumped by the officer. The two struggled as Markov got to his feet, brandishing the SS dagger. Nadia watched as the trooper stabbed the sergeant in the back several times. The officer screamed in agony as the dagger cut organs and flesh alike. Nadia quickly started sucking blood from her palm, as much as she could get into her mouth. Victor and Markov stepped away from the sergeant.

"Damn obstinate bastard. You idiot! You fool! If you were smarter, you wouldn't be bleeding out," shouted Markov. Nadia took a handful of mud and put it into her mouth. She was improvising a spell on the fly. If she could seal someone's mouth using mud, she figured she could seal other things as well.

"Alright let's finish him. I'll shoot him first, then you put a round in him," said Victor. Nadia grasped a handful of mud and held it up toward Victor. She pictured the darkness around the moon and swallowed the mud, grimacing as the grainy earth went down her throat.

"Choke," she whispered before crushing the mud in her palm. Victor was aiming his gun at the screaming sergeant. Then he rocked as if something had hit his chest. A gagging noise emanated from his throat. The gagging gave way to coughing and then a choking noise.

"Victor, what's going on? Damn it, speak to me," said Markov, bending down to check on the mutineer. Nadia kept her grip tight. The magic was tenuous. If she let up for even a moment, the spell would vanish, and Victor would breathe normally. Her arm shook with intense force as if she was choking him with her own hands.

"What's going on? Tell me, man, is it your throat?" said Markov as Victor frantically nodded. "Are you choking?" He nodded again, pointing at his throat. "Damn," mumbled Markov as he got behind and began to press on Victor's belly. A moment later, the man coughed up a glob of grey mud. He continued to choke as mud oozed out of his mouth. The choking man saw Nadia as he started to turn blue in the face. He raised a shaking hand and pointed at Nadia.

"What's going on? Are you doing this?" shouted Markov, letting go of Victor, who collapsed on the ground. Markov pulled her rifle from his shoulder, anger and fear growing on the trooper's face.

"My God, you're a witch, aren't you? It all makes sense: stray woman in the swamp with a cat. How I fell asleep despite it being midday. You probably used your magic to divide us didn't you, enchanted our minds with your poisoned spells." He then pointed her gun at her. "Well, I won't stand for it. Stop whatever you're doing, or I will put a bullet in your throat." If only he hadn't put in a fresh clip. Now was as good a time as any to make a run for it. But she wanted her father's weapon back. She'd made it take flight. She wondered if she had even more control over it.

"Come," she barked, and the rifle jolted out of Markov's hands and flew over to Nadia. It floated in front of her for a moment before she grabbed it. Her hand was so tired, and she wanted to let go. Victor was on the ground, clawing at the earth as mud oozed out of his mouth in a solid log.

"Holy mother of God," muttered Markov as he dropped to his knees and began to pray. Nadia used her rifle to stand, making sure she kept the spell going. Only when Victor stopped struggling did she relax.

"God save me from this evil of Satan. I repent any misdeed and pledge to honor you, in all things," muttered Markov. He looked so pitiful. A part of her told her to kill him. After all, she killed two men already with her magic and possibly a third with Victor. With all that mud in his throat, he would be dead soon. The sergeant was groaning next to Victor. It was clear what she had to do. He had risked his life to save hers. Nadia placed her hand on Markov's head. He winced, clenching his teeth.

"I have the power to kill you with but a word," she lied. She found a way to kill with magic, but it took time and effort. Now was the time for theatrics. "All I wanted was to be left alone. I never wanted to meet any of you in this forest. I know this is all partly my fault. I saw things that I needed, tried to steal from you, and was caught. But this was not my doing. You turned on your comrades in a time when we should be sticking together. When whole villages are being wiped out, you decided to turn on each other. For what?" Nadia found herself getting angry. She then pointed the rifle at the Markov. "Now give me my dagger, and your pistol, with the holster." The man pulled his belt off with pistol and holster.

"Good. Now, look at me." The man did not. "Look at me, you toad!" she shouted. "If you don't look up, I will shoot you, and it might not be a killing shot." Markov complied, looking up at Nadia's face.

"Nadia what are you doing?" meowed Dasha, coming into the camp.

"I'm teaching this man a lesson," she said. She took the dagger covered in the sergeant's blood and wiped it off on Markov's shoulder. "Now I'm going to make a small mark on you. It will only hurt an instant. It won't even be a very large mark. You lost perspective in these woods. I aim to return it to you." She then took the blade of the knife and placed it on his head.

"Oh God," whispered Markov.

"Nadia, this seems excessive," said Dasha, rubbing against her.

"I'm tired of men always trying to take things from me," she said. She placed the tip of the dagger right on Markov's head. After casting one spell of darkness, it seemed so easy to cast another. She planned to blind the man with a rune of darkness. Since he decided to follow blindly, he would live blind.

"Nadia, you're scaring me. You smell like burning metal," meowed Dasha a bit louder. He sounded desperate.

"Good," she snapped around, facing the cat. "If people are afraid of me, they won't destroy the things I love. These dogs are getting what they deserve. For once it is my turn to do the hurting," she hissed. Dasha recoiled, his ears folding back as his grey tail tucked in.

"What happened to your hair?" asked the cat, having backed up against the elderly tree.

"My hair?" said Nadia, momentarily confused.

"I don't know what you and that cat are saying, but if it's about sparing me, I think you should listen," said Markov.

"Shut up!" she yelled at the man. "If you say another word without my say so, I will cut your tongue out and nail it to a tree. Now what about my hair?"

Red-hot anger coursed through her. The uncontrolled hate colored her every action. Dasha's question had grounded Nadia for a moment. She took her braid from behind her neck and examined it. Amidst the river of black hair was a large vein of grey that ran up the length to her head. She stared at it. It was the same white as in Olivia's hair. Nadia always thought it strange how a woman in her mid-forties would have such grey-white hair. Then she remembered what Olivia had said. Those who use foul and profane magic are marked for all the world to see. She had used a spell that had only one purpose, to kill. To kill in a painful and suffocating manner.

Nadia could have used the obscuring black cloud like she did when she escaped Rudolph and his men. Instead, she chose a more direct and permanent solution. The killer magic had left a residual effect on her mind and body. It was affecting all her actions. She squeezed the braid with her week arm, a reminder of who she was. She took a deep breath and closed her eyes. She used the darkness to cast the spell that killed Victor. Now she thought of the moon and its purifying luminescence. She let the light wash over her, cleansing her of the shadows that held sway over her mind.

"Nadia, behind you!" hissed Dasha. Nadia fell back into herself and turned and see Markov lunging at her. She had just enough time to bring the rifle up to shield her. The heavier man hit her, sending them both falling into the mud. They landed with a squelching thud that knocked the wind out of her. Nadia was never a strong or fast girl. Many of her peers were used to heavy labor. With girls even half her age able to throw a goat over their shoulder without difficulty. Nadia was always thin and grew tired faster whenever there was a public works project. Her mother had tried to fix this, convinced that Nadia would be like the others if she just fed her daughter. That was whenever she was sober. This underfed skinny witch was now wrestling with a man who was twice her weight. A man used to hard labor and fighting. Nadia could do little to fend off powerful hands that pulled at the rifle she was using as a shield.

Worse still, her arm was injured from the night before. It was still weak and could do little to defend her. Dasha hissed and charged Markov. He was thrown aside with little difficulty. Nadia tried to push Markov away. She reached for closely cropped hair that couldn't be easily pulled. She tried to gouge out an eye with her thumbs. He swatted her arm aside. The two struggled until he grabbed the gun and threw it aside. It wasn't long before his hands were around her neck, and he began to squeeze. She tried to throw him off. Tried to punch his belly or face. With each hit, her wrists screamed in pain, and the grip on her neck only seemed to tighten. He leaned into her neck, pushing her further in the mud. A choking scream came from her throat that came out as a gurgle. She looked for the dagger. If she could only stab him. The dagger was stuck up in the mud with Markov's pistol just out of reach.

"Nadia," meowed Dasha, his voice a dull thunder in her ears, her pulse deafening in her head like a cascade of boulders.

"You can make the gun float without touching it," yowled Dasha. Dasha had to repeat this several times, as Nadia had trouble concentrating.

Markov pushed down with bared teeth, spit spilling from his mouth and onto her face. Nadia's world was going dark, and her vision collapsed to pinholes. Her struggling became weaker, her strikes hit with less force. She was about to collapse into the darkness when she saw a burning iris above Markov's head. It grew into a circle of fire, so bright against the backdrop of the grey sky above. It grew to the size of a dinner plate and then a window. Markov didn't appear to notice it at all, but it was all Nadia could focus on.

Blood pounded in her ears and skull as the man redoubled efforts crushing her neck. Inside the burning ring of fire, Nadia saw the woman from the previous night. She looked shocked and confused.

"Nadia?" said the woman. Her voice cut through the pounding in Nadia's head. "How do you find yourself in so much trouble?" she said. "I can't save you from this man. You are too far away. But I can give you the strength to save yourself. Now, breathe," she said, holding her hand up and blowing through the corona of fire. A blast of wind hit the pair like a bucket of water. Nadia felt her lungs fill with fresh air.

Markov looked confused. His grip loosened momentarily. Nadia reached out, sensing the magic within her father's rifle. It rose from the mud and slowly aimed at Markov's back. *Load,* she thought. The rifle loudly cocked, the bolt sliding back. Markov turned and saw the gun floating. He looked back down at Nadia. The snarling rage was gone. Now there was concern morphing into panic as he looked down at the young woman. It was a split-second decision. She fired the rifle with a thought, and the gunshot rang out through the woods. The bullet pierced Markov's head, sending blood, bone, and brain splashing onto Nadia's face. The body slumped down on top of her. She could now breathe freely, and she just laid still with the body atop her as she took big gulps of air. Then the shakes started. She was starting to get used to the feeling. After two days of fighting for her life, the feeling was comforting. It proved that she survived. With both arms, she pushed the man off her. The gun remained floating in the air. She took a moment to hug her knees to collect herself. Dasha walked up to her and crawled into her lap. She hugged the cat.

"I'm sorry, Nadia," he said.

"For what?" asked Nadia, feeling the cat's fur against her face.

"I shouldn't have suggested taking those things. It only landed you in a heap of trouble," Dasha said. His fur was smeared with mud from Nadia's dress. She was getting tired of the mud.

"No, it wasn't your fault. It looked like trouble was brewing among them for a while," said Nadia. The sergeant groaned, crawling toward his rifle. Still willing to fight. Nadia stood holding Dasha. She walked over to the sergeant with her own rifle following behind her. She kicked his weapon out of his grasp before crouching down again over the sergeant.

"Well do it, witch, finish me off. Whatever you are planning, I will not be a part of it. If you seek to entrap me with your spells, I will bite my own tongue. I risked my life to defend you and now because of your trickery I'm done for. You turned my men against me with your magic," he said, sweat oozing down his brow.

"I didn't have anything to do with how your men acted," said Nadia. "Whatever was going on between you and those two men was not my fault. I came here on my own business that had nothing to do with any of you. Our meeting was an unfortunate coincidence."

"I would say you're lying, but what would be the point in lying to a dead man," he said, gritting his teeth. "Alright, I'm ready. Make it quick."

"I wasn't planning on killing you. Without your intervention, I would have been in worse trouble. You risked everything to keep those men from doing terrible things to me. I thought all men in the Red Army were bandits and thieves. You showed me that I was wrong. That at least there is one good man in the Red Army," said Nadia, placing her hand on the man's face. "Trust me, this is going to hurt," she said, drawing power for a healing spell. "This tapestry is undone. Make it whole, reknit."

The magic flowed from her hands like water into a cup, the spell seeking out the injuries from the dagger and began to sew them back up. Sergeant

Kolkov screamed. Spittle flew from his mouth as his face turned red. While the man convulsed, Nadia went about collecting her lost supplies, drying herself off with a simple spell, and sending the two bodies of Markov and Victor into the earth. When the sergeant stopped shaking in pain, Nadia was fully dressed in the warm jacket, with as much ammunition and grenades that she could carry. Plus, a new pistol with plenty of ammunition. She helped the sergeant lean against a tree as he continued panting.

"You will be weak for several days. Be sure to eat. Don't go looking for a fight," said Nadia, filling a mess tin full of the soup that Markov had made. She handed the soup to Kolkov before grabbing another mess tin for herself. "I'm going to have a cup of soup as well, if you don't mind. My cat will bite me if I don't eat something when I have a chance."

"I'm not your cat!" said Dasha. "And you are not my witch. We just happen to know each other."

"Quiet you," said Nadia as Dasha curled up on a log next to the fire, stretching his paws to dry off the mud.

"It's not like I can stop you. You have already taken an infantryman's worth of supplies and weapons, why not an infantrymen's ration of soup?" Kolkov said, irritated and tired.

"Just compensation for the trouble of your men," she said.

"That's thinking like a cat," meowed Dasha.

"I think so."

"That is really unsettling," said the sergeant, stirring the soup. He looked at it with suspicion in his eyes and didn't start eating until Nadia took the first bite.

"What is?" said Nadia, eating the thin broth that tasted of barley seeds.

"Talking with a cat. Its unnatural. Everything about you is unnatural."

188

"I bet you wouldn't have said that to your doctor or nurse. I didn't expect thanks, but I hoped I wouldn't have been insulted."

"That was not insult, it's a fact. You dropped in like a bomb, killing two men and leaving me weakened. It's obviously not your first time with conflict or violence, judging by how quickly you have recovered after a brutal strangling. If this is your first time killing, then you are even more deranged then at first glance," he said, forgetting the spoon and sipping the soup from the cup. *Do I really appear so strange to this man?* thought Nadia.

"I'm just trying to survive in a world gone mad," said Nadia.

"Even in a mad world, women don't do the killing, let alone use unknown forces like magic. What if you unleash something terrible? How would you put it back in the bottle?"

"Shows what you know. What you called unknown forces I call a close friend. As for women not doing the killing, men have been killing witches for a very long time. I'm going to defend myself no matter what. But that's not important right now. Right now, an army of murderers has come from far away. They see no distinction between us. We are both on the menu. I have seen firsthand what the Nazis intend to do to us. They will kill us, horribly, and en masse. They are fighting for extermination. We are fighting for survival. We cannot afford to make divisions between us. Saying who is unnatural and who is not. Because in their eyes we are all unnatural, and they will treat us all the way you treated witches."

Sergeant Kolkov said nothing, and the silence of the forest was split by the crackling of the fire.

"Yesterday, my village was destroyed. A Nazi sorcerer sent the ghosts of the dead to stalk me in the night, before unleashing a daemon on me. Oh God, I'm tearing up just thinking about it. Everyone I know is gone, either killed or sent to who knows where." Nadia looked away from the man. "The state has been a millstone around my neck all my life. At least in that system there is room for people to be human. To find kindness, or mercy. But it is still the system that took my father. I do not support the state, but I will fight alongside it. Because there is a foe that will not even give me the hope of finding my loved ones alive. Does that make sense? Do I still seem unnatural?"

"In many ways, it does. The party says that men and women are equal in all things. Yet, no people have used women in combat like we do. If the past few months of conflict are any indication of where this war is headed, then there will be whole divisions of soldier women running through minefields. I believe in Communism, but what we have is perverse. Such perverse things draw in the ilk of the world. Terrible things, like witches who steal children or thugs who imprison men who only wish to protect their homes. Yet, it is a terrible situation when such a thing is your only salvation when a force of utter evil has vowed to destroy not only the idea one carries but the people who carry it.

"I do not think your profane magic and our ideology can coexist, but I also would have said that a Communist state would never ally with the capitalistic states. Now. We fight alongside Britain, the capital of greedy colonialism. No, I do not think what you do is natural. But crises make strange bedfellows."

"You're right. I don't think our two ways of being could ever be compatible. Allies of convenience. But there is one thing I know. My world is one of the moon's. Yours is of the sun. The moon can stand in the sunlight, but the sun is afraid of the night and what it doesn't understand. That is why I can be in your world, even remain hidden, but you will never be in mine. We may not be able to coexist, but at least you cannot ever get rid of us."

"If you say so," he said.

"I do," she said, finishing the soup. "Markov really was a terrible cook." Nadia stood, placing the mess tin down. "You wouldn't happen to have a sheathed knife, would you?"

"Why?" he said.

"Well, I want to trade. This Nazi dagger has been useful, but it keeps trying to cut my belt, and after what I have just experienced, it is more trouble than it is worth. I want a more practical blade, one that has a sheath. A simple trading of blades. I get something that helps me, and you get a war trophy, and proof to your superiors that you hadn't just deserted but were in fact killing Nazis."

"This isn't some magical ruse, is it?" he asked.

"No, I just need a new blade. What is your name, sergeant, your full name?" asked Nadia.

"Some trick to steal my first born," he said.

"No. I just want a more practical blade. So do you have a blade that we can trade or not?" said Nadia, sitting on the floating rifle.

"I do, but it is just a bayonet. Thankfully our rifles are the same, so you should be able to affix it to your weapon," said Kolkov.

"That will work quite well I think," said Nadia, holding out the unsheathed Nazi dagger. Kolkov strained to pull out a leather-sheathed blade with a wooden handle and a ring to attach to a rifle. With some hesitance, they traded blades.

"My name is Constantin, like the old emperor. Sergeant Constantin Kolkov."

"Well, until we meet again, Sergeant Constantin Kolkov. My name is Nadia Voloshyn. Be sure to keep less mutinous men around you. Let's go,

Dasha." The cat yawned and hopped into Nadia's arms.

"Nadia, your bag is full of cans and grenades. I can't fit in it."

"Well, we are just going to have to adjust," said Nadia, kicking off the ground and flying above the tree line.

Part 2

12
Wondering

The mansion had been abandoned. More to the point, it had been condemned. It was a crumbling palace that overlooked the Black Sea. One of the last crumbling vestiges of the old Russian empire. It was a summer home to one of the many Dumas or possibly one of the tsar's properties. Nadia didn't know. But it was vacant, moldy, and long ago stripped of any valuables. Here and there were signs of violence: a large brown splotch baked into the foyer's wood, several bullet holes scarred otherwise pristine wooden walls and plaster. In one of the rooms on the ground floor was a room full of frames without paintings. Their art was taken long ago and redistributed among the Soviet elite.

The furniture had been stolen, leaving a grand empty shell overgrown with weeds and mold. Nadia had stopped only for a night but found herself drifting from one room to the next. She wondered how anyone could live so grand. Even the local party elite's lavish homes looked tiny compared to this grand palace by the sea. Nadia had decided to stay for a while. To give her weakened arm time to recover.

When she had finally settled, throwing her small bag on the lone mattress she had found in the servants' quarters, she slept for a full day. A dark sleep punctuated by nightmares and humming lullabies. She remembered sleeping a lot during the famine of her youth, sleeping through the days of hunger as the waking world held only mashed grass cakes. Nadia had thought that the mansion was a safe place to stay after the third day of being there. It was close enough to a forest so she could start supplying herself with herbs and mushrooms. When Nadia fled her doomed village, there wasn't time to collect essential herbs for her potions. Now she had a safe place to work. The tools were the hard part. She wished she had a mortar and pestle, but a large rock and a kitchen countertop would do. She started with a potion to strengthen her weak arm. She cooked the herbs in a can over a fire and drank the hot concoction.

A daily dose of bitter hot juice was not something she looked forward to, but in less than a week, her arm had regained its strength. Instantaneous magical healing was handy to have, but in many ways, it had too many drawbacks. Potions were much better at healing specific ailments at the cost of time. While the spell of mending may have been quick, she felt drained and exhausted for days after. She slept longer and was tired all the time. It did increase her appetite. However, it wasn't long before they were out of canned food, forcing Nadia to get food from the local forest, a task that took up much of the month. While gathering provisions, Nadia was practicing. She shot with her rifle, taking careful aim, and shooting at a painted bullseye on the garden shed. She learned how to clear a jammed bullet. How to load and maintain the weapon. How to take it apart and put it back together. She was pleased to find out that the magic didn't vanish from the weapon, as the individual parts would hang in the air. It even assembled itself when she ordered it to.

Nadia also learned that the magic in her rifle was affecting it in odd ways. It tended to charge if she didn't keep a firm hand on it while flying. It would idly move its bolt when not loaded. When it was time to practice her shooting, it would forcefully correct her aim. It wanted to shoot, and it would vibrate whenever she pulled out ammunition for a practice session.

Nadia had heard that flying instruments would develop quirks and personalities when infused with magic. Brooms with shafts of oak and mahogany tended to prefer flying in straight lines, while brooms of spruce and pine are more accustomed to sharp turns and more daring acrobatics. Rumor was that a willow broom would never allow its rider to fall. Likewise, the birch of the rifle had its own quirks. Birch was a plentiful wood, perfect for the mass-produced weapons of the Soviet Union and the Russian empire before it. It was a scrappy egalitarian wood that worked well with other forms of magic. She felt she had achieved the most basic forms of shooting and flying but being able to do both had eluded her.

It proved impossible to aim while riding the rifle. The reverse seemed to be more difficult, as to aim while flying required her to grip the gun tightly with her legs flying behind her. Dasha remained unimpressed by the various things Nadia did, preferring to sleep and hunt for mice or birds. When he wasn't hunting, he would pester Nadia to fish and fulfil her bargain. She tried her best to catch a fish, but she had no rod or net, and even if she did, she didn't know how to use either.

In the meantime, Nadia was working on trying to see the spirit plane. Olivia had taught her potions, had taught her to communicate with the dead, and quite a few protective spells. But she had neglected the basics of discovering how magic could be seen. Either that or she intentionally kept that gap in Nadia's education so her pupil would learn it for herself. Knowledge through privation was a cornerstone of Olivia's education.

Now Nadia fumbled and struggled to perceive the other magical world. She felt that there was a veil over her eyes, one that obscured the world that she knew was vibrant as only the lens of magic could be. Nadia had no way of seeing that world. So, she did what any witch would do: fell back on her intuition and asked the natural world.

She spoke to squirrels, who told her to buzz off. She spoke to trees, who said that all she had to do was be quiet and simply be. She asked the deer who said it was best not to be seen. A fox laughed at her and made fun of her. It was the wolf who provided the best information for her.

"Put yourself in mortal danger, then your life will become as clear as moving water," she said, taking a moment away from her pack while the rest watched Nadia from a distance.

"I've had enough of mortal danger. Is there a way of discovering magical sight without risking life and limb?" asked Nadia, scratching the head of a puffed-up, nervous Dasha.

"You are still young. The best things in life are dangerous. It is the pursuit of these dangerous things that give us meaning and definition."

"Says the wolf. If I follow your advice, I would always be getting in and out of trouble. I need some helpful advice."

"I'm a wolf; I have no other way of seeing it. If you want to see the world as a witch, then you best ask one. I can only teach the lessons of a wolf."

"I guess you're right. You wouldn't happen to know any other witches around here, would you?" asked Nadia.

"No, you are the only one this pack has seen in some time," said the wolf. "Now I must go. Our pack travels eastward, as we smell troubles from the west. It stinks of death." The wolf turned and left, rejoining her pack.

"Well, that was awful," said Dasha. "Did you see how they kept licking their chops while looking at me?

"I wouldn't have let them eat you," said Nadia. She sat on the rifle and took off. The rifle jerked forward, wanting to spring off into the sky, but Nadia's firm hand kept it from sprinting upward. Even so, it was always jarring when the gun took off.

"If you ask me, talking with all the critters of the forest is a waste of time and energy. We should find a city. I hear there are lots of cats in Turkish cities. Lots of cute cats looking to make kittens," said Dasha, purring at the thought.

"I don't speak Turkish," said Nadia,

"Details. You speak with all the animals of the forest just fine. It should be easy to pick up another human tongue."

"Says the cat who doesn't even know a single human word," said Nadia.

"Details. Now let's go home and make a fire. That main room it's getting to be one of my favorite places. Warm bricks, the crackle of a fire. Simply divine."

"You might be right. I wish I had a newspaper. The Nazis might be in Moscow by now. Even if I were to get one from a local village, they might think I'm a spy."

"I don't see why they would."

"No travel visa. Technically I'm illegally traveling the country. Right now, I don't want to deal with any more representatives of the state," said Nadia.

"Well, no fur off my tail. The mice here have gotten fat and lazy. I can eat as many as four before the afternoon, and I can spend the rest of the evening by the fire," said Dasha.

The pair flew over the forest and its autumnal colors. Tree shed their leaves with the coming cold, and the air stung her cheeks with its frosted gale. It felt like the temperature dropped with each day. Just a little bit each time with little respite, even on days with sunlight. Winter was approaching, and Nadia could already tell it would be a cold one. She could probably live out in this mansion for the winter, but there was no telling how safe it would be, especially with an invading enemy army that traveled so quickly.

She kept her supplies on her so she could flee at a moment's notice. However, surviving the winter and evading the Nazis didn't help her find the Coven of the Ever-Shining Moon. She wished she had a guide so she could finally find Grandmother's Forest. The wolf was right: to learn witch things, she needed a witch. She suspected she could find Anna the Red by following the army and asking around. That idea was quickly dismissed as she remembered the hands that strangled her neck. But the wolves had another idea: put yourself in harm's way, and everything will become clear. She had tried her best to see the spirit world through meditation like the trees had suggested, but it just left her cramped and sleepy. However, whenever she was in great danger, the woman in the burning corona always showed up to help her. Perhaps Nadia could trigger that so she could ask her how to get into the spirit realm. But how could she trigger it? The last time required a daemon or a man with his hands around her throat. Neither moment was ideal for communication.

She looked down and saw the ground speeding by, the trees becoming a blur of green and brown. If she were to fall, she would indeed be crippled.

She was in danger every time she flew. Perhaps there was a way of tapping into that danger to contact the other witch. When she saw the sea, she had resolved to at least give the idea an attempt. Flying over the crystal waters, she landed on the crumbling porch of the mansion.

"Oh, I can't wait to curl up after a long day of tromping through the mud and speaking with dangerous denizens of the forest," said Dasha.

"That's going to have to wait, I want to try something," said Nadia, putting her bag and bandoleer down.

"No! It's cold! I demand, as holder of your debt, that you get inside and make a fire!" yowled Dasha.

"If what I'm thinking of doing is going to happen, it won't take long and I will want to make a fire immediately," she said, taking off her jacket and skirt as well.

"Why, what are you planning on?" he said, his tail twitching, a sure sign that he felt whatever Nadia was doing was not something to be approved of by a cat.

"I'm going to fall into the sea," she said, suddenly shivering. It was early evening, and the temperature was dropping.

"Well, that's just stupid," said Dasha, his ears folding back.

"I know it is; it's going be freezing. An extremely dangerous thing to do," Nadia said, letting the rifle float in the air. "You can pull me out of the sea, can't you?" she asked her father's gun. The weapon spun before looping as if in a scooping motion. She suspected that meant yes.

"So, why are you doing this very stupid, very wet, very cold, dangerous thing? When we can be warm and safe by a fire?" Dasha said, his tail swishing back and forth.

"Well, every time I was in great danger, that witch showed herself to me. I figure giving the wolves advice a try by putting myself in danger so that she can reveal herself again. That way I can ask her how to find the spirit realm so I can find the Coven of the Ever-Shining Moon."

"What witch?"

"Oh, I guess her magic only showed itself to me," said Nadia. "She only showed up twice when I was in mortal danger."

"So, you're going to do that by swimming in the sea?"

"Falling into the sea. I don't know how to swim, but I figure it would be better than falling to the ground. This way if something goes wrong, I can at least drown instead of crashing into the hard earth," she said, taking off on the gun.

"How is that better?" yowled Dasha as she flew out to the sea.

"Well, with drowning I have a fighting chance," Nadia called back. The palace shrunk as she climbed higher in the sky. Nadia wanted to make sure that she was high enough to trigger whatever spell helped her contact the other witch, but not too high that she would hit the water and die on impact.

A light rain had been falling all day. Now it picked up in full force, pelting her with large, heavy drops. The sea below was rippling as the rain kicked up the surf. It wasn't too late. She could land, go inside, and start that fire that both she and Dasha wanted right this instant. She knew that the cat wouldn't begrudge her for backing out and would berate her for doing something that put her in so much danger. Nadia felt she had no other options.

"Get ready to pull me out of the water," she told the gun. She rubbed the barrel in reassurance and took a deep breath before throwing her leg. The cold bolt dug into the back of her leg. "Alright, on three. One, two, three."

She found that she was still sitting on the rifle. But when the actual moment came, she realized that the shivering she was feeling was not just from the cold but the absolute terror of falling and drowning in the cold dark waters below.

"Alright, let's try again, one, two…"

Before she could finish, the rifle yanked straight up, pointing skyward, causing Nadia to fall off. She desperately grabbed the rifle butt, holding on tight. "What are you doing!" she shouted, trying to pull herself up, using the strap. The gun began to shake, trying to loosen her grip. Her hand slipped from the rifle butt, the rain loosening her grip. She was dangling now from the rifle strap as the rifle began to spin and buck. Then the strap snapped off the butt, leaving her swinging violently. All that was between her and free-fall was the thin connection.

"I changed my mind! We can find out another way!" Nadia shouted in the pouring rain. The rifle's barrel shook as if to say no. The strap began to pull itself from the grip while the rifle stayed in place. She was down to the ragged end when she lost her grip.

She was in free fall. She hadn't realized she had been screaming. It was only with the fast-approaching waves below that her mind caught up with her. Like an unstoppable wall, she dropped toward the cold waves faster than she had expected.

"Alright, miss witch, you can show up now!" Nadia screamed as she looked around for any telltale signs of the burning halo that would allow her to communicate with that woman.

Any further investigations ceased with the sudden impact of the briny water below. Her whole body stung as she plunged into the freezing water. She flailed about beneath the surface, desperately looking for a purchase. The salt stung her eyes and nose. She was now regretting the entire plan as she struggled to get to the surface. Nadia kicked wildly while flailing her arms upward. Panic began to set in as Nadia felt her movements couldn't get to the surface. If anything, she was sinking deeper into the cold sea. She wanted to scream for help, but no help would hear. Her chest tightened up. Her mind flashed back to Markov and his powerful, crushing hands around her neck. All she wanted was to breathe, forget trying to contact whoever was in the halo. If only she could breathe. She remembered the breath the strange witch had filled her lungs with. A spell came into her mind. Magic flared, she felt her chest expand with fresh air, pushing all the old air out in a bubbling mass. The panic receded as she found that she could now breathe underwater. Relief replaced frustration. Yes, she was out of danger, but the danger was the whole point. She flailed upward through the freezing brine.

She broke the surface of the water, inhaling the nonmagical air. The waves attempted to submerge her once again. To pull her down in their cold depths.

"Rifle!" Nadia shouted as the freezing water squeezed the air out of her chest faster than she could breathe it in. "I'm here!" she shouted again. The surf stung her eyes, making her vision blurry. She could not distinguish the sky from the waves that kept pummeling her.

Another wave rolled over Nadia and pushed her below the surface. To her horror, the spell had vanished when she could breath, leaving her once again gulping water. She couldn't focus on casting the spell again. She was flailing in the cold surf. Unable to breathe, unable to think. She was drowning. Looking up, she could see the surface of the world above receding as the sea dragged her downward. She was going to die under these waves. Forgotten. Far from a home that no longer existed.

Then a hope broke the water's surface above like a spear piercing the belly of the vast sea. Her rifle cut through the waves and swam directly toward her. Nadia desperately grasped for the wooden stock and barrel, holding the weapon tightly. She once again erupted from the cold sea, her lungs filling with frigid air. With all her might, Nadia pulled herself up onto the rifle. Her entire body was shaking. She was sucking quick, uncontrolled breaths between hacking coughs. The back of her nose stung, and her eyes were watering.

"Inside," she said. The broom charged toward land as fast as it could, almost knocking Nadia off. She held on, having gotten a death grip on the rifle's barrel and her muscles tensing up. When she made it back to the mansion, she found Dasha at the front door.

"Well, are you happy now, can we go inside?" he said with a chirp. Nadia ignored him and threw the door open, her wet feet squelching onto the hardwood. She was too cold to think as she made her way to the parlor room. Nadia threw logs into the fireplace with broken painting frames for kindling. She then infused her breath with magic and blew on the wood. The wood smoked then caught fire. In minutes, a roaring fire was burning in the fireplace, radiating warmth onto the freezing Nadia and Dasha. The flickering of the fire cast Nadia's shadow about the room. She was still freezing, and her teeth chattered, but at least she was warming up. She was soon warm enough to retrieve her bag and coat from the porch, and with a quick spell she dried herself off. She retrieved a potion from her bag and swallowed it.

The potion was a warmth potion to keep her from freezing to death. It was one of the easier potions to brew. This simple elixir would keep her warm in the coming winter months. The potion spread through her body, thawing all her rigid, freezing limbs. The one drawback was that the potion made her unbearably thirsty. Not a bad trade-off after flying out of a freezing sea.

"So, was that little stunt of yours worth it?" asked Dasha as he spread

fish. Make a living doing that witchy stuff, away from the complications of a violent world. Then I could create litters of kittens all over town."

"First off, you are a lecher," said Nadia. "Second, I have no other home." Nadia hugged her knees, which were chilly to the touch. "There was a witch I met that was nice to me. She accepted me. It was the first time I met someone of the craft outside of my mentor. It made me realize that there was a community outside the suspicious peasants. Or a family that only partially understands the things I did. My mother always wished I would put my witch training aside. To her, it seemed childish, or possibly dangerous.

"She wanted me to become a part of her world and live her life. At the the whims of a brutish state that is both impersonal and overbearing as it seeks to control my thoughts. Now that world has destroyed the family that wanted me to be a part of it. It feels like it just happened yesterday." Nadia did her best to hold back tears. Her grief came in cycles that exploded in quiet moments. Dasha always climbed into her lap whenever this happened, having nothing to say but at least offering a reassuring paw or a fuzzy neck to cry into.

"And Peter! I don't know where he is! I don't know if he is eating, or if he is cold, or if he is even alive. I don't know the spells that would allow me to find him, to learn if he is alright. Even if I did, even if I could find him, how would I protect him? But the coven must know things that will help. If I fled out east and hid, I don't know if I would ever find Peter again. I don't know if I would advance any further as a witch. I would muddle about until I'm killed by some jack-booted fascist thug like Olivia, who was supposed to be some powerful battle witch. But she was cut up like a stupid pig! I can't just wait for death. To hide away and keep my head down. Just wishing people will leave me alone. I have been trying to keep my head down my entire life.

I've been met with only scorn and hate. Where has that gotten me? So, I will learn all I need so that no one tries to make me a victim ever again. If that means diving into somewhere dangerous for the chance of meeting someone who can help me, then so be it," said Nadia, wiping away the tears that ran down her cheek and the snot that came out of her nose. She saw Dasha, his ears back. He looked unsure and perplexed.

"You don't have to follow me if you don't want to. I'm going somewhere dangerous, and I don't know if it's even worth it. But I don't have time to meditate like a tree and discover the secret truths of the universe. There is a pack of murderers hunting my sisters and me. I wouldn't begrudge you if you decided to leave," said Nadia. Dasha's ears pricked up when she started scratching his neck. With a rapid pounce, he grabbed Nadia's hand and bit it. "Ow!"

"'Oh Dasha, the road I travel is so hard and dangerous,'" said the cat mockingly. "'Filled with such interesting and dangerous mysteries that only a witch would understand or appreciate. You can just stay some place safe and boring, and don't worry about that debt I owe you, Dasha. It's just a fish after all, certainly not worth going someplace that could get you killed.' Don't try to trick me, miss witch; I got you figured out. But as long as you have that outstanding debt, I'm not going anywhere. Certainly not because of a little danger. I most certainly wouldn't give up the chance to see something a cat has never seen. Why are you trying to cheat me out of a chance to brag about being a witch's companion? You know what kind of credentials that means in the cat community?"

"No, I don't," said Nadia rubbing the bite.

"Of course not! But doing a stint with a witch gives you one hell of a reputation! It makes you seem mysterious to a species that prides itself on being mysterious. You think I would follow anyone around just for a meal?"

"Yes, I would. I have seen you follow Babushka Olga for meat scraps," said Nadia, once again petting the cat but very wary of his claws and bite.

"Yes, but I wouldn't keep following them."

"I thought your mother said don't associate with witches and that it's best not to put yourself in harm's way."

"Well, cats are a contrarian bunch, and rebellious to boot. If someone says you can't do it, then that is enough of a reason to do it. So, don't you worry, I'm not going anywhere. I will be by your side to give you sage advice and eat any spare delicacies."

Nadia hugged the cat, who squirmed in her arms. "Hey, stop that, it's weird!" he meowed. Nadia tightened the hug before releasing him.

"I'm so glad to hear that, Dasha. We will head out first thing in the morning. It's a full moon tomorrow, so any witch magic that happens will be decisive."

13
Crucible

The next day, the pair left the crumbling mansion by the Black Sea. It wasn't long before they found a road full of fleeing refugees. The winding road had been turned to mud, and numerous carts had been simply abandoned and stripped bare. The line of disheveled people looked like a brown crocodile undulating as it traveled. Nadia examined the line, wary of any Red Army soldiers that may be in the civilians' midst. She wanted to ask someone in that line where the fighting was. While she may have gotten a good response from a soldier, they were a variable she didn't want to deal with, on top of a suspicious mob of people who have lost everything.

"Is this a good idea, Dasha?" asked Nadia, gripping the wood stalk of the rifle as she looked down on the line of refugees.

"Probably not, but you can just fly away if things look ugly," yawned the cat from the small travel bag.

"Well, wish me luck," she said, descending down upon the mass of humanity. The people hadn't notice Nadia, their eyes squarely forward or on the muck that sucked at their feet. "Excuse me?" she said. Several people looked around confused, while others kept trudging. "Up here," she said. Several people looked up and fell back in astonishment. Like a ripple in a pond, the people looked up and saw the flying witch.

"Oh Lord have mercy, the army has sent a witch to punish us for fleeing our homes," wailed a woman, clutching a baby close to her chest. Nadia had forgotten that she was in a Red Army jacket. This caused an additional ripple that had many people backing up from her while slowing down the entire line.

"Please have mercy on us, miss witch, the fascists have taken everything from us," said an old man, who collapsed in the mud. "We are not soldiers or partisans. Just simple people who want nothing to do with the violence."

"Have mercy!" cried another. Soon a cacophony of wailing assailed her. She had never seen this kind of reaction before. She had seen suspicion and mistrust and outright hostility and rage from the peasant and small folk. Never had she invoked such terror and pleading desperation. But then again, she had never worn a stolen Red Army jacket. Even if she wasn't a card-caring Communist Party member, the stolen uniform invoked more terror in these people than any spell she might have cast. It was perplexing for Nadia, to say the least.

"Everyone please, I'm not here to punish you. I just want to ask for some directions," Nadia shouted. Nobody heard her as she shouted at the mass of humanity below.

"It appears they can't hear you," said Dasha, his nose wiggling as he sniffed the air.

"Either that or they aren't listening," sighed Nadia. Nadia curled her free hand into one of the few arcane gestures she knew and placed it in front of her throat. "Silence!" she shouted. Her voice was amplified by the spell made with her hand. "I'm not here to punish you. I simply want to know the direction to the front or the nearest battlefield." The mob went silent, broken by shifting bodies and the soft drizzle of rain.

"Miss witch, my name is Ivan Kovalenko," said an old man stepping out from the crowd. His back hunched forward as he leaned on a cane that sank into the mud, leaving him in a peculiar stance.

"The whole land is a battlefield. Every field and stream behind us are filled with hundreds of the dead and dying. The cities are of no protection as the fascists drop their bombs with no regard for the people. The villages are even worse. Entire towns are murdered for any act of rebellion. From the west comes a murderous tide of rabid animals who bite and kill for their own pleasure, while from the east we have a cold machine that will have you executed for not trying to fight the animals that seek to rip out your throat. If you are looking for a battlefield, you don't have to worry. You are on one," said Ivan.

Nadia lowered down to the earth and hopped off the rifle in front of the man who spoke. The entire crowd stepped back, leaving Nadia at the center. It was only when she was up close that she realized that the old man was injured. More to the point, she could smell the injury on him. It had gone putrid.

"You're injured," said Nadia. The man grimaced and nodded. "Let me see it." The man was suspicious yet complied. He took off his jacket, revealing a poorly bandaged arm. It was wrapped tightly around an injury on his arm and neck. The wound had been festering, and the bandages were dark yellow and brown from dried blood.

"How did you get these injuries?" asked Nadia, pulling out packets of herbs from her bag.

"I was one of the people to be executed in retaliation for partisan activity in the next village over. A sniper shot a Nazi sergeant and in response they lined up everyone over the age of ten and had them shot. The children they rounded up in put in the local schoolhouse before burning it to the ground." Tears began to well up in the man's eyes, falling down his wrinkled cheeks. By now, a number of the crowd had moved on, realizing that the witch was no danger to them. The people kept moving like a river bypassing a pair of rocks.

"May I?" Nadia asked, gesturing to take off the bandages. Ivan nodded. "That's horrible."

"It was," he said, hissing as she peeled the bandages that stuck to the injury with crusted fluids. The smell of putrid flesh was followed by pus and infected fluids around the arm and neck.

"As I said, I was lined up with the rest of the village along a ditch. They set up a machine gun and when their commander gave the order, they fired. The bullet hit my shoulder and I collapsed in the ditch, on top of several people who had been executed already. I lay there among people I have known all my life. I was face first in the back of the grocer; oh God, he smelled of garlic. He already had a thick layer of white powder on him that stung my eyes and nose. I did everything I could to pretend I was dead. I was scared to death that they would see the powder blown away by my breath. I was on the second to last wave of the executed. The body of a friend I knew for over forty years fell on top of me." The man hissed as Nadia placed crushed herbs into the twin injuries, herbs that would fight infection and halt any bleeding, as they had been infused with magic. With a few other spells, the bandages were cleaned of any blood or infected body fluids.

"When they were done with us, the fascists walked the ditch with machine guns, firing into the mass of dead flesh. I can still hear it now, the short bursts of fire, moving closer to my position. I know for a fact if I was a younger man, the fear would have me climbing the edges to run away. It is only my age that kept me alive. That didn't help me from the second shot that grazed my neck." Nadia was reapplying the bandages again, free from infection and filth. "I can only imagine the horrors you have seen following the army. Young women shouldn't be fighting even if they are witches," he said as Nadia pulled out another packet of herbs. "Why are you away from the army?"

"Well, they left me behind," she said.

"Like so many of us. Our army is crumbling in the wake of a terrible foe. I fear for the future. The future was never bright but at least it was our own. Now a foreign people are killing us," he said. He looked into her eyes. They were so old and full of tears. "Is there anything you can do, miss witch? Any spell that can turn back time or turn the fascists into paper dolls?"

"I'm afraid...I...I'm trying. I know of no grand spell that will wish away our problems. But I might be able to help if I can get to the front."

"Then you will want the area around Sevastopol. It is the only city that hasn't been taken by the fascists in the Peninsula. It's many days travel by foot or horse, but I would imagine that flying would be much faster," he said, pointing west. "Follow the coast, and you will eventually make it to the battle. That is the closest front I know of."

"Thank you, Ivan," she said, handing him his coat. "Keep those bandages clean. In about two days put these herbs in your injuries again. The wounds should close up in about a week."

"A week? Impossible."

"Not when magic is involved," said Nadia, sitting down on her rifle.

"God protect you, young witch, for doing this kindness to a lost man."

Nadia nodded and was about to take off when a woman ran up to her with a baby.

"Miss witch, I saw you help that man. I was wondering if you could help me," said the woman.

"What's wrong?" asked Nadia.

"I can no longer produce milk, and my baby is so hungry. I was wondering if you have something in that bag of yours that can help a worried mother." Nadia sighed and began rummaging in her bag. She pulled out more packets of herbs.

"Mix one of these with water and give half to yourself and half to the baby. They will give you nutrients for a week. You should be producing milk by the evening."

"Oh, bless you, miss witch," said the woman retreating to the crowd. Soon more people were stepping forward. The shouting began, and the crowd began to jostle, each screaming for help in a hundred different ways. Some asked to carry the last of their valuables or bring a dead loved one back to life. Some asked for droughts to help them fight the Nazis.

"You can't help them all," said Dasha.

"But I must do something," whispered Nadia as she backed up.

"Will you help each and every one of these hundreds and hundreds of people? Is your bag that full of medicine and herbs?"

"No, it is not," said Nadia, biting her lip.

"Then I think you know what we need to do," said Dasha.

"I think I do," she said. The crowd was closing in on her where once out his entire body next to the fire. His belly faced the flame as he curled his paws by his face.

"No. It was terrifying, but I don't think I was in any real danger. The rifle was there to pull me out, and I was able to create a spell for breathing under the water. It may need work because it popped like a soap bubble when I was able to get real air in my lungs."

"It was still a stupid thing to do, even if you learned a very flimsy spell," he said, stretching his claws out.

"No, the problem was the type of danger I was in. Jus falling into the sea won't do it. The other witch only ever showed up in situation where I had no control. I need to be somewhere dangerous where I can't just cast a spell and change the outcome," said Nadia, scratching Dasha's belly. The cat purred from the attention. As Nadia's fingers danced over the soft fur of Dasha's stomach, the cat suddenly curled out and pounced on Nadia's hand, biting the thumb and lightly digging his claws into her hand.

"Gotcha!" he chirped. "You humans never learn. You always fall for the soft fuzziness of a cat's belly."

"It's too great a temptation," said Nadia, disentangling her hand from the sharp points of the cat.

"Once you learn not to touch things you know are dangerous, then you will be as wise as a cat," he said as he began licking his leg.

"I'm afraid that is my only option. If I want to meet that coven, I need to go somewhere that is overwhelmingly dangerous. Maybe a battlefield. I doubt my spells could alter that," said Nadia.

"Why?" asked Dasha, taking a moment from his leg. "Why are you so intent on meeting up with this coven? What are they to you? Why not just fly out east, find some cozy village where nobody knows you? You can buy me a they feared her. Then they began to climb over themselves to get any miracles she might have. Pointing the rifle skyward, she held on tight before rocketing high above the mass of people. From there, it was easy to get into a sitting position to fly straight. She wanted desperately to look back, but she knew that wasn't the best idea.

"There was nothing you could do for all those people," said Dasha, after some time of silence.

"I know that, but it still doesn't make it any easier. Olivia always said to help people whenever we could. She also said that hiding away from the greedy and hateful people was acceptable. Really what I think she was saying was that a witch must be prepared to make hard decisions," said Nadia, taking a deep breath of the frigid sea air. She could still remember the clawing brine that tried to drag her under the night before. Yet from high above, it was serene. Like a photograph, an image only dangerous up close.

"Sounds complicated," said Dasha, his whiskers wiggling with the breeze.

"Only to a cat, and I guess to a young witch," she said, flying around the steep cliffs of the coast. Down below were jagged rocks that abruptly turned into sand and salty surf. Travel may have been easy. But at top speed, it became exhausting to fly far on the uncomfortable rifle. Nadia had found out it was better to fly slowly. Even so, she wasn't hindered by the terrain and could look over the coast. Occasionally, she would ask for directions from random people, making sure to stay away from any soldiers. She was always met with suspicion, but she found that if she helped out whoever was speaking with, they were willing to direct her to the besieged city.

It was just at the edge of twilight when she discovered a battle in progress. Off in the distance, she could hear the roar of cannonade and the chatter of machine guns. The sky had become a pale grey with pouring rain. Dasha may have been tucked in the travel bag, but Nadia had to fly through the pouring wall of rain, which made her fingers numb as they gripped the shaft of the rifle. The rain kept blinding her, and the wind sought to throw her about. So, it was by accident when she wandered into the battlefield. Down below, she could see two prongs of tanks moving toward a defensive line. Behind them followed squads of infantry that crouched in the wake of several tanks.

"Dasha, wake up. I found the battle!" shouted Nadia over the rain and the roaring of the tank engines. The cat stuck his head out of the bag, looking down at the mass of men and machines.

"I don't think you should go into the middle of this one."

"It might be the best one we will find," said Nadia. Even so, she was having second thoughts. In front of the German armored attack from the woods came an entire mob of saber-wielding horsemen. They charged the tanks head-on, swinging the swords above their heads.

"Oh God, it will be a massacre. I don't think I can watch," said Nadia trying to look away. The rifle in her hands was vibrating as if it sensed the combat down below. A loud roar from the Soviet side erupted as hundreds of men poured out of the forest, charging in a solid wave of men, firing as they ran. The tanks opened fire, and several horses and men were thrown up in the air in a fiery blossom. The horses screamed as missing legs were scattered on the survivors. The Nazi line had erupted in a blaze of gunfire. She had never realized how loud a battle was up close. How much it stank of burned gunpowder. It must be disorientating on the ground. The rifle bolt opened up on its own, like an open mouth waiting to be fed. It wanted the ammunition, but Nadia wasn't even sure she wanted to go down into that meat grinder, let alone fight.

Men were being cut down in waves. The cavalry was an even worse sight. The horses just proved easy targets for the enemy gunners who fired with quick bursts before switching to a long spray of shooting that sounded like a buzz saw.

"Yeah, let's get out of here. Maybe we can find a nice, calm no man's land where they are shooting at each other from really far away," said Dasha.

"I think you're right," said Nadia, watching another group of horses and men explode and gory chunks. The world below was a rainy, muddy mess, with craters that smoked and boiled like cauldrons. Nadia wanted nothing to do with that hell down below. But the rifle had a different idea. Instead of turning away, it dropped in altitude and charged the German tank on the left.

"What are you doing? Don't charge that monster!" hissed Dasha as they charged toward the steel behemoth.

"I'm not! It's the rifle!" shouted Nadia. They dove closer to the rolling tank.

"Pull up, pull up!"

Nadia did her best to change directions, but the weapon was dead set on diving into the center of the carnage below. The tank was slow and plodding, but it felt like it was flying at Nadia as she braced for impact. At the last second, the rifle pulled up, hovering right above the tank. Nadia kicked the tank in an attempt to fly skyward. But the weapon didn't listen. The rifle flew out of her grasp and opened up its bolt. Bullets whizzed by and ricocheted off the armored hull of the tank as several horsemen ran past her, howling as they charged or getting cut down by the whizzing of bullets. Nadia felt like a target on top of the tank, while the tank kept rolling forward.

"Get us out of here!" shouted Dasha as he was jostled in his bag.

"I would if I could!" shouted Nadia. She held tight to the barrel of the cannon. The weapon swiveled, almost throwing her off. She could hear the sound of angry Germans inside the tank. She realized she was blocking the weapon sights. A hatch on the front opened up, and a man in a black uniform emerged. He was young and blond, and there was hate in his eyes as he aimed a pistol at her.

"Break!" She shouted the spell with a reflexive force. The entire tank lurched to a stop and began smoking while the pistol in the man's hand exploded. He swore angrily, gripping his bloody hand with dangling fingers.

"Feuer! Feuer!" said a voice inside the tank. "Wir werden explodieren!" The soldier suddenly had a panicked look on his face as he pulled himself out of the hatch.

"Nadia, this thing's burning!" said Dasha. Nadia kicked the tanker before jumping off the armored vehicle. She wanted to be far away from it as she could. She ran past several soldiers running toward the tanks.

"No, it's going to explode!" she shouted. Several soldiers halted and crouched down to stay out of the line of fire. The black-clad soldiers crawled out of the smoking tank only to be gunned down by Soviet soldiers who kept shooting the bodies, even the burning ones, as if to make sure that they were dead. Then the tank exploded. Nadia's world shook, her ears were ringing, and her nose was assaulted with the smell of burning fuel.

"Good job, sister." One of the soldiers patted her back. "But the battle isn't won yet; there is still another tank. Forward, comrades, for the Motherland! For Stalin! For the people!" A bullet whizzed by and caught him in the chest. He fell to the ground, blood oozing out of his mouth. His tan jacket had a wet red stain that grew with each moment.

"Oh God!" she whispered, crawling up to him, making sure to stay low.

Men were screaming and dying everywhere. She put both hands on the man's chest and focused her mind.

"This tapestry is torn! Reknit." The man screamed as the magic took hold and began to mend his wound.

"I know it hurts but you will live!" she said. The enchanted rifle dropped down and opened its bolt again, waiting for ammunition. "When this is over, we are going to have a talk!" she shouted at the rifle. She pulled out a clip of five rounds and jammed it into the gun. The rifle bolted forward, jumping into her arms. Men were running past her ignoring the witch and the injured soldier. Nadia pulled out a bird feather from her bag, something she found in a nest while staying in the mansion.

"Light as a feather!" The magic moved over the man as the feather burned up into ashes. She grabbed the man by the collar and lifted him with ease, the spell making him light. She was acting on instinct now as she ran toward the burning tank throwing the man down. Several other men were using the tank as cover.

"My God, sister, are you just muscles under that jacket?" joked one of the soldiers as he took aim.

"She would have to be, carrying that ox!" laughed another.

"How can you be laughing?" said Nadia.

"We are already dead, that's why," said the first man.

"Ugh, I have been shot," muttered the man she had carried to safety. "I must be dying I can't feel the injury anymore."

"Where were you hit?"

"In the chest, I fear I'm going to die," moaned the man and clung to the bloody spot on his jacket. "For a moment I was in such unbearable pain. Now I know I will just fade away."

"You will be fine, I fixed the wound," said Nadia, looking up, hoping the burning halo was above her, only to find the pouring rain.

"Bullshit, I was shot!" said the man as he pulled open his jacket, revealing his blood-covered chest with a jagged bullet scar, and a crushed lead bullet resting on his chest.

"See, you're fine. Why won't she show up?" said Nadia.

"Can we leave now!" meowed Dasha.

"Is that a cat?" asked one of the soldiers.

"Yes, it is. Okay, Dasha, I'm going to attack that tank. I'm going to leave you here because it might get rough."

"You are sounding crazier by the minute," said Dasha. "And of course, I will stay right here, right under the burning tank, in the rain, in the middle of a stinking battle."

"My God, it is a cat! Sister, you are one crazy woman!" laughed the soldiers. They couldn't help themselves.

"Make sure no harm comes to that cat, I'm going to take care of that tank," she said, gripping the rifle tightly. The turret of the other tank fired, its cannon deafening Nadia, while its machine gun mowed down men left and right as it advanced.

"Now hold on, girl! Don't do anything too crazy. You're brave enough. No need to prove anything," said one of the soldiers. Nadia couldn't see the halo of light that showed her that strange other witch.

"I think I have to," she said, watching the tank. She had come this far, and she was stuck in it. A part of her wanted to keep hurting these invaders.

"Don't! You'll die, Nadia!" meowed Dasha.

"I won't," she said, kicking off the ground and flying high in the air. The men screamed in shock as she took to the sky. With the rain pelting her face, she soared like a javelin thrown high in the air. She dropped down on the tank's turret.

"Break!" she shouted. She felt the magic go into the tank, yet it kept rolling forward. "Break!" she said frantically, yet the tank kept rolling. Nadia realized she had used too much magic on the first tank and mending the soldier, like a popped bottle of wine gone flat. She didn't think she could do any bigger spells, only little ones. Bullets whizzed over her head, and she realized how exposed she was, so she jumped off the top to land on the chassis. The rain made the metal slick, and Nadia lost her balance, falling directly on the hard metal.

"Sister!" She looked up to see a Red Army soldier waving at her.

"Catch!" He then threw a bundle at her; it looked like several grenades tied together with wire. "Hit the back of the tank, where they are weak!"

"I have a better idea," she shouted. A moment later, the main gun fired, the blast leaving her world a ringing mess. She couldn't hear anything except the breathing in her throat and in her skull. She couldn't focus on anything except the rumbling tank. Grasping around, she found the hatch.

"Open," she said, unable to hear her own words but still feeling the vibrations in her throat. She felt a mental backlash as she forced the magic into the simple spell. Her nose started bleeding, but the hatch opened up. A moment later, she threw the primed bundle of grenades inside the tank. She jumped off the tank, landing in wet grass. A rumbling wave of heat washed over her. All Nadia could do was lay there. Her head pounding from the overuse of magic. The ringing from the explosion slowly vanished, replaced with the cheering of Soviet troops. Above her, a burning halo began to appear.

"Nadia Voloshyn, why do I always find you in such danger?" said the calm witch. The smell of wildflowers cut through the caustic smell of singed flesh and smoky gunpowder.

"This time it's my doing," said Nadia, turning over to look up at the halo of fire and the woman within. "I need to learn how to see the spirit world so I can follow the ley lines and find Grandmother's Forest."

The woman looked surprised. "So, you are a prospect. You wish to join the Coven of the Ever-Shining Moon."

"Sister, are you hurt? Good God your nose is bleeding," said a soldier, running up to her, his head obscuring the witch above her. Nadia pushed him away as his hands sought to find other injuries on her body.

"I'm fine! Sister, please how do I find Grandmother's Forest!" she said.

"What are you talking about?" asked the soldier, his stern face confused.

"This night is a full moon," said the woman. "You will have all the answers you need. Consider this your first test. If you have ears to listen, then you will have answers to hear; seek her out, then quiet yourself. Her light will guide your way."

The halo collapsed, and the smell of flowers was replaced by the caustic stench of battle. The sound of bullets and gunfire and the screams of hundreds of men clashing replaced the serene quiet of the witch's conversation.

"Sister! Get up! We can't stay here," said the soldier. Men ran past or collapsed from the constant machine gun fire. Yet the man felt so far away, like the entire scene around Nadia was not really happening, or it was happening to someone else. That she was just an observer looking into a terrible scene of carnage. "We have to leave!" The man grabbed her by the arm and pulled her to her feet.

"We are on the final push, and we will have them on the run," he shouted, taking aim, and firing with his rifle. Nadia could hear an officer's whistle from a distance, and another wave of soldiers came pouring out of the woods behind her. Dozens were shot down at once as the machine guns of the Germans simply shifted their aim to the large clump of amassing bodies.

"Shoot, sister, shoot!" he shouted. Nadia brought the rifle to her shoulder and took careful aim at one of the many grey blurs in the distance. The enemy looked like grey smudges with the rain, with only the starlight of gunfire to give away their positions. She aimed down at the grey blurs. She was about to take a shot when the rifle jerked to the left. She refocused her shot, and again, the rifle jerked to the left.

"It doesn't matter if you hit anything, just fill the air with lead!" shouted the soldier. She squeezed the trigger, sure that she didn't hit anything. The rifle bolt cocked on its own, ejecting the spent casing before slamming home. She aimed again. The rifle jumped right. She squeezed the trigger, and the rifle kicked into her shoulder. Again, the bolt reloaded. She remembered how the rifle would forcibly correct her aim when she was shooting at cans. Whenever she would relax and let the gun handle the shooting, the can was hit every time.

"Affix bayonets!" she heard an officer shout.

"Damn that blockhead. We are on a suicide run, sister. Good luck to you, may you kill many fascists before you die," said the man, pulling a long blade out and fixing it to the end of his rifle.

"I don't plan on dying, comrade," she screamed back, pulling her own bayonet out and sticking it on the end of the rifle. The gun vibrated as if it enjoyed the fact that it was transformed into a spear.

"I love your optimism, but we are already dead. This war is lost, and our leaders just haven't realized it." Then the man let out a loud "OOOraaa!"

This cry merged with hundreds of others that cut through the sound of gunfire and grenade blasts. If there was a time to escape, this would have been it, she thought. All she had to do was kick off the ground and fly away from this mess. But Dasha was still under that tank. Looking around, she saw that any man who was not charging headlong into German guns was targeted by teams of machine guns from the Soviet side. She doubted she would make it if she charged toward Dasha's hiding place. The momentum was spurring her forward.

"Alright," she said, then gripped the rifle and kicked off the ground. Once again, she was high above the battle with a clear view of things. She scanned the enemy line and found a concentration of fire. *It must be where the machine guns are,* she thought.

She took a deep breath and aimed for that point of flickering light in the grey rain. She burst forward, her rifle flying at top speed. Her bayonet focused right on a target down below. A pair of Nazi soldiers were taking careful aim, the helmets covering their eyes like steel bunkers. While several riflemen flanked and supported the gun, hitting any stragglers, the machine gun missed. It was a precise, merciless formation. But it couldn't account for an opponent in the air. Nadia pulled a grenade from her bag right before the bayonet speared the gunner in the shoulder. The man's partner fell back as he realized the enemy in his midst. In a moment, she pulled the pin and dropped the grenade before once again jumping into the air. Below a loud thump rumbled. Nadia didn't look back as she flew down the line above the German's heads.

Every time she saw a machine-gun nest, she pulled out one of her grenades and dropped it on them. Right as she was about to drop her fourth grenade, something hit her. It felt like a sledgehammer in her leg. She had been shot, and she was knocked off the rifle and was sent into a free fall. She tumbled end over end. She flew toward the ground much too fast. It was going to hurt worse than hitting the water, worse than her impact after the Kindersnatch pulled her off the broom. This time the fall would break her. The spell formed like lightning in her mind. A way of turning the force of her fall into the force that would catch her. She took a deep breath until her lungs were full to bursting. Right before the fall, she exhaled everything in her lungs.

She hit a cushion of air that bounced her up for a moment before dropping her in the mud. A sudden backlash of magic hit her skull again like a punch to the face. It hurt worse every time she cast a spell now. Despite the pain, she pulled herself up, but when she put weight on her right leg, it collapsed under her. It felt like a dull ache that flared into tearing pain as if a tiny razor dug into her leg. As she struggled to her feet, she could see several men in grey running toward her. The soaking, grey-clad Nazi soldiers moved in like a pack of wolves. Four of them were close, but many more followed.

"Hexe!" they shouted, pointing their rifles at her chest. "Hande hoch!" they shouted repeatedly. They weren't shooting at her, she thought clinically. She couldn't reach for her pistol. Not with so many eyes on her. "Hande hoch!"

Nadia made sure her hands were visibly up. She may not have known what they were saying, but she knew that men with guns always made sure that you didn't have any yourself. Her window of escape was closing rapidly. One of the men stepped forward. He grabbed her by the collar, pulling her upright to his face. His eyes were angry.

"You are going to suffer, you beast!" said the man in Russian. That was when the rifle fell bayonet first through the man's helmet. Those angry eyes rolled back in his head as his grip vanished. This was her chance.

"Break!" she shouted, pointing at two of the men, before the mental backlash knocked her off her feet. Her eyes felt they were about to burst, while her chest felt like it was collapsing. The rifle unlinked from the bayonet from the man's head and shot the third. The remaining two soldiers aimed and pulled their triggers. When the weapons wouldn't fire, they threw them aside, going for their knives at their waists. The guns of the German soldiers detonated, blowing the weapons in half, startling one of the men while the floating rifle shot the other. Nadia struggled for her pistol, but the last Nazi jumped on her. The man overpowered her, pushing her down in the grass and mud. She used her arm to keep the hand with the knife from stabbing down on her.

"Shoot him!" she shouted. She could see the rifle opening its bolt to show it had no ammunition. The man on top of her put his weight on the blade and drove down. The knife punched through her padded jacket and into the soft flesh of her collar bone. The blade slipped off the bone and cut into her shoulder. Nadia could only think of putting the pistol to his belly and pulling the trigger. But the weight of the man didn't allow her to grab the weapon. That's when the rifle looped its strap around the soldier's neck before spinning into a noose. With a sudden jerk, the weight was off Nadia, giving her a second to retrieve her pistol. She aimed the gun at his chest, only to find that the gun didn't fire. The soldier then pulled the knife up, cutting the strap with his knife.

Nadia fumbled with the side of the pistol and found the safety. Before the man was able to bring his knife down, Nadia was spraying bullets in his guts and chest, blooms of red erupting from his back. She kept firing until the pistol was empty. The man collapsed on her. She lay on the ground for several moments, as the pounding in her head became a dull roar while her other injuries howled.

Eventually, she pushed with all her might, but the body wouldn't move off her. What was worse was that she could see many more Nazis running toward her. She heaved the body once again but to no effect. Now she would undoubtedly be killed or taken prisoner. She closed her eyes, hearing men run toward her with sporadic gunfire all around. The boots splashing closed in.

She opened her eyes, seeing the pouring rain hitting her face so heavy it almost blinded her. Yet, looking around, she saw that the Nazis weren't even slowing. They ran past her by the dozens. Some stopped only to shoot back. She sat up the best she could and saw a wave of brown-clad Red Army soldiers pouring over the Nazi defenses. When the Nazis were gone, she called out to the closest soldiers.

"I'm here," she cried out. Several Red Army soldiers stopped and pulled the body off her.

"Bloody hell, sister, how did you get back here?" one of them asked.

"Just lucky, I guess," Nadia replied, sitting up and wincing. Her rifle dropped down in her lap.

"Wait a moment. She is the one who took out those tanks, I saw her with my own eyes. She flew around on that rifle of hers," said one of the men that she met behind the tank.

"I saw her as well. She went across the line and destroyed every single machine gun she found. She must be a witch," said another as more men clustered around her. *Oh no,* thought Nadia. This was undoubtedly how she died.

"You're a hero, sister, a true hero!" said one of the soldiers, patting her on the back.

"The witch who saved us this night!" roared another. "The Night Witch!" he shouted. The men cheered as they lifted her up. Beyond her control, she was hoisted high into the air as the men whooped and cheered. As the crowd grew, a chant started rising above the men's cheering. "Night Witch, Night Witch, Night Witch!" cried the crowd. It was in this jubilation and astonishment that Nadia passed out from blood loss.

14
Tyranny's Accomplice

She awoke with a start. Her shoulder and leg throbbed with pain. Dasha was resting on her chest with an open can of meat beside them. Looking around, she found that it was night, and she was inside a tent. She could hear the rumble of artillery and the occasional crack of rifle fire and the sawing noise of machine guns. However, the sound of groaning, howls, and screams of pain were all around her.

"Dasha, you need to get off," said Nadia. Dasha looked up at Nadia, his eyes shining in the flickering of the light from some source outside the tent.

"I hope you're happy. You got your battlefield and left me in the center of it so you could play hero. Under a burning tank no less," said Dasha, stretching his claws out. Nadia realized that her padded jacket wasn't on, leaving her in the clothes she had when she fled the village.

"I guess so. I got in contact with that other witch. Right after I blew up the second tank." With her good arm, Nadia sat up, causing Dasha to move to her lap. A bandage had been wrapped around her shoulder. Her leg also was wrapped up. Clean bandages she knew could do much for an injury. Whoever mended her was not a soldier. Yet conventional medicine was far too slow for her. She needed to get moving. She found her bags and all her armaments resting right beside her with a clean jacket, trousers, and boots.

"Did it ever occur to you to come to find me afterward, so we could be on our way? Now we are in the middle of a camp filled with smelly humans. Do you know how alarming it is to be yanked out of safety by your tail and carried off by the scruff of your neck? I thought I was being kidnapped! Destined for the soup pot!" meowed Dasha. "It was terrible. The only thing worse was finding you unconscious, bleeding like a clawed-up mouse. Thankfully, those human doctors seemed to know what they were doing."

Nadia pulled out several wrappers of medicine. She swallowed one, coughing as the bitter herbs and powdered mushrooms caught in her throat. The other she poured in a nearby canteen and drank the whole mixture in one go. One was to speed healing. The other would allow her to move around without pain. After several minutes, the pain faded, becoming a background hum in her mind.

"Well, it worked out. I'm sorry I wasn't able to get to you I was swept up in the momentum of the battle," said Nadia, pulling on her jacket. She was happy to find it was clean and didn't have the pervasive stink of the man who wore it before her.

"I don't think that was it," said Dasha, moving right up into Nadia's face. "When they brought me to you, you stank of anger and rage and killing intent."

"What? That's preposterous, you can't smell emotions," said Nadia.

"You humans gave up a lot for your sharp eyes and gripping hands. Like a good sense of smell. My point is that I can tell what mood someone's in with a good sniff. When someone is happy, when someone is sad. Each has its own blends and aromas, and anger and rage are red hot. But the killing intent. That is a smell all its own. You can't mistake it. Every creature has it. You reeked of it." Nadia had looked away from her small companion. It was hard to deny what she really felt when he could smell it on her skin.

"I guess I got swept up in more than just the momentum of the battle. I just wanted to hurt those men, for all the terrible things they have done." She then began scratching Dasha's head. Her hands petting over his course fur. "Is that so wrong?"

"I don't know, I'm a cat. You would have to ask a human."

"Miss witch," said a woman's voice from outside the tent. "Are you awake?" She sounded nervous. Nadia was just thankful she could get away from that awkward conversation with Dasha.

"Yes, I'm awake," said Nadia.

"May I come in? I need to check your bandages. I know you may have some strange magic to fix you, but as you know, orders are orders."

"Yes, come in," replied Nadia. A stout nurse in an army uniform crawled into the tent. A bag with a big red cross marked her out as a nurse. The woman was hesitant, as if waiting for something to happen.

"Was it you who did these bandages?" asked Nadia, exposing the bandaged areas of her body, while cold air hit her skin.

"Yes, it was," she said, biting her lip. She was terrified.

"Well, you did a very good job. I can't imagine it has been easy to spare bandages with all the other injured soldiers," said Nadia.

"Well, when the major comes to you and tells you to make sure a particular patient doesn't die, or else, you make sure it's done right. Especially if that patient is a deadly battle witch," said the nurse. *Is that how she sees me?* thought Nadia, unaccustomed to being anything other than unpleasant wallpaper.

"Well, you don't have to worry. I have taken some medicine that will see me well in just a few days."

"You have medicine?" said the nurse leaning forward. "Let me see."

"Unfortunately, it's not something you would recognize," said Nadia. She pulled out one of the small wrappers of medicine.

"Is there any chance you can part with it? We have many injured men out there." The fear was gone as the woman moved closer. Nadia could hear the men outside. Their pain was enough to convince Nadia. She might be mistrustful of soldiers, but they didn't deserve to suffer. Nadia pulled out several packets of medicine wrapped in newspaper.

"These will stop any bleeding, so push them into the wound. These will speed up recovery; you will need to mix them with water. Now, is there any chance I can ask something of you?" Nadia asked.

"What is it?"

"I was wondering if you had any empty medicine vials. I can carry herbs like this, but they become more potent when I can store them in a glass container."

"Oh, okay, yes, I was worried you would ask for my soul or my first born."

"I'm not that kind of witch," replied Nadia, with a bit of smile. "I'm more holistic than that sort of thing. I can keep these bandages clean as well, so you don't need to worry about being punished."

"That's wonderful, but I have another question," said the nurse with a bit of a sigh as she put the various medicines in her bag and gave Nadia several empty vials.

"What is it?"

"Are you able to walk?"

"I should be able to, yes."

"I wish you hadn't said that. You are to report to the major immediately. I will be escorting you. The officers have some questions for you."

"Why?" asked Nadia.

"Well, you're not this company's witch, your hair is not cropped to regulations, and you have nonregulation clothing on you."

"Are they accusing me of something?" said Nadia, wanting to fly away.

"As extra insurance, if you do flee under my watch, I will be punished with service in the penal battalion. Those are death sentences, miss witch. So please don't do anything drastic." Nadia looked down at Dasha, who swished his tail about. The equivalent of a shrug. Nadia sighed.

"Alright, let's go meet this major," said Nadia.

The nurse sighed in relief before crawling out of the tent. Nadia looked at Dasha, who simply hopped in the travel bag.

"This major is going to be trouble," said Dasha.

"Most military men are," said Nadia, gathering her supplies, occasionally wincing from her injuries. Apparently, the magic didn't want her to completely forget that she had indeed been in peril.

She crawled out of the tent into the night. Dozens of fires cast a flickering menagerie of suffering. Medical tents were overflowing with injured men who were laid out in ordered rows with every possible injury imaginable in their ranks. Men who had been scorched with burning fire lay next to men with severed limbs. Others had heavy bandages over cracked skulls and lacerated bowels. The acidic smell of vomit was mixed with the reeking stench of feces and urine and the bitter stink of disinfectant, creating a nauseating cocktail. All around Nadia was the sound of screaming and groaning men. Some wept while others sang folk songs to ease their minds and bodies. Pain and suffering were everywhere. Even the uninjured who carried bloody comrades on stretchers were drenched in blood. Surgeons and nurses could be seen dipping their hands in steaming baths of heated water to remove the gore that had built up to their elbows. These men and women had heavy eyes that had little sleep for many days. Nadia felt guilty that her own nurse was tasked with just overseeing her, dragging her away from the charnel pits of injured and broken men.

"It's not as bad as it could be," said the nurse. "Usually after an attack such as today we would have double this number killed off. With thrice as many injured."

"I don't see how you can possibly deal with so many injured people," replied Nadia.

"One patient at a time. Ten hours can fly by with ten more awaiting you. It's simple how you can deal with so much. It doesn't matter if it's a small injury like yours or a terrible life-threatening one. Now come along, you have places to be," said the nurse, leading Nadia out of the medical camp.

Hundreds of campfires dotted the woods that the Red Army found residence in. The canopy giving enough cover from low flying planes. Yet there were patches of trees that had been reduced to splinters with small craters at their center. From the tree line, Nadia could see flashes of machine gunfire that flickered in the dark, firing at some unknown enemy. The nurse took Nadia's hand and placed it on her shoulder so that they could move through the dark.

"We might need to make a stop or two. I need to check on several patients who were returned to active duty," said the nurse, leading them to one of the campfires.

"Will it take long?" asked Nadia. She had no wish to rush the conversation with this unknown major. But Nadia wanted to make sure there was enough time to seek the light of the Moon.

"Not long, just a quick check up," said the nurse as they approached one of the campfires. The darkness then receded as the light of the campfire illuminated the Red Army soldiers. When the witch and the nurse came into the light, the men lit up.

"Marna Katia!" they cheered.

"Settle down, you animals," the nurse said. "Where is Bataar?"

"He is here, Marna. Who is your cute assistant? Can she carry two men like you, Katia?"

"This is our hero witch, comrade, the one who destroyed the twin tanks from earlier, and broke the machine gun line." said the nurse. The men all got up as one before taking their caps off.

"We are grateful, miss Night Witch. Without you, today's battle would have been a rout," said one of the soldiers.

"If there is anything that you need, simply ask," said another man, stepping forward. Nadia was wary. It was strange being called a hero, too strange to be praised by a soldier of the army who killed her father. She was speechless for a moment, not knowing how to react. Then Dasha popped his head out.

"Are they cooking sausages? Get me one."

"Well," said Nadia, "my cat was wondering if he could have some of that sausage you are cooking." The men all began laughing, and one of the sausages was pulled from the fire. It sizzled as little geysers of grease dripped off the meat. It cleared the stink of the medical tents that clung to Nadia's nose.

"For the cat!" the men cheered. "Now, is there any chance you could bestow a little of your magic on us?"

"Well," said Nadia, trying to think of a way to accommodate these men. She didn't necessarily want to help them, for these men could turn on her. Yet she felt she needed to give them something for the sausage.

"Does anyone have any paper?" asked Nadia. "And a pencil?" Several pairs of hands began rummaging through pockets and bags. One man jumped over the fire to place some letter paper and a pen in her hand. Nadia also noted that the nurse Katia had broken off to look at one of the men who didn't jump up with the rest of them.

"Alright, I'm going to write some luck charms. These will help when the bullets start flying. These won't protect you fully, so don't go charging a fascist machine-gun nest. You can still get hurt, but it will help your chances of not getting hit," replied Nadia, placing Dasha on the ground to eat his sausage.

"Bless you, comrade," cheered one of the men. Nadia wrote down the spells on several pages of letter paper. Soon Nadia was handing out the slips of paper with the luck spells. Some of the men grimaced when looking at the strange, circular runes on the white paper. But they quickly stuffed them in their jackets over their hearts.

"Alright, let's go," said Nurse Katia. "Now, keep Bataar off his feet if possible. When the major says jump, you ask how high, but if anyone of lower rank gives the order, gets someone else to do the work."

"What if it's another charge?" snickered the men.

"Then God be with you all," said Katia, leading Nadia out of the fire.

"Who was the man you were helping?" asked Nadia, trying to make conversation.

"Oh Bataar? He is a Tartar from out east. A lot of the comrades call those men cucumbers. Not in a good way, either. Our union of Communist people still has many problems to sort out. I know on paper we are all one voice and one heart, but the treatment of Bataar calls that into question. The Tartars are used as little more than cannon fodder. Something that can be said for all of us, but it's different with him and the others. I don't know, it seems that whatever happens, Bataar and the other Tartars get the worst of it."

The pair moved into another small campfire of men. The men once again welcomed Katia and Nadia with open arms. Cups of tea were shoved into her hand, and Nadia found herself jotting down several spells of luck once again. The pair zigzagged through the camp, eventually passing the grim Cossacks with sabers at their belts and fur caps on their heads. They ate horse meat and sang sad songs. They found Muscovites, Belarusians, Georgians, Latvians, and drafted Polish troops mixed together like greens in a salad. Their unifying feature was the brown uniform.

There were men with several injuries, but because they could walk were hurriedly patched up and thrown back into service. The injuries and violence crossed all national and ethnic divides. Nadia realized every one of these men met with some loss when dealing with the war. They had seen and endured atrocious things, yet the yoke of the Red Army kept them standing, ready to feel the hammering strike of the fascists, withstanding each violent blow as they were smashed against the red-hot anvil of Soviet discipline.

"I have brought the witch to see the comrade major," Katia replied. The pair had found their way outside a command tent. A pair of guards stood at attention, their faces as cold as the grave.

"We will take it from here, comrade," replied the younger guard. "You can go back to your duties."

"Well, this is where we part ways, sister, good luck to you," said Katia, taking Nadia's hand and shaking it vigorously.

"And to you, sister; may you see the end of the war," said Nadia, shaking the woman's hand. Her grip was firm. *Was it those strong hands that allowed her to withstand the war, or did the war make those strong hands?* thought Nadia.

The guard opened the tent, beckoning Nadia to enter. The tent was a flurry of activity even at this late hour. Men on radios passed orders and reviewed messages. A group of men in the corner read letters and redacted sections. Letters were pulled and marked and added to lists, and Nadia suspected they were marked for either execution or to be punished for subversive thought. Maps were thrown over rickety tables with teacups placed on the corners to keep the map from rolling up. Junior officers made notes with pencils on the map, marking down the location of gun emplacements. One look at the map and Nadia could tell that the Nazis had almost surrounded the army. A small gap was the only thing that could be of any hope. The major had his back turned to Nadia as he spoke with his junior officers.

Nadia just stood back, not knowing what to do in this situation. She opted to look at the portraits of Stalin and Lenin that hung on one of the tent's poles, flanked by two flags of the Soviet Union. The rippling red was pristine. Where everything else had a splotch or two of mud, the flags remained unblemished. Her eyes wandered again to the desk that was placed in the corner. On it, she could see a soldier and his family. A young man and his wife holding a baby. When Nadia saw this man, a ball of dread dropped in her stomach. She recognized the young man. Nadia had nightmares of him. She dreamed that he would come into her home and take the food right out of her mouth. Dreamt that he would grab her mother and brother from their beds and leave her truly alone. Her eyes darted from that picture to the major who spoke of troop movements and their composition.

"Nadia, are you alright? You smell very scared, and angry," meowed Dasha.

"I just found myself in the lion's den," mumbled Nadia.

"Did I just hear a cat?" said one of the junior officers looking up from the map.

The major turned around to see Nadia. Like a wave of freezing water had crushed against her, she recognized the man before her. He had a few years on him. He was no longer the young man he was when Nadia first saw him. She remembered so clearly how this man had ordered her father's arrest. His men had beat her father bloody and dragged him into the back of a truck with the stolen food of her farm. The man who cut a ragged tear in her family, who was just a humble junior lieutenant, was now a major of the Red Army.

"Aw, the imposter shows herself," said the major, stepping up to Nadia. "You have my thanks. Without your help, today's battle would have been a rout," he said, sticking his hand out. Shock and fear turned to rage.

"The major is offering you his thanks, witch," said one of the lieutenants, stepping forward.

"Stand down, lieutenant," said the major, as he pulled his hand back, placing it on his pistol.

"What is your name, comrade?" asked the major.

"Voloshyn, Nadia Voloshyn," she spat.

"I don't think the witch is showing the proper respect for a man of your rank, sir," growled the other officer. The major glanced at the man. "We both know this witch is an imposter. You should have her arrested," Nadia squeezed the rifle. It would be simple enough to fill the tent up with black smoke and shoot these men.

"Don't you have orders to give to the troops?" said the major, turning on the man. "Don't you all have orders to carry out?" The petty officers put their hats on and filed out of the tent, leaving the major and his staff.

"Apologies, Miss Voloshyn. My officers are just on edge from the recent developments. They are angry and wish to take it out on someone. I find myself a bit more even-tempered," he said, adjusting his jacket a little tighter. "I do believe I have failed the most basic courtesy of giving my own name."

"I know who you are," said Nadia. She had dreamed of this moment for years. Reenacted it a thousand times.

"Have we met?" the officer asked.

"Yes, we have, Major Dimitri Volkov," Nadia hissed. "It was a lifetime ago for us both. You were just a junior lieutenant then. I don't know who thought you should be a major."

"Premier Stalin did. When he saw fit to liquidate much of the Red Army's officers. Once war broke out, someone had to fill those uniforms. As for you, I cannot place who you are. You are obviously a witch, but you are not a Red Army witch. Your hair is not regulation, you have no identification tags, and there is no record of who you are. So, I called army command. You are no army witch. In fact, excluding your actions today, you fit the description of a German spy," said the major.

"What? I'm no German spy. I hate them more than you can possibly imagine. I was injured fighting them when I didn't have to."

"That still doesn't mean you're not a spy, Miss Voloshyn. If anything, it might make you a much more dangerous spy. One who is willing to slay their countrymen to ingratiate yourself within our union," he said, turning his back and running his hand over the map on the table.

"Of all the indignities," mumbled Nadia. "From you no less. I'm not a spy of those damned fascists."

"I'm inclined to agree with you, Miss Voloshyn. For one, what is the point of putting a spy among a defeated enemy? On paper, we have already lost this battle. Whatever useful information that can be gleaned from putting a spy among our ranks would be ultimately fruitless as well as jeopardizing a useful operative." He ran fingers over the lines on the page, feeling the slight bumps of raised ink. "That is one reason. The other is that the Germans hate the idea of using women in combat. We know this because the secret police have pulled out all the stops on securing any information from Nazi prisoners. Our own men have also discovered this. After a thorough beating, a Nazi is all too pleased to give any information he can. To a man, the Nazis have been utterly astonished by the existence of our soldier women.

"Sure, the Nazi is willing to let their women work in the factories or on the farm. But you will never find a German woman in a tank, manning a machine gun, or a rifle. They hate the very idea of it. Yet, they will throw injured and sick men out of the top floors of a hospital, or march captured peasants through a mine field. Strange is the animal of man," sighed the major. "No, I don't believe you're a spy. So that begs the question. Who is this witch in my tent, who apparently knows my name and my rank from so long ago? Depending on your answer you will either find a firing squad or your freedom."

"So, I'm under arrest now?" said Nadia, pulling her rifle up in the crook of her arm. "You can't hold me in this tent. You don't have enough men."

"You are being questioned," he said.

"What's the difference?" said Nadia. "With our government, questioning could make you vanish like smoke in the wind."

"Too true." He nodded. "I think I'm getting to the heart of your apparent animosity toward me."

"Animosity doesn't even begin to describe it. I hate the Nazis for what they took from me. But I have hated you for much longer. Hated men like you. Men who blindly rob the people and abduct war heroes, making them disappear from their daughter's life. Never to know if her father was alive or dead. That is the kind of man I hate. That is why I hate you."

"I thought you sounded familiar, Voloshyn. You're the daughter of Alexander Voloshyn." He sighed before turning back to his map. "Your father is dead," he said.

It felt like a glass ball had been dropped and shattered in Nadia's heart. She had not realized that she still secretly hoped that her father was alive. That one day she would find him and learn who he was. So she could discover the man whom her mother loved so much, not the idea of a father she had made over so many long years.

"We executed him and threw his ashes in the river so that there would be no place for anyone to mourn him. If it was just a case of him trying to stop us, he would have most likely found his way into a work camp or at the bottom of a mass grave. As it was, his name was on an execution list. If it were up to me, I would have never allowed such a thing," said Dimitri, looking back at Nadia.

"What do you mean if it was up to you? You were in charge of those men. You could have pled for his case." Nadia hadn't realized she was shouting. When she did, she couldn't stop. "You murdered my father!"

"You think you are the only one who has lost a father!" the major shouted back. The other people in the tent went quiet, turning to look at their commanding officer and the witch in their midst. "My own father was shot right in front of me because he stole grain. Right here, Private Smirnov's father was liquidated for his high rank! My wife lost three brothers and an uncle, who just vanished, no idea where they have gone. There isn't a man or woman in this entire doomed battalion who has not lost someone to the state. You would think that fact alone would have had us all rise up as one and tear down that flag and string up our Premier from a lamp post! But here we are standing, shoulder to shoulder, fighting as one for the people who have killed our loved ones. We are all made accomplices to murder and thuggery, we are all guilty because we participate in the regime. The Nazis may have twisted their citizens' minds, but our country has twisted our souls. We know the actions we do are wrong. We don't have the comfort of deluding ourselves into believing that our horrible actions are in some service to something greater. The state has found validity in our submission. Whoever we were, whatever we believed in, has been coopted by the state. We are the state, and the state is us. Do not try to play the victim and claim that somehow your tragedy is unique. We are all victims. We are condemned prisoners praying that we may one day be pardoned."

The major turned, his fists shaking as he looked down at the maps. He slammed his fist down on the table. "It doesn't matter; we are dead men. It doesn't matter why you are here and what reason you had to fight the Nazis. You gave us another day. Maybe a week; it depends on how fast the Germans can get a couple more tanks. The death blow has been struck. It struck us yesterday, before the Nazis even launched their attack." The man sighed, turning to look at Nadia. He looked so tired, like a man trying to keep his head above water as his muscles slowly gave out.

"What are you talking about?" said Nadia.

"We are surrounded, soon to be cut off. Yesterday we asked command to pull back. Instead, we were ordered not to pull back or surrender. We are to fight to the bitter end so that we can tie up enemy forces. If by some chance you came here to kill me, you are already too late. The state has made sure of that. If you came to kill the enemy, then you are merely delaying the inevitable. I don't plan on having any of us surrender. I plan to obey my orders to the end. As a loyal soldier of the Red Army."

"How can you speak of loyalty after that tirade? Half of the things you said would have gotten you executed for treason. You have no love for the state," said Nadia.

"Because right now, that state is our only salvation. There is no other option. If Napoleon and his army came rolling over those hills, I would gladly surrender to them. If the capitalist countries of England or America flew in, I would surrender. Hell, if the Germany from twenty-five years ago came, I would surrender to them as well. But it isn't any of them; we are fighting a terrible foe who has our backs to the wall. They talk about this being a war to liberate the people from Communism, but every report I have read shows that they seek to destroy us. Annihilate us. And there is no one to save us. England has closed its gates and filled its moat, France has been consumed by the beasts, and central Europe is full of fascist allies and sympathizers. There is no one to save us. We must save ourselves; right now the only thing that will save us is that vary same oppressive state that has condemned me and my men to death. Every day we live, every day they spend their energy trying to kill us is energy not spent on killing civilians. Not spent on desecrating our homeland. I may be dead, and so is every soldier under my command. But you are not under my command. You helped me in my doomed journey, so I'm now going to help you."

"I don't want your help," said Nadia, closing the distance to the major. "I don't want the man who killed my father sticking his hand out in charity."

"If you want to wear that uniform, you will take it. Winter is a stone's throw away. You know this, you could have salvaged another coat, but you still wear our uniform," said the major, staring down at Nadia. He wasn't much taller than her, yet she remembered him being a giant.

"What I choose to wear is no business of yours," replied Nadia.

"But it is the business of the state. Other commanders may not be as lenient as I'm now. Many in my position would have had you shot, regardless of the deed you've done. I have radioed command designating you as a pro-Soviet partisan. Codenamed Night Witch. This will allow you to act as you see fit without any of the state oversight, a designation with unprecedented freedom as long as the war is on."

"You told the state about me?" said Nadia, backing up. "Do you know how many of my sisterhood the state has killed? How many witches met their end in this country in its long history?"

"No doubt innumerable, yet I doubt the state cares about such things at the moment. I doubt any of us are getting out of this alive," he turned, looking at the gap on the map. The slight gap that he and his men could have escaped through. Like a noose closing around his neck. "Go where you wish, Miss Voloshyn. If it's any consolation, I regret what happened to your father. I'm sorry for the pain I have caused you. I wish our world is not the way it is." Major Dimitri Volkov waved his hand and the tent flaps opened to let her out.

15
The Moon

Nadia left the tent, still jittery with anger. She reached down, getting a fistful of mud, and turned back to the tent. It would be so easy to curse him. So easy to fill his lungs with mud. All she had to do was squeeze her fist, and he would start drowning. Would she ever have a chance like this again? A chance to find satisfaction with the death of her father's killer.

"Are we going or not? This place stinks," said Dasha from the bag. "We have dallied here long enough, and while I would love to use your newfound popularity to gorge myself on all the tasty things this camp has to offer, I really don't like how close those artillery explosions are getting."

Nadia sighed and tilted her hand, letting the mud fall back to the wet earth. There was no point in killing a dead man.

"You're right, Dasha," said Nadia. "How did you get so good at keeping perspective?"

"Just lucky I guess," he replied with a chirp.

Without a farewell, Nadia mounted her rifle and shot up into the sky.

Nadia had gotten used to the sharp acceleration, and she flew as fast as she could away from that camp. It was best not to idle in the presence of the dead for too long. The weather had turned into a light drizzle, yet Nadia was getting far too wet. A hazard of being a nomadic witch, she had discovered. She could see the sporadic night fighting. Tracer rounds whizzed out of unseen positions while blossoms of artillery erupted, leaving purple and red after images in Nadia's eyes. Nadia could feel warm tears rolling down her cheek. The warmth was consumed by cold rain.

She hadn't realized how long she carried the hope that her father was still alive. It was painful to feel that hope die, like watching her father get forced into the truck all over again. She didn't think even Peter could understand. Her brother had never known their father. Her mother had never given up hope. But she was no more as well. It seemed the world was conspiring to make Nadia as lonely as possible.

"So, what's our plan now?" asked Dasha. "Maybe finding someplace warm and dry?"

"Not quite yet, I need to seek communion with the moon," she said, pointing the rifle toward the clouds, and flying higher up.

"That's just great," replied Dasha, pulling his head back into the bag. The pair flew through the clouds. Nadia always thought she could grab handfuls of the vapor like she was picking up snow. She was disappointed when she found that the clouds were more akin to fog. The darkness engulfed them. The air grew colder. She thought of the Black Sea as she was pulled down in its cold depths. It was only when the glow of the moon started infusing the clouds around her did those feelings end. That she could catch her breath again. She erupted from the clouds to a silent, serene world, where the moon shone onto a sea of rolling clouds that crashed like waves.

It felt like she was in another world. One far away from the violence and suffering far below. Above the clouds was a calm serenity not seen on the ground. The wind blew on her face in a freezing gale.

"So how does one commune with the moon?" Dasha asked, his voice muffled by the bag.

"I don't know," said Nadia wiping the warm tears from her eyes. "I guess I'm just supposed to feel it out with my intuition."

"And how are you supposed to do that? Isn't this magic stuff supposed to be complicated?"

"Well, yes, but also natural like breathing, and walking."

"That explains everything," said Dasha sarcastically, looking outside the bag and finding it much to his distaste.

"Well, let's it put like this. Did anyone teach you how to catch a mouse?"

"No, it would be undignified," replied Dasha.

"Yet the urge to hunt mice was there," said Nadia, looking at the full, bright moon. "I just have to listen and open myself up. That's the plan."

"I don't understand," said Dasha.

"That's fine, I just need you to be quiet for a while." She stared at the moon, taking in its luminous shine before closing her eyes. Dasha did the same but in the comfort of the bag so that he could nap.

The wind blew around her, and within the darkness of her closed eyes, she pictured the moon. Fat and heavy, it appeared rising upward into the sky of her mind. She was so close. Nadia opened her eyes and found that she was now walking on a field of shadows. She didn't know how she had gotten there. The ground was cold and spongy, and Nadia seemed to be giving off her own light. Nadia was glowing with the same luminescent light that the moon cast on the world.

Nadia took several steps forward. The moon looked so far away there was no way to tell how far she was and how long it would take to reach. With each step, it felt like she was traveling vast distances. Not just kilometers but whole continents. Each step felt like she was crossing the whole of the earth in mighty stride. Soon, she found herself underneath the moon, close enough to touch.

"Hello," she said, her voice sounded so meek, and yet it resounded like thunder echoing outward into the void. The moon began to spin, rotating. The solid surface of hard rock shifted to wavy silver hair. Nadia couldn't say when the moon transformed into a luminescent woman, just that it happened. The Moon was a giant. Taller than the tallest building Nadia had ever seen. Her face was round and her belly pregnant. She wore a gown of starlight that rippled and swayed with her movements. The woman looked down at Nadia as she would look at a mouse. The Moon bent down and shrank to the size of a normal woman.

"Hello." Her voice echoed like the crashing of the tides. The roaring of the ocean sent ripples through the darkness with waves of light.

"I'm Nadia, a witch. I have come to ask how I can perceive the spirit realm, so that I may find my coven," she said. The void echoed her words. When she tried to whisper, her voice sounded like cracking lightning. When she spoke, it vibrated with the sound of a howling blizzard.

"How curious," said the Moon, taking Nadia's hand. "Sit." Nadia complied, sitting in the spongy darkness.

"You seek a way to discover what you have already found," she said. "This is the spirit world, or an aspect of it, or to be more precises, a facet of it."

"I hadn't expected it to be so dark, or so cold," replied Nadia, uneasy with how the Moon's hands felt like cold glass.

"That is how my children like it. It is what makes them happy, so it is what makes me happy," said the Moon, her voice sending waves of light into the darkness.

"Your children? I don't see any of them?" said Nadia, startled by her reverberating voice.

"They are here," she said. She rubbed her hand on the spongy ground. "Here, feel." The Moon took Nadia's hand and placed it on the ground. "You can almost feel them breathing, feel their life."

"I'm on a creature? But how could it be this big?" said Nadia.

"How can you be so small," smiled the Moon. "It depends on where you stand. My children are vast titanic creatures, yet they can shrink to the size of a mouse's shadow. They can wedge themselves in the smallest of crevices."

"I used to tell my little brother about how you gave birth to the darkness; I thought it was just metaphorical," said Nadia, rubbing her glowing hand along the spongy ground.

"And so, it is made true, I'm both a rock in the void as lifeless as cold stone, and dead as the unliving. Yet, I'm also alive and fertile, brimming with the radiance that gives my children life. I'm the man in the Moon and the rabbit fleeing from the coyote. In this place, this spirit realm, I'm what I am. How I'm seen is dependent on who I'm with."

"So, you are not actually a glowing woman?" asked Nadia.

"I am, and I'm not. Just as you are Nadia the witch, and a host of cells. You are what you are, and I love you as one of my own children. I will help you because that is who I am."

"That fills me with so much relief; I didn't think I was worth helping," said Nadia. The Moon reached out and pulled Nadia in, hugging her. Nadia hadn't realized that such cold arms could be so comforting.

"Of course you are. I will keep my promises, especially to someone who shapes magic in my name. You have already shown aptitude in simply finding me. You now know how to traverse the spirit realm. I will give you guidance when I can. You may have to search for other entities. Just know that when I'm at my darkest in the sky, I will be at my least helpful. Now walk with me."

The Moon, holding Nadia's hand, rose with the young witch. The Moon led Nadia into the darkness that shifted and wriggled with each step. The Moon's feet rippled rings of light on the ground like a pebble dropped in a pond. Nadia's own steps had minimal ripples as her feet sank into the cold, spongy ground. Soon the darkness faded and gave way to a forest submerged under a sea. Nadia found that she could breathe in this underwater landscape. The pair moved through the grove of trees as strange entities swam through the air or skittered behind trees or rocks. They were creatures of strange geometries and strange shapes. Nadia could tell right away that one creature was a feeling of melancholy, another a memory of dawn. Nadia didn't know how she knew this.

"We are here," said the Moon. She bent down and pushed aside a shrub. The shrub scampered away, before turning into a jellyfish. A pulsing vein of dawn light was underneath the bush, dipping occasionally into the seafloor. "These are the ley lines. You can follow them your entire life and never find their source. They are a net of energy, akin to the circulatory system of an animal. Within lies the ephemeral energy of magic. The network is too vast to map, but they can lead to specific places quite easily. Your coven, in Grandmother's Forest is here."

The Moon placed Nadia's hand on the vein, and the witch felt she was racing with the magic, traveling along the network till she was in Grandmother's Forest. She saw a trio of women below her. She recognized the woman from the burning halo; the grey-haired witch tended a fire. The other two were unknown to Nadia. One was clad in a shawl of black cobwebs, and an aura of grave stench clung to her. The last woman stood in a purple robe that crackled with lightning. It became so clear how to reach these women. The ley lines told her everything. The Moon had changed and was floating high in the sky. She was in the aspect of a wrinkled matron resplendent in light.

"Do you see where you wish to go," said the Moon, as waves of celestial moonlight rippled across the breadth of the sky like the pulsing of a pale star.

"I do, Mother Moon," replied Nadia. "How could I ever repay you?"

"Your happiness is repayment enough. Now you must wake up. Your injuries are still real, and you need to rest. Remember, for someone like you in a time like this, idling in the spirit realm can be dangerous."

"How so?" asked Nadia. The light started to blind her as it pulsed like a wave. She put her hands up to shield herself. "Wake up, Nadia, you're falling," said the Moon. The spirit realm vanished, and Nadia could feel she had almost slipped off her rifle. She held on to the barrel, as she tilted sideways. Dasha yowled from the sudden jerk as Nadia righted herself.

"Please tell me you didn't almost fall off your flying gun, so very high off the ground?" yowled the cat.

"Don't be ridiculous," said Nadia, her heart racing as she looked down at the sea of clouds down below. "I think it is time we call it a night and find someplace to sleep."

"Correction, you need to find a place to sleep. I was sleeping quite comfortably until you decided to wobble." The bag wiggled as the cat adjusted himself. "Did you find what you were looking in this little sojourn into the clouds? Or did you just look at the moon for an hour?"

"An hour? I couldn't have been in the spirit realm for more than a few minutes," replied Nadia as she began to drop altitude.

"No, you just got really quiet for an hour and stared at the moon. If you don't mind, I'm going back to sleep."

"Well, we are about to get a little wet."

"I'm not, but you are." And with that, the pair were submerged in the clouds, back into the wet, muddy, violent world down below.

16
Death Waltz

It had been a week and a half since Nadia had communion with the moon. Several days of relentless mud and rain, turning the world into a thick soup. She passed numerous columns of fascists bogged down in the sea of mud that sucked up men, machines, and horses alike. Dozens of fascists pulled single carts of supplies that were once carried by hardy, powerful German horses that had died from the adverse conditions of the steppe. It pleased her knowing that the land was doing its part in slowing the Nazi advance.

However, Nadia was very lost. Not lost geographically, for she had a map that told her where villages were. She had, however, lost the trail of where Grandmother's Forest was. She had gotten used to dipping into the spirit realm to find the ley lines, but as the week continued, the spirit realm started taking on the aspects of the physical world. The ley line was covered in mud and took time to locate in the spirit realm. She concluded that she had to venture deeper into the spirit realm to find her way again. A prospect that Nadia was uneasy about, considering the Moon's warning. Nadia didn't want to take any more unnecessary risks. She knew that this was her only option. Nadia made refuge in an abandoned mud hut in a forest.

It was in the evening that she felt comfortable and secure enough to venture once again into the spirit realm. Even Dasha was comfortable, as he had a dry place to lay down and stretch. He made the point that he would have preferred a barn with all the rats he could eat but was content with the bits of rabbit that Nadia had hunted.

Nadia had found an excellent position and drew several wards of protection in the earth that would alert her in the spirit realm if something was close to her body. Magic was becoming easier for her these days, calling upon her teaching and combining it with her experience and intuition. She no longer felt the strain of magical backlash from too much spell work.

She was confident that she would stay safe in the physical world, owning more to her isolation than the precautionary magic that she had put up. She had made herself comfortable within the circle and cleared her mind. She closed her eyes and blocked out the sound of Dasha munching on a rabbit meat.

Nadia took several deep breaths and focused on that other world, using the Moon as a mental and spiritual signpost. It was like being dropped into a hot bath as she found herself in the spirit world. Opening her eyes, she found herself into a vast empty steppe covered in a sea of mud. The hills and forests were gone, replaced with a landscape of mud that swirled and churned in eddies and rivers of wet earth. Stray spirits struggled in the grasping mud as it sucked them underneath the surface. The spirits of the road, spirits of swift running, spirits of expediency found themselves grabbed and pulled by the roiling mud.

Nadia took several steps in the muck that came up to her ankle. This would not be a quick sojourn into the spirit realm. The realm would not allow it. She made her way to a struggling spirit that hobbled in the mud, a great lumbering donkey creature with the face of a man and hands instead of hooves.

"Excuse me, kind spirit could I get a moment of your time? I was wondering if you could direct me to a ley line?" said Nadia, almost collapsing in the mud as she waved down the beast spirit.

"Begone, mortal witch, I'm too busy with this insufferable muck to deal with some wayward peasant girl foolish enough to travel between worlds," said the beast with the voice of man and animal.

"Have I done something to offend you? I was just asking for directions," said Nadia, now right next to the spirit. The mud seemed to climb up Nadia's clothes, clinging to her in heavy clumps that almost pulled her down.

"I would like to reach the realm of hard stone and lush grass, but because of the tyranny of your world, we are stuck with this insufferable mud."

"I'm sorry. I have no control over what my world is, but perhaps I could help you," said Nadia, pulling her legs up and trudging alongside the beast. If she stood in one place, the mud began to pull her down. Almost as if she were slowly eaten by the carnivorous earth.

"Nice try. Then I would be in your debt, a fate more intolerable than this oppressive muck," said the beast, raising one of its hands to wipe its brow. The creature then stopped and rubbed its chin while trudging in place. "Perhaps we could barter instead."

"Barter? I'm afraid I have nothing to barter," said Nadia.

"Oh, but you do. You have the smell of your mother's cooking, the memory of sitting by the fire in December. That feeling of sadness when you look at a dead animal on the side of the road." The beast leaned in with a crooked smile. His breath smelled like rancid butter and garlic.

"I don't know if I could give any of those up, especially for something I could find with just a bit of searching."

"Oh, there must be something that you would be willing to trade. How about your anxiety over food? Famine spirits are always willing to trade for something for such worries. Only a small piece of it."

"That might be something I would be willing to give up," said Nadia.

"Yes, good, good, it is only a piece, it will grow back in time like a piece of liver. You should feel some change in appetite as well."

"So, if I give you this piece, then you will show me where a ley line is?" replied Nadia.

"Yes, yes. So do we have a deal, farm girl?" asked the spirit, sticking out a muddy hand.

"Yes, I guess we do," replied Nadia. Its hand shot out, driving through Nadia's chest. The creature's hand squirmed around its fingers, digging through Nadia's torso like it was rummaging through a bag. The breath was ripped from Nadia as the beast pulled its hand out of her chest. Nadia collapsed into the mud, coughing uncontrollably.

"Oh delightful. These little food traumas are full of despair. That must have been a nasty famine to make such a dreadful little morsel."

Nadia looked up to see what the creature was holding. It looked like a shriveled piece of slimy black carrot broken off at the root. The beast tucked the piece of anxiety away as Nadia pulled herself to her feet.

"Alright, your turn, where is the ley line?" said Nadia, as she took deep breaths of air that wasn't there.

"Indeed. Follow me," said the beast. The two trudged through the mud for what felt like hours or just minutes. They passed fields of corpses whose flesh and bones stuck out of the muck in macabre displays of butchery. They found a field of buildings on fire with the inhabitants weeping as they burned in the hot orange flame.

"Why are there so many scenes of carnage here?" asked Nadia.

"Do you like them? They have been popping up for the past couple of months, or was it the past couple of years? They are the echoes of violent acts. I think they are quite quaint; not the worst I have seen, but it's wonderful that there are so many of them. I can admire the diligence in these acts of violence," said the beast. He pulled an onion from the mud and bit into it. He chewed for a moment before spitting it out and tossing the onion aside. "We are close."

"Thank goodness," said Nadia; trudging through the mud had been exhausting. Her spirit ached from the bargain. They moved forward until they found themselves in front of a tree with dozens of people hanging from the branches with ropes around their necks. An old crone with bird wings, sharp talons, and one burning red eye crowed at them as they approached. She sat on a nest filled with human skulls.

"The one-eyed Liko has made her nest atop the ley line; do not fear her, she will only tear your eyes out if you move to steal her eggs, and I don't think you have any use for those eggs."

"How could human skulls possibly be her eggs?"

"They are the skulls of killers. The Liko whispers horrors into the skulls, dark, twisted desires. When they hatch, they will commit depraved and heinous murders."

"How terrible," replied Nadia.

"Indeed," said the beast. "Such predilections are for the obscenely patient spirit, one that I'm not. If we have no further business, I will be on my way."

The beast turned and trudged off into the vast steppe of mud. Nadia was left with the cawing Liko and the swaying bodies hanging from her tree. Nadia ignored the bird spirit the best she could while not looking up. She went to the base of the tree and began digging through the mud. Taking great handfuls of the muck that dripped between her fingers. A small pile of mud grew as Nadia dug, looking past roots. She wished she was in the underwater forest. Every so often, she would find a bone of a skeleton, sometimes animal, sometimes human.

She eventually found the telltale signs of the ley line. The light that emanated from that pulsing vein glowed through the mud. It pulsed with a warm light, and the smell of sweet fruit wafted into her nose. The Liko above squawked louder, flapping its wings. Its feathers fell on Nadia like snow. Nadia touched the pulsing of the ley line, and it became clear where she needed to go. Grandmother's Forest was just a day's journey from where she was, well outside Ukraine and inside the Russian border. It seemed to be on a cluster of ley lines, but cleverly concealed. The Liko went quiet, and the world began to darken. Nadia looked up to see that the sun above her was becoming eclipsed not by a moon but by an arrogant bulbous black sun.

Looking around, she turned to see a silhouette in the distance. It was a man who advanced with proud, wide steps. Nadia's breath caught in her throat.

It was Rudolph Becker, trudging through mud in shiny black boots and a crisp, clean black uniform. The mud seemed to slide off his clothes, leaving them unblemished. On his hand, he wore his mechanical gauntlet. It hummed and crackled with sparking purple eldritch light. Cables led off to a metal backpack that hooked up to a pair of goggles and headphones. The sorcerer seemed to blink forward, crossing the landscape with ease. All Nadia could think of was how to get away. After all, she didn't know if fighting in the spirit realm was even possible. Nadia closed her eyes and began to fall back into her body.

She fell back, allowing the mud to swallow her whole as she dropped into the physical world. She felt a sudden jerk on her spirit around the throat, halting her. A thin wire had circled her neck and was pulling her up. She was out of breath, but the pain of the wire digging into her skin and pulling her back into the spirit realm was utter agony. A gauntleted hand grabbed her hair and pulled upward. She burst through the oppressive mud of the spirit realm, the wire around her throat felt like hot fire.

"Well, if it isn't the partisan," said Rudolph. "I had almost forgotten about you, until I started hearing reports of a witch blowing up tanks and halting our advance."

He pulled her up by the hair before ripping her out of the mud. Nadia clawed at the white-hot wire around her neck. "That's when I started poking around this place again, setting my little webs of magic to track and find anyone who might be using it. Honestly, I thought all the witches, and magicians of this land had gotten wise to my tricks, but then I remembered a young inexperienced witch who evaded my clutches. So, I cast my net, and low and behold here you are. Now if only we were in the physical world instead of this amusing reflection. Then I could place my luger against your head," he said, pantomiming a gun against Nadia's skull.

"Then pull the trigger. Bang!" he screamed in her ear, causing Nadia to recoil. He laughed as Nadia floundered in the mud. "I'm sorry, I shouldn't tease like that, but when I hear my superiors talk about how the nefarious witches could destroy everything we worked for and then see people like you,

I wonder what all the fuss is about."

"Then why are you here?" spat Nadia.

"Why am I here? In this strange dream realm? Or do you mean in your country? The answer to both is the same: because my nation told me to. Because my leader told me that I was free to do as I wished in these lands if it helped with his goals. I could pursue research I would never even dream of in the west. With the French, the Dutch, the English, our orders were to behave ourselves, relegate our desires to a few minor spheres of study. In Poland, however, we found a wealth of opportunities. Avenues of research that could only be dreamed of. The Reich not only supported our research but gave us resources, lists of undesirables. We were handed the keys to true power. How could we say no to such a thing? The Jews, gypsies, cripples, all the usual undesirables of society were once again free game. All the wealth they had hoarded was given over to the state, their bodies given over to the work camps, and finally their souls were given to me and my colleagues. So, when my leaders said that we need to wipe out all witches in the east, I obeyed. Because the reward was vast, and you and your ilk are just too weak to stop me."

Nadia was leaning up against the Liko tree as Rudolph spoke. He would occasionally slap the goggles, the lenses flickering for a moment.

"There is no one compelling you to do this?" said Nadia, her hands digging into the bark of the tree.

"Well no. But if I didn't tacitly accept the deal, I would have never made it to my position. They would have found some other violent go-getter, who would be standing in front of you now. We aren't operating under your barbarous Bolshevik methods. It is the difference of being commanded by a master and being asked by a friend. It is the difference between 'you will,'" he said, stabbing his finger into Nadia's chest. "Versus 'you may.' Now it is my turn. Why are you here?" he said, tightening the silver cord around her neck. Nadia wished she had a knife, a gun, or even a rock to hit this terrible man.

"Learning what this world looks like," she lied. Above, the Liko scowled at the pair, her wings flapping, a flurry of feathers falling.

"Really? Is that all? Not looking for something, or someone? Admittedly, if I were not so busy, I would explore this world myself. A task made possible by this wonderful contraption," he said gesturing to the goggles on his head. He smelled of machine oil and a charnel house. Nadia, unable to tolerate this any longer, brought up her fist and hit him in the face as hard as she could. The blow struck him, and it felt like all the force in her arms vanished.

"You obviously haven't been here very long. Strength of body means nothing here. Everything is a pale imitation of our world. Only strengthened through words and promises, I'm here through mechanical assistance. You had to make a promise or asked for assistance from something, a deal. So, who was it?"

"A being many times more powerful than you," Nadia hissed.

"Oh, do tell. Was it a spirit? A stray daemon? Some harlot witch passing along superstitions and secrets?"

"No, you oaf," growled Nadia. "The Moon, a being more power than your entire Reich."

"The Moon." He smiled. "Such old-fashioned shamanism seems at odds with your country's declared atheism. So, what possible power can the Moon offer you? I have killed dozens of your sisterhood, all of whom clung desperately to the idea that the Moon was their patron. Yet this Moon couldn't stop even the crudest of indignities that I inflicted on them," he said pulling the wire tight. "I may not have your body, but I can bind your spirit, do what I like with it, leaving your body a vegetable. I can scoop it up as my leisure or just let you die from starvation. I have lots of options, while you have none."

Nadia closed her eyes, pleading with herself to remain strong. She thought of the Moon. She thought of the darkness. How vast and powerful they were, the Moon's children loved by their mother. How titanic. Yet, they could fit inside a mouse's shadow. The darkness could fit inside her mouth.

"Darkness of the Moon, cast out this monster that accosts me."

"Praying to something that won't answer you, how quaint," said Rudolph.

Something in Nadia's gut shifted. It felt like a tide of vomit that climbed out of her throat and pushed out her mouth. A creature of darkness pulled itself from Nadia's mouth. A hand of ash grasped Rudolph by the throat. What sounded like a thousand tiny whispers could be heard from the pitch-black mass. Then an arm followed the hand, growing to the size of a mighty tree, raising Rudolph by the neck. Nadia collapsed to her knees as the darkness pulled itself out of her body through her mouth and nose, the shadow beast threw Rudolph a great distance. He impacted with the ground, bouncing several times. The shadows poured out of Nadia's throat like a mighty river of hot stinking smoke. The darkness grew to the proportions of a leviathan, a vast and dominant presence on the muddy landscape, rising above the Liko's tree of corpses. It towered above the tiny Rudolph and Nadia. The Nazi officer stood up, brushing himself off and looking up at the towering monster above him. The shadow monster raised one of its dozens of hands and brought it crashing down toward Rudolph. Before impact, a javelin of blood shot out of Rudolph's hand, sending the creature reeling.

The screams of the beast echoed through the vast mud steppe, seeming to reach all corners of the universe. Rudolph was throwing those spears of blood now. The darkness retreated with each javelin of red blood magic that was hurled into its being. The shadows started recoiling back into Nadia's body, retreating like a wriggling serpent. Nadia could hardly deal with the expulsion of such an entity. The return was horribly painful. Rudolph threw another bloody javelin at Nadia, who dove out of the way. The magical dart hit the Liko's nest, sending skulls flying everywhere. The creature screamed and charged the Nazi, tackling Rudolph, its wings hitting the magician with all its fury. Nadia could see the rising moon coming over the horizon. The light of the moon clashing with the black light of the eclipsed sun. An aurora of darkness and light poured over the muddy landscape sending rippling waves of dancing light and shadow that swirled over the mud like the reflections of water. Nadia reached out with her hands and grasped a shard of light. It grew hard and translucent like a piece of glass, and she used it to cut the magic wire around her throat, only to find that the threads wouldn't cut. It seemed the way out of the spirit realm was through Rudolph.

The Nazi officer was in the middle of dismembering the Liko with his bare hands while arcane lightning sparked off the battery on his back. Rudolph had made no pacts with this realm. He was here because of the strange technology that was at his command. *That's it,* thought Nadia

That was the chance of banishing Rudolph and escaping his clutches.

She held the shard of light, clutched it as it dug into her spirit's flesh. Nadia picked up a handful of the Liko's feathers that had fallen into the mud around the tree. She then stuffed them into her mouth and devoured them, sucking them down in her gut. The taste of feathers and mud mixing in her mouth was disgusting, but she could feel the magic of the act coursing through her being. She placed a foot on the tree and used it to kick off. The

Liko's feathers transmuted into a burst of flight that sent her flying toward Rudolph, who advanced through the mud in his strange flickering fashion.

The Nazi officer braced for impact as the mud made it impossible to roll out of the way. The two collided right as the moon collided with the black sun above. The pair were sent tumbling, the force of the impact causing a great groove of mud. Nadia was thrown end over end, clutching onto Rudolph with all her might. When the two had found themselves at rest, Nadia was atop the Nazi magician. She brought the glass shard of moonlight downward to Rudolph's face. Yet, the officer had his gauntleted hand up to block Nadia's assault. The blade halted just millimeters from Rudolph's goggles. Nadia placed all her weight down on the blade and gripped the shard as hard as she could. Blood dripped from the shard and down its jagged blade onto Rudolph's face.

"So that is where you have been hiding it, that savage Slavic fury," said Rudolph, his arms straining from the renewed assault. Nadia said nothing and pressed harder down on the shard, touching the right lens of the goggle. "This renewed strength of yours is impressive. Now that we have both bared our teeth, we can stop playing games." The battery began to spark, and Nadia found that she was being pushed off the officer.

"More power!" shouted Rudolph, his voice echoing across the landscape. The backpack hiccupped, and the sound of a child's scream pierced the world. Smoke poured out of the backpack, and Nadia could see a child's face in the red-black smoke. The gloves sparked, singeing Nadia's hands. Rudolph jabbed Nadia's gut, and it felt like she was hit with the force of a sledgehammer, sending her flying up in the air. She was sent spinning from the force of the blow. The Liko's feathers in her stomach kept her floating in the air, giving her a moment to right herself. Rudolph was already on his feet.

His fists crackled with blood-red energy and black lightning. With a casual gesture, a lance of blood shot out of his hands.

It was too fast for Nadia; it impaled her through the stomach. Her entire world went white as the agony coursed through her spirit. She tumbled to the ground, splashing into the mud. Protruding from her gut was an arrow of blood, covered in hundreds of twisted barbs that curled in all directions like savage hooks.

Nadia looked at the arrow in her gut in disbelief. It was like being impaled with hundreds of needles that twisted and wriggled inside her. Being shot was never so painful. Explosive shrapnel was never so painful. All she could do was pant in disbelief. The mud began to pull her downward, into the wet earth of the spirit realm. Above her, the black sun swelled to gargantuan proportions. It pushed the moon out of the sky past the horizon. Then Rudolph appeared over her. He smiled down at her. *How did he remain so clean with not a speck of mud on him?* thought Nadia. But not entirely accurate: on his cheek was a small drop of blood, and the mud mixed with it.

"This was inevitable, you know. No matter how fanatically you fight or how brave your resolve, you and your degenerate race will fail. Even if you had twenty witches at your side, your efforts would amount to nothing," said Rudolph, grasping Nadia by the collar and pulling her up. Nadia could only scream in response. She wanted to strike back, but the barb in her gut made every motion unbearably painful.

"I have seen it everywhere since coming to these lands. No matter how many of you there are, you all burn like ants under a blow torch. You people swarm about, gobbling up everything, and you think that makes you powerful. But you never had a chance when a people with real martial spirit came after you. The German race have been hungry for so long that it has made us lean, it has made us tough. We survived off meager turnips, which focused our minds and bodies. Once all your miserable ilk has been cut from the earth, my people, a deserving people who have known so much pain, so much suffering, will finally be made happy. Finally made whole," said Rudolph. He then gave a slight smile. "But first we need to get rid of the likes of you. It will be like finally curing the common cold."

Inside Nadia, something shifted. The pain in her gut became a distant thing as it was slowly replaced with red-hot anger.

"You think you know what hunger is?" Nadia touched on the hunger inside herself. The part of her mind that she spent so much time trying to hide. Like throwing a rug over a pool of blood. Only to have it seep through the fabric, discoloring the tapestry with an ugly brown splotch. She touched on the hunger that constantly tightened her stomach, made her fear where her next meal would come from. That forced her to hide away food so that she would always be constantly hungry, to avoid the painful memories of the famine. She infused that hunger with magic, then unleashed it on Rudolph Becker. A swarm of insects poured out of her mouth, pushing Rudolph off her. The maddening hunger released the pain of the barb in her gut, pulling her to her feet.

"You know nothing of hunger. Have you ever eaten horse shit because there wasn't a scrap of food in your home? Have you eaten grass cakes? You think eating only turnips make a starving people. You know nothing."

Her voice echoed like the roaring of a typhoon across the land, sending waves of mud out from her. Becker did his best to wipe away the swarm of insects that chewed on his spirit and his arcane equipment.

"I see that you don't know what suffering is. You have never felt it. I'm a master of suffering, so I will be your teacher." Nadia then squeezed the barb in her gut, piercing her spirit's flesh. "I will make it so you and your Thule Society will drown in suffering. Every act of bloodshed will be returned in kind. Every atrocity will be doubled."

Nadia began to raise her arm, and a fist of mud grew out of the earth around Rudolph Becker.

"I will see to it that every Nazi bleeds and is torn asunder. I will have your armies broken and left ragged." She then closed her fist, and the muddy hand did the same, pinning Rudolph in place. "When I'm done, there will be no more Germany. There will be a howling wilderness." She pulled the bloody barb from her belly and held the spell in her grasp. Its barbs pierced through her fingers and palm. Nadia would have dropped it if she could, but seeing the helpless Rudolph gave her an idea. She stumbled over to the pinned Nazi, who wriggled in the muddy grasp. "This is it, I will get my revenge for what you did, for my mother, for Olivia, for my ruined life. It's over," said Nadia, about to bring the barb down into Rudolph's neck.

"I couldn't agree more," said Rudolph.

Nadia brought the barb down, only to be blinded by a flash of light from the blood-red bead of the Philosopher's Stone that hung from his neck. The hot light blew Nadia off her feet. Rudolph's equipment sparked with black electricity that shredded the muddy hand that held him in place. He arose as if pulled up by invisible strings. Nadia coughed and sputtered, attempting to get up, but found Rudolph's boot on her stomach. "You have shown me some interesting things here, but I'm convinced more than ever that you witches need to die. Every single last one of you."

Rudolph pulled a black iron nail from his breast pocket, the Philosopher's Stone still pulsing with hot light. He held and examined the nail in his iron gauntlet. Something about the simple object sent shivers through Nadia's spirit.

"What is that?" she whispered.

"Oh this, just a little something I recreated in the labs. An interesting little object that exists both in the real world and this strange mockery. Apparently, they were first used in Spain, and then brought over to Berlin. They are called the Hexennägel, witch's nails." Rudolph stabbed the nail into Nadia's breast and into her heart. There was no pain at first, just a sudden sensation that her heart had stopped. Then the contractions started, and a pain erupted in her chest that felt like a spool of barbed wire was unwinding inside her. She couldn't scream or breathe. Rudolph took his foot off her arm before leaning down next to her ear.

"You should have known this would happen. Now let's see how many nails we can get into you before your spirit vanishes," said Rudolph, pulling out another black nail. The first nail made her want to die. She didn't know what would happen with another.

With a desperate swing, she slammed the blood dart at Rudolph, but only managed to hit his battery pack. The machine sizzled and cracked as black electricity danced over the pair. Rudolph began to flicker, and when he spoke, only the sound of radio static could be heard. He raised his hand with the nail ready to strike down on Nadia. Nadia pulled the barb from the pack its prongs having dug into the machinery and pulled out sparking cables and globs of oil, causing Rudolph to vanish in a haze of static. The mud sucked her down and dropped her back into her body.

She fell over, completely exhausted, her body numb and cold. She was soaking wet with sweat. Her stomach growled in pain. Her gut felt like it was in knots, and a ravenous hunger overcame her, combined with a wave of exhausting apathy. That left her unable to move. It was nighttime, and the fire had gone out. Fatigue and exhaustion overcame Nadia. She was emotionally drained and left miserable. Too tired to weep, too drained to move, she just curled up where she was and slept.

17
The Muddy Season

A wet paw pressed against Nadia's face, pushing her out of her sleep, waking her to the oppressive cold, out of a world of frantic dreams. She tried to wriggle away from it and tried to ignore the persistent pawing.

"Dasha, leave me alone," moaned Nadia. She was stiff, and cold mud stuck to her long hair. Her hands were numb, and she was unbearable hungry.

"Wake up, lazy bones, I'm utterly miserable. It's time to go," said Dasha. She could feel his weight as he stood on her, leaving muddy footprints on her face. Nadia tried to ignore him, but he kept pestering her. She sat up, her injuries screaming for a moment before receding to a dull roar. Her neck and back were tight knots. It was hard to focus on one specific ache.

It was still raining. Rain had drowned the fire and liquified the floor of her small mud hut. It clung to Nadia's clothes and boots. It covered her rifle and bag. It was like she brought the mud from the spirit realm with her. But her world was plenty muddy without that other world's assistance. A growl erupted from her stomach, which tightened in pain. She pulled out a can of beets and opened it. She ate the rich red beets with her hands. They tasted of pulpy vinegar, and the sticky red juices popped against the grey light.

"Wow, you are wolfing those down. At least I don't have to pester you about it," said Dasha, nibbling on a bird he must have caught before waking her up. She finished off the can by drinking the juice. She threw the can aside and pulled open another can of beets. "Two for breakfast?"

"Yes, Dasha, two for breakfast," she said, devouring the contents. The juice was cold, and the beets burst with vinegar as she bit into them. She forced herself to slow as the beets got caught in her throat. She drained her canteen of water. She was still hungry after eating, but with only two cans of beets left, it was not a good plan to eat them. She didn't know when she would get another chance to supply herself with canned food. After eating, she laid back down in the mud. She wanted desperately to go back to sleep. She wanted to close her eyes and forget the muddy world and the violence in it.

"Hey, lazy bones, are we going or not?" asked Dasha, licking his chops.

"You can if you want," said Nadia. "I think I should get some more sleep."

"It's already midday, miss sleeps in mud," replied the cat. He climbed on her once again. He was leaving muddy footprints on the few patches of her clothes not already covered in wet mud.

"I'm sorry I just need a few more hours, away from all this wet," replied Nadia, resting her face in her arm.

"Sleeping won't get you away from the cold and mud. If anything, it's going to make you even colder if you keep laying on the ground like that," said Dasha.

"I don't care," said Nadia, mumbling. Dasha sat on top of Nadia for a moment. He moved up to her head and sniffed her. His whiskers wiggled as they dripped with damp.

"Nadia are you alright?" asked Dasha. There were several moments where all that could be heard was the rain.

"No," replied Nadia after a while. Adjusting her head, she looked outside at the grey rain and birch wood. The green of the undergrowth was muted by the pale sky, causing it to blur with the rest of the scenery. "He attacked me last night."

"Who did?" asked Dasha. "I was here with you the entire time you were doing your witch business in the other world."

"Rudolph Becker. He attacked me in the spirit world," said Nadia. Her stomach cramped up. She usually didn't eat so much, eating maybe a can of food a day, with half a can in the morning and the other half throughout the day. With maybe some wild nuts to snack on. The sudden filling of her stomach hurt.

"Oh," said Dasha. "I take it you won?"

"I didn't lose," said Nadia. "Yet fighting him in that place was exhausting and painful. He was so dangerous, so corrosive, I felt myself becoming undone as I fought him. Felt myself becoming something different. The rage and anger and hate I felt in that place. It overwhelmed me. I can barely recognize the woman in that strange place. But I'm that woman. When did I become her? I can barely recognize myself anymore. Two months ago, I was a nobody. I was helping on the communal farms, while avoiding the attention of people who both hated and despised me. But I was also with a loving family, making a broom in secret." Nadia pulled herself up and pulled Dasha in, scratching his head. He was very wet from the rain and mud. Nadia cast a quick spell to dry him off. He instantly puffed out, all his hair standing on end.

"Mraa! Next time tell me when you're going to do that. It feels so weird." Nadia petted the cat, flattening out his fur, running her hand along his back to the tip of his tail.

"Sorry. I don't even feel like a woman. I look like a mess. I always feel dirty and ugly. Who could ever love a creature that looks like me? I know that's probably not important right now, with the war and everything. All the same I hate it. I even stopped having my woman's times. My cycle was like a watch. Now it's just vanished. Like I regressed back into a little girl. I don't feel like a witch, or a woman, or even Nadia. This war has transformed me into some other animal that bears Nadia's likeness. Everything feels so strange. I don't know what to do," she said, having pulled Dasha close. "That scares me, more than the sound of gunfire, more than the fascist horde, more than any bit of dark magic that pierces my flesh or spirit. I'm afraid of what I'm becoming. I'm afraid of what this world, and what this war, is making me become."

"My little kitten is growing up," Dasha said, snuggling up against her face.

"I'm older than you by quite a few years," said Nadia as Dasha put a paw on Nadia's mouth.

"It's not the length of time, it's how you use it," he said, "I know what you are feeling right now."

"No, you don't."

"It's true. I wasn't always Dasha the tomcat, who prowled around stealing morsels from unwary townsfolk and seducing all the lady cats about town. I was once a barn cat. After ten weeks of life with my mother and brothers and sisters, I was yanked out and thrown into a barn. If I wanted to sleep, I had the barn. If I wanted to eat, I had to hunt. I had to learn quickly, and I did. I got good at it. If I hadn't, I wouldn't be here yammering about it with you. I went two winters living like that. Then they tore the barn down. I don't know why they did. I was left destitute. So, I took my skills on the road.

"I hunted where I could, in fields, in city streets and eventually I found myself on a train. Horrible contraptions they are, so noisy. I rode who knows how far. I didn't dare jump off, so I rode that train until it finally stopped. I ran out as fast as I could, avoiding the brute of a dog they used to hunt up stowaways. It was then I found myself in your town."

"I could have sworn you were a local cat," said Nadia, feeling sheepish that she didn't know this fact about her friend.

"Shows what you know. Anyway, I started carving a place for myself. All the cats of the town were house cats, never worked a day in their life. They didn't know how to tussle like I could. So, it was quite easy to carve a place for myself as the town's hooligan cat. If you asked me when I was a kitten if I could ever see myself outside of the barn, I would have told you to go jump in a pond. When there was no more barn, I learned new things, I had to change if I was going to survive. It was the skills I learned in the barn that helped me survive. But it was my life after the barn that made me the dashing rogue that extorts fish from a young, naive witch. Which I have yet to see, by the way. My point being is that you are still you, it's just you are building on an existing foundation. Growing your claws, as a cat would say."

"Thank you, Dasha, I think I needed to hear that," said Nadia. She still felt terrible, but at least she didn't want to wallow in the mud any longer. "Let's get packed up and get going, we are going to have to cross the border if we want to get to Grandmother's Forest."

274

"You're the one who needs to pack up," said Dasha, swishing his tail back and forth. "I have a bird I need to finish."

Nadia put her friend down and began scooping up her supplies. She drank a potion made of nut oil and moss that warmed and rejuvenated her tired limbs. Nadia could feel the magic of the drink spreading through her chest and body like warm tea.

Then once Dasha got himself ready for travel, the two took off into the rain. Nadia had indeed slept through most of the day, and the daylight was thinning. Even so, she flew fast over the muddy steppe northward. From the air, the roads looked like trenches, carved up with jagged trowels. Veins of running water sliced through the mud creating small streams that would be gone next week replaced by a new formation of streams. The mud adjusted like the tides of the sea. Little fighting was done as all the major German offensives had ground to a halt. The mud sucked up all the momentum, leaving only local battalions battling it out here and there. Even so, she flew across large swaths of no man's land as the Nazis and the Red Army exchanged artillery shells and gunfire, while snipers dueled for optimal ground. The land between the armies became a strange, cratered landscape that reminded Nadia of a sea of broken cups.

She flew by villages turned to cinders, the black and grey ash mixing with the mud to look like a cigarette burn on the ground from overhead. Huge trenches were carved out next to them. She dared not go down there, knowing the kind of horrors she would see up close. So, she flew northward, tightly gripping the rifles barrel.

It was uncomfortable to fly so long. The weather changed from rain to a light snow, still warm enough to not stick to the ground and adding to the morass of mud that was now freezing. It was so cold that Nadia couldn't bear to fly for much longer, and she touched down in an empty battlefield as hundreds of birds dined on the bodies of the numerous Soviet and Nazi dead.

"Why are we stopping?" Dasha asked as Nadia's feet sank into the mud.

"Because I ache everywhere and can barely keep warm. These potions may keep me from getting colds or freezing to death. But I still feel the chill, unlike you, who's curled up in a cozy bag and your fur."

"I'm plenty cold in here. Now let me out, I want to stretch as well."

Soon the pair were walking the battlefield, stretching their legs. The field smelled of decaying flesh, as rotting bodies mixed with the smell of gun powder and burned gasoline. The ground had been turned red. The blood having mixed with the soil. The earth held an acrid stench, turning the land sour. Everything was poisoned with all the dead flesh. Nadia could tell that several soldiers had winter jackets while the Germans were still wearing their grey summer uniforms.

"Didn't they know that it was going to get cold in winter?" Dasha asked, sniffing the dead German, whose face had been mauled by a bullet. His eyes having liquefied, leaving empty sockets.

"I don't know. All my interactions with the Nazis have shown an utter disdain for the eastern people. They might have thought that they would have won already. How far did you walk to get here?" she said to the eyeless body. "How far did you have to go to die here?" said Nadia before spitting on the corpse.

"This place is gross, when are we going to get out of here?" asked Dasha.

"When I find a warmer jacket and hat, and if I'm lucky, a good pair of gloves. My ears and fingers have gone totally numb."

"You're not going to take clothes from a dead person, are you? It's weird enough that humans where the fur of dead things. But for some reason it just seems weirder."

"How so?" said Nadia, spotting a soldier who had been shot through the chest. Yet his ushanka was still intact. She pulled it off the man's head and cleaned it with a spell.

"Because it's like you're taking human fur. I don't know. I know the god of cats stole your fur. You got to work with what you can get."

"So, he is to blame for our lack of fur?" said Nadia, thankful that the spell got rid of that smell. She could already feel her ears warming up.

"That is the word in cat myth; you should have heard what the cat god did to the rabbit," said Dasha. Nadia pulled all the ammo she could from the soldiers she came across. There was precious little with some soldiers only getting a rifle and nothing else. Others weren't even that lucky, having only been given a clip of ammunition that they clutched in their hand when they died. She came across several pairs of men who had apparently fought over a rifle only to be gunned down by some Nazi soldier.

"What happened to the rabbits?" asked Nadia, not really listening as she scavenged.

"Rabbits used to have much longer legs. They were as tall as deer. The rabbit would mock the god of cats by leaping over him during the hunts, or when he slept. So, the god of cats swapped the rabbit's legs with deer. Now the god of cats can chase down the rabbit without it hopping over the cat, while the deer were always to boring to hunt with their stubby legs. So now the cat can hunt both and feel challenged."

"Do all cat myths involve changing the world to better suit cats?" asked Nadia, pulling the coat off a headless soldier. The body was rancid, and Nadia had to hold her nose as she unclothed the man.

"Don't all human myths do that?" asked the cat.

"Hands up!" shouted a young voice behind them. Nadia turned to see a young boy of about fourteen rising up from behind a mound of dead bodies.

"Dasha, why didn't you tell me someone was around?" whispered Nadia, raising her hand in the air, still clutching the coat.

"He was up-wind, and the bodies here are overwhelming," said Dasha.

"Put that coat down," said the boy. He was dressed in a Red Army uniform that was far too big for him. His head was shaved, and his aim was all over the place. Nadia dropped the coat, keeping her hands raised high. The rifle vibrated on her back as if itching for battle.

"You are now my prisoner," he said hesitantly.

"Am I now?" replied Nadia. "Am I to be taken to the children's brigade?"

"Don't laugh! All these things belong to the Soviet Liberation League. If anyone is found looting these things, they are to be taken captive," the boy stuttered, unused to the language that was obviously written by someone else.

"You're a partisan? It's okay, I'm a partisan too," replied Nadia, taking a few steps forward.

"No closer," shouted the boy as Nadia stopped.

"Nadia, what's our plan to get out of here?" Dasha asked.

"It's alright. The safety on that rifle is on, the bolt is twisted to the left. That boy is not shooting anything."

"What are you muttering?" the boy asked, stepping forward.

"I'm just consulting with my cat," said Nadia.

The boy looked perplexed for just a moment. "No tricks or lies. I have never seen you before, so you're not part of our movement. You are no partisan."

"It's true, I'm a partisan, I was made one only a little while ago," replied

Nadia.

"Oh yeah, which front are you apart of?" asked the boy.

"None, really. I guess you could say I'm the sole member of the witch's liberation army," said Nadia.

She then smiled for a moment, finding the idea humorous. The boy did not. His face turned to one of abject terror. Nadia suspected he was remembering all the strange and terrible tales of Baba Yaga and witches who eat little children who don't obey their parents. He pulled the trigger. Or tried to. Nadia sighed, dropped her arms, and advanced on the boy as he struggled with the rifle. Nadia pulled out her bayonet, walking right up to the boy who struggled to undo the safety on his rifle. Nadia pushed him down, making him fall into the snowy mud with a squelch. She put a foot on his rifle, pushing it into his chest.

"Nadia, you better not hurt that poor mixed up boy," cried Dasha, standing on a dead body.

"Just going to give him a scare. Give him a lesson," said Nadia, pointing the bayonet at his neck. He winced and closed his eyes and gritted his teeth.

"Make it quick." He winced as steam began to rise from his groin, and Nadia noticed that he had wet himself. She placed the tip of the bayonet on his cheek. He was breathing heavily. She made a small cut on the bone of his cheek before taking her foot off his chest.

"Come on, let's get you standing," she said, helping the boy to his feet. The boy didn't look her in the face as he pulled the rifle close to his chest. "Let this be a lesson about the proper use of your firearm." She then placed the bayonet on his shoulder. "Clean, and dry," she said, casting the twin spells to dry the boy's pants, and instantly the mud and urine vanished from his clothes.

"Does this mean I'm now your mortal servant? Or are you going to eat me?"

"Neither," replied Nadia, sheathing her bayonet. "I'm going to take my coat and leave if that's alright with the Soviet Liberation League," she said.

"I, I guess," he said. Nadia felt the boy had been adequately humiliated.

"How about this, you're out here collecting supplies, right?" The boy nodded. "Did you happen to find any paper, maybe a pen?"

"I have both on me. I was also writing down the names of any dog tags I found."

"Well, how about this? I can write several luck charms down, and you can say you haggled with a witch to get a hold of them in exchange for this hat and coat."

"I don't know if they will believe me," he replied.

"Hmmm, a very real possibility," she said. "Best keep them for yourself, and when you manage to survive where others perish, you could say you had the devil's luck. How about that?"

"I guess that will work."

She wrote the charms down and handed them back to the boy, remembering how the soldiers reacted.

"Cheer up, young soldier, you just had the blessing of the Night Witch."

She picked up her jacket and Dasha and took off into the sky.

"Why did you have to scare that boy?" asked Dasha as Nadia put her new jacket on. The jacket was frigid and stiff but began to slowly warm her.

"I don't know," she said. "I have had so many guns pointed at me that it has become depressingly familiar. If I were anyone else, that boy might not be alive right now. I just gave him a hard lesson that if he is going to live this violent life as a partisan, he would have to expect a violent end."

"You're lying," meowed Dasha. "I can smell it."

"Okay, I wanted to scare him, really scare him. I hate that everyone I meet out here is trying to kill me," said Nadia. "I'm tired of being terrified whenever I encounter someone else. Always wondering if they are going to try to kill me, or worse. I wanted to do the scaring for once. I wanted to be the frightening one. To not be the victim for once. Is that so wrong?"

"By victimizing others?" asked Dasha.

"Yes."

"Something has been different about you since you came out of the spirit realm," said Dasha.

"We talked about this already," said Nadia, starting to feel cozy within her new coat.

"Yes, now it is becoming apparent. I don't know if you would have cut a kid's face before. You would have reasoned with him or maybe flew away. Not teach him a hard lesson. So, I'm wondering if everything is alright?"

"No. everything is not alright. I don't know how it could be. I'm just so tired, Dasha. I just want a warm bed with clean sheets. I want to use a bathroom, a proper one. I want a warm bath to scrub off all the mud, dirt, and sweat. I want to cook a meal for my mother who is dead. I want to tell my little brother a bedtime story. I don't want to wonder if every person I meet is going to kill me. I'm tired of flying through freezing rain, looking for a group of women who might not accept me amongst them. I'm tired of hating so much, hating the men who have burned and murdered across our country. But they make it so easy to hate them. My own government is no less horrible, but if we kept our heads down and didn't make a fuss, I could have lived my life. Yet, I can't imagine ever going back to that life. To any of it. All I see is mud and cold. There is no such thing as an easy life anymore. It's all just feels so unbearable, but I know I have to. I have to because the only alternative is a quick end. If not by the Nazis, then someone else. I just want to rest."

Nadia had laid down on the rifle as they flew across the muddy landscape. The snow melted as it touched her numb skin. The ice crystals were so small and delicate they were destroyed by the much stronger heavy raindrops that fell with it.

"I'm sorry," said Dasha. "I know that it all seems so helpless, but we are getting so close to the forest. These witches you are going to meet in Grandmother's Forest must have answers."

"I hope so, Dasha," said Nadia.

18
Grandmother's Forest

Nothing more was said as they flew over the steppes and forests. Dasha occasionally tried to start conversations by talking about some terrain features or the types of fish he liked. Nadia mumbled short responses to these comments. After a while, Dasha curled up in the bag and fell asleep. Nadia was left alone with her thoughts and the howling wind as she flew in the slowly darkening sky, eventually flying by a sliver of red light that cut under the clouds as it sank into the horizon. The dark once again covered the landscape. Villages doused their lights and hid from the bombers and soldiers.

The Red Army and the Wehrmacht continued fighting, with plumes of explosions breaking up the landscape below. The two armies ground against each other like a pair of steel buzzsaws, sending sparks everywhere.

Nadia used quick peeks into the spirit world to find the ley lines that pulsed in that land to find her way. Eventually, she found a cluster of them, like the center of a spider web. *This must be Grandmother's Forest*, thought Nadia. She dropped speed and began to descend. Finding herself on the edge of the forests. She found a decent stick that could be made into a torch. She blew on the end, setting the branch alight as a torch that pushed back the darkness. Nadia's body was stiff as she raised her torch, each step sending shooting pains into her leg. She couldn't bear to fly any longer. Nadia pulled out her pistol and unclicked the safety as she moved through the dark. She had no idea what she would encounter out here, but she didn't want to be on the short end of a firefight.

"Are we there yet?" asked Dasha, yawning as he stuck his head out of the bag.

"Yes, but I have no idea what to expect out here. This is home to some powerful witches, and I have no idea where they could be. This forest could be massive, and I would never know exactly where they could be hiding."

"Maybe you could ask an animal or a tree," he yawned again.

"Smart cat," she replied, walking up to a large tree. "Excuse me, I was wondering if you knew where the Coven of the Ever-Shining Moon would be?" The tree groaned and cracked as a face began to form on its surface. Its eyebrows furrowed as it looked Nadia over.

"Outsiders do not belong here. Begone. You are not welcome in these woods," the tree groaned.

"Excuse me? I was invited here. Do you know what I had to do to get here?"

"I don't care, leave, Grandmother doesn't want you in her forest." The tree's face sank back into the wood. Nadia kicked the tree with her foot, only managing to stub her toe.

"Ow, rude tree," said Nadia.

"I guess it didn't go well?" asked Dasha.

"No, it didn't," said Nadia as she began to move deeper into the forest.

"Maybe you could do the stone trick, like when you first left the village?" said Dasha.

Nadia didn't have high hopes but brought the torch close to the ground, looking for any stones that might be sticking out of the soil. Most were part of various rock formations that either made up part of a hill or were so large that they jutted out of the ground. These rocks tended to not be so helpful and were difficult to wake. The smaller rocks tended to be easier to rouse, and these were apparently hard to find. Dasha helped by searching in the undergrowth, his vision more accustomed to the night.

"Hey, I found one!" he chirped. Nadia trudged over, her feet squishing in the mud. She pushed the undergrowth aside while keeping her torch high, so it casts its orange light over the spot. Sure enough, there was a rock sitting in the mud. Nadia reached down and grasped the tiny stone. She found only a glob of mud. The stone had vanished as if it sank straight into the earth.

"What? Where did it go?" Nadia asked.

"It doesn't want to help you, outsider," said a tree, its face growing out of the bark. "You should leave before the shrikes find you."

"I'm not leaving," replied Nadia, wiping the mud on the bark of the tree. "What are these shrikes anyway? I doubt they could be worse than a Thule sorcerer or German tank."

"There is much you don't know, little witch. Come back in ten years and maybe then you will be worthy of entering Grandmother's Forest," said another tree.

"What are they saying? They are just making those weird groaning noises to me," said Dasha. His tail swished in the undergrowth.

"They are saying we are not wanted. Well, I don't plan to run," said Nadia as they trudged away from that cluster of trees. "We will get no help from the trees. They are terrible gossips, at least amongst each other."

"Well, are they threatening us in any way?" said Dasha with a meow of concern.

"No but they alluded to some sort of danger, and something called a shrike might come and find us," said Nadia. Something caught her eye in the distance hanging from the trees.

"Do you see what those things in the trees are?" asked Nadia.

"Yes, but you aren't going to like it."

The pair moved forward for a closer look. Nadia had noticed that rain had stopped, as well as the wind, making the strange objects in the darkness ominous. She came close enough. She couldn't help letting out a small gasp. A skinless deer head had been nailed to a tree with dozens of skinned human faces nailed to the tree's trunk. Some had the texture of leather, while others looked shiny and wet. They covered the tree, rising high in the branches.

Overhead, hanging from the leafless limbs of the tree, were long ropes of intestines. Hearts impaled on tree limbs; a whole sheet of dripping human skin was draped on a branch.

"I think we should leave," said Dasha. "I don't smell or hear any animals about."

"Yeah, we should definitely go," said Nadia, walking past the tree and heading deeper into the forest.

"What in the cat god's nine tails was that?" asked Dasha. "Was it a human that did that? I know humans do strange and terrible stuff to animals and humans alike."

"It wasn't fascist handiwork, if that's what you're asking, or Soviet.

Both of those tend to be pretty direct. Shoot, burn, stab, hang. That's how they deal with people. This is something different, a carefully crafted scene of horror. It's almost as if someone wanted it to be seen," said Nadia.

"Like a warning," asked Dasha.

"Or a monument," replied Nadia.

"Hey," said Dasha after several minutes of quiet. "Can I ride on your shoulder? You know, so we don't get lost."

"Yeah," said Nadia, picking up the cat and placing him on her shoulder. "So, do you know what a shrike is?"

"It's a bird," said Dasha. "Tasty enough, but they are a hunter of an unusual sort."

"How so?"

"When a shrike catches its prey, it will find some thorny bush or branch and impale it on some thorns. It will then eat the skewered prey. They will do this with bugs and mice. I always knew when one was around whenever I found their impaled prey on a barbed wire fence," said Dasha, with nervous chirps.

"The tree said that we might draw the attention of the shrikes, and I don't think he was referring to a bird," said Nadia.

"Do you think these shrikes are the ones that made the tree of body parts?"

"I don't know. Maybe. Regardless, I don't want to meet whatever made that display."

The forest had become oppressively dark. The torch offered little light, leaving Nadia in a pool of orange inside a sea of ink-black night.

From the darkness, a gaunt cough erupted like a groan of pain siphoned through a trumpet. A consecutive whooping followed. Nadia went stiff as a board.

"What was that?" asked Dasha. In the distance, the sound continued in response.

"I don't know," said Nadia, raising the pistol up. "Let's keep moving." In the night air, breaking the silence were the coughing cries. Nadia picked up her pace, tromping through the undergrowth as quickly as she could. It moved closer in the darkness, at times sounding kilometers away or just out of torchlight. "I think we are being followed," said Nadia.

"It's that torch you have, it's probably attracting every spooky apparition in these forests," said Dasha.

"I think you're right, but I would rather have a ready source of fire, just in case," said Nadia. She moved away from the mysterious cries in the woods. The trees seemed to close in on her. She was left with game trails and tightly packed trees that hemmed her in from the growing entities at her back.

"Nadia, move faster, I think I can smell them," said Dasha with a high-pitched yowl. Nadia turned and pointed the gun into the darkness. Beyond the torchlight, she could hear panting. Nadia fired her pistol, the crack of the round echoing throughout the forest. Something in the night howled like a deer that had been injured. Several other howls erupted in the distance in response to the apparent pain of the unseen creature. A pair of eyes could be seen that were pearl white and glowed with the luminescence of the moon. Nothing was comforting about the shine in those eyes.

Another pair joined the first. Then a third. Then they started moving toward Nadia. The creatures coughed and howled in unison. Nadia felt like she was being hunted, like a hare chased by a pack of wolves. She ran as fast as she could. Thankfully, the earth started to harden and was absent of any mud. The trees got thinner as her path narrowed in front of her. The trail narrowed to a point where she had to turn to the side to move forward. All the while, the sounds of whatever was in the dark grew closer. She heard the clack of antlers as they scraped against the narrow trees. Nadia could hear the scraping of claws against wood and the splintering of trees. Nadia didn't look back, instead choosing to navigate her way through the tight tangle of trees that seemed to grab at her clothes and straps. Then it happened. She ran into a pair of trees that were almost too close to pass through.

"What are you waiting for? Keep going!" yowled Dasha. Nadia pushed herself forward between the pair of trees that blocked her path. The torch lit up a clearing. If she could just get out of these trees, she would be free. She shoved herself inside, pushing her body through the hole. She saw those eyes moving closer. Dozens of them now, all pressing through the grove of trees. She fired her pistol three times into the mass of eyes. The response was a howl of pain, slowing those creatures long enough that she could get her body through. Something yanked her back as she made it past the pair of trees. She found that the rifle had been caught at an angle and with the strap holding her back.

One of the creatures advanced to the edge of the torchlight. Dasha yowled in terror upon seeing the ghastly visage of what perused them. Nadia had to stifle a cry in terror as the beast moved toward her. The creature had the head of a skinned deer, with glass claws attached to boney hands, and a pair of large antlers with dangling, bloody felt. Dozens of animals were impaled on the tips of the protruding bone. Human faces were stretched between the antlers' prongs. Its gargled cry was followed by a coughing whoop as it moved on her from almost a meter away. Nadia unloaded the remaining bullets into the creature. It was hard to miss at this range, especially when aiming at the center of its mass covered in strips of skin, meant to look like feathers. The creature recoiled and screeched, its eyes vanishing, growing dim as it collapsed. It was quickly replaced by another creature covered in the same grisly trophies as the first. Nadia unhooked the rifle as the monster lunged at her.

Nadia fell flat on her back, hitting the hard earth. She watched as the creature stuck its arm through the gap of the trees, desperately clawing at Nadia. The creature then stopped and examined the two trees blocking its movement. The creature began to push the twin trees apart so they could fit between the gaps. Such monstrous strength would certainly tear her to pieces. Unslinging the rifle from her back, she quickly twisted the safety off and took aim at the creature. The rifle corrected her aim when she pulled the trigger, jerking upward away from the creature's chest. The deer head exploded, throwing antlers and bone outward.

The rifle cocked back on its own, chambering the next round. The creature, absent a skull, was pulled back into the dark. There was a cry followed by the sound of snapping bone and tearing flesh. Nadia pointed at the gap with her rifle, finding that there was no further attack for the moment. She reloaded her pistol and pulled a grenade from her satchel. Nadia pulled the pin and threw it into the dark. She picked up the torch as she ran away from the explosion.

"Dasha, get down," she yelled, having lost track of him when she fell. She threw herself to the ground, the impact sending jarring pain through her body, especially the injured shoulder and leg. She hissed in pain, but that was soon forgotten by the grenade's concussive bang. A howl of pain came from the dark, followed by the coughing whoops of the antlered beasts. The injured monster screamed in the dark while Nadia pulled herself up, the tormented screaming clawing in her ears. The scream was halted suddenly as something impacted the injured beast in the dark. A choking gurgle was met with the snapping and tearing of flesh followed by the sound of crunching, like something biting the head of a chicken. Nadia raised the torch high, thankful it didn't set the undergrowth alight.

"Dasha, where are you?" whispered Nadia. The rifle then hopped out of her hand, floating in the air while scanning for monsters. She pulled out her pistol once again, keeping her eyes open for any oncoming attacker.

"Over here," cried Dasha. Nadia followed his voice to the edge of the clearing, where she found an opposing wall of trees. "We're trapped! Hemmed in at all sides."

"What do you mean trapped?"

"The trees made a perfect circle around us."

"Are there any gaps I can squeeze through?" asked Nadia, listening to the skirmish of rustling at the tree's edge while dozens of pairs of eyes looked on her.

"There isn't even a gap I could squeeze through. It feels like we were herded into this place," said Dasha.

"I think you're right," said Nadia. "I think these things, these shrikes, are smarter than they look. But they are so vicious. I think they are eating their own fallen."

"Oh, they are. If you could see what I could your hair would turn white," he replied.

"I can barely see anything with this flame. Maybe we should just fly out of here, come back in daylight."

"I like this idea, let's go," said Dasha, hopping into Nadia's arms.

The rifle moved down so Nadia could mount it. With a quick kick, they shot up in the air. Before they could get any distance up, they found the branches of the trees had been cut into a ceiling of needle point thorns. There were hundreds of birds and animals impaled on the long branches. It took all of Nadia's energy to pull back on the rifle to keep her and Dasha from adding to those spikes. Unfortunately, she lost her balance when she pulled back, causing her to fall. She exhaled the spell that would catch her fall, and she and Dasha landed on a cushion of air, before dropping back to earth.

"A canopy of thorns. We really are trapped," panted Nadia.

"What are we going to do?" asked Dasha, his tail puffed out and his back arched.

"We have no choice but to fight these creatures. But I'm going to need a bit of your fur so I can better see them. Then I can make a ward."

"Well, do it quickly, they are starting to get bored with what is left of the fallen shrikes," said Dasha. Nadia reached down and plucked a pinch of fur from Dasha's back, the cat swearing as she did so. The rifle fired on its own, making Nadia jump. It cocked itself as a shrike scrambled into the clearing. Nadia stuffed the piece of fur into her mouth and swallowed it in one gulp.

"Eyes of the night," she whispered, shutting her eyes. When she opened her lids, the world had turned to grey and white. Darkness became visible, and she could clearly see the monsters that menaced her. She pulled another grenade out and threw it into the nearest clump of shrikes in the tree. They scurried away from the fist-sized explosive, but a shrike was shredded from the concussive force. Whenever a shrike fell, two or three of their fellows would pounce and begin tearing the creature limb from limb.

Nadia pulled her bayonet out and placed the torch on the ground. She dug the bayonet in the earth and began to form a circle. The rifle shot any of the shrikes that got into the clearing.

"Nadia, can you hurry it up? They are starting to get past the wall of trees."

"I'm going as fast as I can," mumbled Nadia as she had to stop to reload the rifle or throw a grenade into the monsters' midst. Nadia gritted her teeth, making the proper symbols in the proper arrangement. She winced whenever the rifle fired an unexpected shot.

"Behind us," shouted Dasha. Nadia turned to find one of the shrikes had gotten through the wooden wall on the other side of the clearing, having pushed the pair of trees aside like window curtains. Nadia pointed the pistol and began to pull the trigger in rapid succession. The pistol bucking in her hand with each shot. The creature collapsed at her feet. A lucky round cracked its skull. None of the body shots seemed to do anything to these beasts except when it hit the skulls—then they fell like everything else.

A gurgling cough came from the breach that the shrike had made as two more of the creatures stepped into the clearing. The rifle killed the first that jumped in, its head exploding with a pinpoint shot. The rifle opened its bolt to signal that it was out of ammunition. Her pistol had no more ammo, and it would take too long to prime a grenade.

She picked up the torch, brandishing it at the creatures, who recoiled from the flame. But more began to gather. As many as eight had climbed through the hole, bolstering their numbers. Nadia felt her breath quicken in her chest as she watched the monsters attempting to surround her. She couldn't allow that. Nadia had an idea but didn't know if it would work. Nadia thought of the same principle that allowed her to light a fire with an ignition spell. She wondered if she could amplify it. Nadia took a deep breath and summoned the southern wind in her lungs. She would use it to carry the flame.

Nadia exhaled on the torch; a great river of flame shot out, engulfing the shrikes. Their gargling, coughing screams were only outmatched by the woosh of flame that erupted from Nadia's chest. The smell of burning hair and skin filled the air as the creatures burned like dry wood. The flame clung to them as they thrashed about. The momentum of the creatures was halted for a moment, but more kept climbing through the breach. Nadia took the extra moment to finish the circle on the ground.

"Alright, I'm done!" shouted Nadia. She didn't know if she could summon the southern wind again as it left her gasping for air afterward. The shrikes ran about, burning bodies illuminating the night, casting flickering shadows on the trees. All the while more gaps were created in the walls of the clearing that the shrikes entered from. They were relentless and so numerous that she was now utterly surrounded. With growing numbers, their fear of fire dwindled as they skulked between the piles of burning abominations. Nadia gripped the blade of the bayonet as tightly as she could, then pulled outward. The cut was both painful and quickly forgotten as the menacing shrikes advanced on her. She then squeezed her fist, letting the blood drop to the earth.

"I bring down this circle of protection to shield me from malignant spirits that skulk in the dark. With my blood as offering, I bring this circle alive. Let it be my shield. Let it be my protection and repel that which is not of this world."

The shrikes howled as they flexed their glass claws as if they had realized what Nadia had done. They charged in reckless abandon. Their claws outstretched to grasp Nadia. To rip her to pieces and skin flesh and face.

"Repel!" shouted Nadia.

The sound of birds hitting glass filled the clearing as the shrikes slammed into an invisible barrier that ignited the creatures' flesh with cold white fire. The creatures began to crumble, the fire consuming them, their limbs turning into white ash. The monsters that had charged collapsed into piles of white ash. The circle at her feet glowed with the light of a full moon. From these runes, a low reverberating hum of a bell could be heard. The remaining shrikes kept their distance. A tiny ripple of light pulsed out of the circle, and the shrikes retreated from this slow-moving wave of dim light, back to the gaps in the trees. They pushed and clamored over each other to get away from the advancing ring. Those that couldn't squeeze through were consumed in the expanding ring and set alight with the white flame. They disintegrated like the other foolhardy shrikes that had attacked. Nadia, taking deep breaths, began to laugh.

"We did it, we are alive, Dasha!" she laughed, picking up that cat and squeezing him.

"For which I'm very grateful," replied Dasha. "But I don't think it's over just yet." He pointed with his paw at mound of the dead shrikes that had become a large pile of ash. A rumbling series of steps came from it with the snaping of trees. With her magical infused vision, she saw a towering creature pushing aside the trees like grass. It was easily the height of a chimney stack. Nadia reached into her bag and pulled out a fresh clip for her rifle and a her last grenade. She hadn't realized she had used so many of them. Between the battle with the fascists and her dealing with the smaller shrikes, she had burned through her stock of explosives.

She pulled the pin and threw it into the grove of trees before ducking down. The concussive blast sent ash everywhere. Looking up, Nadia could see the giant had not slowed. From its chest, a rumbling cough erupted from the creature raising its head skyward. The creature's eyes were pure white. It wore a cloak of skin made of a patchwork of creatures. Some deer, or bear, while other patches were of cow and human skin. Its curling, twisted antlers had dozens of impaled creatures, from squirrels and birds to dead soldiers and dogs.

"Is that a shrike?" asked Dasha.

"I hope not. It's the biggest creature I have ever seen," replied Nadia. "If it is a shrike, all we have to do is break that skull." Nadia took aim with the rifle for the center of the creature's eyes. When she pulled the trigger, the rifle sent painful reverberations into her injured shoulder. The creature seemed to flicker as if it turned into smoke. She quickly chambered the next round pulling the bolt back. She fired. Again, the creature flickered as if turning to smoke.

"What in the moon's name?"

"It's shifting!" yowled Dasha. The creature bent down and ripped one of the smaller trees out of the ground before smashing away any branches.

"It's what?" said Nadia firing again, trying to block out the various sources of pain. Her rifle was now slick with blood from the cut on her hand.

"Shifting! Only the most serious of cats can do it. It's when you transport your body into the spirit realm but leave your spirit behind. It's like the opposite of what you do," yowled Dasha. The creature plodded forward, holding the tree in its hand as it shouldered its way into the clearing.

"How are we supposed to stop it?"

"I don't know. I don't know of any cats that have actually achieved it," said Dasha. "At least he can't get us in the circle."

"Unless he hits us with that tree he is carrying," said Nadia picking up the torch, wincing as the bark rubbed against the cut on her hand.

"Well, don't get hit," said Dasha, running out of the circle away from the giant monster.

"Great advice," mumbled Nadia. The giant shrike was fully illuminated now by the piles of its burning kin. It raised the tree and swung it like a club, trying to knock Nadia out of the circle. Nadia, in response, jumped up while the rifle flew her out of danger of the massive tree. Flaming ash was thrown into the air with each swing, and Nadia was covered in dirt that stung her eyes. The distraction making her lose her grip, and she fell back to earth. Looking down, she could see that the circle was now broken. Her wayward fall disrupted the delicate lines of magic. The creature howled, tossing the tree aside, and with wide steps, advanced on Nadia. Nadia hoped she had enough breath in her lungs to blow another blast of flame from the torch.

Overhead, the rifle took careful shots at the giant shrike as it blinked into smoke before returning to physicality. Nadia grabbed the torch and brought it before her mouth. Inhaling, she was about to release the southern wind to cover this abomination in a hot flame. The creature was abominably fast. It darted out and smacked the torch out of her hand with a kick.

Nadia pointed the pistol at the creature's head and fired. The same flickering shadow form appeared, and Nadia dove through the creature's smoke. The creature turned around and gurgled, advancing on Nadia. Another shot from the rifle rang out over the clearing. The giant shrike reacted when the shot actually hit flesh. *Of course,* thought Nadia, *it can't avoid an attack it can't see.* Nadia also knew that the rifle had one more round in it.

"Shoot it again!" Nadia shouted.

The rifle complied and fired into the creature's back. The creature flickered as it turned to face the perceived attacker. The bullet passed through it and kicked up dirt into the air. Nadia took a moment to inhale and fill her breath up. With the southern wind in her lungs, she stood in front of a burning pile of one of the lesser shrikes. She then exhaled, and the wind carried the flame and covered the unaware shrike. It gave a guttural wail that echoed through the forest. It flickered into black smoke, but even in that other world, it still burned. As did her throat. The creature materialized with hot flames covering its back. It sank to all fours and charged Nadia. The witch tried to get out of the way, but a wayward swipe of the creature's giant clawed hand slammed into her. The claws sank into her padded coat, but a single claw cut into her skin. The force of the swipe sent her flying, colliding with the wall of trees. She bounced off the trees and fell into the earth. Her whole body was in pain after the impact, leaving her unable to move. She could see the creature hulking forward, its large shoulders bobbing as it moved in on the vulnerable Nadia. She did her best to lift her pistol and fire. She could hear Dasha from somewhere, yelling at her to get up. To not die. She pointed the pistol at the creature, aiming the best she could.

She pulled the trigger, feeling the gun click. Looking at the gun, she saw that a bullet had jammed. She let the gun go and sank her head in the dirt. This was it. She couldn't move. Given time and space, she might be able to put a spell together to stop the advancing monster. But battered and beaten, she could think of nothing. The creature's large hands gripped her. Its claws dug into her belly. It held her like a doll, bringing Nadia up to its face. Nadia could see the glow in the monster's eyes, and a gurgling rumble came from the beast's throat before it clicked its teeth together. It lifted her above its head, well above the ground. Dasha meowed in anguish below as he watched Nadia raised high over the shrike's antlered head. Nadia knew that the piercing of the antler would hurt. She could do nothing to stop it. The beast lowered her down. Then Nadia saw something out of a fairy tale.

A hut with chicken legs stood behind the creature, its chimney puffing smoke as the cabin bounced and bobbed. With a powerful kick, the hut struck the shrike into the wall of trees. Nadia fell to the ground, bouncing off the hard earth with a painful thud.

Looking up, Nadia could see the shrike turn to face the walking cottage. The creature gargled before lunging at the bulky house. It was met by a taloned foot that grabbed the shrike by its antlered head and slammed it into the earth. Nadia could barely keep her eyes open as she watched the pair battle in the clearing. Her eyes flickered, trying to stay open. Fatigue and blood loss proved too much as she faded. Her last image of the night was of Dasha sprinting toward her, pleading for her not to die. Nadia could do nothing but fade to unconsciousness.

19
The Eye of the Ever-Shining Moon

Nadia felt warmth for the first time in months. A warmth that covered her and weighed down her entire body. She knew she was in pain as she wavered in and out of consciousness. A distant pain separated by the gulf of unconsciousness. Her eyelids would only occasionally open to see firelight on Dasha's grey fur. A brief glimpse of a warm world before she faded back into a dreamscape of violence and fear. The real world was only breaths of fresh air before she was again submerged into the uncertainty of dreams.

She couldn't remember any of the events that happened while going in and out of sleep. But she remembered Rudolph. He sat in a chair watching her as she ran through a field of blood or was covered in a swarm of ants. He was there when lions tore her apart or when the fascists buried her alive. He was the doctor in her dream that had her tied down while he dissected her flesh before removing her eyes and limbs. Then she would wake up for no more than a minute as a foul-tasting slurry of bitter plant matter was pushed into her mouth with a hand that gently rubbed her throat, forcing her to swallow the foul paste. Then she would fall back into a dream. Some dreams were of her mother and brother. She dreamed of her father, who had come back. He whispered a secret that she couldn't remember. She was distracted by an army of soldiers that forced a rifle into her hands. She pleaded with them to let her go see her father that she hadn't seen in so many years. They pushed her into an open grave, and then shot her for treason.

She woke up.

Tears were running from her eyes. Tears from a quickly vanishing dream that shook her to her core. Her tears covered a warm goose feather pillow. She could see that she was in a bed of brightly colored checkered blankets with an intricate mosaic of reds, yellows, and blues. Beyond that was the grey Dasha, absent of mud and sleeping on her lap. The hut was filled with herbs and plants hanging from the roof, nailed to the walls, organized into small boxes were hundreds of plants from across the width and depth of the forest. The whole place smelled of wildflowers, mint, and firewood. At the center of it all was the white-haired witch she saw in the burning corona. Nadia was groggy and still unused to the comfort of a bed. She wanted to savor the feeling of being in a warm, safe place. Nadia said nothing as she watched the witch that for so long had only visited her in desperate moments. Whenever the woman turned to adjust herself, she instinctively closed her eyes. Making it seem as if she was still sleeping. Nadia knew she was prolonging the inevitable conversation with this strange woman. All of which was sabotaged by a growling stomach. The sound carried through the little cabin, over the crackling fire. The woman turned, and Nadia could hear her get up, walking over to her bed. A warm hand touched her head. It felt reassuring.

"I see that you are feeling much better. Your injuries kept you under for a while. It's been a long time since I've seen those kinds of injuries. A bullet had to be pulled out, and there were numerous cuts and bruises. Then there were the broken bones you received from the shrike. The scars of snapped bone on your arm. Knife wounds on your collar bone. Plenty of wooden splinters. How did you get so many injuries?" asked the woman.

Nadia opened her eyes. The woman was old, but not the ancient babushka hunched over with a cane. The witch had wrinkles, yet she seemed much younger in the right light.

"Can you sit up?" she asked. Nadia nodded and pulled herself up with great effort. Her body was stiff and her limbs heavy. Dasha had woken up with the jostling of the bed. His ears pricked up when he saw Nadia, and he hopped up and ran into Nadia's arms.

"Nadia!" he meowed, leaping up on his hind legs as he started licking her face. "I'm so glad you're alright. I was so worried that you would just lay there like a vegetable for the rest of your days," he said as Nadia began to scratch his neck.

"I assured Dasha that you where alright and simply needed time to recover. The magic would not allow you to fade into death."

"Where am I?" Nadia croaked.

"You are in my hut," said the woman, standing up and moving to the fire with a bubbling cauldron over it. She filled a bowl up with steaming liquid.

"Please, no more bitter medicine, I doubt I can take it," croaked Nadia.

"It's the most important medicine I know, chicken dumpling soup with paprika," said the woman. She handed the bowl to Nadia, who dug in immediately. Apparently, her deal with the spirit creature still had sway on her as she felt ravenous without the usual anxiety about saving the meal for later.

"It has been a week since I found you and the shrikes. I know you are hungry, but don't eat so fast. I did my best to give you porridge with your medicine, but you ate very little."

"It's very good. I don't know how to thank you. I don't even know who you are."

"Of course." She smiled. "We never had any time for introductions with our correspondence."

"I saw the chicken-legged hut. Are you Baba Yaga?" asked Nadia in a hushed tone.

"Goodness no," laughed the woman. "I'm a simple guardian of this hut; my name is Lydia. Witch of the hearth and forest. I have watched over this sacred place for many years. I'm the one who tends the groves of trees, reenforcing them with protective spells that deter outsiders from cutting these woods."

"So, you are the one that made those shrikes?" asked Nadia, wiping her mouth with her sleeve. She was wearing the dress and shirt that she had left her village in. Her coat was neatly folded with her pack by the bed.

"No, that is Esmeralda's handiwork, a sister of our coven," said Lydia, scratching Dasha's back and tail. His rump rose with the extra attention while Nadia's own hands were occupied with eating.

"The Coven of the Ever-Shining Moon?" asked Nadia.

"Yes."

"I have gone through so much to be here, you see. A witch named Anna said I was now a part of the coven," said Nadia in a rush of words. "I don't know if I would have even come here if the fascists hadn't pushed me here, and killed my mentor, and everyone else." She took a deep breath. "That is, I'm happy that I have some where to go, and I will do my best to help the coven in any way I can." Lydia saw that Nadia's bowl was now empty. She took it and returned it to the cauldron.

"I'm afraid you are not yet part of our coven," said Lydia.

"What? But I have nowhere else to go," said Nadia, getting out of bed. Her legs were wobbly as she stood up. "You can't just cast me out like yesterday's rubbish."

"I wasn't planning on it," replied the wizened witch. "But tradition demands that you are reviewed. It is an ironclad tradition. You are a prospect to our coven. One of our members feels you are capable and are worthy to be a member of our ranks. However, that remains to be seen with the rest of us. Now get dressed. The faster we get this process going, the better," said Lydia. As she headed to the door, she turned to look back at Nadia with a smile. "I, for one, am excited about your upcoming trials. The hearth has never been so persistent with anyone else," said Lydia before she left the hut.

"I like her," said Dasha, rolling around the bed. "She tended to you for three days straight making sure you were alright. Also, she had some very tasty deer meat."

"I bet she did," said Nadia, sitting back down on the bed, putting her hands on her face. "I have spent so many months just getting here I don't know what will happen if I fail this examination. It's like going into school and finding out you have a test to see if you know your numbers."

"I have never had to do that," said Dasha. "I wouldn't worry too much."

"I can't help it. If I fail this, what am I going to do? Where will I go? Do I join the army? Do I go further east to avoid the fascists as they continue marauding? What am I going to do if I fail?"

"You aren't going to fail. You are the most capable witch I know," said Dasha, purring on the bed as he rolled around on his back. His tail swished back and forth. Nadia couldn't help petting his exposed stomach.

"It feels too soon, though. I just want to go back to sleep. Maybe have a few days to collect myself, but apparently, I don't have time for that," sighed Nadia.

"I don't see why it has to be done so quickly."

"Me neither," said Nadia, leaving the brightly colored bed to get dressed.

The Red Army jacket had been cleaned and smelled of summer flowers. Her clothes from her village felt so constricting. So light and delicate, but the damage they had suffered had been repaired. Bullet holes were patched, and slashes had been sewn shut. The tapestry of violence she had endured was clear on her clothing. Violence made abundantly clear on her body. Savage and terrible injuries sat next to benign cuts. Lacerations from enemies stood out against the backdrop of her flesh, with the largest scars being on her arms and hands. Her hands, in particular, had impressive array of scars from the numerous times she cut her hand to power a spell. It wasn't long ago when she would only make the tiniest cuts on the sides of her palms to get a few droplets of blood. Those tiny marks had been obliterated by huge white slashes and a landscape of callouses that she never had, not even when she was doing hard labor for state work projects.

She didn't know when her delicate body had become as hard as wood. Didn't know when her mind had become a steel fortress, but she had changed. So, she dressed, put her stolen uniform on, and equipped all her weapons, ensuring they were loaded and safely stored. Her ammunition was low, and she had no more grenades. She was starting to feel under-equipped. Regardless, her bayonet was still sharp. So, fully clothed, and fully equipped, she picked Dasha up and left the hut.

"Why do I have to come? Can I stay in the warm hut, with the fire and the deer jerky?" whined the cat as he went limp in defiance.

"If I'm to be judged, I would like at least one friend by my side or on my shoulder," she said, taking a comprehensive view of where she was. The chicken hut was sitting down with a set of stairs held up by rope and pulleys. The stairs deployed so she could step down. The hut seemed to shift and with her exit, the stairs pulled up on their own.

The air was warm, much warmer than it should be. Much more akin to late summer than the middle of fall. High above, a full moon shone down on a massive clearing; there was no way that she slept long enough for another full moon to appear. But the full moon dominated the sky, pushing to the horizon with a galaxy of stars and comets. At the center of the massive clearing, ringed by towering ancient trees, was a huge metal disk in the shape of an eye.

Nadia couldn't tell what type of metal it was. Beside it, huddled around a fire, were three women. The first was Lydia. Another was clothed in a rippling purple cloak. The last one wore a black dress and shawl made of cobwebs. Nadia took slow steps, wishing that there was a sea of mud between her and them so she could delay this meeting. The witch in black broke off from the small group and marched toward her. She had a hurried walk that was still concerned with seeming graceful. The woman had black hair and skin as pale as a corpse. She carried a broom of withered wood. She moved in front of Nadia.

"Greetings, sister," said Nadia. The woman pursed her lips, furrowed her brow, and slapped Nadia in the face. Nadia was both astonished and infuriated.

"So, you are the one that made a mess of my shrikes. Any half-competent witch would know how to avoid them. All you had to do was carry a branch of prickle weed and they would have left you alone. But you and your blundering stirred them up and destroyed them. Do you have any idea how long it takes to bind a spirit to a physical construct?" she said, moving right into Nadia's face poking a finger in her chest.

"No, sister, I don't. My most humble apologies," said Nadia, wanting to be diplomatic, though every instinct told her to punch this woman in the mouth.

"Of course not," said the woman, grabbing Nadia by the upper arm and dragging her to the fire like a child. Nadia tried her best to shake off the woman's grasp, but her grip was shockingly firm. "Look at this," she hissed to the other two women. "Look at this. Is this the caliber of witch we want amongst our ranks? First the hot-headed Anna and now this wisp of a songbird."

"Get your hand off me," growled Nadia as she pulled her arm away. The woman in purple watched silently. Her cloak rippled softly while the taste of a charged battery surrounded her. Lydia, who sat on a log by the fire, poked it with an iron spike.

"The caliber of this illustrious coven is decreasing with each passing candidate. Some army brat learns a spell or two and thinks herself among equals. It is tearing me away from my important work, right when subjects are so plentiful."

"Do you not think our coven's work isn't worth your time, Esmeralda?" asked Lydia placing a small branch in the fire.

"Do not play those games with me, Lydia. You may have been selected to be the hearth bearer, but in many ways, you are still just a girl."

"Sister, must we go over this now?" sighed Lydia. "Your position as high crone is not under threat. Every one of our little number of witches knows the importance you bring to our gathering. Surely overseeing a prospect is a reasonable diversion."

Nadia was about to step in and start pleading her case when a gust of wind blew her backward. The purple-clad witch placed a finger to her lips. Seeing this, Nadia shook her head and stepped back.

"That's not the point. Our coven was composed of the most revered witches of any age. We can't just let in any peasant girl. Especially one reeking of Communist iconography."

"It is the age we live in. It will pass with the setting sun. As for the caliber of witches, not all who joined so long ago were considered illustrious, just humble witches looking for a place to belong. I remember both you and I were such know-nothing peasant girls."

"That was different, and you know it was. The pogroms made us especially skilled in in short amount of time," said Esmeralda.

"So, they have now. If what I see in the flame is true, the pogroms are even greater now than ever before," replied Lydia. Esmeralda spat.

"It would throw off our numbers; it was risky when Anna was invited. Too many more and we could draw the attention of the state." Esmeralda was pacing now.

"The state is too busy right now; that gives us a chance to restore our numbers. We used to be a coven of as many as twelve," said Lydia, standing up and going to Esmeralda. The white-haired woman clutched Esmeralda's hand before placing it on her own face.

"It brought to much attention to us. We are safer when we can hide in the shadows. Just the three of us," said Esmeralda.

"She has been recognized. Recognized by a member of our coven. We have our traditions. We cannot throw them away just for the chance at safety, we wouldn't be living. Only surviving. By keeping with our traditions, we thrive in the harshest of ages." The two touched foreheads, their hands intertwining.

"Alright, but I will not go easy on her. I will be upholding the strictest standards of our coven," said Esmeralda, stepping away.

"No one is asking you to do otherwise," replied Lydia, taking her place by the fire once again.

"Alright, farmgirl, as high crone I will begin by asking you about your pedigree, your training, and why you believe you should be accepted amongst our number. First off, declare yourself," said Esmeralda, circling Nadia, looking her over like a spider examining a captured insect.

"I'm Nadia Voloshyn. Called by some, the Night Witch," said Nadia as Esmeralda ran a finger over Nadia's rifle.

"I see you have enchanted your weapon to fly, how *modern*. Are you self-taught or did you have a mentor?" she asked, taking Nadia's hand, and examining it.

"The former witch Olivia Yosonivitch, known as the Mockingbird, who was murdered by the Thule sorcerer Rudolph Becker," replied Nadia. Esmeralda recoiled, while Lydia put her hand to her mouth. A crackling of electricity charged off the purple witch.

"You lie. There is no way a little sparrow such as yourself would ever be the Mockingbird's apprentice," hissed Esmeralda.

"It's true," said Nadia. "Until two months ago I was under Baba Olivia's tutelage, until the fascists of the German Reich came to her home and killed her." She had not expected to say that with such bitterness. Yet remembering Olivia gutted like an animal filled her with a shaking rage that burned her up inside.

"If true, then this fascist menace is even more potent a threat than I had ever imagined. The Mockingbird came out of the war and the ensuing revolutions covered in blood. Many powerful wizards met their end at her hands," said Esmeralda.

"A conversation must be had about this," said Lydia.

"Later," said the purple-clad witch. "We must continue."

"Quite right, Umbra," said Lydia poking the fire.

"Normally, this would be the place where we question you about your abilities. Your magical focus, but I'm being drawn to a very particular feature about you," said Esmeralda. As quick as a mantis, she plucked a hair from Nadia's silver lock.

"Ow!"

"Hush," replied Esmeralda. She stretched the hair up to the light of the fire, examining the strand. Esmeralda then ate it, felt it with her tongue before grimacing. She spat into the fire, turning the flame a deathly green.

"As I thought, you have been marked. You have used a death curse," said Esmeralda. The green flame silhouetted in emerald before it died down and was replaced with the warm glow of the hearth. "Explain yourself."

"I…it just happened," replied Nadia. All eyes were now centered on the strip that cut through her black hair like a river of silver. "When I was searching for you, I ran into a trio of soldiers, separated from their company. I would have rather not had any contact with them, but they had other ideas. I don't want to think too long on what those ideas were. One of them disagreed with the others and a fight broke out. I helped out the best way I could, so I filled one of the soldier's lungs with mud. I then fought off the other. It all happened so fast that I had little options, so I improvised a spell," replied Nadia. Esmeralda took several steps closer to Nadia. Far too close to the young witches liking.

"You improvised a killing spell. Right on the spot?" said the pale witch. Esmeralda clutched Nadia's chin. But Nadia pulled back from her touch.

"It appears we have a viper in our midst," said Esmeralda. "A witch who flies on a firearm, able improvise a death curse, and clever enough to track us down. But not clever enough to notice the nail in her spirit."

"Nail? What nail?" replied Nadia.

"The nail in your spirit. Some malicious spirit or sorcerer has pierced your soul with a witch's nail, an insidious dart, and you haven't even noticed."

"I fought a Thule sorcerer when I was in the spirit realm, if that's what you mean," replied Nadia.

"Now that nail as wheedled its way into your soul, like a parasite wriggling in your flesh. Dug in so deep that only the most extreme rituals will be able to remove that little piece of magic in your soul."

"I don't feel any different," said Nadia,

"Well, you are, we all see it as plain as day. Have you been feeling depressed, sleepy, out of sorts? Maybe more cruel or vicious?" asked Esmeralda.

"She has, now that you mention it," replied Dasha.

"See, even your familiar has noticed it," said Esmeralda.

"I thought you were on my side," Nadia hissed at Dasha.

"I am. It's just you have been acting strangely," replied the cat, whipping his tail in agitation. "It's not my fault."

"Save any side conversations for later," replied Lydia.

"Indeed, as high crone my assessment of this young witch is that she is reckless. She will use violence over other methods. Skilled violence, yes, but her inexperience has left her open to other attacks. That may prove dangerous to our coven. This witch is an inferno that will burn herself out. I don't know if she should be placed among our ranks. What say you, sisters?"

"I see a talented young witch used to violence in a dangerous world, learning as she goes," replied Lydia. "A most talented witch, though very inexperienced. She will require a firm hand to bring the best out of her. An experienced sisterhood that can make this young witch flower into something beautiful."

"And what say you, Umbra?" asked Esmeralda, pointing her broom at the purple-clad witch. Umbra stood, a wave of wind blowing off her as she did. The fire bent with the breeze. Umbra floated over the ground to Nadia before leaning forward.

"Was it worth it?" asked Umbra. Her voice was as soft as a light rain.

"Was what worth it?" asked Nadia, holding her ground as this laconic woman moved closer to her.

"The death curse. Do you feel it was worth it?" replied Umbra, meeting Nadia's eyes. Umbra's eyes were dark with glowing blue veins. Her hair was a curly tangle. Nadia felt her breath pulled from her chest like she was standing next to a bolt of lightning.

"I'm here, aren't I?" said Nadia. "No matter what else you may think of me, I'm alive." Umbra turned to the other two women. A warm gale washed over the small group.

"She is a survivor. We need survivors," said Umbra, taking her place around the fire.

"It seems that a vote has been cast. With two against my own, with the inclusion of Anna's nomination, this young witch may begin her trials." Esmeralda turned, placing a hand on her hip. "As high crone I now call you sister in waiting. You will go to each member of our coven and offer your

312

services to them by order of their rank within our sisterhood. They will in turn give you a trial that can be reasonably completed by the standards of our coven. There will be no stealing of the sun's hair, but neither will you be fetching mushrooms from the woods."

"I thought a coven was supposed to be a gathering of equal witches," asked Nadia.

"It is," replied Lydia. "But there are traditional positions of a spiritual nature that must be filled, and any organization must give way to some instance of hierarchical practicality. Especially with larger covens. So, you will first seek out Anna, then you will meet with Umbra, then Esmeralda, and finally myself," said Lydia. "In the future you may be called upon to issue a trial for a prospective witch. In this way we can judge the capabilities of new members. If at any point you are deemed unable to meet the requirements of our organization—"

"Then you will be cast out," interrupted Esmeralda. "Unable to return or seek application to our coven for another ten years."

"What?" replied Nadia. "How is that fair?"

"It is a way of seasoning a witch. Normally a witch is not asked to join a coven at such a young age, unless that coven is made up of younger witches. These are practices that engender self-reliance. With solitude, the world becomes your teacher. You will learn and have much to teach when you are finally admitted into a group."

"Olivia should have told you such things, then again, she had always been a secretive witch. A much better witch alone then as a teacher, if you are any judge of her capabilities." Said Esmeralda

"Say what you want about me, but I will not have you talk any more disrespect about the woman who taught me everything."

"Or you will what?" asked Esmeralda. "Will you silence me? Like one of those goose-stepping Communists? Make me vanish for speaking my mind? I'm free to express myself however I wish, and I won't be chastised for it."

"Esmeralda, please," said Lydia with a sigh. Esmeralda looked at her sister and then at Nadia. Her imperious glare softened for a moment.

"I suppose it is not prudent to speak ill of the dead, even if they are a brainless bunch," said Esmeralda. She returned to her place by the fire. "I suppose it is time we begin the ritual."

"What ritual?" asked Nadia.

"The ritual of recognition," said Lydia. "Come with us." She offered her hand to Nadia. Nadia paused for a moment before taking Lydia's hand. The three witches led Nadia to the edge of the giant metal disk. "Dasha may go no further, for he cannot be recognized in this space."

"Wherever I go, Dasha goes," said Nadia.

"It's okay, Nadia, I would rather stay out of the way of spooky witch things," he said, hopping off her shoulder.

"But…alright," replied Nadia.

"Leave your weapons as well as any stray symbols," said Esmeralda.

"No, I'm not leaving myself unarmed."

"She doesn't understand the basics of what's going on, does she?" scoffed Esmeralda.

"She will learn," replied Umbra.

"Nadia," said Lydia, squeezing her hand. "Right now, you are about to undergo a ritual of recognition. You must bring nothing with you to this event. This ritual is a declaration to the world. A confession of who you are. You must be stripped of any spiritual and martial trappings. To reveal your soul as pure and unspoiled as the moonlight. We have all undergone this ritual. Think of it as your stated intent to join the coven."

"But I have already done that! I have told you I want to join," said Nadia.

"Yes, but not to her," said Lydia, pointing to the Moon above. She then leaned in, stepping close to Nadia, who instinctually stepped away from the gentle witch.

"I sense that the trials you have undergone have left you guarded. Left you uncomfortable unless you have weapon within easy reach. The nail in your spirit must not help. But in this place, you have no need to fear. This is a sacred place, the heart of our coven's power. You can trust us to protect you, as in time we will trust you to protect us."

"I would rather not," whispered Nadia. Lydia took Nadia's hand and placed it on her cheek, before placing her hand on Nadia's.

"It is no easy thing to let your guard down. Not easy to let others see who you really are. But don't worry, whatever we see with in you I'm sure we will love the being that is you."

"What kind of ritual is this?" whispered Nadia.

"A ritual of seeing, so that we will know the caliber of the woman who seeks to be among us."

"I don't know if you will like what you see," said Nadia.

"Don't think such things. For she will love you no matter what," said Lydia, looking upward at the gargantuan moon. Nadia joined her. The Moon was huge and heavy, her light shown down on Nadia's face. As warm and comforting as daylight.

"Alright," said Nadia, "I will leave my things behind. But shouldn't Anna be a part of this?"

"It's alright, Anna has other obligations. Only the most senior members need be present."

Slowly Nadia placed her bag and pistol on the grass at her feet. She then gently placed her rifle on the ground with it. Finally, she discarded her coat. Without a word, Lydia took Nadia's hand and was led to the center of the great disk. A great eye was carved on its surface. She stood in the pupil as the other three witches formed a triangle at the edge of the iris. Nadia felt cold despite the warm metal-air within the clearing.

"We have gathered here as sisters of the Coven of the Ever-Shining Moon to cast our gaze on an outsider known as Nadia Voloshyn," said Lydia, taking precise steps. While her hands made strange shapes crossing fingers and making symbols.

"She has been seen by one of our own and comes before us now," said Esmeralda, mirroring the gestures of Lydia.

"Speak, outsider, what is your intent? Speak truthfully less you be rent asunder by our hands," said Umbra. Nadia didn't know if they would actually attack her. The words and movements were ceremonial. Even so, she hoped her answer was truthful. That it was what she really wanted.

"I seek admission into the Coven of the Ever-Shining Moon."

The three other witches moved and changed places.

"The outsider seeks admission," said the three women in unison. "Then let her be seen. We call upon our mother, our teacher, our guide. Come to us, Moon of the Earth. Let us know this outsider's spirit. Should she be a daemon, cast her out. But if she be friend, then show her as such."

All three women held out their hands, and a low resonating hum filled the air. From their hands, a pale moonlight gathered around them, forming an orb of light. These balls of light coalesced into a smaller version of the Moon.

The three women then began to sing, a high-pitched resonation that reminded Nadia of the opera that could occasionally be heard on the radio. These voices grew to a rising crescendo and merged into one resonate hum. The miniature moon floated toward Nadia and stopped above her head. All the hairs on Nadia's body stood up and shivers ran up Nadia's back and neck. The light from the miniature moon began to grow brighter. Soon it felt like the whole clearing was consumed with this pure blinding light. Nadia couldn't keep her eyes open and squeeze them shut. Something tugged at her gut, as though someone was pulling on her spirit like fishermen pulling on a line. The light was so bright that it burned through her eyelids.

"You may open your eyes," said a calm voice that sounded like rain in the desert. Nadia opened one eye, and then the tugging at her heart becoming more persistent. However, that was soon forgotten when she saw an elderly woman who glowed with lunar radiance.

"I see you are doing well, and you found what you were looking for," said the old woman. Nadia looked around and found that she was in the same place of absolute darkness that she met the Moon the first time. The old woman rocked back in a rocking chair while she knitted a shawl of shadows with a pair of large needles.

"Mother Moon?" said Nadia hesitantly. The woman smiled and nodded her head.

"Yes, it is me," she said, clicking her needles together.

"How did you get so old?" Nadia asked, kneeling down next to the elderly apparition.

"This is how I'm seen by them, that little circle of sisters who grew together so long ago. You should do something about that."

"About what?" said Nadia. The tugging at her chest had become even more persistent. The Moon took one of the long needles and pointed at Nadia's chest. Nadia looked down to see a swastika the size of a coin over her heart. It burned and sizzled, scorching the flesh around her skin. A small thread led from it out into the blackness of the void.

"When you were struck with that hateful little nail, the sorcerer marked you. Awful little man that one. With that sigil he can learn when you enter the spirit realm, he can examine your dreams and explore your memories. He is doing his best to reel you in right this instant. Yet as long as you are with me, you will be as safe as a bear cub with its mother," said the Moon. "Even so, you should deal with it as soon as you can. You won't be safe as long as you are on that man's line."

"I don't know how," said Nadia as she probed the edge of the mark. It stung like an electric shock when she touched it, the pain quickly vanishing.

"You will in time; you are quite the clever one. I'm proud of you."

"I don't feel so clever," said Nadia. "I feel like a cord that has been stretched for too long and with too much force. That I will split at any moment."

"But you don't," the Moon said as she stitched.

"But how long can I keep it up? I have barely made it to this point. If I fail these trials, I don't know if I can keep going for another ten years. How do I keep going?"

"One day at a time, my dear. I have seen terrible things you humans have done to one another. Yet they survived, and they didn't have half the skills and talent you do. I have no doubt of your capabilities or the strength you possess. I remember when you were just a small tulip among a bed of flowers. When that flower bed was set ablaze, you remained; a little singed admittedly, but you remained nonetheless."

"I survived by luck. I don't know how long I can rely on something so fickle," said Nadia.

"A little luck and a lot of capability can bring someone far. You will do fine on your tests. I have seen many capable witches in my time, and I know the really great ones at a glance. You have the strength to be a truly great witch, an important woman that will have her fingers on the threads of fate."

"What does that mean, Baba?"

"It means that the destinies of your world are like spinning plates, held precariously by the hands of giants. But a tiny mouse can upset the configuration, provided the mouse has the courage to risk the giant's wrath."

"You ask too much," said Nadia, resting her head on the Moon's lap as she looked out in the great nothing of shadow.

"I ask nothing. I'm merely telling you of the curious position you find yourself in. What you do is up to you," said the Moon. She placed a hand on Nadia's head. Her hand was oddly warm, yet it left a chill.

"There were many avenues of your destiny that you could have chosen. You chose the most interesting one, and the most difficult one by far. I see many moments in your coming years, many sad, difficult ones, but some truly joyous times. They must be fought for. They must be seized with both hands. Very few could envision the path before you now, let alone walk it. So, I will give you my blessing," said the Moon. She then stood up. This tiny lady who seemed to tower over Nadia leaned down and kissed Nadia on the forehead. "Now wherever you may go, I will be there with you."

Nadia wanted to respond, to thank the Moon for her reassurance, but she began to fall. Fall out of the spirit realm, past the vast menagerie of portents, symbols, and personifications, back into Grandmother's Forest. Her body caught hers, making her collapse to the earth.

Nadia was covered in sweat while her whole body shook. Her forehead felt like a white-hot blade had been pushed into her skull. She was freezing. Clouds of white smoke came out from her mouth.

"By the goddess," whispered Umbra.

"Impossible," hissed Esmeralda.

"Nadia, what have you done?" said Lydia, grabbing Nadia by the shoulders. Nadia's whole body shook.

"What do you mean?" asked Nadia, her teeth chattering.

"This!" shouted Esmeralda poking her forehead. Nadia touched her brow an area was tender.

"Is there something on my forehead?" said Nadia, looking at the three women. Esmeralda looked like she would burst with outrage, while Umbra and Lydia appeared to be in utter shock.

"Umbra, there is a small mirror in the hut. Will you please fetch it for me?" The purple-clad witch nodded before rising off the ground and gliding to the chicken-legged hut.

"As for you, let's get you to the fire. You look like you have just been pulled out of a frozen lake," said Lydia, helping Nadia to her feet.

For a moment, Nadia could barely walk, but with Lydia's help, she managed to stumble off the steel disk and sit down next to the fire. The waves of heat washed over her as Nadia watched into the crackling fire. Lydia left Nadia by the fire and returned to place Nadia's jacket over her shoulders. Umbra returned and handed a small mirror to Nadia. Nadia took the mirror and looked at her face in the reflection. On her forehead, glowing dimly, was the moon in miniature. It was full and glowed with a soft light.

"What did you see during the ritual?" Lydia asked, taking the mirror back.

"I went to the place where the Moon lives in the great field of shadows. There we spoke and she gave me her blessing," said Nadia.

"This must be some kind of trick, some ruse she has pulled to ingratiate herself among us," said Esmeralda. "Possibly a spy meant to pray on our omens."

"I'm no spy," shouted Nadia. "I'm tired of everyone assuming I'm a spy."

"What's all the fuss about?" Dasha asked, leaping onto Nadia's lap. "And why do you have a piece of the moon in your forehead?"

"Even the cat can recognize the goddess's blessing," said Umbra, stepping up to Nadia, taking her hand and kissing it.

"Stop that," Nadia said, pulling her hand away. "Will someone please tell me what is going on?"

"You have been marked by the Moon, and a piece of her has been imprinted on you," said Lydia.

"Is that what that is?" said Nadia. "She could have asked before doing that."

"Unbelievable, one ritual and she receives the Moon's blessing. I have spent my life trying to commune with our patron, and she brushes it off like it is nothing," said Esmeralda, now pacing.

"This isn't the first time I have spoken with her, you know," said Nadia. "Lydia was the one who showed me how."

"I thought you would get an omen to guide you on your journey. I never expected you to actually speak with our patron," said Lydia. Esmeralda sneered before turning and walking off. After a bit of distance away from the group, Esmeralda screamed.

"Did I do something wrong?" asked Nadia.

"You have done nothing wrong. It's just many of us spend our whole lives to get to the point where we can hold a few words with the Moon. The mark you were supposed to get would normally look like a small blotch on your skin," said Lydia, pulling up her sleeve. Nadia could see a patch of discolored skin in the shape of a moon's crescent.

"This is the sign of the Moon's acceptance of the applicant. Never before has a prospect come back with the blessing of the Moon in so powerful a form. Surely this means that she is a definitive member of the coven," said Umbra.

"What!" shouted Esmeralda, marching back to the fire. "As high crone I won't allow it. She must undergo the trials like all the witches who want to be members."

"Surely the goddess's blessing supersedes that?" said Umbra.

"I must side with Esmeralda on this," said Lydia.

"Thank you, I'm glad centuries of tradition haven't been thrown out the window over a farm girl," said Esmeralda.

"I'm right here," said Nadia.

"Don't think I haven't noticed. We need to converse about this. You stay put," said Esmeralda. The three other witches left the fire, went off a little way, and spoke in hushed tones.

"What do you think they are saying?" asked Dasha.

"I honestly couldn't say. I wish I had more of those dumplings. I feel so famished."

"I'm glad you have an appetite, especially after such a long recovery."

"I don't know how long it will last."

"That moon on your head is really weird."

"It's already causing problems. I'm going to have to cover it if I want to get any sleep at night. Why did it have to glow? So inconvenient."

"Don't knock it just yet," said Dasha. "You might not have to bump your toes in the dark ever again."

"I don't think that is what the Moon's blessing is supposed to provide."

"Says the woman who keeps stubbing her toes in the dark," yawned Dasha.

"We have come to a conclusion," replied Lydia, stepping back into the light of the fire. "You will seek out Anna the Red immediately and begin your trials with her."

"What's the rush?" asked Nadia, standing up.

"We wish to expedite this process somewhat," replied Lydia.

"You are not a full member of our coven and your presence requires reconsideration of our group's purpose," said Esmeralda.

"I don't understand," replied Nadia.

"It involves divining our futures, analyzing the portents and what our coven is meant to do. Your mark is a sure sign that maybe we should not be reclusive and that we need to be more a part of the surrounding world."

"These are private rituals," said Esmeralda. "Sacred acts that are for the coven's eyes only, not meant for outsiders, even ones who wish to join us."

"Well, do I have time to get supplies? I used up a lot to get here," said Nadia.

"Take what you wish from my hut, but you must leave here tonight," said Lydia.

"I can never have a moment's peace, can I?" sighed Nadia.

"Nor will you," said Umbra. "The blessing on your brow marks you as one meant for great things. I fear you will never have a moment's peace again."

"Fine, I guess I will get going."

"That would be best," replied Lydia. "I will be praying for your return and success in your trial with Anna the Red."

"As well as I," said Umbra.

"Don't waste this opportunity that you have been given," sneered Esmeralda.

Nadia left the fire and headed to the cabin with Dasha trailing behind. After collecting a bag full of supplies, the two jumped off to the sky, leaving the magically enchanted forest and returning to the world.

Part 3

20
Pomp of the Red Star

Moscow was suffering in November, as the entire city was turned into a fortress. This was no longer a city where people lived; it was now a citadel, and its inhabitants were its garrison. On Nadia's approach to the city, the surrounding countryside transformed from agricultural farmland to killing fields. An army of conscripted laborers dug massive trenches. The majority were women. With sheer force of muscle, several great rings grew around the city. The pits were so deep in some places that a whole house could be put at the bottom.

The Red Army dug in around roads and strategically vital crossings between these great moats of dirt. The defense was monumental in its scope and desperately thin, as these formations were hastily thrown together. Yet, as thin as it was, Nadia could see that it was hardening by the day. All the while vast army formations left Moscow, marching down the central rows to block the approaching enemy's advance.

Witch of the Winter Moon

To Nadia's surprise, she still found Moscow beautiful. It was a sprawling metropolis with tall buildings and wide boulevards. Statues of Lenin, Stalin, and Marx sat in the center of intersections, while people in their hundreds of thousands swarmed in and out of repurposed factories. Automobile shops worked on tanks instead of cars, chocolate factories made rations instead of sweets. A clock factory turned out bullets like grains of sand. Once a shining example of the socialist experiment, Moscow was now a weapon of war, aimed at the heart of the incoming Nazi threat.

Ever since she was a little girl, she wanted to see this shining city in the propaganda films and newspapers. This city of such ancient history was reinvented as a beacon of the future. Now as beautiful as it was, it seemed alien and deadly. The threat turned the inhabitants into prisoners. Nadia watched as soldiers went to every tenth apartment complex and pulled out the apartment administrator. They were lined up against a wall and shot. The men seeking to numb the world around them with alcohol were thrown against the wall and executed. Order and morality would be maintained under pain of death.

Nadia could do nothing to help these poor souls. As the machine of the state turned, it crushed those who didn't fall in line. There was only one drive in Moscow: the will to repel the invaders. To throw back the fascists that sought to destroy the life of the Soviet people. Any sentiment of peace, surrender, or humanity was crushed under the iron-shod heel of the state. Anyone opposed to the will of the people was lined up against the wall.

Nadia felt that the city was suffocating. As if a poison gas had filled the streets and everyone was desperately trying to breathe as they did their best to remain unnoticed. To obey was to live. Moscow was a dangerous place for a witch who was not part of the formal structure. She hid on rooftops and only moved about at nighttime, using the cover of darkness to avoid the commissars and military police.

Being a partisan witch out in the wilds of the Ukrainian and Russian steppe was one thing. It was quite different in the capital of a worldwide Communist Revolution. She had already had several close calls when the military police raided the roof she was sleeping on. She was startled awake when a soldier kicked the door to the roof open. She hastily jumped off the roof and hung on to the flying rifle beneath the building's edge. She hugged the wall in case any nosy soldiers decided to look over the side. Nadia became a very light sleeper in Moscow.

The only reason she was in the city was to meet with Anna the Red. It had taken Nadia the better part of the month to get in contact with Anna. Using birds to send messages, she tracked down Anna. She also traded luck charms to groups of soldiers to find out where she might be. It seemed that Anna the Red was everywhere. She fought with besieged peoples of Leningrad, bringing supplies to the northern city as the Nazis tried to starve out the inhabitants. The following week Anna was in the south, killing officers with hexes and bullets. She was leading counterattacks against the brunt of Nazi advances. Wherever they needed magical support, Anna was there.

Slowly, Nadia began to contact the battle-hardened witch. Birds would return with messages to meet in specific places, at specific times of the day. The information was usually a week out of date, and the window to meet up was missed. However, this dance of messages began to bear fruit. The windows shrunk, and soon they were only a day or two apart. Nadia wished that Anna would just stay in one place, but the army's rigors kept her sister moving. However, these missed meetups were not in vain. Small gifts were left behind. A lock of red hair, a ration can or strip of ammunition were left in place of the witch. Whatever Anna could spare. So, for much of October and early November, the pair were drawn inexorably to Moscow. The city was a vortex that sucked in the best troops it could to man the defensive, and a magical witch was something you invariably wanted to keep close to the city.

It was on the seventh when the pair could finally get a chance to meet up, on a building overlooking Red Square and the annual parade of the October Revolution. A strange twist of the old calendar made the parade fall in November. Vast blocks of men marched with British-made guns from the Great War, looted from old storehouses and museums with only a single clip of ammunition in their weapons. The men paraded in front of the leaders of the Soviet Union before they marched straight to the front. Not even the Nazis' great invasion would stop this annual celebration. Yet, from where Nadia watched, she could see none of the mighty men who ruled her country. She could only see the mass of soldiers that marched out. Nadia and Dasha chewed on sausages and scraps as they watched the procession.

The blocks of soldiers became a rolling mass as they marched in unison. It was numbing watching the endless lines of soldiers. Their individual stories and struggles were rendered meaningless once they were in these great formations. Their passions, joys, and worries were erased underneath those brown coats and winter hats. Their faces might as well have been smooth porcelain from where Nadia was standing.

"Nadia is that you?" said a voice she hadn't heard in months. Nadia looked up to see Anna the Red floating above her on her broom. She was in her winter uniform now, the heavy overcoat replacing her tan summer uniform. She had a fur ushanka, and on her collar were several buttons made of gold.

The witch landed onto the rooftop, and Nadia could see that Anna the

Red had gone through much. Half her face was covered in scar tissue. Her hair that was once cropped had grown much longer, her red locks sticking out of the ushanka, and her smile had a missing tooth. Anna ran up and hugged Nadia. A warm embrace that she had not expected.

"My goodness, you have changed in such a short amount of time," said Anna, pulling back and looking at Nadia. Anna rested her broom on the ledge of the building. "I brought candy." She smiled. It was unsettling to Nadia to see the woman she thought so brave and gallant and beautiful become so scarred.

"My goodness, sister, what happened to you?" asked Nadia, sitting with Anna on the building's ledge.

"You like?" smiled Anna, shoving a handful of the blue wrapped candy into Nadia's hand. "I think it makes me look roguish; the men love it. They think it fits with their archetype of a witch."

"But what happened?" asked Nadia, clutching the handful of candy.

"Don't mind that, sister, it's a badge of honor. A mark of my resourcefulness. Now let me see your broom…wait, don't tell me you hitched a ride here? That's an almost nine-hundred-kilometer journey."

"Well, I did ride here, but not on a broom or train," said Nadia, pulling out her rifle.

"You enchanted a rifle? My, you are a clever one. I knew you were special after your first little demonstration in the field outside of your village. I still am trying to figure out that little hex you placed on that commissar's gun," said Anna, popping a piece of candy in her mouth. "Go on, eat, I have been saving these up since I found out you were looking for me. I'm going to feel like a pig if I eat them by myself."

Nadia shrugged and unwrapped a coffee-colored toffee. The candy was hard in her hand but softened as soon as she placed it in her mouth.

"Oh my goodness!" said Nadia as she chewed the candy.

"Do you like it?" Anna put a piece of candy in her own mouth, throwing the wrappers off the side of the building.

"It's so sweet! It almost hurts my mouth," said Nadia.

"More?"

"Please!"

Anna reached into her pockets and pulled out even more candy, stuffing it into Nadia's hand. These little morsels of sweetness were more beautiful than gold.

"So, you have met with the rest of the coven?" said Anna. "What do you think? Was it everything you imagined?

"I don't know what I expected. I'm pretty sure Esmeralda hates me," said Nadia. Dasha had hopped on the ledge and began to nuzzle her hand. His polite way of interrupting a conversation so he could get his head scratched.

"She is like that with everybody. I don't know, maybe it has something to do with being over four hundred years old," said Anna.

"Four hundred? There is no way she is even thirty, let alone four hundred," said Nadia, popping another toffee in her mouth.

"You flew here on a magic rifle; what is possible doesn't really matter as far as magic is concerned. Who knows how she is able to look so young?"

"Maybe a glamor, they are simple enough to put on objects, I guess it would be possible to put on a person."

"Hmm, figures. You really are quite the resourceful one; no doubt that is Olivia's doing. How is the Mockingbird? No doubt fighting the Germans like in the old days?"

"She is dead," said Nadia flatly, scratching Dasha behind the ears. "A

Thule sorcerer got her."

"Oh, I'm sorry," said Anna. "Did she take any down with her?"

"Yeah," said Nadia, "She took out a few of them." She remembered the stickmen in uniforms. The old cat hanging by a shoelace. The butchered remains of her mentor. The candy didn't taste as sweet anymore.

"That's good," said Anna. The pair fell silent for a moment. The continuous sound of marching could be heard behind them.

"The coven sent me to meet with you to begin my initiation," said Nadia.

"Ah, the trials," said Anna. Dasha had crossed over to Nadia and was sitting between the pair of witches, happy that he was getting attention from both.

"They are apparently going to be made very difficult," said Nadia.

"Well, they were no walk in the park when I did them. But I know you are capable."

"That's wonderful to hear. You should probably know something before we begin."

"What's that?" said Anna, her mouth full of toffee. Nadia pulled off her hat. Her black hair with a sliver of grey fell to her shoulders, revealing the glowing moon on her forehead. Anna licked her fingers, tossing another wrapper over the edge.

"Well, that's interesting. How did you get that?" asked Anna.

"You're not surprised? The others of the coven fell over themselves when they saw it," said Nadia. Anna leaned in as she chewed, reaching out with her hand.

"May I?" Nadia nodded in response as Anna touched the moon on Nadia's forehead. "Weird, it so cold. Well, I don't think this will have very much impact on what I want to do with you," she said, tossing a handful of wrappers over the edge.

"What are we going to do?" asked Nadia.

"Since you have been searching for me out anyway, I was going to ask you a favor. Now that you're a recognized applicant, I can make it a trial. We are going to kill a Nazi wizard," smiled Anna.

"Oh."

"Not exciting enough for you?" asked Anna.

"No, it's just I thought we would be doing something more, you know, witchy," replied Nadia. Anna got up off the ledge and turned to face the rows of marching soldiers. Great blocks of cavalrymen marched behind columns of infantry. They left steaming dung piles that stuck out in the trampled white snow when the horses passed.

"You know I didn't pick the nickname Anna the Red," said Anna as she watched the parade. "It was given to me by Esmeralda. She thought joining the Red Army was foolish, that I would be corrupted with its ideology. I tried to explain what I had seen out west, what the Nazis were planning. Old acquaintances that I had met when I traveled Europe had simply vanished. I saw the ghettos so many people had been forced into. I heard the Reich's radios as they denounced the enemies of the German people. Even when the Molotov Ribbentrop pact was declared, I wasn't fooled. I could feel it coming. A fight with the Nazis. They couldn't allow folks like us to exist in any country. So, I joined up with the Red Army, despite the caution of the other three. They spoke of Stalin's purges, his superstition, and his hatred for all things magical. But I knew that when they came, there would be a need for fighters. I didn't know Moscow's Arcanum had been purged. That the officer corps had been depleted and that so many had been removed. That we had been left so utterly unprepared for the Nazi attack. But I believed that we could survive. That we would endure. We would be victorious. So that is what the test will be. We will fight the enemy. The death stroke doesn't exist anymore. The idea of a quick war is dead and gone. To beat the monster, we need to take pieces out of him. We will blunt his claws with our broken bones. We tire him out by retreating along the endless roads.

"We cripple him by killing important members among their ranks. My test is to see if you can endure, to see if you can fight. Because we need fighters among us. What Esmeralda didn't know was that I'm not a party member. I know that Hitler and Stalin are the same type of man. Once this war is finished, the man of steel will turn his attention on us again. I may believe in Communism and the people, but I don't believe in tyranny. I will gladly help one tyrant kill another, but I have not forgotten that the man in charge of this land is also a tyrant. I want to make sure you can fight both Adolf and Joseph. We can hide in our forest. Avoid the gaze of the world to practice our craft in secret. But I don't want to practice in secret. I want us to be strong enough that no one will persecute us. So, we are going to kill a wizard. To sharpen our own claws and to dull the claws of our enemy."

The wind blew as Anna turned back to Nadia. To Nadia, she looked so strong, so sure of her course. While she felt fragile, like glass. Maybe by being with Anna, she might gain some of that strength. To become so sure of things.

Down below, angry shouting could be heard. Anna looked over the edge, and Nadia turned to do the same. Several uniformed men were examining the pile of wrappers that had gathered in the snow. The bright blue wrappers were a dead giveaway that someone had been littering. A man in a peaked cap looked up and pulled out his pistol.

"You two, up there! You are under arrest, for negligence of duty, littering, and theft of state resources," he shouted.

"Oh shit," laughed Anna ducking down below the lip. "It's the military police."

"What are we going to do?" asked Nadia, ducking down while scooping up Dasha.

"What else? We leave. Last time I checked, they can't fly." Anna grabbed her broom and ran over to the other side of the roof. Nadia grabbed her rifle and followed as Dasha meowed in complaint about being shoved into the bag. "Come on, we are going to meet the boys."

She then hopped off the roof and flew up into the sky.

"I like her," said Dasha, peeking out from the bag. "She is like a cat."

"Yeah, she kind of is," said Nadia before jumping off a ledge and shooting off after Anna. The two witches flew over Moscow over the massive parade of men, horses, and tanks.

21
Magicians of the Court

"Isn't that thing uncomfortable?" shouted Anna as she flew up next to Nadia. The wind hit the pair with flakes of snow that made everything incredibly cold. "I mean a broom is not that comfortable to ride on, but it doesn't have all those sharp metal bits or knobs."

"Oh, it's incredibly uncomfortable. I put a cloth over the sights to help, though I can't really do anything about the bolt. But it can shoot and fight without my help."

"Naturally, a weapon of war would want to be feisty. It probably turns like an ox, right?" said Anna.

"I wouldn't know, I have never flown on anything else," shouted Nadia.

"Well can it do this?" said Anna making a short loop in the air, twisting, and bobbing with great elegance. The rifle had never flown like that.

"Wow, that's amazing, I don't think I could do any of that. It's too bad you fly so slow," laughed Nadia.

"Slow! I'll show you slow," said Anna, bending down and speeding off.

"She thinks she is going fast, doesn't she?" meowed Dasha.

"She does. Do you think we should give her a little time to make it challenging?" asked Nadia, leaning down on the rifle.

"Only fair I think," he chirped before hunching down in the bag. Nadia smiled and counted to ten. The rifle jittered in anticipation. Right when she said ten, the weapon burst forward with dizzying speed. She quickly started gaining on Anna, who turned back and looked surprised. She kicked her broom like she would a horse and went a little bit faster. As Nadia began to close the distance, she rested her heels on the rifle and gripped tightly. The rifle went faster and matched speed with Anna, flying right next to her.

"I can go faster if you want," said Nadia as she shouted over the roaring wind.

"I'm sure you can," replied Anna and slowed down. Nadia had to pull back on the barrel of the rifle to keep it from zooming off past Anna, and once again, they were moving at a comfortable speed.

"No wonder you made it to Moscow so quickly. Here I'm puttering around on the equivalent of a biplane and you're moving like a modern engine."

"To think this gun is older than I am," laughed Nadia.

"Older than both of us put together from the looks of it," said Anna.

The two flew across the countryside while the snow became heavier. Nadia pulled out a potion that would warm her up. She had gotten quite good a brewing them over the past month as the temperature began to drop.

"What is that?" shouted Anna.

"It's a warmth potion, it will keep you nice and cozy in a blizzard."

"Can I get one of those?" shouted Anna. Nadia tossed the potion over, and she drank it in one big gulp. "Oh my God, it's disgusting!"

"Yeah, that taste doesn't go away either," said Nadia. "Get used to the taste of burned medicine and wilted cabbages."

"You can keep your potions to yourself," said Anna. "We are getting close to the front. Soon you will meet the boys."

"Who are the boys?"

"The last remnants of the Moscow College of Magic. They were conscripted en masse. They are a bunch of college boys around your age. Decent magicians, much better riflemen. They have been put into a unit to help kill our Nazi wizard."

"You still haven't told me who we are going to be targeting," shouted Nadia as they began to drop in altitude.

"His name is Arnold Ropke; he is one of the old timers of the German army. Back when they had the Kaiser. He is a career soldier who fought on the western and eastern fronts in the last great war. The Germans don't have a lot of magicians, but the ones they do have are very dangerous."

Nadia thought of Rudolph and the nail he had in her spirit. She shuddered at what kind of magician this Arnold would be.

The pair landed in the center of the camp. Gone was the sea of mud, replaced with the hard frozen earth. In the previous months, speed was sapped from armored fighting. Now, mobile combat was once again possible as the Nazis began their drive toward Moscow.

The whole camp was active as they examined the horizon and prepared for war. Artillerymen found their range as they fired shells into the distance. Men of all sorts dug into the ground with pickaxes while sawing down trees to make a medieval cover that would absorb the onslaught of bullets and shrapnel. Nadia and Anna walked past a group of soldiers cleaning their weapons. At first glance, Nadia thought they were men but found they were women. There were lots of women. Men still outnumbered them at least five to one, but there were plenty. Some were operating heavy machine guns and anti-aircraft turrets. Others did the laundry as they leaned over vats of frothing hot liquid to clean clothes or make the meals to feed the vast multitude of soldiers. Nadia caught sight of a burned-out German tank that was used to train dogs to attack.

"Why are they using dogs to attack a tank?" asked Nadia as they moved through the camp.

"They are going to strap bombs to the dog to blow up Nazi tanks," said Anna. "Personally, I think its barbaric, but this whole war is barbarism."

"Yeah, I guess it is," replied Nadia as she watched the trainer pat the dog's head for a job well done. The pair made the way to a huge tent that had a dozen men milling about. They looked like riflemen and officers, but they drew on chalkboards with obvious magical incantations while debating this or that occult theory. One pair was practicing turning snow into water and returning it back to snow. Another gaggle were busy throwing knives at dummies that moved on their own.

"Are these the boys?" asked Nadia.

"They try so hard, don't they?" said Anna. A trio of the magicians who were drawing on a chalkboard looked up and saw the witches.

"Anna you're back, and you brought a friend," said one of the soldiers, waving at them. "But you know the rules: non-magicians can't be in our camp."

"It's okay, Petrov, she is a witch as well. She is going to help us with our little project," said Anna. One of the men who turned from the chalkboard looked very unimpressed with Nadia and Anna. He was tall, dark haired and filled out his uniform with broad shoulders and muscles.

"Well, if it's alright with you, Anna, I don't mind," said Petrov.

"Is this the witch you gush about?" said the tall soldier. *He's going to be a problem*, Nadia thought as she rested her hand on her pistol. He slowly walked up to Nadia and Anna, specifically to Anna.

"Don't mind him," said Petrov. "He has just been transferred here; he already solved this magical equation that has been puzzling us for months."

"Did he now?" said Anna stepping up and offering her hand. "Magician first-class Anna." The man spat on the ground.

"Did you fuck the captain to get that ranking? Maybe not with that face."

"Oh, it's like that is it?" said Anna.

"Vladimir, you should apologize right now," said Petrov. A third trooper signaled to the others about the brewing confrontation.

"I don't think so. I studied for many years at the Leningrad Institute of Magic and then in Moscow. I did the work, did the time, and this whore has a rank with all the privileges. Letting women serve in the army is one thing. Someone has to do the laundry and put the guts back into dying men, but magic is a different story. It's common knowledge why they don't let women into any of the colleges of magic. Their menstrual cycle spoils spell work. That's why they have to retreat to the forest to be witches. The magic knows you shouldn't be practicing and has twisted you to look like this. You, girl!" he barked at Nadia. "If you are some acolyte of this charlatan, you should quit magic now. You're pretty enough to find a decent husband. It's not right for a woman to be doing magic."

"Is this some joke I'm not getting, Anna?" asked Nadia, thumbing the safety on her pistol. By now, a crowd of magicians was gathering, some nodding in disapproval, while others were already taking bets.

"No, he's serious. It's some nonsense they teach in the ivory towers of academia. When I first met magicians, it was like this for a full week straight," said Anna.

"Don't ignore me when I'm talking to you," said the man, stepping into Anna's space. Anna turned and punched the man in the face, dropping him like a bag of potatoes. Anna shook her hand in obvious pain.

"Was there anything else in that potion you brewed?" asked Anna. Vladimir was groaning as he tried to sit up, touching his nose that was gushing blood.

"A few herbs that boost strength and stamina. I got tired of people jumping on me and trying to strangle or stab me," shrugged Nadia.

"What have you been doing the past couple months?" asked Anna. She pulled out a wicked curved dagger and closed in on the injured man. Nadia flicked the safety back on her pistol before taking her hand off it. Anna crouched down on the man's chest with one knee. She then stuck the point of the blade in the man's nose. With a quick flick of the wrist, the blade cut through the man's nostril. He screamed, clutching his face with both hands as blood gushed down from his face.

"Now listen here. I have a bit of your blood and I can do terrible things with it. I can make you break out in so many lesions that you will scratch yourself to the bone. I can make it so that you only see nightmares in your waking hours. I have so many ways of being an unholy terror to you it would make your head spin. So, if I hear any impolite comments out of you, I might turn you into a chicken, are we clear?"

The man nodded as Anna got off his chest. She took a strip of paper and dabbed it in the blood before writing the man's name on it. Several others stepped forward to help the injured Vladimir up. "That's how I keep these boys in line," said Anna, sheathing her dagger.

An officer stepped out of the tent. He was clean-shaven and about the same age as Anna. Maybe a few years older. Regardless he looked over the small camp of magicians and spotted the man bleeding from his nostrils.

"What the hell is this?" he shouted, pointing a riding crop at the bleeding man.

"Nothing, captain, I was simply reminding one of the men the proper respect that you need to show a superior officer," said Anna saluting.

"Fine, fine, whatever. Have you finished looking for your contact? Is this the other witch?"

"It is, captain," said Anna, pushing Nadia forward. Nadia didn't care for being the sudden center of attention, scrutinized by an army officer.

"Hmmm, where did you get that uniform, girl, and that weapon of yours? I've heard from Anna that you are not part of the army."

"I salvaged them off the battlefield, and the gun was my father's. He kept it after the Great War."

"Hmmm," he said as he looked her over. "Do you have any actual experience fighting?"

"Yes, I'm a registered partisan. I helped with a battle down south, near Sevastopol," replied Nadia.

"Well give me your name and I will run it through headquarters," said the captain, pulling out a piece of paper and a pencil.

"Nadia Voloshyn, captain."

"I'm sorry, could you repeat that?" asked the officer. Nadia did so. "I'll be right back," he said, disappearing into the tent. Nadia looked at Anna, confused. Anna shrugged. The officer came out with a massive stack of paper and a pen.

"Your first job will be to write those luck charms you have been passing out as you have been moving north. You can do them while we do our briefing," he said, hoisting the massive stack of paper in her hand.

"How do you know about the luck charms I have been trading?"

"You are Nadia Voloshyn, the Night Witch? You're famous, and those charms you have been passing out have become more valuable than bullets. 'The charms of the Night Witch.' If you would be so inclined, I will be wanting the first in that stack."

"What?" laughed Anna. "If it's luck charms you wanted, I could have written you dozens already."

"You don't understand," said the officer. "Wherever these charms have been passed out, the holders have given obscene supernatural luck. They survive things that should have killed them. The Germans overran a squad who got them down south, but they held the bastards back in a farm for almost three whole weeks. They kept radioing that the Night Witch's charms had saved them again. Suddenly everyone wanted them. There was a partisan boy who got one and is now a master marksman who never misses his shot."

"Well, I can make those myself. It's one of the simplest spells to do." Many of the other magicians nodded in agreement.

"Yes, but soldiers are a superstitious lot, and it's best not to mess with the precedent. It might spoil the luck."

"My wrist is going to be in so much pain," mumbled Nadia.

"Psss," hissed Dasha. "Ask for something tasty in exchange. Like a fish!"

"Well, I'm going to need a fish to do it right," said Nadia. "It helps with the magical ley lines." She didn't know if that was true. But her cat wanted a fish, and she still owed him one. The other magicians overhearing this simply shrugged and returned to their studies.

"Done. I will see if I can scrounge something from the officers' mess," he said. "Well let's get started then." He led them to the front area where he grabbed the chalkboard and flipped it over.

"You little minx," said Anna up close. "You have gotten famous by passing around the easiest two-ruble spells. I would call you a con artist, and if swiping a fish for your cat is any indication, I wouldn't be far off."

"I didn't know they were going to be such a hot commodity. Magic works off intent. If the soldiers are betting their entire lives on a tiny luck spell, they are going to be more effective."

"Alright," said the captain clearing his throat. "Now that it seems we are all in attendance…oh for God's sake, Vladimir, put some gauze on it and quit your belly aching. There will be a lot more blood spilt out there. As I was saying, now that we have everyone in attendance, we can begin the briefing."

Nadia found a chair. While the captain talked, she scribbled out spells. "Our target is Arnold Ropke, also known as 'the Boar.' Just be glad our assignment isn't against 'the Eagle' or 'the Wolf.' British spies have made it clear they are in Africa. Arnold is one of the Reich's premier magicians. After the first war, he was required to take off that uniform. However, Hitler worked around the Versailles Treaty by redesignating him as volunteer instructor. But make no mistake, despite his age, he is more dangerous than ever. He is a master magician. Word is he declined a position as head of the college of Berlin because it didn't give him a chance to stretch his magical expertise."

The captain then hung a picture of the man on the board. In it was an aged man with a bushy mustache wearing an old German officer's uniform. He had a dozen medals on his breast.

"The Boar is an expert in battlefield magic. Able to catch bullets and artillery shells alike. While the very earth at his feet is a weapon, he made a cliff side fall on an Italian brigade during the 12th Battle of the Isonzo. On top of that, he is a crack marksman, with enchanted bullets that hit like an artillery round."

"Holy hell how are we supposed to stop this monster?" asked one of the magicians.

"By any means necessary. Right now, the Boar is operating with the 4th Panzer Army. It seems the weather is not affecting that army as dearly. Most likely thanks to the Boar's magic. If we kill him, we slow the army down. Apparently, Russia's winter is a little too rough for German equipment." The men laughed. "We will be attacking tomorrow. Our army group will engage the 4th Panzer Army, while we go after the Boar. Make no mistake, gentlemen, this entire offensive is designed to kill the Boar, so there is no going back. If we fail, there will surely be a firing squad waiting for all of us."

The entire group of men was silent. The enormity of the task and the risks sank in for them. Nadia's hand cramped as she jotted down another spell.

"Sir, may I ask why so much importance is placed on killing this man? I mean, the Germans will get here when they get here. It's not like killing one man will change that," said one of the magicians.

"Our backs are against the wall. Premier Stalin wants a propaganda victory and has already printed the celebratory newspapers declaring the Boar's defeat. There is no room for failure in this operation. The Germans are powerful, aggressive, and brutal. But they are stretched dangerously thin. If we can at least slow them down, dig our heals in, we could stop their advance. This battle will be a steppingstone to throwing back the fascists. So, make sure you get your rest, and be sure your wills are up to date." The captain slapped the picture with his riding crop. "Tomorrow, we go on a Boar hunt

22
Winter War

The army moved out in the dark of the predawn. The magicians rode in a truck, one of the few that could work in these conditions. Nadia was exhausted, as she had only gotten a few hours of sleep. Upon finding out that the Night Witch was in their camp, she was swarmed by a host of soldiers pleading for the lucky charms that had given the vital edge to so many soldiers. She was up very late as she wrote out the simple spells of luck and fortune. Eventually, they became a scribbled scraw of illegible Cyrillic. The men didn't mind. One even cried, so sure that he was a dead man walking. Even so, she couldn't get any rest until two hours before the army shipped out. Eventually, Anna burst into her tent with a cup filled with soup. Nadia drank the meager meal before she was shuffled off to the truck.

The men were checking their firearms or reading small spell books so that they could memorize spells and concepts for the coming fight. Nadia was fascinated by the approach of academic magicians. They had externalized so much knowledge in books that they never needed to keep anything memorized, unlike Nadia and the rest of the witches, who gained their knowledge through mentors—a witch had to memorize every spell and technique. This is followed by an intuitive study of the natural world. As a result, many of the established wizards could be expected to know the same spells. Every witch was an enigma of knowledge and capability with wildly varying skills and talents. This was a passing interest as she tried to keep her eyes open to avoid falling asleep on the truck.

She had failed in that task as she was shaken awake by one of the magicians. The truck had stopped. The morning dawn's dim light shown through a fresh snowfall.

"Are we there yet?" asked Nadia, stretching her back. Dasha had been resting on her lap, and he stretched as his claws, digging into the padded jacket.

"Sister," said a magician. It was Petrov, the man who was with Vladimir. "The truck has broken down. Some damn fool had forgotten to fuel it up. Now we walk with the rest of the foot sloggers. If we are lucky, we might be able to hitch a ride on a tank.

"What a pain," sighed Nadia. "If only you people knew how to fly."

"We magicians have been trying to crack that chestnut for centuries. Until the hot air balloon and the Wright brothers, you witches have been the only ones to fly. With the odd exception here and there," said Petrov.

"What? But it's so easy to enchant something to fly," said Nadia. "All you need is—"

"Nadia!" barked Anna. Nadia jumped from this, looking at her senior witch. Anna signaled Nadia to come to her, hopping out of the truck into the snowy morning. Her feet crunched with each step. "As a rule, don't tell the boys anything about our craft," said Anna.

"Why not?" asked Nadia.

"If you tell them how to make spells, they will write it down. If they write it down, it will get passed around rather quickly," Anna said as her breath danced through the snowflakes. "Think of it like a germ. It will spread in universities, with professors and students examining it, poking at it, replicating the spell. Eventually finding ways of counteracting our magic. We witches have survived this long by keeping our tricks to ourselves. You must always remember that no matter much they celebrate us now, or how much they are glad of our achievements, they are always a potential pogrom. The power of flight is easy for us, but we have made it quite difficult for them to achieve. All so we can retain our edge."

"When do you think there will be a time when we won't have to guard our knowledge so closely?"

"I don't know. But unless you are speaking with another witch or you are teaching your own apprentice, say nothing."

Nadia nodded as she watched her sister rub her hands together for the meager scrap of warmth.

"Good, let's get moving. We got a four-kilometer march ahead of us," said Anna, sliding her broom in a sling on her back. She then unslung a machine gun with a round drum clip.

"I now know why Dasha calls us trundle feet," said Nadia. "That reminds me." She went over to a crop of trees, "This will do, Dasha." The cat stuck his head out of the bag, shaking his head as snow fell on him.

"I was trying to get some sleep!" said Dasha as Nadia pulled him out of the bag before placing him on the ground.

"I need to leave you here for a little while," said Nadia, scratching his head.

"No!" he yowled. "Are you trying to run out on your obligation again?"

"You silly cat," she said, rubbing his ears. "I would have hoped we have traveled long enough for you to know I wouldn't do that." Dasha couldn't help himself as he began purring when she started petting his back. "I'm going into another battle, and I don't want you to huddle underneath a tank again for protection. A battlefield is no place for a cat," she said.

"It's no place for a human. We have both seen them I don't understand why you would want to go back," replied Dasha.

"There are too many forces pushing me into it. I would rather not risk my life to kill some old fascist wizard. But if I'm to continue this path, I need to do this. But just because I must go into danger doesn't mean you have to. So, I'm going to ask this tree to give you sanctuary and if I'm not back within the week, you go on your way."

"Why wouldn't you come back before then?" he asked.

"Well, I could be injured, or I could be, you know…" she said, petting his back. He hopped up, putting his paws on her knee, his face getting close to hers.

"Don't talk like that, Nadia, you are the cleverest witch I know, and you are coming back safe and sound. Maybe even bringing something tasty."

"I'm thinking practically. If I do die, I don't want you to be in a place where you will soon follow me," she said.

"You're making me really worried," said Dasha. "I don't like when you talk like this."

"I'm sorry, I didn't mean to. But we have cut it close before. I just don't want to put you in unnecessary danger."

"That is exactly what I don't want you to do, either! I most certainly don't want to be left at the wayside while you risk your life. I have been on a lot of crazy adventures in my time. But the craziest, most interesting, most amazing adventure I have ever had has been with you. I don't want this to be a goodbye."

Nadia stopped scratching Dasha. She picked him up and embraced him. He squirmed, unused to this sort of human affection. He licked the silent tears that rolled down her face.

"I know I said I don't want to be afraid anymore," she whispered. "But I can't help it. I know going into danger is not the best thing for me. But I couldn't stand if you went in there with me and got hurt. I could let the world tear me to pieces, and I would endure it. But I would die if that happened to you. In many ways you have been my guide as well as my friend. You help me understand who I am when I have yet to figure it out. So, I'm asking you to wait here. Far away from the violence. That way I won't have to worry about you when the bullets start to fly. I will at least know that your safe and that you will carry on even if I won't. If I could have done that with Mama, Peter, and Olivia…" She wiped away a tear with her palm. "I don't know if life would have been different. I can't do that with any of them. But I can do that with you. I can leave you this can of fish and have this tree give you some place to sleep when you feel like it. If I come back within a week then we won't have to worry. If I don't, move on, continue with your adventures. If I'm injured and can't move, I can still find you with piece of your fur. Can you do this for me, Dasha?"

"Well, I don't like it, and you usually need someone watching your back, but that Anna seems dependable enough. So yes, I will stay here, eat my fill of mice who are too stupid to avoid me, and wait for your return. Just don't get yourself killed. You're not the only one who lost everything."

He finished licking up the tears on her face as Nadia gave him one last hug. It was easy to convince a tree to give Dasha sanctuary. With one final hug, they parted ways. Nadia looked at the group of trees, doing her best to memorize the surrounding terrain and land. She had to quickly catch up with the magicians, who had already started off without her. However, with her flying rifle and following the tracks, she met up with the group.

The magician soldiers marched across open fields and clusters of trees and over a small frozen stream. Occasionally, Nadia and Anna had to fly high up to scout, giving the others a comprehensive view of the surrounding countryside. High above, planes were flying westward. Nadia had assumed that they were German planes. Anna laughed, saying it was the Red Air Force.

"I thought that all of our planes were destroyed," said Nadia.

"Initially we took a pounding, but now that it's winter and near Moscow, our planes can fly freely from their heated hangars. Like most of the German equipment, their planes may be nice, but they can't handle our weather at all," smiled Anna.

That was at least some good news, as they wouldn't have to dodge low-level fighters or worry about being bombed. Having experienced it once, Nadia never wanted to never be under a bombardment ever again.

It was mid-morning when they finally caught sight of the enemy. The whole troop had stopped, and radio signals were sent to the tanks, while homing pigeons were sent to the cavalry.

However, responses were haphazard. A column of tanks had already made it to the edge of the forest where battle would happen far from the rest of the infantry, who were much further behind. Only the tanks, cavalry, and magicians would be taking part in the conflict that was quickly closing in on them.

The magicians got to work using their magic to dig a great ditch that they could use for cover. They set up several machine guns and used their magic to create a giant cannon that looked like it came from the fourteenth century.

"Alright, men, we wait for the enemy to break into the clearing. Then we will let the tanks and cavalry engage first. Only when we have caught sight of the Boar will we move out. Until then we hold position and defend ourselves. Maybe throw a few harassment shots. Once the Boar reveals himself, we will move in on him. Then neutralize him," said the captain as he walked up and down the trench.

The field was a vast stretch of farmland that had been burned to cinders. All that was left was a vast field of soot-covered snow. A farmhouse sat in the center of the field, yet it was a farmhouse in name only. The house had been put to the torch. It was twisted black wood now, with a solitary standing chimney.

All along the edge of the tree line, they made a makeshift defense. Men on horses milled about waiting for their scouts to return while tanks struggled to remain in formation. A sense of unease began to fall over Nadia. Something about this felt very wrong. Off in the distance, coming out of a hot haze, dozens of tanks could be seen advancing on the Red Army position.

Something in Nadia's stomach tightened to a knot. She had been forced into fighting before, but she never had to wait for it. It was thrust upon her, or she brazenly dove into an existing fight. Nadia cheeked her weapons, wishing she had more ammunition, even if the bullets would do nothing to the advancing tanks.

Petrov was quivering, and his teeth chattered despite the warmth of his jacket. Vladimir, with his cut nose with several stitches and gauze over his face, stood with him. He remained level-headed. He may have been a chauvinist fool, thought Nadia, but at least he didn't scare easily. The magicians that had conjured a cannon from the earth were now forming balls of dirt transformed into heavy iron cannonballs, which were then enchanted again to fly further, hit harder, and with more accuracy. The team worked as an assembly line. Each wizard formed a chain, creating the munitions to be thrown at the modern tanks in the distance.

"Ready to fire at your command, captain," said the magical gunner.

"Fire at will," said the captain. He held up his binoculars to his eyes as he looked over the battlefield before looking at his watch.

"You're going to love this, it's positively vulgar," said Anna. One of the magicians loaded one of the enchanted cannonballs into the barrel. No gun powder was necessary, for this magical contraption had runic bands that propelled the munition.

"Raising the gun," shouted one of the magicians. He then stamped the ground with his foot, and a column of earth moved the gun above the trench.

"Fire!" With a tap of an iron wand, the cannon fired without an explosion. The cannon rang with sturdy steel rubbing up against iron, followed by the release of air. The ball went flying off toward the column of tanks. The ball impacted a distant tank, stopping the vehicle in its tracks, the giant ball in its turret.

"Direct hit, sir!" shouted one of the magician gunners.

"Excellent work. Now we can wear them down, bit by bit, and maybe draw out the Boar," he said. A thunderous rumbling followed by a bugle came from across the tree line as thousands of cavalry rode out of the forest. Like a wave of flashing sabers and thundering hooves, they rode into the vast distance, kicking up snow and soot in their wake. From the look on the captain's face, something had gone terribly wrong.

"Damn foolish cavalry," he yelled. "It's too soon! The idiots have mistaken the cannon for the signal to attack."

The German line erupted in a blaze of fire into the mass of charging cavalry that threw men and horses in the air. Charred body parts flew everywhere.

Then a single Soviet tank lurched out of the forest, then another tank; in dribs and drabs the armored column rolled out of the forest protect in tiny, disorganized knots, creating a jagged line of advancing armor. The battle began to heat up as bullets zipped overhead and tanks fired their shells.

"Welcome to the Red Army, Nadia," shouted Anna. "The most disorganized power in the world!"

"Is it usually so chaotic!" yelled Nadia as another magical cannon round fired off.

"We are doing well, all things considered; at least half our force isn't running in the opposite direction."

A tank round flew overhead and hit a nearby tree, sending thousands of wooden shards raining down on the magicians. Men popped out the tops of Nazi tanks to man machine guns, firing into the mass of sword-wielding cavalry. Blooms of fire erupted on German tanks as handheld firebombs were thrown at the gunners and at the rear, stopping the vehicles dead. Nadia could see one cavalryman's horse had been shot, sending it falling to the earth. The man ran away before he was gunned down. The horse, however, was still alive as it struggled to its feet. It couldn't get its bearing. The tank kept rolling toward it. The horse screamed with confusion, unable to flee the steel behemoth as it slowly rolled over the animal. Nadia looked away from the gruesome murder. This scene was happening everywhere. No matter where

Nadia looked, all she could see was the pain and misery of man and beast.

"Captain, I think we found the Boar!" shouted a gunner. Nadia looked over where the man was pointing, standing from the hatch of a turret. A man in a curved helm shouted and pointed at the various advancing cavalry that swarmed around his tank. He operated the machine gun, pouring rounds into the mass of men and horses, killing with impunity.

"Send a cannon ball his way; that will be a sure test of his ability," said the captain.

The men complied, loading a round and sending it hurtling across the battlefield. Nadia watched as the man sensed the incoming projectile. He held up his hand, gestured, and the cannonball stopped in midair. He gestured again in a circle. The cannonball became a focal point of gravitational pull as stray bullets, fallen sabers, tank scraps, and shrapnel were pulled until it became a spinning mass of debris. With another gesture and a punch, the ball flew back toward the cannon at high speed. Anna grabbed Nadia by the collar, throwing her to the earth. Men dove out of the way as the mass of twisted metal impacted the cannon before it magnetically detonated, sending shrapnel everywhere, killing several and injuring dozens.

"Oh God, he is going to kill us!" shouted Petrov. "We don't stand a chance." He threw his rifle down and scurried out the back of the trench.

"Hell!" shouted Vladimir, clutching a bleeding arm. "Witch! We have to shoot him!"

"Why?" said Nadia, pulling herself to her feet. Anna was busy firing her weapon to notice what was going on.

"Orders from the top! Malicious deserters must be shot. As the commander is occupied, it falls to us to carry out the order."

"That's insane. I'm not even part of the army!" shouted Nadia.

"You think that matters? I would do it myself, but I can't aim a rifle with this injury. Listen, witch, if we don't kill him, every tenth man will be shot in his place, and if you don't shoot him, I must shoot you," he said, raising a pistol.

"Don't you dare," said Nadia, pointing her own rifle at Vladimir.

"I would rather not, but I have little choice, time is of the essence. If we don't act many more will be executed. Do you want that on your conscience?" shouted Vladimir.

"Nadia, for the mother's sake, shoot the coward and be done with it," shouted Anna. "We have a war to fight." Before Nadia could respond, the rifle jerked on its own toward Petrov and fired. The man died, his head exploding in chunky gore.

"Good job," said Vladimir.

Nadia collapsed to her knees. She told herself that she hadn't wanted to shoot the man. That given a chance, she might also have run away. Yet, Nadia knew that the magic in the rifle might have picked up on her true intention. That she would rather kill a fleeing man than risk confrontation or retribution. How did she internalize the will of the state's violent policy of absolute control? Her hands shook, and all she could do was ball them into fists.

It was in the cold earth that she noticed something was wrong. The walls of the trench began to vibrate. They were shuddering so much that rocks began to jiggle out of the wall. She closed her eyes and dropped into the spirit realm. There were hundreds of earth spirits of brawny, oxen-shaped beasts that had ropes tied to their horns, hooked to a giant gash to the earth. They were trying to close the tear in the ground. Nadia fell back into herself as more of the rocks vibrated out of the wall.

"Everyone get out of the trench, its being sealed up!" Nadia shouted. "The Boar is trying to seal us into the trench."

Right as she finished, the earth began to close together. The magicians scrambled out of the trench, some with magic, others with grit. The injured stood no chance of hoisting themselves out while the more agile could do very little besides pulling a man or two out of the trench. Nadia and Anna took to the air, bouncing out of the trench with a quick hop on their flying instruments. Others were not so lucky. Half of the magicians had been caught inside the closing trench. The walls swallowed up the men like a mouth slurping them into the ground. A few hands and heads stuck out. They flailed about as their comrades tried to dig them free to no avail.

"I have never seen earth shaping so potent," whispered Anna.

All the major players of the magicians' cadre were gone. The captain was sucked into the earth with a piece of shrapnel in his neck. The remaining magicians were diving into the cold snow to keep from getting shot.

From high above, Nadia could now get a clear view of the battlefield. The tanks of the Red Army drove onward in a mob of armor. The rugged tanks often blocked the sights of their comrades' tanks. By contrast, the German vehicles moved like a wolf pack as tanks split off from the leading group, driving past the Red Army counterparts. Their machine guns were blazing as they mowed down any remaining cavalry that had not started fleeing.

The Germans were surrounding the Soviet tanks like the mandibles of giant bugs. The Nazi tanks dodged and weaved at the biting edge, taking careful aim at the vulnerable spots on the Soviet tanks. Often a tank's rounds would simply bounce off the thick Soviet armor. But there were German tanks at another angle that would punch through the lighter-armed flanks and back. The fascists began to dismantle the Soviet armor piecemeal. To Nadia, it was plain as day that the Germans were better organized in so many ways.

If the Red Army's attack was better organized, they could have least stalled the Germans. As it was, it was barely slowing them down. At the center of it all, the Boar rode forward, his magic catching bullets and shells before hurling the ball of shrapnel at tanks and cavalry alike.

"The battle is lost," muttered Anna. "But maybe we can salvage a strategic victory if we kill the Boar."

"Is that even feasible now? Our group is so depleted," said Nadia.

"We have no other option. If we come back empty-handed, that would be a death sentence. The Kremlin already doesn't trust us. If we don't start showing definitive results, they may just put us on a firing line."

"Not you, you can just leave," said Nadia.

"I can't, I fought with those boys for months now. I can't just leave them to their fate. And what kind of witch would I be if I issued you a challenge that even I couldn't overcome?" She smiled. "We have no other options but to dig our heels in. The defensive rings around Moscow will just have to do. But we can still blunt the Reich's magical capability. 'The Tiger,' the Reich's closest comparative wizard, is over three hundred kilometers away. If we succeed, we will have the edge in the battle for Moscow. So, knowing this, do you still think we should run? Or do you want to go on a Boar hunt?"

Nadia looked back to the German wizard as he rode forward on his tank. He raised his arm, and a pillar of stone shot up underneath a Soviet tank, sending it high into the air before it fell back on its side.

"Alright, you go rally the other magicians. I will make a smoke screen to shield them as they advance," said Nadia.

"That's what i like to hear," shouted Anna, diving down to the remainder of the magicians.

Nadia pulled out her bayonet and affixed it to the end of the rifle. She gripped the blade and made a decent-sized cut on her palm to match the scars that covered her hand. Blood oozed from her palm. Only a little bit was needed for this spell to achieve its results. Back at the village, the blood in her mouth was enough to fill the town center with acrid black smoke. The blood from her palm would do the job of turning the battlefield into a black haze. She sucked the blood out of the gash.

She tapped the butt of the rifle, and the weapon shot forward at a blazing speed. Through magical alchemy, she shaped the blood in her mouth and released it as a noxious black smoke. Like crop dusting, the black smoke covered her path in a stinging, blinding cloud. On seeing this, the Germans stopped their advance, unsure if this was a chemical attack or some other trick. Only the Boar's tank rolled forward. He had pulled out a gas mask and had placed it on his face with a veteran's speed. He then operated the machine gun at the top, trying to shoot Nadia out of the air.

Nadia dodged and weaved the best she could. The rifle couldn't make quick turns, but she could corkscrew and speed through the barrage of bullets. On seeing the German wizard, other tanks added to the fire of machine guns. Nadia's saving grace was the smokescreen that half covered her as she charged across the battlefield. The remaining cavalry found refuge in the black smoke. Not wishing to fight German armor any longer, they risked an unknown fate in the black smoke to escape the rumbling behemoths.

Soon the tanks ceased focusing on her. She had outpaced many of them and would have to circle back around to deal with the Boar. Using the smokescreen as cover, she doubled back, the cavalry that had made it to the other side cheering her as she flew past them. Only half of the horsemen remained after that mighty charge that started just minutes ago. Many riders doubled up on horses that look crazed and panicked. The riders were just happy to survive as they retreated into the forest. Anna and the boys had already charged into the black smoke. A bright flare pierced the veil of noxious, choking mist. Nadia flew over the cloud to get a better view of what was going on.

Nadia watched the squad of magicians charge the Boar's tank head-on. They projected shimmering blue shields in front of them as they ran at full speed. Bullets reflected off the glowing blue barriers, bouncing back to their source. There was just a dozen of the Soviet wizards in all, with Anna flying close by. Many of the German tanks ignored them and rolled right by as they pursued the scattered Soviet cavalry or finished off the few Soviet tanks that still fired at their German counterparts. At the center of the German formation was the magical battle avoided by the tankers. They ground forward, reforming into the battle formations, slowing only to machine-gun the survivors of destroyed Soviet tanks. One Soviet tanker was leaning out the top of the tank, firing his pistol at an oncoming German tank that slowly turned its turret before firing into the now burning hulk. The fire and force of the explosion sent the turret into the air before falling back to earth.

Nadia dug her heels into the rifle butt to get it to speed toward the advancing wizard formation. They closed in on the tank while the Boar poured machine-gun fire onto the shimmering blue wall of the Soviet wizards. The bullets ricocheted and were caught in one of the balls of twisted metal that floated in front of the German wizard. His gas mask made him a menacing figure. Six of the wizards began a chant, while the others used their blue shields to protect them while they cast their spell. Anna, for her part, flew around the tank, pouring fire from her machine gun, trying to get a glancing shot on the Boar to no effect, as the bullets from her gun simply veered off into the ball of bullets that began to glow orange with the friction of so much grinding metal. Nadia darted toward the fighting, hugging low to the ground, a landscape of charred dirt and white snow an arm's length away.

The Boar's tank slowly began to rise off the ground thanks to the concentrated efforts of the six magicians as they kept chanting in unison. Nadia could see that it was like the spell she had learned to catch herself off the ground if she fell off her rifle, only the spell employed by the wizards seemed more interested in raising the tank off the ground. Not quite flight, but a forceful levitation. The Boar ceased his machine-gun fire, taking in the combat scene before him, one hand continually gesturing. He reached down, pulled out a rifle, and slung it to his back. The other tank members crawled out through hatches on the front, jumping out onto the snow, only to be gunned down by the circling Anna. The tank continued to rise in the air, further up than a house, the Soviet wizards straining to keep it up. Once at a sufficient height, the magicians ceased, and the tank dropped back down to earth. The Boar stepped out of the falling tank as he dropped with it. He simply pulled his arms and legs in his body, magically rotating, so his feet faced the ground. With a thunderous smash of crumpling metal, the tank bounced off the earth. The Boar's descent slowed to a halt, unlike the armored machine. The Boar landed gently to the ground on both feet. Then the panting magicians stared at the Boar, who seemed unfazed by this development.

"Amateurs," said the masked Boar, his voice muffled as he spoke in heavily accented Russian. "I applaud your bravery and the efforts you have made, but you are all very much outmatched. Surrender now, and I can guarantee your safety."

"He is lying," shouted one of the magicians. "Affix bayonets. I would like to see him catch hard steel."

"So be it," he shouted as a dozen men charged him.

"No, scatter!" shouted Anna. The ball of shrapnel and bullets that had been forming from the Boar's continuous casting fell into the center of the mass of magicians before exploding. Both Nadia and Anna flew upward. White-hot shrapnel burst among the magicians as white streaks followed the burning projectiles. Melted bullets whizzed through several wizards who couldn't get their magical shields up. The six who lifted the tank were cut to ribbons as the burning rounds tore through their bodies, burning so hot that their clothes caught fire. The men collapsed, their charred flesh and burning clothing sent billowing hot steam into the air.

The surviving wizards, who had barely kept their shields up, recoiled in horror at the detonation in their midst. Outrage fueled the survivors as they charged the Boar. The Boar placed the butt of his rifle at his shoulder, took careful aim, and fired. The front of the rifle burst with the strength of a blinding sun, followed by a wave of pressure that sent snow and dirt flying from the epicenter. The bullet tore through the first magician's shield, shattering it like an egg. Without further resistance, the bullet, like a jet of liquid metal, passed through the man. The force of the impact was so extreme it sent him flying back.

The utter annihilation made one of the men pause before he was shot with an enchanted round, sending him sprawling head over heel, a ragged crater punched through his chest. The Boar, with mechanical, practiced movements, cocked the next round into the rifle's chamber, taking careful aim at the two remaining men. The men reenforced their magical shields, dropping their rifles to gesture with both hands. The Boar cocked his head and fired at the men's feet, the force of the blast throwing them in the air. The Boar fired again once they were on the ground. The magical round made a man-sized crater, with the former magician's limbs flying off in different directions. The Boar turned to the last magician as he pulled himself to his feet. His coat was splattered with chunks of gore from his comrades.

"You should get running, young man," said the Boar as he pulled another clip of ammunition from his belt. "If you stay there, I will have no choice but to shoot you, and we both know how that will turn out."

The last magician dropped his rifle and ran as fast as he could. The Boar crammed the cartridges into his weapon before turning to look at the two witches in the sky.

"I don't have to shoot the man running away, do I?" asked Nadia.

"No more shooting. I don't want another one of those shrapnel bombs to go off," replied Anna. She pulled her curved dagger out of her belt.

"If we can get a bit of his blood, we can put a hex on him. Make him vulnerable to more mundane attacks. As it is I don't think we can do anything from a distance."

"So, do we just charge him and hope for the best," asked Nadia. The Boar was pacing, holding his rifle as he watched the two witches.

"You should run, young ladies. I have no wish to hurt any women," he shouted through the mask.

"He is like something out of another era," said Anna. "Like a medieval knight or gentlemen general from the last century."

"He is still a fascist," said Nadia.

"Still a fascist," echoed Anna. "You take the right. I will hit him from the left. Once you get his blood on your blade give it to me, and for the coven's sake, don't die."

"Is that the plan we are going with?" replied Nadia.

"Have you ever tried shooting two hawks attacking your eyes at the same time?"

"Point taken," said Nadia. The two charged toward the German magician. He braced his stance, aimed with his rifle, and fired. The two witches corkscrewed away from the deadly round as it whizzed by. The bullet's trail heated up like an oven. When the round passed, the hairs on Nadia's neck stood up with the potency of the magic. The rifle quickly pulled ahead of Anna's slower broom.

The Boar tried to aim at her, and he fired again. Nadia dove down as the bullet whizzed over her, the wave of heat following it, the force of the bullet pulling her hat off her head. The Boar tilted his head and stretched his arm to the tank behind him. With a grip, the wrecked tank lifted off the ground. The Red Army magicians strained to keep it up with six men. He lifted it with ease by himself. Like he was hurling a shotput, he threw his arm forward, and the tank flew toward Nadia. The object was too big and too bulky to veer around. The rifle just couldn't maneuver out of the way fast enough. Even a corkscrew would throw her from the rifle at this speed. She pulled up on the barrel to get above it. The rifle did its best to climb up in the sky.

The bulk of the tank passed under her, but the turret's mangled gun smashed into her. She bounced off the tank top and was sent falling to the earth. She spun end over end and lost track of where she was.

23
The Boar

Somewhere Anna was screaming her name. It was all happening so fast. She didn't have time to think. The pale light from the Moon in her forehead flared to life, and it seemed that the world began to slow. Nadia was pulled from her body and into the spirit realm. The Moon, sitting as a kindly mother in a rocking chair, was there, her long grey hair bunched up around her feet.

"What's going on?" asked Nadia.

"You look like you need to talk. Maybe a bit of advice is in order," said the Moon as she rocked. This current form reminded Nadia too much of her mother.

"No, I can't be doing this. I'm going to hit the ground," said Nadia, looking around frantically.

"Not necessarily. Time works differently here," said the Moon.

"Alright, if you have advice, let's hear it. I don't mean to be disrespectful, Mother Moon, but I'm fighting for my life," said Nadia.

"All creatures are in some way, my dear. What makes this struggle so different?" said the Moon. A chair of pure light was pulled forth from the darkness. Nadia hesitated for a second before sitting down.

"I feel overmatched. Again. But this time it's against a true fighter. The daemon I fought acted on instinct and malicious intent. Rudolph is a fanatic at heart. A dangerous, cruel fanatic, to be sure, but he was never a soldier. Never a warrior. This Arnold Ropke is both a wizard and a warrior. He is someone comfortable with fighting. He hasn't shot any man while they were running, and said he disliked the idea of fighting women, yet he seems utterly merciless when he has the mind to fight. He lifted a tank with a spell that took the magical strength of six other magicians to lift. This is my first year on my own, and my magic doesn't feel up to the task. It was not designed to fight in a war, while his magic and spell work seemed to have been tailor made for a modern battlefield. What do I do against that kind of magician?"

"You should play to your strengths," said the Moon.

"But I have none. He has so many. At distance, I'm completely outmatched."

"Well, if that is the case, then grab him by the belt, and don't let go," smiled the Moon, leaning toward Nadia.

"But how do I get close to him?" asked Nadia, uncomfortable with the advancing Moon. "He will just knock me out of the sky." The Moon moved close to Nadia, right up to her ear.

"My children are always there to help," said the Moon. Then Nadia felt herself falling. She was back to the material world, and the ground was closing in fast.

Reflexively she threw out the spell that would catch her fall as she hurtled toward the ground. She hit a cushion of air before dropping a short distance to the snow. Looking up, she saw the Boar trying a similar attack against Anna. Her maneuvering was superb, and she dodged and weaved out of the way of the thrown tank hulks. It seemed that the Boar had forgotten about Nadia. Another tank was rolling up on her. Upon seeing Nadia, the gunner swiveled the weapon getting ready to mow her down.

"Break," sighed Nadia, throwing the spell out of her mouth with an exhausted sigh. The sign on her forehead flashed when the spell was cast. Nadia felt a sudden swell of power infuse the spell and the tank lurched to a halt. Nothing happened when the gunner pulled the trigger. He slapped the weapon. Then the tank exploded.

Nadia was thrown back with the force. She suspected the spell had worked its way into the fuel and engine as it caught fire, igniting the stored ammunition. The turret shot into the air before falling back down, slamming right next to Nadia. Nadia realized she would have to be careful with certain spells in the future, lest her crest decided to give it some extra magic. The other tanks in the column veered away, giving her a wide berth as the drivers gunned the engines.

Her magically enchanted rifle flew down from the sky and landed in her hands. The Boar was a short distance away. Great pillars of dirt and snow were shooting out like giant darts trying to impale Anna as she buzzed around the Boar like a pesky fly. Nadia hopped onto the rifle and launched toward the Boar. She flew closer and closer, her coat rippling with the wind. The world was so hot and so cold. Her whole body felt like it was on fire. She was going to stab him in the chest. She was the bullet that would kill him.

The Boar was tracking Anna but caught sight of the witch with the Moon's crest speeding toward him as fast as she could. He stamped his foot, and a wall of dirt rose between them. She couldn't slow down or change direction over the wall, so she flew faster, throwing up the spell she used to save her from falling. The cushion of air caught her before she hit the dirt barricade. The rifle bayonet embedded itself through the wall punching through the hard frozen dirt. Nadia placed her hands on the wall.

"Spirits of earth, I release you from your service," she said, speaking into the spirit realm. Her voice gained an otherworldly timbre. The wall disintegrated into a heap, revealing the Boar once again. While he was distracted, Anna charged the Boar. Her dagger was out as she attempted to cut the rival wizard and get some of his blood. This was Nadia's chance as well. When his back was turned, she would attack with the bayonet. She thrust forward using the rifle like a spear. It was a sure hit as she threw her weight into the attack.

He turned just enough to avoid the blade while he brought the butt of his own weapon into her face. For a moment, her mind went blank with the throbbing pain and the sensation of falling. Somewhere she heard Anna screaming with rage. A warm liquid ran down her mouth and neck, and it took her several moments to reorientate herself to the world around her. Pulling herself out of the snow, she could see drops of blood in the snow; more blood followed, falling from her chin. Her jaw and nose throbbed. A sudden urgency reminded her she was fighting. She looked around, trying to steady herself till she found the Boar throwing Anna over his shoulder and onto the ground. With a small adjustment he put his weight on her arm, snapping it at the joint. Anna screamed, dropping her dagger in the snow. He then backed away from Anna, putting distance between him and the two witches.

"By God, you fight like hell cats. There is nothing honorable or noble about fighting you people. It's all savagery and brutality," said the Boar. He picked up his rifle out of the snow. He must have dropped it in his scuffle with Anna. "It's not like it was in the old days, there was honor in fighting the tsar's forces. What have the Communists done to you people to make you like rabid beasts?"

"If you don't like it, you can leave," hissed Anna, crawling back toward Nadia, clutching her broken arm close to her chest.

"I'm afraid my duties don't allow me that luxury. My government has told me to come and make war. So that is what I must do." The Boar raised his rifle up, pointing it at the pair. "At this range, I don't have to be terribly accurate with these rounds. If you surrender now, I can guarantee your safety."

"Don't you listen to him, Nadia, I have seen what they do to fighting women. Hanging and mutilations are just a release, after hours of torture," hissed Anna, pulling herself to her feet.

"False propaganda, girl, don't listen to her. We are a civilized people. You can join the world of reason once again. I can free you from the psychosis of Communism," he said. "If you keep fighting, I will shoot. You may be able to escape but with your friend the way she is I'm afraid she will be turned into pulped meat. There is no need to die for that despot Stalin."

"Don't pretend like I haven't seen the violence your 'civilized' people have visited upon this land. Murdering civilians, setting fire to their homes. You make a wasteland wherever you go!" shouted Nadia.

"We are doing what we must to minimize the suffering," shouted the Boar. His voice sounded pained as he spoke through the mask. His aim never wavered. "You sit in a trench for four years as bombs fall like rain! Let the poison gas wash over your friends as it chokes the air out of their lungs. You haven't seen the landscape turned into a polluted hell. Water is made undrinkable from the bodies and chemicals floating in artillery craters. A short, violent, cruel war is preferable to the never-ending hell of a meat grinder! Now, do you surrender or must I do the humane thing and end you!"

"You speak as if you have no other option. We do not, we cannot yield to the likes of you. You and your people have done too much evil for that to ever be an option," said Anna.

"That is unfortunate to hear, young ladies," he said.

"Break!" shouted Nadia throwing the spell at the Boar's rifle. He pulled the trigger, looked down at it before throwing it aside. The rifle burst, breaking in half, pieces of wood and metal flying everywhere.

"Clever girl," said the Boar. He held out his hand, and metal shards began to fly into a point in the air collecting into a ball. Nadia didn't want to give him time to create that magical shrapnel bomb of his. She took a lock of her hair, using the bayonet to cut it. Nadia blew on the tip of her hair, setting it on fire with a fire starter spell. She then took a deep breath, filling her lungs with the southern wind, and blew a giant cone of flame. The Boar stamped his foot again, creating a wall of dirt blocking the flame.

There must be lots of darkness in that mask of his, thought Nadia as she jumped onto her rifle, tossing the burning hair aside into the snow. She darted over the wall and saw the Boar pulling out a small pistol. Nadia suspected that pistol was full of enchanted bullets.

"Children of the Moon, blind my foe," whispered Nadia. Her voice for a moment sounded otherworldly. As if she wasn't speaking with her own voice but that of the Moon. A shimmering black force began to leak outside the Boar's gasmask. Not smoke, but a liquid black. It had no substance, yet it clung to him, devouring the light. He fired several times at where he thought Nadia was, the bullet creating melon sized holes at the top of the dirt wall. The Boar threw his helmet to the ground as he desperately tried to rip his mask off. Digging his fingers under the lip of the mask, he pulled it upward off the back of his head, taking a deep breath. The dark leaped off his head. When exposed to the light of day, the darkness crawled into the Boar's shadow, merging with it. He had just enough time to look up and see Nadia falling on him from above. The Moon on her forehead was full and beautiful. Her face was full of rage and hate.

The bayonet's blade pierced his shoulder, cushioning her fall. She quickly drew her pistol and fired every bullet in the clip right into the Boar's chest. The shrapnel bomb fell into the snow, causing a sizzling of steam from evaporated ice. Nadia could see the details of the Boar's face that were hidden by the mask. He was clean-shaven, with weary brown eyes. The Boar looked like a man who would be comfortable in a rocking chair. His uniform turned dark red from the seven holes in his jacket. Nadia's hand shook as she watched the dying man at her feet. Blood dripped from her palm and nose.

"You were trouble. I knew it when I saw the moon's crest on your head. Yet you are so young," coughed the Boar, blood oozing out of his mouth. "I underestimated you. I thought your youth and power could be beaten by my experience. You remind me of a witch I fought many years ago. Went by the name Mockingbird." He coughed. "Do you know her?"

"Yes, your Thule Society killed her," said Nadia, gripping the pistol tightly.

"Oh," he said, breath heavy. "I'm sorry. She was something special. Fighting you reminded me of the old days. Had we known there was witches and magicians of your caliber in the Red Army I would have done everything I could to keep us from invading. I doubt it would have had any impact. A man can only do so much in the face of the machine," he said, coughing up blood.

"Alright. Do it. If I taught you anything, it's that conflict should be short. Short and brutal, I believe you a have achieved the second part, now you just need to end my suffering."

Nadia reloaded her pistol and fired. The bullet punched into the Boar's skull, killing him. His body twitched, blood oozing out of his injuries. The wall of dirt collapsed, revealing Anna clutching her arm. Nadia began to pull the belt off of the Boar's body. She wanted that ammunition. If she could figure out how to make her own, she would be safer.

"Well, you passed your test," said Anna, looking down at the body. "Grab the identification tags as well. We need the proof. Even if we can't take the body with us," Nadia ripped the identification tags of the dead man.

"We should get going," said Nadia, looking up and seeing the second wave of tanks rumbling up. The gunners operating the machine guns were taking aim. Armored cars filled with German soldiers passed them, blitzing forward to get ahold of the lone witches in the center of the smoking battlefield.

Nadia mounted her rifle and flew away. Anna followed behind, keeping her arm close to her body. They flew back to the Soviet lines in the cloudy early morning.

24

A Small Victory

Dasha was overjoyed to see that Nadia had come back in one piece. That didn't stop him from biting her for showing up injured.

"All things considered, a bloody nose is not so bad," said Dasha. "What happened to your hat?" The shining moon crest on her head lit up the snowflakes that went by.

"Lost in the struggle," said Nadia.

It was an afternoon's journey before they returned to Soviet lines. By then, Anna was gritting her teeth and grinding them as a way of dealing with her broken hand. They finally found safety and a medic was sought out. Nadia, however, was unimpressed with the Red Army's previous treatment of her coven sister, so she began without them.

"This is going to hurt," said Nadia. She sat next to her sister beside the fire.

"What will?" asked Anna, looking very worried.

"The spell to fix your arm," said Nadia, pulling out a potion. "Drink this, it will ease the pain and make you feel better."

"You already gave me one."

"You're going to want another."

Anna drank the vial of liquid. She grimaced and hissed, shaking her head. While Anna was distracted by the horrible taste, Nadia acted.

"This tapestry is torn. Reknit," said Nadia, placing her hand on the injury. Anna screamed in pain as the magic forced pieces of shattered arm and torn ligaments back together. Anna grabbed Nadia by the collar, pulling her close to scream in the younger witch's shoulder. The muffled cry was soon followed by frantic panting.

"You are the worst doctor I have ever had," said Anna, through tears.

"I'm not a doctor," said Nadia, delicately rotating the healed arm making sure that it was working as it was supposed to. Several soldiers had come by to watch, before shrugging and walking off, assuming the injury wasn't as bad as it looked. It didn't matter to Nadia much what they thought, just that her friend had full use of her arm again.

"Are all your spells so to the point?" asked Anna.

"That was one of Olivia's spells, Mine are a bit different. More frantic."

"You didn't look frantic in the battle today. Watching you was like watching a conductor of an opera. I have never seen another witch or magician fight like you. You were a master of the battlefield. Throwing spells out that would take a witch or magician a lifetime to learn. Like that one spell of the shadows filling the Boar's mask. Hell, you blew up a tank with a word."

"You are just saying that to a novice witch," said Nadia, looking away from her friend. Anna reached over and grabbed Nadia's hand.

"Nadia, my sister. We were in a life-or-death struggle that stripped away all the unnecessary falsehoods, leaving only the truth. What I saw was a woman in her element. Not only did you survive blows that would have taken out a normal soldier, but you stood up and kept fighting. You killed the most dangerous wizard I have ever met. Right now, I feel like the novice. Seeing you working your magic let me know I still have much to learn. There is very little I can teach you from here on out. You have passed my trial, and you may leave to continue your journey."

Anna sliced off a tiny lock of her hair with her thin dagger. She then tied it to a bullet and handed it to Nadia. "This is my token of acceptance. From here on out, I call you sister. As I have from the moment I first laid eyes on you in that goat pasture all those months ago."

Nadia couldn't help herself and hugged Anna. The moment of intimate acceptance was broken by a wolf whistle.

"Kiss her, make a woman out of her, little girl," laughed a passing soldier.

"Pardon me, Nadia, I need to punch a disrespectful trooper," said Anna, breaking the embrace.

"Allow me this time," said Nadia, pulling Anna back into her seat. "I don't want you to hurt your arm I just fixed."

"Shadows of the moon," said Nadia, her hair blowing up with unseen air. "Torment this oaf for one full hour."

Black tendrils of hands began to reach out to the catcaller's shadow.

He screamed and bolted, trying to shake the shadowy assailants that found purchase under his clothes. They clung to his shadow as he ran through the camp. Anna smiled at the other soldiers trying not to be noticed by the magician in their midst.

"You might want to head back to the forest," said Anna. "But first I'm going to need the Boar's dog tags. You know, so I don't get shot for failing to carry out orders." She laughed. Nadia couldn't help but join her. It was a laugh that had no reason to be funny. But once they started, they couldn't stop, like all the pent-up stress that had felt over the past months had been released like a flood gate, leaving them laughing and giggling against each other. They then shared goodbyes, and Nadia was off, flying to the Coven of the Ever-Shining Moon and Grandmother's Forest.

"Will you stop sniffling?" yowled Dasha. "How is a cat supposed to get any shut eye when you keep snorting and spitting like a cow?"

"Oh, I do apologize for my nose filling with dried blood after getting hit in the face with a rifle butt. I should have thought of how my cat's sleeping habits would be affected," replied Nadia.

"Apology accepted," meowed Dasha. "Did we really have to stop for those herbs? I mean, it's cold!"

"Well, there are special herbs that are only grown in the snow. If you have a problem, take it up with them.

"I just might now that you mention it. Next time I see those weird plants I will pee on them," said Dasha, his whiskers twitching.

"Please don't, they're hard to find," said Nadia.

"Okay, I'll figure out another away to get my vengeance on them," he said, sticking his head deep in the bag. "I like that one herb you got. It's making me loopy, but it sure is nice."

"Catnip. Call it my apology for leaving you in the woods while I risked my life on the trials," said Nadia. She had been flying by night for hours using cat's eye spell to guide her flight. The sooner Nadia got to Grandmother's Forest, the sooner she could sleep properly. The sooner she could get working on the subsequent trial.

"Well, I don't mind if you do more of those dangerous missions if I can get that stuff afterward."

The hairs on Nadia's neck stood on end, and an electric tang hit her nose and tongue. Nadia looked up and saw the purple-clad Umbra floating overhead. She was descending towards Nadia. She flew without a broom or anything else.

"Umbra, I completed Anna's trial," said Nadia, holding up the bullet with the lock of hair.

"As I thought you would," she said. The air grew colder, and the wind picked up. "Our trial, however, must wait."

"That's fine, I could use a little rest," said Nadia.

"Unfortunately, you can't. Events have moved faster than we have expected. You will be taking your trial with Esmeralda before mine," said Umbra, flying close to Nadia as a powerful updraft blew underneath the purple-clad witch. Her robes seemed so light and airy, ill-suited to the cold temperature, yet she didn't seem to mind at all.

"I thought that I was supposed to go from youngest to oldest," said Nadia, shivering a bit with the gust of air that radiated out from Umbra.

"Esmeralda has changed the order, as is her right as high crone. Considering your favor of the Moon, you're coming challenges will be taxing."

"I didn't choose to get blessed by the Moon during your ritual. Why should I be treated any different?"

"Yeah," meowed Dasha. "At the very least we deserve a rest."

"I wish I could give it to you. I will say this however: Esmeralda's trials are dangerous. There is no shame in preserving your life and seeking us out in another ten years," said Umbra, rising to the air. Nadia rose with her.

"Wait, have other witches died doing Esmeralda's trial?"

"I can say no more. You must go east, where the ley lines take on the aspect of the dead. Esmeralda will be at their convergence. Once you have completed her task, I will find you," she said.

"How will you know where I am?" shouted Nadia.

"The storm about you is easy to spot," said Umbra. She flew off, great winds buffeting Nadia back, forcing her to keep her balance. Streaks of lightning emitted from Umbra as she flew off into the distance. It looked like she was riding a stag made of lightning.

"Mama always said stay away from witches, they are a capricious bunch. But did I listen? No," said Dasha. "Now we have to ride hither and yon without so much as a campfire."

"I wouldn't say that. The Nazis haven't made it this far east, so we can at least have a fire going."

"Best news I have heard all night," chirped Dasha as he squeezed himself back into the bag.

25
Esmeralda of the Grave

It took Nadia weeks as she searched the width and depths of the east. The terrain was so vast, and the further east she went, the fewer markers of civilization existed. Roads turned into trails and posts that held up powerlines disappeared. Modern equipment seemed to vanish. Flying overhead, she could occasionally spot work camps. Tiny compounds of modernity in name only. They either worked in forests or the sides of hills. It was clear that these camps were not voluntary places of work. Many men were being whipped and beaten as they lugged giant trees by hand with dozens of other worker prisoners. So far away from the modernized center, away from the eyes of the world. Here, the Soviet Union extracted its resources off the backs of dissidents and enemies of the state. Nadia tried not to think about them, but it was impossible as she kept running into these work camps.

"How can this system continue on?" said Nadia around a roaring campfire at the end of their long journey. Dasha was face first in a sausage.

"Pardon?" said Dasha.

"The Soviet system, how can it keep going? I was never a supporter of the Communist Party. But I never imagined that the philosophy of the liberated worker would be so twisted. Maybe I did; from what my mother told me, the idealism of bolshevism died with Lenin. They were not necessarily good times under him, but at least the idea of a brighter future existed. But I grew up around images of Stalin's bright vision. It always seemed at odds with the posters and the news reels. It all just seems like a cheap mask over a battered face."

"I have never trusted the Communists," said Esmeralda, emerging from the dark of the forests. Both Nadia and Dasha jumped.

"Esmeralda, you startled me," said Nadia, relaxing a bit. The black-clad witch stepped into the light of the campfire. Each step emphasized the sway of her hips.

"I expected to see you sooner, yet you took your time. Were you touring the locales of the east? Don't you know we have a schedule?" said Esmeralda, sitting on her broom by the fire. She crossed her legs. Her dress split open, revealing a long slender limb that looked incredibly smooth. The snow was falling faintly, and the evening temperature had dropped considerably. Yet Esmeralda wore a dress that was spider web thin. Even bundled up in her own greatcoat and drinking a portion of warmth, Nadia couldn't help but shiver.

"Aren't you cold at all?" asked Nadia.

"The cold is an old friend to me now. It is you who is shivering like a newborn lamb." Dasha had hopped onto Esmeralda's lap and began nuzzling her hand while purring. *Traitor,* Nadia thought as she watched her friend rub against a woman that made her feel uneasy.

"What's this about a schedule? Umbra implied something was

happening. That I needed to meet you first. What's going on?" asked Nadia scooting in.

"That is not for you to know, not yet anyway. Suffice it to say we have had to make a few adjustments on your trials, and that the coven has resolved to change its course," said Esmeralda, her hands trailing over Dasha's soft fur.

"If it concerns me, I would like to know what is going on," said Nadia.

"Well, that is your problem. If you don't like it, you can be on your way." Nadia couldn't help but grimace as she watched Esmeralda pick up Dasha and rub her face against his fur. "Who is a pretty kitty?" said Esmeralda, rubbing his neck.

"I am," purred Dasha as he rubbed his cheek against Esmeralda. "Being with you is like being with Nadia's catnip."

"I'm sure it is," smiled Esmeralda, before locking eyes with Nadia. "So, are we going to gab like schoolgirls all night or do you want to get your trial done?"

"What, now? I have been flying all day," said Nadia, rubbing her hands to warm them up a bit. Her potions may keep her from freezing to death, but they certainly didn't make her comfortable with the cold.

"Would you prefer that you slept on a lush bed of goose feathers, while servants offer you grapes, so you can do this trial at your convenience? Should I, a full-fledged coven member, bow to the whims of an applicant?" said Esmeralda. She was now scratching Dasha's belly.

"I didn't say that. I have just been traveling nonstop and would like a chance to collect myself first," said Nadia.

"Well, we don't have time for that. Living on the frontier was common practice for an aspiring witch back in my day. So, I will lay things out as they stand. If you don't come with me now, I will fail you. You can wait the ten years to try again and maybe learn a little respect for your betters." Nadia wanted to rebuke this woman, but instead, she chewed her lip before standing up.

"Douse," she said, extinguishing the fire with a quick spell. She then ate a piece of Dasha's fur to give her night vision. "Fine, let's get going," said Nadia, grabbing her bags and rifle.

"Smart girl," said Esmeralda, shoving Dasha into Nadia's arms. She threw one of her legs over her own broom and took off. She flew fast, but Nadia could tell she wasn't flying as fast as Nadia could go.

"I like her," said Dasha, rubbing up against Nadia's chin.

"I'm sure you do," said Nadia, taking flight with a jump as Dasha yowled in panic with the acceleration.

"I take it you don't," said Dasha.

"No, I don't, she has been rude and snobbish since we first met," replied Nadia, as she was catching up with Esmeralda. Flecks of snow stuck to her as she flew, yet they seemed to roll right off Esmeralda.

"Maybe it's just you; I feel so warm and comfortable around her," replied the cat as he purred. "But to be fair, I'm a cat who loves attention, and she was giving me plenty of it."

"Hedonist," replied Nadia. Little conversation was had between Nadia and Esmeralda as they flew across the steppes and rolling forests. The wind had picked up, and it began to snow more. The spit around Nadia's mouth began to freeze, and her teeth couldn't stop chattering. Her whole body was tense as the wind buffeted her about.

"Where are we even going!"

"To my devil's cauldron," said Esmeralda.

"What is that?" Nadia yelled over the wind.

"You will see." The two witches began to descend to the earth. The cold air began to vanish, and in its place was a sweltering heat. Snow pooled into the water at the edge of the storm, creating a great moat. The water had a rainbow shimmer like it was mixed with oil. The earth itself was charred black, with twisted grey grass. Dozens of animal skeletons lay scattered around this patch of blighted earth. Small rabbits and birds were placed every few feet from each other. The body of a decaying bear had several scavenging birds that had also perished while picking clean the carcass.

"What happened here?" asked Nadia as her feet touched the ground. She sank into it, her feet pressing the earth, releasing a black oil. "Is this place safe?"

"It most certainly isn't. Don't drink the water, and most certainly don't let Dasha touch the ground. The ground is poisonous and will occasionally release pockets of toxic gas. Not immediately fatal, but if we wait too long, well, the bones are testament enough to the effects of this place," said Esmeralda.

"I mean, is it even safe for us?" asked Nadia.

"We won't be here for long, and I wouldn't let anything happen to Dasha," smiled Esmeralda. They walked through the polluted plain. In the distance was a small forest that had no leaves and foliage, and the bark was cracked and warped.

"You still haven't told me what happened to this place," said Nadia as they entered the grove of trees. Nadia noticed several human skeletons tied to these trees, child-sized ones.

"This place is my handiwork. Well, the changing of the land at least," said Esmeralda, picking up a skull. "The locals were so fearful that the land would consume their farms. They sacrificed their children to appease the daemons that live here." She then laughed a wicked, musical laugh. "The best part is their herds and crops were still consumed by the blight."

"But why, though? What is there to gain from destroying this swath of land?" asked Nadia giving the skeletons a wide birth.

"My moniker is 'of the Grave.' Esmeralda of the Grave. My studies have taken me to the doors of death a long time ago, and I have been trying to pick the lock ever since. This is just one of many examples of making a key." An object began to be visible through the forest of trees and skeletons. At the center was a great submerged bowl almost the size of a house, like a teacup pushed sideways into the mud made of rusted metal that shed off its surface, covering the ground with red sand.

"So, what do you think applicant?" asked Esmeralda. Nadia approached the giant bowl, touching the rims and edge. She felt a stinging pain in her hand. She could see a cut on her palm. The edges of the bowl were razor-sharp. "Careful, the cauldron is not a benevolent artifact."

"Is this the devil cauldron you spoke of? Did it make this wasteland?"

"You ask a lot of questions. I suppose that is at least one admirable trait you have. I can respect a questioning mind." Esmeralda walked up to Nadia. "May I?" She said already grabbing her hand. Before Nadia knew what was happening, Esmeralda licked the blood off her hand, sending a wave of stinging pain up her arm and spine.

"Ow!" shouted Nadia, pulling her hand back from the other woman. She looked at her hand. She could see that when Esmeralda licked away her blood, the cut had vanished. All that remained was the tapestry of scars on the palm.

"If you are going to keep using your blood to power your spells, you should really learn how to close a wound like I just did. It will save your arms from becoming like mine." Esmeralda ran a finger along her arm, and the glamor that covered her was peeled back. The magic rippled like water, showing a horrific collection of self-inflicted scars. The glamor dribbled shut like water filling a glass, leaving unblemished skin.

"Don't look so upset," said Esmeralda. "A little blood to restore my youth is a small price for a demonstration of a useful spell." Nadia stepped back, keeping her arms away from Esmeralda. The beautiful witch chuckled. "You were wondering what a devil's cauldron is. I first discovered them a hundred years ago," said Esmeralda, running her hand on the rusted surface, red rust flaking off and falling into the toxic mud.

"A hundred years ago?" asked Dasha.

"Hush, cat, a lady is talking. I was driven out of my last home in Saint Petersburg. I needed time to collect, to peruse my work without distractions. The boundless east with is sparse population of steppe nomads and mining villages proved useful for my exploration of death. One day, exploring a stretch of land, I came across my first devil cauldron. It was very much as you see it now. I was intrigued for it seemed to produce the kind of magic that was linked to death. Unlike the magic found in ley lines or just floating in the air, these devil's cauldrons produced a corrosive but potent magic. It grows like a cancer undetected, and yet they keep their malignancies in check lest nature wipes them away. It is a powerful nexus point between the living world, the world of death and the spirit world."

"Why would you want to use such evil magic?" said Nadia, knowing that she had used deadly malignant magic in the past. But only in the direst of circumstances with the deserters in the woods.

"It is no eviler than a tumor, or blade in the belly," replied Esmeralda.

"It is a window into death, a way of seeing the other side without having to awaken those dreadful walking corpses to question. That look on your face says you know what I'm talking about," smiled Esmeralda. She stepped forward, pushing Nadia back against the rounded wall of the cauldron. "That hungry, lustful, manners of the dead. Their personality eroding, and their intellect shrinking to the most primal needs of feeding and consuming of flesh. So, tell me. Who did you bring back to life?"

"Olivia," she said. Esmeralda sneered and stepped away from Nadia.

"My point stands," said Esmeralda, turning away looking over the forest of dead trees. "After a century of dealing with those creatures, one seeks out alternatives. Any alternatives. So, I blight the land to learn more of that mysterious other plane of existence. Of the land of the dead."

"Why are you so curious?" asked Nadia.

"You ask too many of the wrong questions," scoffed Esmeralda. "We are not yet sisters, we might never be. My motives are my own. We shall see if you are one day worthy of knowing who I am. Until then, you are nobody. A disruptive force, a vessel for this," she said, tapping the shining crest on Nadia's forehead. The light of the moon washed over the glamor on Esmeralda's hand, peeling back and revealing a long boney hand underneath. An old hand of thin scarred skin pulled taut over cold bones. Esmeralda recoiled her hand from the crest. For a moment, Esmeralda had shown Nadia a glimpse of terror before the glamor reasserted itself.

"We have a schedule to keep," muttered Esmeralda. "Your trial as it stands is to spend a night in the cauldron, you may sleep, eat, whatever you wish. But you must stay in there for the rest of the night. In the morning you will tell me everything you have seen down there. Oh, but first you must drink this," said Esmeralda, pulling a vial of white liquid from between her cleavage.

"What is it?" asked Nadia, taking the vial.

"I see you drinking those potions like water. This will flush your system of any magical concoctions that you have been consuming. How your body can withstand so many numerous alchemical ingredients is beyond me."

"Why do I have to cleanse myself? Is there something in there that reacts negatively to it?"

"On the contrary, those potions you brew will make it more difficult for the cauldron to affect you. The cauldron naturally produces gases and poisons, they are a necessary component when interacting with it. Without them, you are just spending a night in underground room."

"I don't know how comfortable I'm going down there now. It sounds incredibly dangerous."

"It is. I only ever spend an hour at a time down there. But if you don't want to go down there then you can be on your way, and I won't have to deal with you for another ten years. I'm not forcing you down there, but if you want to be a member of the Coven of the Ever-Shining Moon, you will drink this potion and go into the cauldron." Esmeralda held the small vial out to Nadia, her hand as smooth and delicate as a newborn's. "Well?" said the older witch. Nadia grimaced but took the vial.

"Good girl. I suppose I should warn you that you might die down there. The cauldron can be treacherous to both the body and the spirit," said Esmeralda as Nadia uncorked the vial before drinking the dram of liquid. It tasted like medicine and iodine.

"I'm here, aren't I?" said Nadia, exhaling in disgust.

"Yes, you are, Now give me your cat, I have some venison that I know you will love," she said, taking the cat, who was all too happy to jump into

Esmeralda's arms.

"By the king of cat's nine tails, I'm in love!" meowed Dasha. "Nadia still owes me a proper fish."

"Hmm is that so? A real witch pays her debts promptly. Now, come along little one, it's best you don't stay here to long, lest you join the crows and rabbits. Oh, and Moon Bearer, it gets cold here at night. You best make it inside the cauldron where it will be nice and hot," Esmeralda turned and flew off on her broom, leaving Nadia feeling suddenly sick.

Her stomach gurgled as the draught began to force the contents of her stomach out of her body. She leaned on the cauldron's side as she vomited her meals of the past day and every potion she had ingested. She was sweating profusely. Not since the oxen bane had she felt so sick. She took several deep breaths and straightened herself.

"Stupid cat, just leaving without a word of good luck," mumbled Nadia as she looked inside the black darkness of the maw of the cauldron. With a deep breath, Nadia entered the darkness.

26
Fear of the Hammer

In the back of the cauldron was a spiral staircase that descended into a circular chamber below the cup. The ground was covered with shreds of red metal shavings that crackled underfoot. A man-sized pedestal sat in the center of the chamber. Nadia thought it strange the pedestal remained free of the red metal that seemed to cover the interior of the cauldron. If she had to be anywhere tonight, the pedestal would surely be the most comfortable place. There were about twelve indents in the walls of the circular chamber where sat the mummified remains of dead bodies. Their skin was pulled back in horrible rictus that revealed their teeth between thin tight lips. Their skin was the texture of leather, and their clothes were a mix of peasant and nobility. All of them were women. The corpses were unnerving as Nadia recoiled from their sight. Nadia wondered how many people Esmeralda had sent down into this awful place.

Already, the fumes were giving Nadia a headache, and it was becoming too warm to wear her heavy winter greatcoat any longer. She took off her coat and folded it and planned to use the pillow if necessary. Not that she would get any sleep with so many corpses watching her. Nadia hopped up onto the pedestal and decided to spend the night preparing.

Nadia started examining the bullets she had taken from the Boar. The spells carved into the cartridges were pretty rudimentary in their arcane constructions. Just a simple principle of amplifying the potential energy of the bullet, with explosive results. Once she found the underlying intent, it was a simple affair of inscribing the runes on her own cartridges. It was pretty clear that this wasn't a modern spell, either. A spell from long ago in the tribal past that one could inscribe on sling stone, now turned to destructive force with modern technology. Nadia made as many as she could, but a painful pounding in her skull became too much for her. Like the ticking of a clock, her head pulsed with a pain that spread from her head to her neck and jaw. Nadia's lungs felt like they were burning in her chest. It became too much. Even the cat's eyes were giving her nausea. All she could do was lay back on the uncomfortable pedestal and curl up on the jacket. She closed her eyes tight. She just wanted to get out of this place. She wanted it to be morning and for the pain in her head to end. She was forced to live in each dreadful moment. Nadia chided herself, knowing she had survived much worse and endured greater pains, yet she couldn't help but groan in the dark.

When the darkness finally closed in on her, and she was falling into herself, she opened her eyes to find that the interior of the cauldron had changed. It was like she was taken to a completely different room. The pedestal remained, but the staircase and the metal shavings had vanished. The room was still circular and made of red rusted metal, but the ground had been changed to hard red clay. The pain in her skull subsided to an aching roar that lightly throbbed behind her eyes. Nadia raised her rifle and turned the safety off. The room held burning metal torches that flickered and popped from underground gas. From the looks of it, the stairway had been replaced with a hexagonal pillar, made of the same red metal the cauldron was made of. It was covered in strange glyphs that pulsed with intense red light. The runes seemed to attack her eyes, causing them to ache.

A cackling laugh broke the silence, and Nadia immediately turned with her gun to face a potential threat. In one of the indents was a laughing corpse dressed like a Russian fairy tale princess. Her dress was red with intricate floral patterns edged with white lace. Atop her head was a bejeweled blue crown with a vail that covered the eyes. Her lips had turned black, and her flesh had greyed. Her eyes were leaking yellow fluids in sunken sockets that stained and crusted the veil over her eyes. Her teeth were stained with rotting pus. The corpse woman laughed at Nadia, pointing at her with a scraped bony finger. Heavy chains held her neck, wrists, and ankles. At least she didn't have to worry about being attacked by this dead creature.

"Stop it, why are you laughing?" shouted Nadia, keeping her rifle leveled at the head of the chained corpse.

"Because I get to pass on soon, and you will take my place," said the cackling corpse.

"I don't think I would like that," replied Nadia, looking around making sure some other dead thing wasn't sneaking up on her.

"Well, that's too bad, you look like such a delicate little thing, so skinny. You won't survive one hit from Chernobog's Juggernaut. Like a baby bird crushed with a wooden mallet." The corpse brought her fist to her hand for emphasis before erupting in howling laughter again.

"Then I better not meet this Juggernaut. I wish Esmeralda told me I would be socializing with the dead." Nadia, seeing that the corpse was not a threat, lowered her weapon. The dead woman erupted forward. Nadia fell backward on her rump. The corpse was pulling its chains taut as it lasciviously licked its teeth and lips.

"Oh, did Esmeralda tell you nothing when you came down here? Big surprise," said the corpse. "That haggard old buzzard didn't tell me anything, either; she said how I would find such great secrets. Yet I was too much of a dullard to escape."

"Escape? Listen, I'm spending the night down here, so I can move on with my trials," said Nadia, keeping her distance. The corpse relaxed her chains and sashayed backward to her place in the wall.

"Well, that's not an option. You are at the heart of the labyrinth in the spirit realm. You must escape if you want to see the land of the living again. Fear not, you won't die of starvation or thirst in this place. The Juggernaut will squish you long before that."

To punctuate her words, a loud ringing clang reverberated out of the central metal pillar. The runes pulsed with the reverberations of ringing metal. "There it is. Better start running," cackled the corpse, pointing at the exit. Another strike, with another ringing smash from inside the central pillar. Panic erupted within Nadia.

"What do I need to do to get out of here?" asked Nadia, her voice rising over the striking metal.

"How should I know? The place twists and turns and tailors itself to the traveler. But take too long and the Juggernaut will hit you dead!"

A large hammer smashed through the metal surface, and Nadia could see a glimpse of Chernobog's Juggernaut. A pulsing red eye of molten metal peeked through the wound of the central pillar.

"Here he comes, better start running."

"Please any detail you can give me before I leave, anything at all, the Juggernaut, the labyrinth, anything."

The Juggernaut had put his hand between the place where his hammer struck, and he began to tear it open, ripping the metal like it was silk.

"If you want to get out of here, you must look within yourself, or you will be sitting where I am, laughing at the next fool Esmeralda sends down here!"

The Juggernaut was tearing its way through now, and Nadia could now see the creature. It was a giant, armored monster with a molten cyclopean eye. Its face was a bronze mask in the mold of a mustached cassock. On its head was a rounded helm with chainmail that sunk into fish scaled armor that covered its body. In its hand were a large construction hammer and a farming sickle on its waistband.

"Here it comes, little bird," cackled the corpse. "Smash her for me, metal man! Set me free!"

Nadia was now running, looking back to see the Juggernaut taking a long stride forward into the hallway after Nadia. Nadia knew she would be faster on her rifle, so she threw her leg over the rifle butt and kicked off the ground only to fall back to the clay floor, hurting her knees in the process.

"Rifle fly," she shouted, shaking the weapon. The rifle remained motionless. As the Juggernaut began to close on her. Nadia scrambled to her feet and began to run down the hall. The monster was quickly outpaced, yet it continued its persistent stride. When there was enough distance between her and it, she turned and pointed her rifle at the Juggernaut. She squeezed the trigger, taking aim at its massive frame. The rifle kicked like a donkey into her shoulder. The bullet struck the Juggernaut in the chest, bouncing off the armor. Nadia fired the remaining shots into the approaching monster with no effect. She turned and ran again, trying to get more distance between her and it, taking several twists and turns down a singular corridor. She then loaded the Boar's enchanted rounds, got in her crouch, and waited. The Juggernaut turned a corner, only to be hit by the enchanted bullet. But the round bounced off the beast like a drop of rain. There was none of that dramatic destruction she saw on that battlefield while fighting the wizard. Nadia suspected this place had robbed her of her magic, and fighting was not an option. All she could do was run. She shouldered her rifle and began to jog down the winding path.

At several turns, it felt like she had made a perfect square. A bullet in the wall made it clear that she had not circled back on herself. Instead, the labyrinth didn't obey the fundamental law of space, with passages twisting back on themselves. She was much faster than the metal-clad monster, yet there was nowhere to run. No way to evade or escape the inevitable march. All the while, the exertion of her escape made her body feel sick. Each breath felt like it was filled with burning coal, and her head throbbed with crushing pain. Nadia couldn't stop to catch her breath. The Juggernaut always seemed just a hallway away, just around the corner, as she turned her own.

The fear was forgotten for a moment as Nadia found that the floor had been changed to mud. The clay mixed with a red liquid. Something in her said that the clay was mixed with blood. With each jogging step, the horrific mixture splattered. It caked onto her boots, building up to make her feet heavy and slow. Nadia looked behind her and saw that the Juggernaut was quickly closing the distance, the mud proving no impediment to the titanic monster. With each step, a cloud of steam arose, the creature running so hot that it evaporated the muck. Nadia quickened her pace till her legs screamed, and her breathing was ragged. She was practically crawling when she rounded another one of the labyrinth's many corners into a room ahead. The mud clung to her shoes. With all her might, she tried to pull her feet from the mud, only to go nowhere. The Juggernaut was closing on her. Nadia thought it was better to lose the boots than get killed, so she cut the laces on her boots and pulled her feet free. She trudged through the muck, finding that she moved more easily without the boots, even if each slimy step sent a shiver up her spine. She trudged for what felt like hours, but it could have been the moment-to-moment exertion that made it feel longer. But with a sudden shift in the ground, she found she was walking on hard clay again. She collapsed on the ground, taking a moment to look behind her. The mud had been no impediment to the Juggernaut and was only far enough away for Nadia to catch her breath for a moment.

Her lungs burned with exertion. She was exhausted and just wanted to lie there for but a moment to catch her breath, but she had no such luxury. She pulled herself into a sprinter's starting position and kicked off the hard clay. She ran flat out down the long hallway that lay before her. Her rifle banged against her back while her feet pounded the hard clay. There were no rocks or thorns to hurt her feet, just the collision of skin against of earth. She kept running. Thought and reason were gone as she used every muscle to get away from the unstoppable creature. She didn't know how long she ran. But when it felt like she could run no further, she fell. Nadia looked behind her and found the Juggernaut was a great distance away. His molten red eye was a bare flicker in the distance of this incredibly long hallway.

Nadia rolled on her back and just panted. Mud and dust were caked onto her clothes, weighing her down. She had no clue where the exit was. But she knew if she kept moving forward, she would find something. Looking straight up, she could see that the great hall she was in had no ceiling. The walls simply went on forever into the darkness. No stars, no moon, just all-consuming dark…and paintings? Nadia got to her feet and could see hundreds of paintings hanging on the walls of the hallway. They appeared with a blink of an eye. She approached one, first checking on her pursuer, who was still a great distance from her. The painting was in the style of orthodox painted icons. Nadia gasped when she realized what the painting was of.

It was an image of her watching her mother being executed by Rudolph. She couldn't help but put her hands to her mouth to stifle a cry. Sadness and despair welled up within her as she was confronted with the memory of watching her mother die. *Who would make this?* she thought. *Why is it here of all places?* Her tears cut through the cake of mud and dust on her face. She wiped the tears away quickly so as not to sob. She had to control herself. There was a monster coming after her. Even so, the tears came, but the sobbing was contained. With a deep breath, she turned to another of the painted icons. It was another portrait of her past. Her mother holding her back as her father was taken away in the back of a truck. Soldiers carrying bags of turnips and potatoes loaded into another. Her mother's face had a black eye, and her clothes were dirty. One of the soldiers stood out as Dimitri Volkov, a very different man from the one in charge of the doomed army she met months ago. A young man of stony disposition. She turned away to find the third painting of her falling into the Black Sea from a great height and the cold brine below.

All the paintings were of her life, so many hundreds of moments were made on wooden panels. There were many moments of sadness but many happy moments. There were images of her telling stories to her brother. Other peaceful moments in the woods as she collected herbs. One portrait was a collage of her making brooms that would never fly. Her first full meal after so many months of famine, a perogy filled with lamb and cabbage. The painted icon had captured how the meal was too hot to eat, even as Nadia stuffed the food in her mouth. It was disorientating to see her life laid out in such a fashion. A fear she couldn't explain came over her.

She began to jog, to get away from the Juggernaut and the paintings that took up so much space on the red iron walls. She tried not to look at them as she moved forward. She didn't want to look, so she stared forward. After what felt like hours, she found a grand archway that led to a large room.

Nadia passed through the archway before it sealed itself with a massive sheet of dense clear ice. The Juggernaut could be seen through the clear cold surface that smoked amidst the heat of the room. The beast moved slowly down the hall. She had some time before the Juggernaut arrived. Nadia turned to see dozens of scarecrows in the chamber. Each of them wore a different garb. On the far wall was doorway with key painted on it. On a pedestal before the scarecrows was a sickle designed to cut wheat. The curved edge was sharp to the touch, with Cyrillic script on the blade.

"To know yourself is to free yourself. Cut away the false disguises to find the heart of who you are and find the key to set you free," read Nadia aloud. A wave of nausea returned; she felt like she was breathing in smoke, and her head felt like it was spinning. Her stomach cramped up from the exertion and wanted to push out its meager contents onto the earthen floor. Nadia would not allow it. With gritted teeth, she advanced on the closest scarecrow with the large sickle in her hand.

The closest scarecrow was her height, with a plain dress and a broom in its twig hand. The dress was so familiar, far too familiar. Nadia bent down and lifted up the skirt, searching the length. She didn't want to find what she was looking for, then she found it. A small patch with red thread. She knew exactly what happened to this dress. It was torn when a stray branch ripped it after a fall from a new broom. The patch was then mended with red thread that was a gift from a remorseful mother. She knew these things because she was the one that made the patch. This was her dress fitted to this scarecrow. A quick look around told Nadia that all of these scarecrows were dressed as her. With her clothes.

There were dozens, some dressed up for the holidays. Nadia's school uniform was on a smaller scarecrow at a desk. A scarecrow with a much cleaner Soviet army uniform held a wooden replica of her father's rifle. One scarecrow stabbed another dressed as a German soldier, the knife raised over its head, ready for a downward strike.

Straw cats surrounded one scarecrow. Another was held a straw-covered dung paddy to its mouth. All of these appeared to be aspects of her life. Holding back nausea, she looked at the sickle in her hand. It was dark yellow, reminiscent of the gold on the Soviet flag. She pondered the inscription and looked back at the door of ice. The Juggernaut was still a ways away; with so many scarecrows, she had to work quickly. Nadia returned to the scarecrow dressed in the aspect of the witch. She took the sickle and began to cut open the scarecrow's chest.

Nadia suspected the key to the door was inside one of the scarecrows where the heart was, the sickle blade's inscription most likely being both literal and figurative. She had to pick the right scarecrow to find the key at its heart.

The blade sank deep into the straw and cloth of the scarecrow with a rough downward cut. Nadia pulled the blade out and pulled open the cavity, only to find straw. This had to be the scarecrow with the key. Nadia was a witch. After all, Nadia spent so much of her life on this path. If Nadia wasn't a witch, then who was she? She didn't want to ask these questions. She wanted to advance forward and get out of this horrible place. If she had the means, she would simply burn up all these scarecrows and take the key from the ashes.

Her head pounded in pain, and she wanted to throw up. She moved on to another scarecrow of the soldier. She cut into the crisp uniform that had never known mud or blood. The buttons and straw fell to the hard clay floor. She breathed a sigh of relief when she found no key in the chest of the straw doll. She was no soldier of the Soviet Union. She may wear the uniform, but it was refreshing to know that that uniform hadn't overtaken her. So, Nadia moved from scarecrow to scarecrow, cutting open the cloth and straw with a butcher's precision.

She cut into the lover of cats and the alchemist and found no key. Nor was she the withered scarecrow, a survivor of famine. Two effigies filled her with utter dread, the scarecrow killing a Nazi soldier and one child reaching for her doomed father.

A mighty crash of hammer against ice pulled her attention from the straw scene before her. The Juggernaut reared back and slammed his great hammer against the thick ice barrier, sending spider webs through the ice with each strike. Nadia ran to the murderous straw replica and cut open the back with the golden sickle, the cloth and straw slicing like paper. She opened the ragged tear and felt a mixture of relief and anxiety.

There was no key in the killer scarecrow, so she was no killer. A loud crash echoed through the chamber. The Juggernaut had smashed through the barrier and had entered the chamber. It roared as hot fire bled through the scales of its armor.

The hulking monster surveyed the room. Its red molten eye passed over all the straw constructs of Nadia. Its eye fell on the effigy of the witch, and it roared before it smashed the straw personification of Nadia. The straw body flew, crashing into the alchemist construct. The beast smoldered as it advanced on another straw Nadia. With its great hammer, it crushed the lover of cats into the clay floor.

For the moment, the Juggernaut was less interested in her, but this was the only reprieve she was likely to get. She moved to the effigy of the scared girl reaching for her doomed father. She then stabbed the blade into the straw chest. Looking inside the straw, she found a key made of rubies and silver. A wave of sudden anger flashed in her chest. Was this all she was? Just a frightened little girl? A smoldering glow covered her. Looking up, she could saw Chernobog's Juggernaut. Its single glowing red eye dripped molten fire over a metal mustache. The beast then raised its hammer in the air to strike Nadia. Nadia felt paralyzed. She knew she should move, but with the monster right there, she didn't know how. Then, like she was witnessing some other woman, her body moved out of the striking path of the hammer. The heavy maul crushed the effigy of the scared girl, sending straw flying.

Key in hand, Nadia ran to the door that would offer her escape. The giant pursued with long strides with slow, methodical steps. With a casual backhand swing of the hammer, it destroyed the effigy of Nadia killing the German soldier, advancing on her as she slid the key home in the lock. The door also made of ice melted like the spring, and Nadia ran into a grand chamber. The chamber was kilometers long with polished stone-grey stone floors and a domed ceiling. Atop the dome was an iris casting diffused pale light across the chamber.

The Juggernaut continued its advance on Nadia, who ran further into the grand chamber. Fatigue ate at her again, but she pushed past it. The flood of adrenalin only made the throbbing in her head worse. This place was toxic. It was making her feel physically ill as well as straining her spirit to the breaking point. She knew she was more than just a frightened girl. This place and whatever strange magic it had couldn't be right. But she remembered what Olivia once told her. One of her very last lessons. That magic was, in many ways, a mirror. It fed off the intentions and secret desires of the wielder. If this place was saying that she was a frightened girl distraught at the loss of her father, then somewhere inside her must have felt the same. She didn't know how she could feel more ill. But the thought that she was a creature driven by nothing more than fear made her fall to the polished stone floor. She struck the ground with her fists, heedless of the danger that followed her every step.

"I hate this place. I hate Esmeralda for sending me here. Why did I even enter this horrible place?" she whispered.

"Because you are nothing more than a stupid little witch," said a voice she had never expected to hear again. Looking up, she could see Vera, the owner of the tea shop from her village. Her face was marred by the two bullet holes.

"Vera?" said Nadia. "What happened to your face?"

"It's your fault. A Nazi soldier placed a pistol to my face and fired twice."

"What? How is it my fault? I didn't hold that pistol."

"But you did attempt to throw a grenade at the German commander. Our village would have been spared if you weren't such a capricious dullard."

"When I had that grenade there were already people hanging from lampposts. I was avenging the horrible mutilation of my mentor; you are delusional if you thought the Nazis were going to spare us," Nadia shouted.

"I'm delusional? You thought you could attack an army officer without consequence! Just like your idiot father. Nothing changes in your family, just a clan of fools."

"That's not fair! You have always been a closed-minded, suspicious hag."

"What's not fair is how you, of all people, get to live while we had to die," said Vera.

"We?"

From the darkness stepped out her classmate Ivanka. Her clothes were ripped, and her face had been severely beaten, with blotchy bruises on her neck.

"All of us are here, Nadia," said Ivanka.

"Not all of us were so lucky as to get a bullet," said Vera.

"They shot me in the belly, I wish it had killed me," said another voice behind her.

Nadia gasped when she saw the charred body of her classmate Sofia. "I was still alive when they poured gas over us in the killing trench. Then they set us all ablaze," said the soft-spoken Sofia.

In ones and twos, the people of her small village stepped out of the shadows. Most were riddled with bullet wounds.

"I'm sorry this happened to you all, but don't you see? It was the fascists that did this to you," pleaded Nadia.

"Yes, but why do you get to live?" asked Ivanka.

"Why did you get to escape the horrors?" asked Sofia.

"What was so special about you?" asked Vera.

"Because you're not," said Mykola, stepping from the shadows with his slashed throat. "You are just lucky."

"She was never one of us," said Sofia. "She proved it when she left us to die."

"You were too stupid to know that you shouldn't attack a military officer," said Vera.

"Too much the coward to face the consequences of your stupidity," said Ivanka.

"You think I wanted you to die?" shouted Nadia. "I had to avenge my mentor, and now I'm trying to avenge all of you as well!"

"You are a fool to think you are anything but a disaster to everything you touch," said Sofia.

"If you want to avenge our deaths, then lay down and let the Juggernaut step on your neck," said Mykola.

"I can't do that," whispered Nadia.

"Because you deserve to live?" asked Ivanka.

"We deserved to live as well," said Sofia. All the people of the village stared at Nadia, and she could see all the horrible mistreatment at the hands of her enemy.

If I hadn't fought back, would they still be alive now? she asked herself. Nadia shouldered her way through the crowd, and nobody stopped her. There were so many people. So many dead. As she moved away from the familiar dead, Nadia could see hundreds of men in the chambers, and many of them were soldiers of the Red Army and the Nazi army.

"You killed me when you threw a grenade at my machine gun nest," said a German soldier, grabbing her arm.

"Let go of me," said Nadia, pulling her pistol on the man.

"I had no interests in Nazi ideology. I just wanted to see my friends through the war," said the soldier.

Nadia shot him in the head. He stumbled with the impact before swaying forward. Another hand rested on her shoulder. She turned to see the officer who tried to stab her with a knife.

"You shot me with that pistol. I was trying to kill you because you were witch-kin and you deserved to die," he said. Nadia shot him as well.

"I was in the tank you ignited with your magic," said a scorched soldier.

"Then you shouldn't have come to my land and murdered my people," said Nadia.

"I had no choice. I was conscripted by the army. If I disobeyed, I would have been thrown into a work camp just like my father."

"You think this is supposed to make me feel sympathy for you?" shouted Nadia. "As far as I'm concerned, you are all murderers."

"What about you?" said Victor, the treacherous deserter camped by Eldernaut. "You drowned me with mud and your profane magic. How many of us have you killed directly?"

"And how many of us did you leave to die?" said Marna Katia, the nurse of the doomed army. "What you don't kill you abandon."

"When the fear overtook me, you shot me in the back because someone told you to," said the magician Petrov.

"Murder and death follow you wherever you go," said a charred Nazi soldier.

"That's not fair, I would have never done any of this if you all hadn't had your stupid bloody war."

"But we did, and you jumped in like a bomb. You are a plague on our battlefield."

"I'm not!" shouted Nadia. She fired her pistol at anyone that came too close. The dead soldiers stumbled with each shot. The light of the oculus above stared down on Nadia. She fired until her pistol was empty. The mob of dead closed in on her, each accusing her of a thousand misdeeds. They were so many she couldn't push her way through the mass. Their accusations became an indecipherable roar, and Nadia sank to her knees and pressed her head to the floor. *What if they're right?* she thought. *If I had not interfered, would these people still be alive?*

I have been running and fighting for so long but was it worth it. Was my quest for acceptance as a witch worth all this death and suffering? Was my revenge worth all these dead? Maybe it would be better if I just lay down and let the Juggernaut take me.

"Get up," said a gruff voice. A pair of hands grabbed Nadia and pulled her to her feet. "Ignore the words of the jealous dead."

Nadia looked at the man who pulled her to her feet. He was a man she had seen so often in black and white photographs. A man with strong hands and wind-burned skin and eyes the color of clashing sabers.

"Papa?"

The man took ahold of her hands and examined her palms and fingers, running his finger across her skin.

"You have strong, calloused hands," he said. "They have seen much, done even more. Such telling scars."

"Papa, if you were to admonish me now with all the other specters, it would kill me," said Nadia.

"Forget them. They are of no consequence," said Alexander. "Breathe deep and banish them."

Nadia took a breath and exhaled. The chamber was filled with a strong breeze that dissolved the dead, leaving a vast empty space. The moonlight from the oculus stared down at the pair. The fiery Juggernaut slowly approached in the distance.

"Where did they go?"

"They are a part of your shadow, as am I."

"Then you are not my father?" asked Nadia.

"Does it matter?" he replied.

"I don't know, but if you are, then…"

"I have made my journey through the land of the dead long ago. All that remains of me lies within you."

"But you were killed, your ashes were thrown into a river. When you vanished from my life, Mama crawled into a bottle and never left. I had to raise Peter on my own. The day you were taken from us was the day my childhood ended."

"You blame me for this?" he asked. Nadia met his eyes, and she was unable to keep her own from filling with tears. She fell to his chest, striking him with her fists.

"Why did you have to fight them?" she wailed. "We could have endured the famine together, as a family. But you had to be the hero everyone said you were. We thought you would return one day. You became a ragged wound that would never heal."

"I'm sorry if my absence caused you pain. I wish I could have remained in your life, to watch you grow, to see you happy, maybe making a family of your own with someone you love. But that is not the life you were given.

"Yours was the life of endurance, and struggle. You have become strong. I see before me a true child of the steppe, a survivor. The strength I see within you is not a common one. It is a strength honed by a knife's edge."

"Then why do I feel so weak, why do I feel like I'm being crushed under the weight of the world?" asked Nadia.

"Because there is doubt in your heart. Rudolph has placed a nail of darkness in your soul. It is tearing your spirit to pieces. He hopes to slow you down, so he can place a precise death blow," said Alexander.

"I don't know how to get rid of it."

"I can help you, but it will be painful."

"Almost everything in my life has been painful."

Alexander nodded, and placed his hand over her heart, and pressed. His hand pushed through her clothing and flesh. Nadia couldn't breathe as her father's hand wriggled inside her heart. He made a fist, and he pulled. Nadia screamed as his hand left her body. He pulled what felt like broken glass from her chest. He opened his hand to reveal a nail covered in clotted blood.

"This is the curse Rudolph placed on your heart. Take it."

"I don't want it," said Nadia.

"You will need it to defeat Chernobog's Juggernaut," said Alexander, pointing at the approaching beast.

"Papa, I have already tried killing the beast; there is no stopping it."

"There is a way," he said, placing the nail in her hand.

Nadia looked to find the bloody nail had turned into an obsidian cartridge in a jacket of red brass. "You want me to shoot this?"

"I want you to free yourself. All you have to do is aim for the eye."

"Papa, I'm not that good of a shot."

"Once you take aim, you will know that is not true," said her father.

"I don't think I can do it. What if I miss?"

"Then you will die."

Nadia turned to the approaching beast and loaded the cartridge before sliding the bolt home. She crouched down to steady her aim.

"Right as you are about to fire, hold your breath," said Alexander. "Then exhale after you pull the trigger."

Nadia breathed deep and took aim at the approaching Juggernaut. The shard of moonlight in her head glowed brighter as she inhaled. The Juggernaut began a loping run. If she missed, she would be crushed. But the doubt and unease in her heart were gone. So, she took another deep breath and held it. She fired. A trail of black flame left the barrel, and with it, the sensation of a snapping wire in her chest.

The bullet struck the Juggernaut in the eye. The beast fell forward, crashing down onto the polished stone, cracking the floor with its weight. The chamber began to rumble, and a large crack ripped across the floor from Juggernauts corpse and up the roof of the dome. Large chunks of stone began to fall, crashing into a large pile.

"I hit it! Papa, did you see?" she said, turning back to her father. He was gone. Nadia realized that she felt peace at that moment. She knew that he was dead and accepted it and forgiven him.

Large chunks of the roof crashed down into a rising mountain. The rubble merged into a set of spiraling stairs. Nadia climbed the growing rubble stairs, higher and higher. The light of the oculus was as bright as daylight. The air felt less acidic as she climbed upward. It wasn't long before she was high above the chamber floor. Down below were the hundreds of specters that silently watched Nadia ascend. She continued to climb, her muscle screaming and her head pounding. The oculus was within reach. Nadia jumped up and pulled herself through the passage out the maw of the cauldron. She clawed at the black sand and pulled herself forward.

"Nadia!" yowled Dasha. The cat was in the arms of Esmeralda. "Where are her things?"

"No doubt strewn about the bottom of the cauldron," said Esmeralda. "Stand up, you just past my test."

Nadia stood up on shaking legs. Esmeralda stepped forward and put Dasha in Nadia's arms. Her disapproving attitude dropped into a pleased smirk.

"Since you are obviously in a state, I will do you a kindness and retrieve your belongings from the cauldron." Esmeralda descended into the back of the cauldron and down the spiral staircase.

"So, how was it?" asked the grey cat.

Nadia said nothing and just stared out at the desiccated forest, poisoned by the cauldron's existence. Dasha pushed his paw in Nadia's cheek.

"Are you alright? You smell different."

"I'm going to be fine, Dasha. I just need some time."

27
Through Another's Eyes

Esmeralda eventually returned to the surface with Nadia's jacket, bag, and boots. She threw them at the feet of the young witch before taking Dasha out of Nadia's arms.

"Would you mind explaining to me why my cauldron is covered in bullet holes?" said Esmeralda.

"I had to shoot a few specters," said Nadia.

"Next time I send someone down there I will have to search them for weapons," sighed Esmeralda. Dasha purred as Esmeralda stroked his fur. Nadia tightened her jacket and made everything secure. "Can you fly?"

"I can fly. Where are we going?"

"To the home of one of my apprentices. She is the one who keeps watch over the cauldron," said Esmeralda, mounting her broom.

"You have apprentices?" asked Nadia.

"Dozens," said Esmeralda before handing Dasha to Nadia before taking flight. Nadia kicked off the ground, relieved that the power of flight had returned to her rifle. A feeling of peace began to grow in her heart as she climbed higher in the sky. She was tired, emotionally drained, and physically ill, but she was flying once again. It wasn't long until Nadia caught up to Esmeralda, her rifle being much faster. They left the poisoned grounds and returned to the howling blizzard. Nadia stayed close to Esmeralda. The storm was so thick that one could vanish in an instant. Nadia did her best to brace against the razor wind, but Esmeralda seemed to luxuriate in the freezing gale. The cold was no more hindrance to her than light rain.

They flew for a while, and Nadia had no idea which direction she was flying. The fluttering black dress of the other witch was her only reference point on the roiling blizzard. Nadia almost lost her guide when Esmeralda took a sudden dive toward the ground. She followed downward. She scanned for the telltale flutter of Esmeralda's black dress but couldn't see it through the whipping wind and blinding snow. Nadia spotted a cabin with a smoking chimney. It seemed a safe bet that was her destination. The assumption was correct when she met Esmeralda on the porch.

"Good, you haven't gotten lost," said Esmeralda, entering the cabin. Nadia followed her inside. The usual living accommodations were squeezed next to the tools of witchcraft. Herbology and vials for potions leaned against scrying mirrors and bundles of sage and a raven's foot. However, unlike her mentor's shop, there were more items related to the magic of death. There were skulls for the questioning of the dead and sharp blades for the practice of haruspex. Plenty of grave moss and rare hallucinogenic mushrooms that could only be found in graveyards and other burial sites.

"Ilsiya must be hunting," said Esmeralda. With a quick sweep of her hand and word of incantation, her clothes dried out. Nadia repeated the motion, her words drying her own.

"I would like to get out now," said the muffled Dasha within Nadia's coat.

"Oh yes," said Nadia, taking her coat off and letting Dasha sit on the table in the center of the room. "Do you think your apprentice would mind if I made some potions?"

"What's hers is mine. Whatever you do, you best make enough for me as payment," said Esmeralda.

"Yes, but will she mind?"

"No. We have some time before she comes back; you can tell me of your experience in the cauldron then."

Nadia put her coat by the fire. She still had the poisonous black sand and red clay under her nails. She cleaned herself in the washbasin before working.

"What do you plan on making over there?" asked Esmeralda.

"A tonic that can clear the toxins from my system," said Nadia. "The tinctures I have are only good for stopping surface level infections from injury; the cauldron's toxins have no doubt dug deep into my body. I need to use a more specific concoction to counteract the cauldron's effects."

"You mean the nausea, headaches, and fatigue? You're welcome to try, but I have never been able to get the right mixture to counteract all three," said Esmeralda.

Nadia worked while Esmeralda fed the fire and began preparing a meal. The smell of soups and flatbread caused Nadia's stomach to rumble and twist with hunger. When she was done, she swallowed a dram of the concoction. When it hit her stomach, the knots receded and the thundering in her skull subsided.

"Here," said Nadia, handing Esmeralda a corked vial. Esmeralda held it up to the firelight.

"Is that all? You were using lots of herbs."

"I need a lot to extract the oils. That substance is good vehicle to counteract the cauldron's effects. Now if you don't mind, I'm ravenous." Nadia grabbed a bowl and a slice of flatbread and began to eat.

The pair sat for some time. Nadia had no desire to talk now, and her counterpart spent the time mixing ink to transcribe Nadia's account. She wrote some notes with a vulture's quill; her script was no cresylic but a much older Uyghur alphabet.

A sudden opening of the door let a gale of freezing air into the warm cabin. Esmeralda's apprentice was dressed in animal furs, and in her hands, she held a trio of rabbits and a curved bow. Upon spotting the two guests, she dropped the rabbits and ran over to hug her mentor.

"Baba Esmeralda! You should have told me you were coming. I would have hunted something bigger for the table," said the woman.

"Don't even fret, my tulip. Ilsiya, this is Nadia," said Esmeralda.

"Is she another of your apprentices?" asked Ilsiya.

"No, she is an applicant for the coven." A hush fell over the room, with only the crackling of the fire and howling storm outside. Ilsiya looked Nadia up and down.

"She doesn't look like much. Just barely out of her girlhood," said Ilsiya.

"She has already mastered flight, while you have yet to understand the basics of enchantment," said Esmeralda. Ilsiya puffed out her chest, her hands squarely on her hips.

"I forget myself, Baba. Apologies to my esteemed guest."

"No need for any of that. I hope you don't mind I took some of your soup," said Nadia, turning toward Ilsiya. The apprentice gasped when she saw the shard of the moon glowing from Nadia's forehead.

"You, you should have waited for the rabbit," said Ilsiya. "It, it would have tasted better."

"I'm sure it would have been; unfortunately I was famished," said Nadia.

"I sent her into the cauldron," said Esmeralda.

"You what?" Ilya ran over to the table, taking Nadia's hand. "How was it? Did you get the visions?"

"I did. It was awful," said Nadia.

"Are you ready to tell me what you saw down there?" asked Esmeralda. Nadia wiped up the last drop of stew with the flatbread. The wooden bowl clunked on the table. Nadia went in depth about what she saw in the cauldron. In many ways recalling the details was like trying to remember a hazy dream. The details held firm in her mind, yet on their retelling sounded incomplete. Esmeralda would occasionally ask specific details, "What was the color of the mud?" or "Were the painted icons of modern or medieval design?"

"Honestly, I don't know what more I can tell you," said Nadia. "I really didn't have time to take any notes."

"It's just as well," said Esmeralda. "What you experienced is pretty common for those who enter the cauldron. The cauldron and the land of death is not keen to give up its secrets so easily. It also hates it when others keep secrets from it."

"So how many of our sisters have you sacrificed for this knowledge?" asked Nadia.

"I'm sorry?"

"The cauldron's interior was lined with what I assumed to be other witches. How many have you sent to their death?"

"That is not fair!" said Ilsiya, "It is a great honor and a privilege to even go see the cauldron. Baba doesn't just send anyone in there."

"If you went in there, you wouldn't think it such an honor."

"Twelve," said Esmeralda to a suddenly hushed cabin. "I lost twelve sisters to the cauldron. Five sisters and six apprentices. The first time I lost an apprentice was because of ignorance. I had just finished duplicating the cauldron. I had no idea of its potency. I left her in there overnight, just like I did with you. I found her the next morning. She had died, unable to cope with the artifact's power. I questioned her corpse and learned that the cyclopean giant crushed her. I never saw such a thing when I entered it on my own.

"Over the years I learned that only those strong of spirit could endure the cauldron's trials. I lost several more. I gave ample warning to everyone I sent down there, but the inevitable happens."

"I have been training for years to explore the cauldron," said Ilsiya. "Baba hasn't let anyone in there for ten years."

A knock on the door made everyone turn. The howling storm outside almost muffled it. Ilsiya looked at Esmeralda, her mentor giving her a nod.

"I would hate to be whoever is out there," said Dasha, who had busied himself with a leg of fresh rabbit. Ilsiya opened the door to find a purple cloaked figure in the doorway. The freezing wind flooded the cabin and threatened to kill the fire. Ice crystals formed on dew and condensation, and the air crackled with static.

"Hello, sister," said Esmeralda, standing to greet her.

"We must speak," said Umbra.

"One moment," said Esmeralda. She took out a small, curved blade and cut a lock of her hair; she then tied it to one the rabbit's bones and handed it to Nadia. "This is my token, proof of passing my trial."

"Thank you. As you said, it wasn't easy." Nadia replied. Esmeralda then stood and joined Umbra. The door was closed, leaving Ilsiya and Nadia inside.

"Lots of interesting people coming to my doorstep today," said Ilsiya. "Do you know who the woman in purple is?"

"Umbra," said Nadia.

"Umbra? As in Umbra of the Storm?" asked Ilsiya.

"I guess, I have only ever met her twice," replied Nadia.

"Who are you?"

"Pardon?"

"Who are you?" said Ilya sitting back at the table. "I have not seen my mentor in over a year and then she arrives with an applicant with a shard of the moon in her head. A witch who not only passed the cauldron trial but who is also much younger than I."

"You are not much older," said Nadia.

"But you can fly, have the blessing of the Moon, and you are on the path of joining one of the most noble and august covens in the history of our craft. I feel like I should have heard of you, but you are like a thunderbolt on a sunny day."

"I don't know what to say. I'm just Nadia. Some soldiers have taken to calling me the Night Witch. Not a moniker I'm too keen on."

"Nor am I, but the opinions of the unenlightened don't matter to me. Who was your mentor?" Nadia had to hold her breath before she could answer. She still missed her mentor terribly.

"Olivia Yosonivitch, I have heard her called the Mockingbird."

"I know of her. A dangerous witch."

"She never seemed that dangerous to me. She was always very firm in her tutelage but in many ways, she was my second mother. I miss her terribly."

"Did she pass?"

"A Nazi sorcerer killed her. He then went on to murder my mother in front of me. That was two months ago," said Nadia.

"By the three worlds, that was two months ago? By the goddess."

The door swung open, letting in the cold air once again. Umbra and Esmeralda stood in the doorway.

"My sister says you have finished her test," said Umbra. "It is time we go."

28
Grandfather Winter

Umbra, Nadia, and Dasha traveled to the howling ice winds of the northeast. The falling snow blew with fierce wrath. The weather relentlessly battered Nadia as she flew. Snow clung to her coat, and ice froze on her eyelashes and eyebrows. Her warmth potion that warded off the effects of cold could only do so much in the face of a blizzard. If it wasn't for Umbra's swirling purple clock, Nadia would have gotten lost. The storm made conversation impossible, even with Dasha, who sat within the warmth of her greatcoat.

There were several points when Nadia tore the skin on her hands where they had frozen to the rifle barrel. A few strips of cloth fixed the problem, but her hands ached when they weren't frozen numb. It was on the third morning of travel when the dawn broke the storm. The landscape that had been obscured by the blizzard was now visible in its stark barren majesty. The rolling hills of the steppe were replaced with an outcropping of blue ice and jagged rock. Trees covered in snow rose like arrowheads from the snow.

"That mountain," said Umbra, gazing northward.

"What about it?" asked Dasha.

"Your trial is there," she said, her delicate purple cloak flowing within the wind as flecks of light snow spun around her.

"What's on the mountain?" asked Nadia, kicking snow on the last of the embers of the night's fire.

"What do you know of weather magic?" asked Umbra.

"Very little. I can call upon the four cardinal winds to help with the banishing of spirits. As well as using the southern wind as a carrier of flame. But not much else. Olivia said that it is a fickle art, one best not attempted for its perils. She was very good at preparing me in the fundamentals, but I still feel there is much beyond my purview."

Umbra turned back and watched Nadia as she broke down the camp. Nadia was so busy that she was startled when Umbra put a hand on her shoulder. Looking up at Umbra, Nadia could finally get a good look at her face. She could see a pair of gentle, sad eyes.

"Prepared enough," Umbra said, pulling her hand back with a sparking static shock. "Most magic works against inert forces. You make a rifle fly when it should not move. You know to shift the properties of plants to help the body. You also know how to exaggerate forces like creating a fire by blowing on wood. From what the others tell me, you know how to break down forces, especially that machine curse. A most surprising talent you have.

"But weather magic is different. It is constantly in flux. The firmament cannot be easily held. The weather may seem like it is chaos, but it is tended by the forces of the spirit world. A spirit may control the easterly wind that blew in from the sea, another controls the baking heat of the steppe in high summer. These spirits in turn have made agreements with one another in their fashion. Agreements that make up the seasons, that form the basis for the cycles of nature. If one wishes to control the weather, to change the course laid out by these spirits, you must negotiate with them. To extract boons from these entities is no easy feat. Even the most minor spirits could prove a danger to an inexperienced witch. Your trial will involve extracting a boon from one of the most powerful weather spirits."

"Which one?" asked Dasha.

"Grandfather."

"No! You can't send her after him!" hissed Dasha.

"Who is Grandfather?" said Nadia, shouldering her bag.

"Grandfather Winter, King of Blizzards," said Umbra, "He is an old and powerful entity, who has ruled the eastern steppes for eons. He delights in sending storms to freeze anyone not near a fire in winter. I would not normally ask an applicant to extract a boon from such a fickle and dangerous spirit. But the coming challenges will require all the power we can muster. A hazardous task. But that crest on your head shows that you have a knack for negotiating with powerful beings."

"The crest of the Moon?" Nadia said. "I don't remember ever negotiating for it?"

"Even so," said Umbra. "You have spoken with our coven's namesake, an honor few of our order has ever achieved, but you an outsider, wear her mark. That is why I think you are capable of this task. You must go into the mountain glacier and into the halls of Grandfather Winter. You may choose whatever boon you wish. For the danger is yours to bear, and the prize yours to keep. I will know when you return whether you have completed your task."

"How are you going to do that?" asked Dasha.

"Boons are not subtle things," said Umbra as several arcs of electricity sparked off her, melting the snow at her feet.

"Alright," said Nadia, readying her rifle to fly. "I have come this far."

"You must leave your weapons," said Umbra.

"What?" yowled Dasha. "That is crazy! What if something happens?"

"Grandfather is tyrannical, and he sees any weapons as a threat to him. It is sure death to carry one in his presence."

Nadia looked at the mountain across the frozen lake. A cold wind blew down from that mountain. As if the glacier was cutting the wind in half.

"I will have no means of quick escape if I leave my rifle," said Nadia as she turned back to Umbra. The purple-clad witch said nothing as the wind whipped her thin cloak about. Nadia looked down at the rifle. She felt safe with it in her hands. It had been in her care for months, and Nadia never went anywhere without it. Nadia took a deep breath and handed the rifle to Umbra. Nadia began to disarm herself, taking out her pistol and bayonet. A small pile of armaments had built up at their camp.

"Well, I'm going with you this time!" said Dasha.

"Dasha, I can't risk your life in these tests."

"Dog spit," said Dasha, his tail poofed out. "I know why you left me in the woods during that warzone, and the cauldron was too dangerous for a cat. But this is different. I'm coming with you into that mountain and that is final."

"Grandfather probably won't care," said Umbra.

"See, even she says it's okay," said Dasha. "Now let's get going, that mountain is pretty far off, and I don't want to be caught out there when its dark." Dasha jumped into Nadia's bag, so he didn't have to walk in the snow.

"Do you want me to light a fire before I leave?" asked Nadia.

"Do not worry. I don't feel the cold," said Umbra, sitting in the snow. "I will meditate and pray for your safe return." Nadia nodded and began her trek toward the mountain.

"Do you think that lake is safe to cross?" asked Nadia as they approached the large lake that spilt out of the mountain glacier. "I mean is it frozen solid?"

"I don't know. It's deep winter, and we are really far north," said Dasha. "I think we will be fine."

Nadia slid down the embankment to find the white ice of the lake. She placed a foot on the ice testing its strength and finding it acceptable.

"Are you sure you aren't going to slip on that? Maybe this isn't such a good idea," said Dasha as Nadia found her footing.

"I think I have an idea for that." Nadia returned to the shore and began to dig through the heavy snow. When she found a jagged rock, she returned to the wide, slick surface of the lake. She began to chip away at the ice until she had a good handful.

"The balance of earth to the balance of ice," she said, infusing her words with magic. She then swallowed the ice that tasted minerally and of wood pulp. She grimaced as she swallowed the last of the ice as it changed from snow to cold water in her throat. Nadia took several hesitant steps and found it like walking on solid ground. She then crouched down and carved a rune of stability in the ice before tossing the stone aside.

"Dasha, I need you to bite or scratch me enough to draw a little blood," she said, holding out her arm to the cat.

"I suppose it's better than you opening up your hand with a knife," he said, resting a paw on her arm before swiping it, leaving several harsh red lines.

"That will do." She took the blood and traced the rune on the ice. "Ice of the lake, please bear our weight." The blood solidified with the spell.

"As long as that rune remains, the lake will be stable," she said. The early morning sun shone down on the ice, turning it dark blue. Light snow swirled on the surface with the gentle wind. The two trekked across the frozen expanse.

Nadia was already feeling the strain. She was so used to flying over obstacles that she didn't usually feel the weight of her bag or the cat that had tucked himself inside it. Months of the flight made her feel slow and clumsy, even with the magically enchanted ice. She huffed and puffed most of that day, often stopping to drink from her canteen or eat to regain energy. It was early evening when she made it to the glacier's maw. A cave in the ice poured out a frozen river.

"I'm going to need a bit of your hair," she said.

"No! It always hurts when you pluck it," yowled Dasha as he retreated further in the bag.

"Just a small pinch so I can see in the cave," she said, adjusting the bag.

"No! Throw some sunlight on a rock like you did when we first fled our village," hissed Dasha.

"Alright, Dasha," she said, taking out a can of food and bound some sunlight to it. It glowed with the afternoon light that played havoc with her shadow.

"So, Grandfather is in there?" asked Nadia.

"I would assume so; it has the look of a foreboding entrance if I ever saw it," said Dasha, poking his head out of the bag. "You know, it's not too late. We can find some other spirit and get their boon and claim it was Grandfather's."

"No. Umbra would know."

"Alright then," sighed Dasha. "But if things get too dangerous, I want us to run."

"I'm done running, Dasha."

The light from the enchanted can cast a golden wash over the bright blue walls of ice that surrounded Nadia. Sunbeams shown through Nadia's fingers, making shafts of shadow play on the rippling sapphire surface. There was no snow inside the cave, so Dasha could once again walk on the ground.

"I thought you would be complaining about the ice on your paws," said Nadia in a whisper. Every sound rang out and bounced off the walls and ceiling.

"I'm an all-weather cat; a little bit of ice is no hinderance to me. What about you? You're practically shivering."

"It's not the cold that's making me shiver," said Nadia.

"Then what is it?"

"I don't know. Every time I went into danger for the past several months, I have had something to protect myself. My rifle, pistol, grenade, a knife, even a bit of mud was a means of protecting myself. But I have nothing. I do not even know any spells that could shape ice. Not that it would do any good against a powerful spirit of winter," said Nadia.

"You would be correct," chirped Dasha.

"How do you know about Grandfather? I'm a witch and I hadn't even heard of him until Umbra said I would be extracting a boon from him."

"I'm a cat, I know these things," said Dasha with a tail swish.

"Well, what can you tell me about Grandfather, since you seem to know so much? I need to know everything I can about this spirit."

"Well, I have heard around the streams and creeks that he has a temper. That, more than anything, should tell you what kind of spirit he is. When he is upset, he can unleash blizzards across the land. Rumor was that Grandfather was smitten with an air spirit, and when that affection wasn't returned, he raged all winter. He is lord of the storms, who will brook no insults and is a stickler for etiquette, even if he is as rude as a ram."

"That's not a good sign," Nadia said, climbing over a boulder of ice. "Is he generous?"

"Only with his storms."

The tunnel expanded and rose upward and into a wide crevasse that opened to the sky. Nadia had to hold her hair tight as the wind pushed against her. The ground sloped down into the earth. Unlike the cauldron, whose darkness choked and smothered everything, the halls of Grandfather grew brighter the further down they went. The ice gave off a blue glow that burned Nadia's eyes. She had shut her eyes tight on several occasions where the reds and yellows of her eyelids could provide refuge from the burning blue.

"Nadia, I smell death up ahead," said Dasha as they approached an ever-widening chamber of ice.

"Is it fresh?"

"No, rotten, but preserved."

"What does that mean?"

"It means that something is dead but it's not breaking down," he said. "If you don't mind, I think I will get back in your bag." He crawled into the satchel.

"Is there anything more I should know about Grandfather's lair?" asked Nadia as they moved further into the ever-expanding hall.

"It's not a lair, it's a court."

"Well, I guess that helps," said Nadia as the full scale of the great hall became clear. The floor of the hall was made smooth like an ice-skating rink.

The walls of ice were no longer opaque and were glass clear with shimmering ripples of blue. With each step, the ice cracked before becoming smooth again as she took another step. But it was what was within the ice that made Nadia gasp. Below the surface were hundreds of frozen bodies. Perfectly preserved people with their arms crossed as if in bed or in a coffin. They were merchants, Cossacks, steppe landers, whole families. All dead beneath the ice.

"Oh," said Dasha. "Grandfather also considers himself an artist."

"This is no art I have ever seen."

"Of course not. Spirit art isn't meant to make sense to mortals."

Pillars of ice rose, each containing people inside. Some wore weapons and were mid-charge. Others groveled on their knees, while one or two appeared to be in mid-dance. They increased in frequency to a central point that led to a pool of water. Large chunks of ice floated within its depths.

"Is this the place where Grandfather rests?" asked Nadia.

"I think so," said Dasha, hopping out of the bag, his feet making four different spider webs of ice.

"Well, how do we get him out?"

"An offering perhaps?"

"I didn't bring one?"

"Just give him whatever you have?"

Nadia rummaged through her bag and found some canned food, a few drams of stimulant potions, a bundle of herbs, and a few bullets. Nothing she couldn't live without. She emptied the bag into the pool, many of the items sinking down into the blue water.

"Hmmm," said Dasha, sniffing the water. "I was sure that would work."

"What? If you weren't sure about it, you should have told me! We could have used those supplies," said Nadia, the sound echoing in the hall and reverberating back at them.

"Do not speak so loudly in my domain," rumbled the pool. Both Nadia and Dasha turned to the water that began to roil. A giant hand, the size of a cow, gripped the edge, and a giant emerged from the pool. His hair and beard were long and dripping with ice and water. He wore an ancient grey tunic lined with silver, and his skin was the white grey of fresh snow under clouds. His eyes were the color of a frozen river with the demeanor of an executioner.

"What are these baubles you have brought to my dominion, little maiden?"

"They are offerings…Grandfather," said Nadia, taking a knee.

"Meager offerings, from a meager supplicant," growled Grandfather. A hand reached outward, and all the supplies Nadia offered rested on that giant's hand. "The herbs I recognize, but what of the others?"

"Canned food, Grandfather, ammunition for a weapon, and potions."

"Potions!" boomed Grandfather. "The herbs make more sense. You are a practitioner of the feeble mortal arcane! Be you sorcerer? Wizard? Alchemist? Occultist?"

"Witch, Grandfather," said Nadia.

"A witch! I should have guessed, then I must assume this is no social call to pay tribute to the lord of the howling blizzard. You want something! Something that is mine!" Grandfather brought his fist down, smashing the ice sheet that Nadia stood on. Nadia wobbled and lost her footing, falling hard onto the ice, bruising her arms. Dasha then scurried away from the impact.

"Witch! Now you hide your allies from me! What are you playing at? Do you plan to trick me in some way? Speak or I will add you to my gallery of statues."

"I'm Nadia, Grandfather. I have no intention of deceiving you in any way. Please overlook my breach of etiquette, I'm not accustomed of interacting with spirits of any stature, let alone one who is so wise and lordly."

"Flattery," said Grandfather, spitting. "I have no need of it. You only say the thing fables tell you to say. You have no imagination. You are like so many empty headed bumkin witches that crawled out of a peasant's latrine. You have given me this meager offering, so by the ancient laws you will have your audience. Now speak!"

"I seek a favorable boon, Grandfather," said Nadia, looking up at the gigantic spirit.

"My boon! You interrupt my solitude for this! If you came to me every day for ten years with offerings of goose and goat, I would consider it. What makes a dunce like you even worthy of my favor?"

Nadia moved her hair aside, revealing the glowing moon crest. Grandfather grumbled and leaned forward, his massive face towering over Nadia. A finger rose and gently tapped the glowing crest on her head.

"Intriguing. The Moon has taken an interest in you?" said Grandfather raising to his full height. "I always enjoyed the Moon's choice of aesthetics. A true artist, that Moon. A spirit who rarely if ever gives out her gifts. Which begs the question: why you? What makes you so different, so deserving of her attention? Speak, little witch!"

The walls and ceiling thundered and shuddered with Grandfather's bark. Hundreds of cracks raced across the ice before sealing themselves up. Nadia was thrown off balance with the concussive force of Grandfather's voice. She fell again on the hard ice.

"Get up! You are as clumsy as a small child," snarled Grandfather. A flash of anger overcame Nadia.

"I'm not a child, you oafish bully!" shouted Nadia as she rose to her feet.

"Nadia, remember your etiquette!" hissed Dasha.

"No, I have been dealing with men like him my entire life. So caught up in his own petty power that everyone else looks weak or pathetic."

"You dare in mine own home to criticize me!" Grandfather inhaled, his cheeks growing large and round before he exhaled a blizzard.

Savage winds of ice and snow buffeted and blew Nadia off her feet. The force of the gale blowing her across the ice. "I'm rightful heir of Marzanna, Queen of Winter, I have held up the mantel of the raging storm long before you witches even knew the rudiments of magic. What makes you so arrogant as to show me such disrespect?"

Nadia was covered in ice that clung to her eyelashes and hair. The cold blew through her protective coat. Her muscles became stiff with the sudden shock of freezing wind. She arose again. Giant clouds of hot breath froze in midair before settling down as a light mist of snow that once again melted on her skin. Nadia marched toward Grandfather, each step careful and precise as the wind attempted to knock her over again.

"You are not the only one who bears an ancient and respected lineage. I'm a practitioner of the ancient sisterhood of Tanya. We have been dubbed enemy, and we are the masters of our own destiny. You want to know if I'm worthy? Then judge me by my enemies, a totalitarian state that seeks to wipe out all magic that is deemed profane. Numerous suspicious, xenophobic peasants who have distrusted and abused me since I was born. A demon-trafficking sorcerer who has killed my mentor. All the while his people wage a war of annihilation. If they succeed, then there will be no one left to offer you tribute. You will be forgotten, just a bad dream of a dead people."

Grandfather continued to scowl as the wind died down around him. Nadia once again stood in front of Grandfather as he looked her over. He sneered as he bent down to Nadia's level.

"You apparently have some backbone. But your enemies are nothing new for your kind. You are brave, but it is tempered by foolishness and desperation. Tell me, what would you do with my boon?" asked Grandfather.

"I would..." said Nadia but found that her voice was caught in her throat. The obvious answer was that it would help her into the Coven of the Ever-Shining Moon. But beyond that, her mind went blank. Grandfather waited for a moment, then began a deep boisterous laugh that shook the halls of the ice.

"You came to my domain, risking your scrawny hide, and you don't even know what you want my boon for?" laughed Grandfather.

"I hadn't considered it!" shouted Nadia, growing flush with embarrassment.

"Then we shall see what you really want," said Grandfather as he submerged himself in the pool.

"Maybe we should get out of here while we still have a chance," said Dasha.

"I don't think we can; we have come too far."

"At least Grandfather's tempered has cooled," he snickered.

The bubbling pool roiled with deep pockets of air exploding to the surface. Grandfather arose as water spilled off his body and fell on the outer edge of the pool. He held two great silver mirrors bejeweled with diamonds, rubies, and emeralds in each of his hands.

"Tell me, do the peasants still tell each other's fortune in winter?" asked Grandfather.

"They do, it works best on Christmas, but it's not even December," said Nadia.

"Baa, these spells will work fine anytime in the winter," said Grandfather, positioning the mirrors on either side of Nadia, creating a tunnel of infinite reflections. "Did you ever do any fortune telling as a child?"

"I did as a little girl, but I never liked what I saw."

"Most people don't," laughed Grandfather. "The Romanovs gifted me these mirrors over three hundred years ago. In exchange I gave them their crown. I found these reflections make excellent tools for fortunetelling. All you must do is use a little of your magic and ask your question. The mirrors will do the rest."

"What question do I ask?"

"Isn't it obvious? What do you want, witch?" said Grandfather as he slowly began to submerge in the ice. "Now, when you're done just push the mirrors back into the pool."

"If you don't mind, Nadia, I'm going to hop out of the way of the magic mirrors. As a cat, I don't need to know my fortune."

"Aren't you even a little curious?"

"I already know what I want. It's only humans that seem to be ever confused on that point." Dasha curled himself up and promptly began to nap.

Nadia looked at herself reflected infinitely, the scrawny woman in a brown coat with a shining crest of a nearly full moon. The traditional Christmas fortunetelling required her to put her hair down, but there was no need for that. Nadia crouched down and ran her fingers through her long black hair with its streak of white. She plucked two strands, one black and one white, and held them up to her lips. She held the spell of ignition in her mind and blew on the twin strands, lighting the strand on fire in a breath of steam. Her nostrils flared as the smell of burning hair hit them.

"With this offering of my own self I beseech this space between mirrors to reveal my fortune." Taking a deep breath, she exhaled a cloud of hot air. "What is it I desire?"

She then stared intently into the infinite reflection of mirrors. Nadia examined each iteration of herself in that grey, ever-darkening world of reflections. This was a spell that children could do, but with limited results as the proper aptitude or training in magic was essential. Nadia closed her eyes and evoked a meditative trance. When she felt herself shifting, she opened her eyes to a world of mirrored surfaces. The spirit world was influenced by the magic she cast on the mirrors, and like panes of glass, facets of a diamond, or pools of water, the world gave back images of Nadia. Reflections of Nadia biting into a juicy apple or walking in a forest on a summer's day. She saw herself with apprentices as they trekked through the forest, examining plants and toadstools.

A giant mirror embossed with reflective ice flowers showed Nadia with her mother and brother by the open fire, relaxing together after a long day. She had to look away as the sight saddened her greatly.

A stream of water at her feet showed a vision of Nadia alone in the woods. This was a much older version of herself with wrinkled lines like deep grooves across her face. Nadia moved through this reflective world. The images began to shift from the domestic to the violent. Images of burning German cities dominated panels of glass. Weeping mothers holding dead the bodies of SS soldiers filled a diamond the size of a house. Sights of Nadia stabbing, shooting, and burning dominated a ceiling. These sights horrified her as she witnessed the atrocities that she took part in. These were her desires. Nadia realized that great anger and hate had taken seed in her soul. *Is this what I want? Do I just want to take revenge for the atrocities inflicted on me and my home?* Inside, she knew she did. Tenfold. She moved on.

However, one panel amid the bloody horrors caught her eye. A vision of Nadia standing above Rudolph Becker. The sorcerer's eyes were rolled back in his head as he twitched and convulsed while Nadia looked on. But it was the look of the other self that drew her in. It wasn't one of hate or rage. That other Nadia was self-assured. Content. Unafraid. Nadia reached out and touched that panel of glass. It melted into a pool of water, and with a sudden tug, Nadia was pulled into the liquid.

She tried pulling herself out, but her efforts were futile as she was sucked into the glass. Then she was the other Nadia. The Nazi sorcerer at her feet convulsed and gurgled red foam from his mouth. Her heart was filled with relief and sadness. She never wanted to know this man. He had taken so much from her. Well, he couldn't take from her anymore. No one would ever make her feel helpless, ever again. She was not his victim. She was nobody's victim.

She took Rudolph's dagger from his limp grip and sliced his throat with cold, controlled hands. She then let the dagger fall into the snow. With a sudden tug on her heart, she was pulled back into the waking world. She had her answer. Nadia took the mirrors, sliding them along the ice, leaving a trail of scratches that quickly became smooth. Nadia pushed the mirrors into the pool, watching them sink down into the black-blue water.

"That took too long," said Dasha. "It is far too cold in here."

"It took as long as it needed."

"Do you know what you want?" said Grandfather as he arose from the pool's depths.

"I do, Grandfather. I want to never be a victim again," she said.

"You don't ask for small boons," said Grandfather. He furrowed his brow and stroked his beard in contemplation. "The Moon has marked you. Whatever she has planned for you will be great. I want to be a part of whatever that is. I can offer you this boon, but it will be on my terms. As you said, if things stay as they are, I will never get any offering again. You must remind the people of this land and the invaders that they are in my power. I offer you the power of my storms; in exchange you will give yourself over to winter. You will be exchanging power for solitude. But as a witch, I expect you are used to that."

"I am, Grandfather."

"Then do we have a deal, Nadia?" asked Grandfather.

"We have a deal."

"Then give me your hand," said Grandfather. Nadia extended her scarred hand, Grandfather with the lightest touch, tapped her palm with the tip of his massive finger. His touch was colder than anything Nadia had ever felt. So cold it burned her flesh. She screamed in pain as she grabbed her palm, only for the cold to spread to her other hand. While a band of blue runes circled her ring finger.

"What is happening? What have you done to her?" hissed Dasha.

"It is not any easy thing being the beneficiary of winter," said Grandfather as he submerged into the icy pool. "It is a cold and ruthless season, as are its gifts."

The frost on her hands climbed up her body, leaving Nadia panting and hissing. She collapsed to her knees as the frost crawled in her clothes, covering her body. The frost thickened as it climbed her neck and covered her head, leaving her immobile. She was made into a frozen, conscious statue. Dasha's anxious meows could only be heard faintly through the ice. Nadia was wracked with fear. She couldn't breathe, let alone move. Only her heart seemed unfrozen as she could hear the rhythmic thumping in her ears. Soon even that began to slow and grow sluggish, and the freezing cold that burned her seemed to infuse every cell in her body. The cold held her tight before it began to fade in its intensity. Her body adjusted to the paradigm of winter. It was in this chrysalis of ice that Nadia began to sense the cold. How it wanted to trap and hold its shape. But she sensed it could be convinced to change with the help of a little magic. She held the intent in her mind. She channeled her will into the ice, which melted in an instant. The ice water fell from Nadia, leaving her coughing and panting.

"Nadia!" yowled Dasha as he began to lick her face.

"I'm alright," coughed Nadia. "I'm alright, I just…need a moment."

"That scared the whiskers off me," he said. "You're soaking wet; we need to get you near a fire before you freeze to death."

"I…don't think we need to…" she said. "I don't feel cold at all."

"What?" Dasha said, placing a paw on her hand. "You're cold to the touch."

"I don't feel it. If anything, I feel a little warm."

29
Winter's Herald

"You have succeeded," said Umbra when Nadia returned.

"I think so," said Nadia, sitting down next to the fire.

"You have, the pressure around you is different," said Umbra, taking a seat next to Nadia. "Has Grandfather left any marks on you?"

"Just this." Nadia held out her hand with the blue ring. Umbra grasped her wrist and looked at the mark on her finger.

"I see," said Umbra. "You have done well. You have passed my trial. How do you feel?"

"Well, I don't feel the cold anymore," said Nadia. "It's a little creepy."

"This is part of the boon. The attention of the spirits is not easy thing to acclimate to."

"I'll say," said Dasha. "Do you have anything to eat? Nadia gave all our food as an offering."

"I do not, but the trees have plenty of resting birds."

"Well, I will leave you two witches to talk about witchy things while I do far more sensible cat activities," said Dasha, slinking away in the dark.

"He seems disturbed by your recent ordeal," said Umbra.

"The last two tests he was out of the way of any danger. Now he saw what dealing with Grandfather was like. He doesn't like seeing me in danger."

"A loyal friend."

"He is, even if he is uneasy."

"He will adjust. You have shown yourself quite capable of protecting yourself; he will see that."

"I just hope that this was all worth it. Protection from the cold, while extraordinary, will do little against the fascists," said Nadia. Umbra was silent as she looked at the ring of runes on Nadia's hand.

"I want you to think of falling snow."

"Why?"

"Humor me," said Umbra. Nadia closed her eyes and thought of snow. "Think of snowflakes in their individual uniqueness and imagine them falling from the sky. Think of crystalline shapes catching the wind and falling to earth."

Nadia concentrated on what Umbra was telling her. She saw the water in the cloud freezing and slowly drifting toward the earth, where it clumped up. After a minute of this meditation, Nadia felt the tickling brush of snow on her skin. Opening her eyes, she saw that it was lightly snowing.

"I did this?" asked Nadia to a nodding Umbra. "But I didn't use any spells or incantations."

"A powerful boon indeed. I suspect that if you put your mind to it, you can create a powerful blizzard."

"And the fascists are still in their summer uniforms."

"A most unfortunate circumstance for them. For your success, I offer you my token." Umbra held out her hand that held a piece of purple cloth tied around a lock of curly hair.

"Thank you, Umbra. I guess that all I have left is Lydia's trial."

"Indeed, but for the moment you must rest. You have a long way to travel to meet up with Lydia, and I have my own preparations to make."

"What kind of preparations?"

"You think that you and Anna are the only witches that hate the Nazi invaders?" said Umbra as a thunder bolt struck beside them. Nadia didn't know what startled her more. The concussive blast, or the stag made of lightning that Umbra mounted and flew away on.

30
The Hearth's Omens

The flight back to the sacred forest of the coven was uneventful. It was easy for Nadia to avoid the constant fighting on the ground. She watched as Nazi soldiers fought desperately to get into any warm building held by Soviet fighters, making the fascists pay for every scrap of ground. For her part, she concentrated on making storms. Umbra had shown her that it was easy to make it snow. With extended concentration, she could whip up a howling blizzard that grew and compounded on itself. With a breath, she could release the storm howling across the fascists' front.

One peculiarity was the presence of Soviet planes flying sorties and reconnaissance. When they caught sight, the pilots often waved to her, and several blew kisses, yet there was no time to tarry as the planes quickly outpaced her rifle.

"Can you ease up on the snowstorms!" meowed Dasha amid the maelstrom. "I'm freezing."

"How can you be freezing? You're in my coat," said Nadia.

"How can you not? Even with both our coats, I have never been this cold," said Dasha, wiggling his face closer to her body.

"I don't know, the boon has made this weather quite comfortable. If anything, I'm a little warm."

"By the ninety-nine-tailed god of cats, what is the next trial going to do to you?" he said, tucking his head in the coat.

What indeed? thought Nadia as she followed telltale signs that led her back to the sacred forest. She arrived at nightfall and found the chicken-legged hut covered in snow. She drifted down to the doorstep and knocked on the door. Lydia opened the door. Her calm and serene face was clearly distressed and fatigued.

"Come inside quickly. You are letting the storm in," said Lydia. Nadia stepped inside, and Dasha jumped out of her coat to sit by the fire. "Goodness, child, were you flying around in that soup?"

"It's not so bad. Not anymore," said Nadia, taking off her greatcoat. The inside of the hut was very warm. Nadia could feel herself sweating as the fire roared under a small cauldron. Soon, Lydia had pushed her into a chair and put a bowl of cabbage soup in her hands with a slice of rye bread. Nadia thanked her host and began to eat. Dasha was given a few slices of salt pork, which he ate, chirping with delight.

"You have passed all your tests, much more quickly than I anticipated," sighed Lydia.

"Is something wrong?" asked Nadia between bites.

"I fear the next trial before you will be too much. I have gazed into my hearth and found that the task before you will of utmost importance," said Lydia, taking a log and throwing it in the fire.

"It can't be any worse than fighting on the front or Esmeralda's cauldron," said Nadia.

"Or Umbra's spirit negotiations," meowed Dasha.

"This is different," said Lydia. "What do you know of the magic of the sorcerers of Thule?"

Nadia stopped eating and pushed the bowl away from her. Her hands balled up into fists. She squeezed them so hard that her fists shook her fingers, turning red with the effort.

"I have only ever encountered one of the Thule sorcerers," said Nadia. "A man who has given himself over completely to profane magic. He consorts with daemons, practices human sacrifice, and augments his power with occult technology. Worst of all, he has the full power of a nation behind him that approves of what he does, and even exults it."

"Is this the Thule sorcerer you spoke of when you were first being judged?" asked Lydia.

"The very same, Rudolph Becker. He is also the one who killed and mutilated Baba Olivia," replied Nadia. Lydia was silent as she fetched several herbs and mushrooms around the hut.

"It always astounds me how magic pushes and pulls us at its whims. Come sit by the fire," said Lydia, taking the cauldron off the fire. Nadia brought her chair over to sit next to Dasha, who was stretching out to warm his belly.

"It has taken me many years to read the hearth with any degree of skill. It has taken many more years to be able to show you the visions in the flame," said Lydia, tossing the herbs and fungi into the fire. "Look into the flame."

Nadia scooted forward and tuning out the howling of the storm outside and the smell of cooked cabbage. The fire flickered and popped as it crawled over the wood, devouring the bark and the knots within. Amid the orange and red, Nadia could see a black-uniformed figure. He walked down the line of villagers and partisans, stopping just long enough to shoot each in turn. The bodies collapsed like dolls. Nadia was beyond horrified, filled with angry indignation. The last person in line was spared, a young woman who looked more accustomed to living in the woods. The man turned to Nadia, showing Rudolph Becker with his red jeweled talisman around his neck. He laughed for a moment before drawing his knife and mutilating the young woman. Nadia turned from the fire, not wishing to see the young woman's horrific fate.

"This man is hunting our extended sisterhood. In truth, several Thule sorcerers are assigned to the task. But this Rudolph Becker is the most successful. This man must be stopped, so I'm tasked with the destruction of his tools."

Nadia recalled all the trauma this man had inflicted on her. The beating she took. The murder of her loved ones, and the violation of her spirit. She had grown so much in these last few months, but had she grown enough? He always seemed to have her at a disadvantage, but he had yet to kill her. Maybe that was her edge. The fact that with all his murderous guile, he was still unable to stop her.

"Must I do this alone? This man is a danger to us all. Shouldn't we all be trying to kill him?" asked Nadia. Lydia looked deep into the fire. She didn't flinch while watching the terrible things Becker did to that witch.

"If only it were that simple. I have been reading the flames. I use it to divine the future, to some extent. I have not seen our coven cross paths with Rudolph; I only ever see you. I see you fighting and dying, you surviving but crippled. Always alone with not even Dasha by your side. In all my visions you were very different iterations of yourself. None ever looked anything like the young woman who sits before me. The strings of fate are not set like marks on a stone, but there are some certainties. Anna, Esmeralda, Umbra, and I are all pulled elsewhere. My divination doesn't give clear directions, only possibilities and uncertainties. It saddens me that the task before you is so dangerous. But our world has always been a troubled one. As for your task, you need not kill him, but you must destroy his tools that allow him to find us so effectively. Otherwise, he most certainly will interfere with the plans we have set into motion."

"I don't know if I'm strong enough for the task," said Nadia, looking at her scarred hands. "He has bested me at every turn. I hate him so much, but he frightens me. I don't want to meet my end by his hands."

"There is another option," said Lydia.

"There is?"

"Yes, you can forfeit your trial. You will not have a chance of entering our coven for another ten years, but it will give you time to grow and learn. We will find our way of dealing with this man. Even if we must flee this sacred place. Never to return for another hundred years. You are not beholden to complete the tasks we set before you. If you cannot face this man, then you must find your own way without the aid of our coven."

"I don't think I can do that," said Nadia, looking at the blue band on her finger. "I have traveled too long on this path to leave it. I need to see it through."

"I suspected that this would be your decision," said Lydia. "The Mockingbird's influence is all over you. You may stay until the storm lets up. But the sooner your task is complete, the better."

That night, the wind howled against the cabin. Ice built up in the crack under the door. There was a solitary bed that both women and cat slept in. The fire had burned low, clinging to two large logs that smoldered with black wood and veined lines of ash. Lydia and Dasha had fallen asleep rather quickly, leaving Nadia alone in the flickering orange dark. Anxiety had reached into Nadia's heart at the prospect of facing down Rudolph. Memories of his handiwork on Olivia's body leaped into detailed life behind her eyes. Skeins of magic were drawing them together for some strange purpose. She closed her eyes and sank into the spirit world.

When she opened her eyes, she found the endless field of dark. Her soul's body was luminescent and tinged with a blue pale of ice. With a deep breath, she called out in the darkness.

"Mother Moon!" she yelled. "I wish for an audience."

The Moon, in the aspect of the gentle mother, arose from the dark as if rising from the horizon.

"I'm here, Nadia, no need to shout," said the Moon, dropping down to Nadia. "You seem distressed. What is the matter?"

"I'm filled with dread of my coming task," said Nadia. "These past few tasks I have done for the coven shown I have grown so much. Anna's task showed that I'm capable in combat against experienced magicians. Esmeralda's task helped me come to terms with the turmoil I have in my heart, and Umbra's task showed me what I wanted and gave me the power to achieve it. Now it seems I alone must save our sisterhood. I don't know if I'm up to the task."

"Why is that?" asked the Moon.

"I know what will happen to me if I fail," said Nadia. "I will be slowly mutilated and killed. I fear that I won't be able to keep my tongue from revealing valuable information. Not only will I be butchered, but I will be putting more of my sisters at risk. For several months, the only risks have been to me. What do I do?"

"A difficult task. You feel the weight of a grave trial. One that will have you risk everything. However, you are not alone. My children are there to help you when you need it. Now you must go, for he is watching you."

"Rudolph?" asked Nadia.

"Yes." The Moon tapped the crest on her head, and Nadia collapsed back into the waking world. Nadia looked up at the flickering shadows on the ceiling as the wind howled outside. Slowly she got out of bed and began to dress.

"What are you doing?" yawned Dasha.

"I need to use the bathroom," lied Nadia, as she grabbed her coat and bag.

"Well use the chamber pot."

"I would rather go outside," said Nadia, taking her rifle in hand.

"Nadia, are you going somewhere?"

"Dasha please," said Nadia. "Don't make this harder than it has to be."

"You are! You were going to leave without me, even when I said I wouldn't allow that ever again!" hissed Dasha as he hopped off the bed and trotted right up to Nadia. "Well, you are not abandoning me that easily."

"I'm not abandoning you," said Nadia. "I'm trying to keep you safe. I don't know if I will be coming back from this fight. I don't want to see you hung from a tree like Petrenko."

"Do not be so angry with her, Dasha," said Lydia, getting up from the bed. "She has a difficult task before her. I think she was trying to protect both you and her."

"By leaving in the middle of the night without a goodbye?" hissed

Dasha.

"I wanted to make sure you were safe," said Nadia. "If I didn't come back, I knew you would have a warm home. I don't know if I will ever come back. If I don't, I think I would be happy knowing that you are safe."

"You are just trying to wriggle your way out of getting me a fish," meowed Dasha as he rubbed his face in her hands.

"I love you, too, Dasha," said Nadia. "You have made these painful months bearable. We both lost our home. I want to make sure you are safe while I fight for our new home."

"He will be taken care of, sister," said Lydia. Nadia took ahold of Dasha and held him in her arms.

"If you don't come back, I will find you in the land of the dead and make sure you pay your debt," he meowed softly in her ears.

"When I come back, I will get you the biggest, tastiest fish you have ever seen," said Nadia. With one final squeeze, she let Dasha down on the floor.

"Sister, before you go, I have something before you," said Lydia taking a small chest out from under her bed. Inside was a pouch with a cord. "Here, it is filled with holy herbs that that can protect you from malevolent daemons." Nadia took the pouch and put the cord around her neck.

"Thank you."

Nadia opened the door, letting the storm in with a blast of freezing wind and snow. She quickly closed it and let the freezing air wash over her. Nadia mounted her rifle and took flight. Tears were frozen to her face as she climbed higher in the sky.

31
Witch of the Winter Moon

It took over a week before Nadia could track down the theater where Rudolph and his men were. He was near Moscow, where the fighting was fiercest. Rockets screamed across the horizon, landing in Axis-held territory as the Nazis fought in the city suburbs. Anti-aircraft guns thundered away at advancing German troops, while tanks blitzed across barbed wire and machine-gun embankments. Human waves of thousands of soldiers were thrown into the teeth of buzzing German machine guns, and hundreds of thousands more dug into fortified positions.

Nadia had been focusing a blizzard on this very front, one that was so intense it set record temperature drops. The Soviet kit was prepared for this cold, but the Germans were trapped in their summer uniforms. With Grandfather's boon, she pulled down a storm that made German advance impossible. This gave her time.

Nadia had found a German communications post. She waited for the cover of night before she attacked. The blizzard provided fantastic cover, but the assistance of the Moon's children covered her in the darkness that allowed Nadia to sneak up on the Nazi outpost. She landed on a search tower and bayonetted a lookout. As he died, Nadia took his dog tag that told her his name.

"I call upon the soul that has resided in this body. May no daemon or malignant spirit of this world or the next inhabit this flesh. I call upon Private Hugo Fischer, soldier of the Third Reich, invader of the Soviet Union, and lookout for his comrades. Private Hugo Fischer, return to your body for as long as your body is capable of fighting." She kissed him on the forehead and almost immediately felt his body awaken with life.

"I live!" he exhaled as he awoke.

"You don't. I have killed you, and now you are in my thrall," she said with a magical altered voice so he could understand her. "I'm looking for the leader of an Einsatzgruppe unit by the name of Rudolph Becker. He is a Thule sorcerer and I plan to see his end. Do you know where he is, Hugo?"

"I have heard that name, but I don't know where he is," said Hugo as he coughed up blood. "Our colonel was speaking to him on the radio…you have such tender lips." Hugo's eyes were pinholes of intense focus.

"Hugo, you don't have much time before your hunger for life takes you over. Is your colonel still here?"

"He is," he said through a smiling snarl, baring teeth that wanted to bite and devour.

"Tell me where he is, Hugo."

"I will, once I get that pretty tongue out of your head."

"You will behave yourself or you will be sent back to the land of the dead without the taste of human flesh. Now where is your colonel?"

Hugo ground his teeth so tight that they begin to crack and splinter, oozing blood. With a shaking hand, he pointed at a school covered in Nazi banners.

"Alright, Hugo, you are to only devour your comrades. If you eat anyone unarmed or not wearing a Nazi uniform, you will go up in cinders," said Nadia before wrapping herself in a shroud of darkness and taking flight. With magical vision, she could see Hugo climbing down from his tower and attacking his former comrades. The magic animating him would keep him fighting and killing until they destroyed his body. Probably with flame throwers or explosives. She waited. She could hear the gunshots of the other soldiers before breaking into a darkened room of the school. Inside the classroom was dozens of swastika-emblazoned army crates, most ripped open and empty. There was a single grenade resting on one of the crates; Nadia took it and placed it in her bag.

Draped in the darkness, Nadia moved into the hallways, checking for any soldiers. The hallways were empty, but panicked cries could be heard throughout the building as soldiers began to fire on the undead abomination that was once Private Hugo. One soldier came out of a door with his back turned to her.

Nadia hopped on her rifle, and in absolute silence flew over to the soldier and bayonetted him in the back. With the weight of the impact, the two hit the ground, the blade running him clean through. He yelped in pain as Nadia twisted the blade.

"That scream of yours is not nearly loud enough," she said, her magical voice translating her words. "Where is your colonel?"

"I'm not telling you anything." He yelped when Nadia pulled the blade out of his back and slammed her pistol in the back of his head.

"You will," she said, showing him the bloody blade. "With this blood of yours I can do terrible things to you. I can make your insides as hot as an inferno." She blew a spell of heat onto the bloodied blade, and the dying man under her yelped with pain before screaming. His veins pulsed flame red in his body. His eyes were wild with terror and pain. A pair of soldiers left another room to see who was screaming.

"Nachthexe!" shouted the man as his blood caught fire, turning the man into a smoldering corpse. Nadia charged the two men as they readied their rifles.

"Break!" shouted Nadia, casting the mechanical curse on the pair of weapons. With an explosive crack, the weapons burst apart, sending shrapnel into their hands, faces, and chests. This gave her time to sink her bayonet into the neck of the first guard and deliver three close-range shots from her pistol. A bullet whizzed by her as another soldier from inside a classroom took a hurried shot. He was a young man in his late teens struggling with his weapon's bolt.

"It seems your bolt is frozen shut," said Nadia before shooting the heads of the two men at her feet. The burning man smoldered between them, and the young soldier pulled out a knife in his shaking hands. Nadia's rifle hovered over her shoulder, taking aim at the boy's head. With a thought, she could have killed him. But she needed her answers. Nadia took a deep, magical breath and exhaled. The temperature of the hallway dropped to well below freezing. She summoned the Moon's dark children to blot out the electric lights so that only the light from her crest could be seen in the hallway. Nadia walked to the boy, his entire body shaking from the cold and the terrifying witch. All very unnecessary, but a bit of theatrics was part of a witch's arsenal.

"You think you can kill me with that?" said Nadia. The light of her crest illuminated the frightened soldier.

"Please...I'm still young," chattered the boy, the knife having frozen to his hand.

"Still young? I think you have plenty of blood on your hands."

"No, I was sent up a week ago, I haven't killed anyone."

"Liar," she said, pointing her pistol at his forehead. "If you lie to me again, I will make maggots erupt from your eyes and have the earth devour you."

"Please God, don't let my soul be taken by this abomination," he whispered to himself.

"What is your name?" said Nadia, crouching down to him.

"It's William," he said as Nadia's rifle shot another man who came rushing around the corner.

"Well, William, I need to know where your colonel is, I'm after a dangerous man. I want him dead. Your commander knows where he is, now you can tell me what I want to know, or I can get creative with some magic."

"Dear God in Heaven forgive me, Colonel Brotz is in the administrative office. It's on this floor, down the hall and to the left," he said. His breath coming out in clouds that froze in the air.

"Smart boy," said Nadia, before shooting him in the knee. "Now you will be sent home never to hurt anyone in this land again." The boy screamed in pain, clutching his knee. "Feel free to tell others about me. Tell all of Germany that once we are done with your army here, we will be coming for them, and that no one will be safe." She wrapped herself in darkness and left the screaming boy in the freezing hallway.

Nadia reloaded her weapon as she made her way to the administrative offices. A machine gun could be heard outside, shooting in intermittent bursts before laying out a long, continuous buzz of bullets. At the administrative office, she could hear someone shouting on the other side of the door.

"Yes, we are under attack! I don't know! An unknown magician! How do I know? One of my men is attacking our soldiers and is apparently unable to die, and the lights have gone out. If that wasn't enough, the aetheric monitor is going wild!"

Nadia opened the door and saw three men dressed in the aristocratic officer's uniform that reminded Nadia of the Boar. They worked next to a radio and a device that showed wriggling lines. She shot the two soldiers closest to her.

"Get off the radio," said Nadia, the shadows writhing around her like coiled serpents. The colonel slowly lowered the headset, hand twitching toward the pistol at his hip. Nadia shot Brotz's hand, blowing a finger off.

"Next one is going in your knee," she said, making sure there was no one else in the room.

"You must be that witch that has been giving Rudolph so much difficulty," hissed Brotz while gripping his hand. "The one that got away, the Night Witch that has been harassing our troops for months."

"I'm surprised anyone took notice," said Nadia, stepping in the room.

"You killed the Boar in front of an entire Panzer division. We took notice, and I can't think of anyone else who has escaped the witch finder. Rudolph was still quite sore about that."

"Where is he?" said Nadia, cocking the pistol's hammer for emphasis.

"Let me guess: you will do something utterly terrible to me if I don't say? If I do, I will be spared? I know how this war has been fought. I don't think I will be leaving this room alive."

"How perceptive of you."

"Might I get something to drink? I think better when I've had a drink," said Brotz. Nadia shot the man's ear.

"Shit! You pig whore!"

"Tell me where Rudolph is," said Nadia. The device next to the radio saw considerable spikes in its readings.

"You are a barbarous bitch. You people are defeated. Why do you keep fighting? You are not humans, you are gangsters and brutes, robotic machines that refuse to roll over and die! Once we rid the world of you Jewish controlled Communists, we will finally know a world of true liberation. I'm glad to die in the pursuit of erasing you from this world."

"What are you even talking about?" said Nadia. "Your head has been filled with so many evil symbols and ideas that it has driven you from your humanity. Now where is Rudolph?"

"Why don't you ask him? He is on the radio," he said. Nadia walked over, gesturing for Brotz to move. He moved over as Nadia took the headset and put it on her ears.

"Rudolph?"

"Hello Nadia." When she heard Rudolph's voice, she shot the colonel in the head. He collapsed to the ground, twitching with blood oozing on the floor. "I take it you have just killed our mutual acquaintance?"

"I have," said Nadia, the sudden rage flaring in her heart.

"I didn't think you would make it this far, I thought for sure that nail I put in your heart would drive you to suicide. Looks like I was wrong about you again."

"You keep making those kinds of mistakes, it will get you killed," she said.

"I think you are correct. You see that device next to the radio? I helped design it. It picks up aetheric energy and is a useful early warning system against magicians, wizards, witches, really any users of the occult. It's also linked to the radio, and it is showing me that you are giving off a massive amount of magical energy. I think I killed the wrong witch when we first met. I hadn't anticipated this kind of growth in such short amount of time. Now here we are. You are making such a mess of our Fuhrer's operation. I think after I kill you, the rest of Moscow will be a forgone conclusion, as well as cleaning up the last of your unclean breed."

"You were right about one thing. You did kill the wrong witch. Now tell me where you are so we can finish this."

The crackle of the storm could hear over the radio could be heard as Rudolph paused. The spikes of energy on the etheric monitor pulsed and spiked with the storm.

"The sooner the better," he said. "I'm at the Museum of the Revolution. I'm so glad it has come to this. It is so very rare that a witch would just walk into my tender care."

"That is why you people will lose this war. You have only joy in your heart when you kill, while I'm only left with hate." She threw the radio receiver aside before leaving the room. "Break," she whispered, and the radio and the aetheric monitor started sparking and sputtering. The spark set a fire that began to grow. Nadia flew out of the burning building, leaving the survivors nothing but the rumors of a powerful witch with control over ice and darkness.

The Museum of the Revolution was several kilometers west in the occupied territory of the city. Nadia could see low-level fighting within the raging storms of freezing ice. The occasional explosion of a hand grenade in house-to-house fighting punctuated the cracking of machine guns. Bullet tracers lit up the falling snow like a shooting star in the fog.

While the world fought and froze, Nadia caught sight of the museum. Amidst the storm and the night, Nadia landed unseen on the roof of the building.

Nadia's magically assisted eyes caught sight of a solitary man on his belly looking out over the square. He held a rifle with a high-powered scope that he used to survey the square below. With practiced stealth, Nadia flew over to the man before dropping on him with her bayonet. The man groaned in pain as his breath was expelled from him with the blade. Nadia didn't give him any more time as she took the blade to his neck. She had a commanding view of the museum square that would have once looked splendid but was now covered in rubble, bomb craters, and shell casings. A concrete statue of Vladimir Lenin remained untouched as he pointed off into the horizon. Nazi soldiers patrolled the outer perimeter while others sat at machine-gun nests. Unlike their summer-uniformed counterparts, these men had adequate winter protection and green, brown camouflage that stuck out in the snow but did well enough at night.

Nadia counted the number of patrolling guards before loading the special ammunition that she made from the Boar's spell. She took aim at the machine-gun nests and fired. The bullet left a hot trail through the air, melting the falling snow and turning it to steam. When it hit the machine-gun nest, it exploded, leaving a small crater.

"Artillery barrage," shouted the soldiers as they all ran for cover. Nadia lined up her shot, took out the next machine gun nest, and systematically crippled the static defense.

"This isn't artillery, it's a magical attack!" one of the soldiers shouted. Nadia loaded a fresh clip and fired five more rounds. Each shot turned a Nazi soldier into gory chunks, leaving her alone in the courtyard.

"That's it for the Boar's ammunition," she said, loading a fresh clip of standard rounds. "No need to be stingy."

The door to the museum opened, and Rudolph and a squad of men exited the building. The same squad of killers that had taken everything from her moved with practiced ease, covering each other as they spread out to look for attackers. Rudolph was wearing additional equipment over a long grey wool coat. Cables connected his metal gantlet to a large battery on his back. The gauntlet crackled with occult energy, giving off a powerful stench of ozone. On his head was a pair of goggles connected to the battery. Their function was unknown to her, and she didn't want to give him time to use them.

She took aim and fired. The bullet's aim was true, but the space around Rudolph twisted and distorted, turning the bullet around him, striking the bricks instead. She repeatedly fired; each time the bullet struck the bricks, with one striking the foot of an elite Nazi soldier. The man collapsed, clutching his foot while his comrades finally pinpointed the shots' source and returned fire. Nadia took cover, rolling back into the roof. The crack of shots continued as Nadia frantically reloaded, taking note of her ammunition count.

She had five more shots for the rifle and two clips remaining for her pistol, with a solitary grenade. Nadia pulled the pin on the grenade and threw it over the edge. She waited expectantly for the explosion, but instead all she heard was the crunching of metal and the splintering of the wooden grenade handle.

"Nadia? Is that you? Come down here. Stop this childish skirmishing."

Nadia took a quick look over the edge and saw that the grenade was held in Rudolph's gauntlet. A field of black lightning crackled around the grenade before it was crushed into a ball, its parts turning to rust and splinters. "Are you worried that we would turn you into Swiss cheese? Well, maybe, but I want to get a good look at you."

Nadia cloaked herself in shadow and flew off the building, landing in front of the concrete statue of Lenin. The soldiers all pointed their rifles at Nadia but didn't fire. The shadows melted off her, the massive floodlights casting her shadow on the concrete statue behind her.

"So, here we are," said Rudolph, taking a few steps forward. "I didn't think you would actually come. I have the tactical advantage, with men, technology, skill. You must be very stupid, desperate, or you think you have an ace up your sleeve."

Nadia said nothing, her rifle floating over her shoulder. She then slowly let her long hair down and revealed the glowing crest of the moon. Rudolph took a moment to laugh, his laughter carrying over the muffled quiet of the winter night.

"So, you found some pagan spirit to make a deal with? These superstitious women. Shoot her and bring her body to me," he said.

"Break!" shouted Nadia, the dozen rifles aimed at her immediately jammed and cracked. The floodlights that filled the square with light burned out and fizzled. Only Rudolph's equipment seemed unfazed by Nadia's spell.

"Impressive. Cast your weapons aside before they explode in your face," said Rudolph. His men complied with grim efficiency, throwing the weapons aside as they burst apart.

"So, you have some power to play around with," he said. "Men of the Waffen SS, this woman has dishonored our organization, and the only possible justice is that she meets her end by the daggers bestowed on you by Henrich Himmler himself. As he commanded, we are to use these weapons against anyone who has besmirched our honor." The men began to pull out their ceremonial daggers.

"Now bring this witch to her end with the tips of your Ehrendolchs!"

The men charged forward, not in a frenzied rush but in a methodical attempt to surround her. Two men stayed behind with Rudolph. Their own daggers were drawn in preparation. Nadia pulled out her bayonet and blew on its tip to heat up the blade to a red-hot glow while also flicking the holster of her pistol. When the SS soldiers saw this small action, they charged from all sides. With a thought, the rifle started shooting, taking a man's head off with each shot. Nadia dropped to her knee and took a deep breath, readying a spell in her mind. With an exhale of the southern wind on the tip of the burning bayonet, a jet of flame consumed a trio of men and stopping several more in their tracks. She drew her pistol and began to fire on the oncoming soldiers. She fired until the pistol was empty. These men who were temporarily halted rushed her again. The rifle fired twice before it was empty, which left a single soldier charging her with brandished steel. Once again, she took a deep breath and sent out another blast of fire that enveloped the man completely.

Nadia was so concentrated on the conflagration that she didn't notice another soldier she thought dead had crawled forward and stabbed her in the leg with his dagger. She screamed in pain before turning on the man and stabbing him in the neck with her red-hot bayonet. Steam and blood erupted from the man's wound, but he had just enough life to grab her by the collar and pull her to the ground. The pain in her leg exploded as the dagger dug deeper with the fall, slicing muscle and cutting bone. The three men she had set fire to had put themselves out and began to stalk forward like hunters on a wounded doe. Nadia, unable to reproduce the flame spell with a cooled dagger, ejected the magazine from her pistol and loaded a new one.

The SS men ran into her gunfire without hesitation or fear. Her aim was good, as she felled two of the men before filling the third with bullets. To her horror, the pistol clicked several times.

The last man practically threw himself down on her, the dagger plunging into her shoulder, cutting her collar bone. The soldier was in her face, blood oozing from his mouth. Nadia pulled the dagger out of her leg and stabbed the guts of the man on top of her. She stabbed again and again until he went limp. With her one good arm, Nadia pushed the man off her. She was bleeding profusely from her injuries. She searched her pockets, pulled out a vial of magical elixir and poured it on her injuries. She hissed as the wound began to clot and seal up on its own, she then pulled herself to her feet. The dozen or so men lay dead or dying around her. They had fought with fury and fanaticism that she had not seen in other German troops. Nadia took hold of her floating rifle to steady herself.

Rudolph began to clap while his remaining men unzipped their jackets and discarded their helmets. The pain in her shoulder and leg ached, and she felt weak. She didn't know if she could take these last three men head-on.

"What a wonderful display of applied magical combat," said Rudolph. "Were you not a Slavic witch, I would enthusiastically accept you into our ranks. But seeing as you are an abomination, you must be destroyed by whatever means necessary."

The two remaining soldiers had stripped off their shirts, their bodies covered in repugnant runes that crawled on their flesh like cancerous spider limbs.

"You're one to talk of abominations. I don't traffic with daemons or use human sacrifice as components for my spells," shouted Nadia.

"It's funny you should mention daemons," said Rudolph. He snapped his fingers, and the two soldiers brought the daggers up to their necks and sliced their throats. The men fell to their knees, blood pooling in the snow. "I see the horror in your eyes. You are thinking to yourself, 'Why would they willingly do this?' The answer, witch, is when you are fighting for honor and the future of your race, how could you not?"

The blood pooled into a small pond, and two pairs of finned hands climbed out. Toad-like beasts crawled out into the snow, reeking of rotting flesh and fetid blood. Their long spindly legs were bent and twisted in the wrong way a toad would typically be, more akin to a grasshopper than the toad or frog they mimicked. The pouches under their necks swelled with grotesque sores that wheezed when they expanded. When they opened their mouths, they began to sing like monks in a choir.

"We have been brought to this place, oh lord, what is our task, oh lord," the daemon toads sang in unison.

"Kill the witch," said Rudolph.

With these words, a pair of tongues shot out of the daemons' massive mouths. The unnaturally long appendages grabbed Nadia and pulled off her feet. They threw Nadia into the lobby of the museum. Pain spiked in her shoulder and leg, which overwhelmed her for a moment. Through gritted teeth, she pulled herself up. The images of Soviet exultation of the worker were behind her. She took a moment to collect herself as the sound of wet, webbed feet hit the smooth stone floor. The two daemons hopped on their unnatural legs.

"Oh lord," sang the toads, "your sins are ours to bear, oh lord, we will eat her bones and hair. The blood of maidens will gush like tears and wine."

Nadia did her best to clamber to her feet, looking for anything use as spell components. In desperation, Nadia stabbed her fingers into her injured shoulder and found the blood she needed. Nadia stuck the fingers in her mouth, tasting the iron in the thickening blood. She transformed the blood into a concealing smog and spat it out in a large cloud.

"Hide, oh maiden, hide from our eyes, but you cannot hide from God's sight," chanted the toads as they bounced into the cloud of smoke. Nadia limped away from the monsters. She was not equipped to fight these creatures. She had no ammunition, no explosives. The Kindersnatch in the woods almost killed her. These were very different from that monster, but their parodies of religion mimicked the Kindersnatch's parody of maternal care.

Toads shouldn't be out in the winter, thought Nadia as she limped into a room filled with uniforms and photos of the 1917 Revolution. The weapons and armaments have long been gutted for the current war effort. Maybe that was why they brought her inside. Maybe the cold was too much for them. Looking up, she could see that the room had a giant skylight that was well beyond her reach. With concentrated effort, she summoned her rifle with her will.

Nadia was pelted between her shoulder blades, knocking her off her feet. One of the toads had struck her with his tongue before moving in with quick hops. The monster landed right on top of Nadia's legs, astride her body. The beast loomed over her, his slimy hands flipping her over to face it.

"Oh lord, I thank you for this feast that will quell these famished urges."

Nadia tried to wriggle out of the beast's hands, but his strength was too great. The beast opened his mouth and moved to devour her headfirst. She couldn't help screaming as the beast slipped his large mouth over her head. But when the creature's tongue brushed against the crest of the moon, it recoiled, spitting her out.

"Tastes of purified moonlight, oh lord, best break the neck and pity the wastage," said the frog, gripping Nadia's neck to kill Nadia with its great strength.

A crash and shattering glass rained down, followed by snow and a rush of freezing cold air. Nadia was given a moment to think as her flying rifle began to club itself against the creature's head. Nadia took a deep breath of the winter air and exhaled a freezing eastern wind that knocked the daemon off its feet. Nadia had to grab ahold of her rifle to stand up, and with a kick off the ground, she was out of the skylight. If the daemons wanted to fight, they would have to do so on her terms, outside.

Nadia waited for a moment above the museum, the storm gathering intensity around her. The toads jumped up through the skylight. They were visibly distressed as they held their hands in mock prayer. They sniffed around with their broad snouts.

"The purity of the moon," said Nadia aloud. She focused on the moon's light, on its clean properties. With this thought came the image of the moon, large and swollen with light. It was a full moon tonight. She gripped the pouch of herbs given to her by Lydia. The herbs spoke to her in the language of plants.

"It's time," said the dried herbs in the pouch. Nadia took its contents and swallowed the bitter herbs. Then it became so clear to her; the storm was suddenly peaceful, the light from her head grew brighter, and the storm grew in strength. Moonlight shown bright in her eyes, and magical power pulsed off her. She was like a stone sending ripples in the water of the world around her. The daemons looked up, and Nadia thought she felt fear as they dropped to their crooked knees.

She was the storm. She was the moon.

She descended on the beasts as they were knocked down. They cowered as the light spread over them.

"Have mercy, high priestess!" shouted the toads.

"I can see that these are not your true forms," said Nadia. "That you have been twisted by ignorance and hate, frogs covered in the oil stink of putrid spiritual energy. I will say your true name, Vodyanoy."

She placed her hands on the heads of the creatures, and a light black smoke erupted from the mouths of the daemons. The shapes reduced in size, and their legs snapped back into position more akin to a frog. They adjusted themselves and squatted, looking up at Nadia.

"We thank you high priestess of the Winter Moon, we no longer bear the sins of the mortals, we return to the great river for penance."

The Vodyanoy traced a circle on the ground that melted into water. With a high jump, they dove into the small pools and vanished, leaving only rapidly freezing puddle. Nadia returned to the edge of the building and looked down at Rudolph still in front of the museum. Even in the dark of the storm, Nadia could see his aura of black light. She flew off the roof to find Rudolph looking over his men. Above him, Nadia could see a small sun of black light. Nadia wondered why she didn't see it earlier, but then she realized that she saw the spirit and physical realms overlapping.

"Your daemons have been purified," said Nadia, landing on her feet, the pain in her leg and arms a vague suggestion. "Your men are dead, you are alone."

"What is this?" said Rudolph turning to see Nadia. "Still alive? Why is a little pagan whore so difficult to handle? Am I surrounded by incompetence?" He kicked one of the charred soldiers. "No, there is no faith in their vision. The vision of a pure world, absent of fear and hatred and the degradations of an inferior people. Maybe your vision is somehow purer in its subhuman way."

"Mine is clearer," said Nadia, pulling her bayonet out of the soldier's neck and hooking it on the end of her rifle. "Mine was guided by survival."

"Then we have the same vision, only from different angles. For every true Nazi is fighting for the preservation of the Aryan race and its way of life. By rooting out Communism, and degenerates, and malcontents. By wiping these people out we are ensuring our survival. The Slavs are clearly doing the same with our own German race."

"You call murder survival?" said Nadia, "You know nothing of survival. You have only lived as the persecutor for your own perverse fantasies. I have always lived on the outside, as a woman, as a daughter of disgraced war hero, as an ancient practitioner of a sacred craft. I have known suspicion, and mistrust from people like you my entire life. You loudly proclaim yourself the victim as you place your boot on another's neck. I have felt the weight of that boot. Now the boot is on your neck, and I'm no longer your victim."

"No, you are not," he said. The sun above him began to grow and swell with bulbous and warped arrogance. "But you must still be killed because our coexistence is impossible. Even if it means my death, I will fight on, for my honor is loyalty."

Rudolph's talisman pulsed with a bright red light, blinding Nadia with its unnatural flash. Rudolph was bigger than her, and with a quick, fluid motion, he punched her in the gut, pulling her off the ground. It was much stronger than a regular punch, and she felt a rib break. She coughed and hacked on the ground. The snow pressed against her face. A sharp kick to her hand sent searing pain in her fingers, making her lose her grip on the rifle. The metal gauntlet grabbed her by the collar, lifting her up off the ground.

"This device I created feeds on background pain and suffering. Every

464

gunshot and bomb blast keeps this device filled with readily available power, giving me the strength of three men, as well as the fuel for certain spells," said Rudolph. His other bare hand began to strike Nadia in the face.

"I may not be as adept at combat magic like yourself, but I find clever workarounds." Like an Olympic discus thrower, Rudolph spun three times before throwing Nadia. She tumbled head over heel and barely managed to throw out the spell that kept her floating above the ground.

"I was wondering if you had any more tricks, but it seems you're out. That little spell that sabotages machines doesn't seem to work on my equipment. No ammo, no more clever spells, just a weak girl who should have stayed in her place and never looked for mysteries in the hedge."

Nadia hit the ground coughing. She was severely injured, even if the pain felt far away. She struggled to her feet on shaking legs.

"Children of the Moon, I call on your aid." The shadows began to peel off the walls and statues and surged toward Rudolph like a swarm of wolves.

"What is this?" said Rudolph, striking the shadows with his gauntlet to little effect.

"Grandfather, I invoke your storms." The wind picked up, and a gale of ice washed over Rudolph, making him brace as the shadows grabbed ahold and blinded him.

"Father, bring me my rifle," she said, and the flying weapon flew into her broken hands.

"What manner of creatures have you been consorting with!" shouted Rudolph as the shadow clung to his head.

"Mother Moon, lend me your light," she said, breaking off a shard of the moonlight from her crest and placing it on her bayonet. She held tight with broken fingers, and taking a deep breath, charged Rudolph.

In a blind panic, the Nazi officer began to fire bursts of blinding black light that skipped and repelled off the moonlight bayonet. She moved with the freezing gale; her hair was wild and glowing luminescent from the light of the moon crest in her head.

"Get off me, you grotesque spirits!" shouted Rudolph as he pulled the shadow from his face with the sparking gauntlet.

The bayonet hit a magical barrier. Rudolph was staggered for a moment as the light from the bayonet grew. The battery on Rudolph's back began to spark and hum before a flash of moonlight burst the shield and the battery like a bubble.

Nadia's bayonet pierced Rudolph's gut, the light shining through the sudden rivulets of blood. Rudolph was knocked off his feet with the impact. He looked shocked to find that he had been stabbed. He looked up a Nadia in fearful amazement.

"Not yet! I have not seen the Fuhrer's work complete!" said Rudolph, and rage broke through Nadia's clarity. She pulled the bayonet from his gut and stabbed him again. Growls of rage turned to savage yells and then into wailing tears. She stabbed him over and over before slipping in his blood, landing on Rudolph's body. Crawling up to him, she put her hands around his neck and began to squeeze his throat while screaming with rage. He was very much dead when her strength gave out. Rolling from him, she lay in the snow.

She had gotten her revenge, killing the man who destroyed her life, but she felt empty and tired. Her injuries could no longer be ignored, and the lack of blood was making her feel woozy. She got up to her knees and pulled the glowing red pendant off of Rudolph's neck. It pulsed with the throbbing beat of a heart. With what little strength she had left, she pulled herself to her feet and walked toward the museum. She needed to rest. Find shelter. But as she walked, her feet began to drag, her head became light, and she collapsed into the snow.

32
Sisterhood

Nadia's eyes fluttered open into the cold air of a hospital hall. She was in a bed with scratchy sheets, and her arm was in a sling. She was bandaged up, yet she was in no pain. Her head felt exquisitely cloudy. She was surprised that she had her own room, as her experience with hospitals was always in a public space, with dozens of hospital beds stacked right next to each other. This level of privacy was an unexpected luxury. Her clothes and jacket were folded and placed on a small table, while her rifle leaned against the wall below several portraits of Lenin, Stalin, and Marx. A nurse peeked her head in and was about to leave before realizing Nadia was awake.

"Girls, she is awake!" shouted the nurse, who came in with a clipboard. "How do you feel, sister?"

"I feel fuzzy," croaked Nadia as the nurse took notes.

"Well, you have been given a full ration of morphine. Others have been getting much less, if at all," said the nurse. "It will wear off in a few hours."

A few other nurses came into the room, asking if she was alright and if she needed anything.

"How long was I out?" asked Nadia.

"A week!" said one of the nurses. "A patrol of soldiers found you surrounded by dead Nazis, including one of their state sorcerers. They are going to give you a medal, even though everyone thought it would be awarded after your death. It's a miracle you didn't freeze to death."

"That's not even the best news! The fascists are being driven back!" said one of the nurses.

"What?" said Nadia in astonishment.

"The Premier Stalin unleashed a secret army of tanks and soldiers on the fifth. The Nazis are retreating!"

"They are not out yet, but for the first time in this terrible war we are on the attack!"

"That's wonderful news," said Nadia closing her eyes.

"So, tell us, are you a witch?" asked one of the excited nurses. Nadia was hesitant for a moment. It was never something you wanted to admit to, and her instincts told her to lie. But something in the nurse's expression changed her mind.

"Yes," she said to squeals of delight.

"That must explain those other women!"

"She must be part of a coven!"

"Other women?" asked Nadia.

"Oh, dear me, yes, you have visitors! We will go fetch them."

"Isn't that against protocol?" asked one of the nurses.

"She is a hero, they get special treatment," said the nurses. Nadia was meticulously checked and rechecked before the Coven of the Ever-Shining

Moon walked in. Anna, Esmeralda, Umbra, and Lydia entered the room as if they stepped out of a painting. Dasha was riding on Lydia's shoulder.

"Nadia!" meowed Dasha jumping on the bed, bouncing over to rub his face on Nadia. "I thought you were a goner!"

"I guess it takes more than that to get rid of me," laughed Nadia as she stroked Dasha with her good hand.

"Leave us," said Esmeralda to the gaggle of nurses.

"We still need to make sure she has no lasting damage," said one of the nurses.

"Leave us or suffer the consequences," said Esmeralda.

"This conversation is not yours to hear," smiled Anna. "After all, you don't want the secret police to come to your door asking what you heard."

"I take your meaning," said the nurse. "Girls, let's give the hero and her guests some space." The room emptied except for the small coven of witches.

"I don't have to go do I?" asked Dasha.

"Of course not," said Esmeralda, running her hand across his back to an audible purr.

"I have completed my—" started Nadia before Umbra place a finger on her lip. Anna looked behind the portraits and found a hidden microphone and recording device. With a whispered spell, the recording device sputtered before stopping entirely.

"Did you know it took me three months of continuous practice to learn that spell you made up on the spot?" said Anna.

"I didn't," said Nadia.

"That was why I thought you should join us, and now here you are," said Anna.

"Have you completed your task?" asked Lydia, clutching a lantern with a small flame inside.

"I have. Rudolph Becker is dead, and his amulet is hopefully in the pocket of my coat," said Nadia, pointing with her good hand. Umbra searched the pockets of the jacket and pulled out the blood-red pendant. They all gasped in disgust as they looked at the marble hanging from the silver chain.

"We will see to its destruction," said Lydia and placed the amulet in a small pouch. She then took a bundle of burned sage tied with a lock of her hair and handed it to Nadia. "My token for the completion of your trial."

"You were instrumental in our plan, sister," said Anna. "If you hadn't tied down Rudolph, then there was a chance he would have disrupted our strikes on the fifth."

"You all helped with the offensive?" asked Nadia.

"Of course. Why do you think we had such a strict timetable?" said Esmeralda.

"On the fifth, we attacked the backlines of the nazis hindering them enough for the Red Army to do some real damage." Said Anna.

"Now they are in retreat. All thanks to you," said Lydia.

"Can you stand?" asked Umbra.

"I think so," said Nadia, carefully uncovering herself as Dasha bounced to the foot of the bed. Anna took a step closer as Nadia wobbled onto her feet.

"Steady, they have been working on you with crude medicine," said Esmeralda.

"I'm alright."

"Good," said Lydia. "Stand here please." She gestured to the empty space in the room. Nadia took several shaky steps closer, her bare feet hitting the cold tile. The four witches stood around her in the cardinal directions: Anna in the west, Esmeralda in the east, Lydia in the south, and Umbra in the north. They each took a candle and lit it with the tiny flame in Lydia's lantern.

"What are you doing?" asked Dasha

"Quiet, feline," said Esmeralda.

"I, Anna, envoy to the kingdom have tasked this sister of our craft an ordeal of battle. She has slain a deadly warrior and proved she is prepared in protecting our coven, I give her my blessing."

"I, Esmeralda, high crone of the Ever-Shining Moon, have tasked this sister of our craft with an ordeal of spirit. She has traveled to a place where the spirits dwell, where the land of the dead and the waking world intersect. By navigating this dangerous terrain, she has proved that she can discover deeper mysteries. I give her my blessing."

"I, Umbra, guardian of the storm, have tasked this sister of our craft with an ordeal of diplomacy. She entered the halls of Grandfather and negotiated a boon to the benefit of herself and the coven. She has my blessing."

"I, Lydia, tender of the sacred hearth, have tasked this sister of our craft with an ordeal of cleansing. She has retrieved a profane artifact that was a threat to all the sisters of our craft. She has my blessing."

The witches tilted their candles, letting the wax fall to the tiled floor. The four women reached out and placed a hand on Nadia. The coven then spoke in unison.

"With our blessing we accept this sister into our ranks, and dub her Nadia, Witch of the Winter Moon." The candles were blown out. There was silence as the smoke rose from black wicks.

"Congratulations, sister," said Umbra.

"So now what do we do, now that I'm a member?" asked Nadia.

"There is a war to finish," said Anna.

"Secret police to evade," said Umbra.

"Mysteries to uncover," said Esmeralda.

"There are other witches that need guidance and protection," said Lydia.

"I'm ready," said Nadia.

"We know you are."

Epilogue

February 28th, 1953. Five days before Premier Stalin's death.

Peter split another log for the fire before throwing the split wood into a steadily growing pile. He was anxious as it would soon be spring. The winter felt much longer. Three professors from his university had vanished, as well as the obstetrician that would help his wife deliver their first-born child. Words could get you in a lot of trouble, and Peter had been taught what to say in public a long time ago. As an engineer, he was preparing for a profession that wouldn't get him into any trouble. He made sure to speak laconically in public, yes or no answers, nothing that would draw too much attention to himself or his wife. A precaution that had kept him and his slowly growing family safe for the time being.

The rebuilding efforts from the great patriotic war kept him busy, and because of his skill in construction, he was given a small cottage for his current job. It had none of the modern amenities, and it reminded him of his home growing up. Years later, when he returned to that place, he found that the whole town had been leveled. There were only splinters, overgrowth, and a monument to all the people killed there.

He took another log and split it. The rhythm of hacking wood did a passible job of keeping his mind off of complex things…like the ending of winter.

"You are looking healthy," said a woman's voice behind him. He turned, and all the anxiety in him vanished in an instant.

Having arrived as quietly as a light wind, his older sister, Nadia, stood in his yard with an elderly Dasha on her shoulder. She wore a dress that had her medals of valor pinned to her chest, including medals of magical excellence, her sharpshooter badge, the "People's Hero" partisan medal, Moscow's medal, Stalingrad's medal, and so many more. There were scars on her arms, neck, and few nicks on her lips and face. Their father's rifle, now very much her rifle, was slung over her shoulder. While he wore a heavy sweater, she wore no winter clothing. He tossed the ax aside and ran over, picking her up with a great big hug.

"Nadia! I missed you so much!" he said, spinning her around in a circle. Dasha meowed angrily in protest but kept his footing. "Goodness gracious, how is that cat still alive!"

"Determination," said Nadia with a laugh as he placed her back on the ground. "How is your Klara? Last time we spoke you said you were planning on having a child."

"She is doing wonderfully, our doctor said we would have a summer child." He smiled, trying not to think too hard about where the doctor was right now. "Oh, please come in, come in! We will warm you up with a fire," he said, leading her inside.

"I think that would be nice," she said, following him. While drab and plain outside, the inside was filled with colorful blankets and hand-painted portraits of flowers from the countryside. Nothing that would get him in trouble with the state.

"I was afraid you wouldn't be coming this year," he said, placing several logs in the fireplace. "Now, where did I put those matches?" Before he could search for them, Nadia blew on the logs, setting them alight. "Silly me, I forgot."

"It's alright," she said, sitting at the table. "I had some errands to run before we could meet, and I didn't want to jeopardize you with the secret police."

"Are they after you?" he whispered, suddenly worried for his sister's safety.

"Possibly," she said, scratching Dasha's head. "In the war, we witches were warmly welcomed against the fascists. Now we are grudgingly given accolades while they erase our efforts from the history books. I don't mind, it is something I'm used to. Do you have a plate? I went to the market and got a nice fish for Dasha; he gets a little messy when he eats."

Happy for the change of subject, Peter fetched a plate for the elderly cat and his large fatty fish.

"I suspected that you would be getting Klara pregnant, so I brought some elixirs that will promote health in her and the baby. Just a drop of it in her tea once a day should do the trick," she said, taking several bottles to from her bag and placing them on the table.

"What a relief. We have not been able to get an appointment with our obstetrician. Until we find a new one, this will put our mind at ease."

"The police took him?"

"It seems so." He sighed. "You know I was half tempted to lie, say that he might have been sick, but if I can't speak truthfully to family, then what kind of man am I?"

"One who loves his family," smiled Nadia. "But soon, you won't have to hide your words so carefully."

"Why is that?" he asked.

"I plan on having a meeting with Premier Stalin today. I expect it will be quite productive."

Author Bio

Stuart Mascair is a self-published author, and proud member of the Cherokee Nation. He lives in Albuquerque, New Mexico where he enjoys hiking local trails. Stuart graduated from Evergreen State College with a Bachelor of Arts in political science with an emphasis on literature. In 2021, he received his Master of Fine Arts in creative writing from the Institute of American Indian Arts in Santa Fe.

When not writing, Stuart can be found jamming out to some tunes, painting little army men, trying out a new recipe, or looking for a new digital artist to inspire him.